"Hogan writes with tangible energy, capturing the trials of divided loyalties in the midst of global war... Fans of military SF will enjoy Hogan's fresh take on the genre."

Publishers Weekly

Reese Hogan

SHROUDED LOYALTIES

**ANGRY
ROBOT**

ANGRY ROBOT
An imprint of Watkins Media Ltd

Unit 11, Shepperton House
89 Shepperton Road
London N1 3DF
UK

angryrobotbooks.com
twitter.com/angryrobotbooks
Hold on tight

An Angry Robot paperback original, 2019

Cover by Francesca Corsini
Set in Meridien

ISBN 978 0 85766 829 5
Ebook ISBN 978 0 85766 830 1

Printed and bound in the United Kingdom by TJ International.

9 8 7 6 5 4 3 2 1

For Michael
Brother, fellow artist, and forever friend

MARROSE OCEAN

KHEPPRA ISLE

TRIEVANIC SEA

MARLDOX

BELZEN

★ ELLEMKO

RIACHMAR   ARTORA

SOHOS

WINSTOW

★ POAHA

DESCAR

★ KELD

VASSIS

SULSY

AMMIESISCH

FAOLENAMINE

DHAVNAKIR

BRICSIANYA

★ CORVENYON

CRIESUCE

PIILYAR ★

TREA

★ YOLNOARA

CRIESUCE

RAENTALLA

ISLING OCEAN

Chapter 1

BLACKWOOD'S NEW RECRUIT

There were better ways to end a watch than being summoned straight to the captain's stateroom. Chief Sea Officer Mila Blackwood could think of three right off the top of her head: eating breakfast, snatching a short nap before diving drills, or going over the procedures for the upcoming mission. She ran a hand over her tired eyes, wishing she'd at least had time to grab a mug of nettlebark tea, but she thought she knew why she'd been called, and she didn't wish to prolong this anymore than she had to. *First we're so short-staffed I have to take on watches, and now this.*

She delivered three knocks to Captain Rosen's door, harder than she meant to.

"Enter!" the submarine captain called.

Blackwood turned the knob and pushed open the stateroom door, stepping into the room serving as both the captain's private quarters and office. Right now, there were only two people at the small table opposite the bunk.

The captain of the *BZS Desert Crab* sat on the far side of the table, wearing a dark blue jacket with gold-embroidered stripes on the cuffs. Her hard-brimmed hat bore the sigil of two moons, one in crescent phase and one broken, picked out in blue and yellow thread. The skin around the captain's eyes was creased with a perpetual harshness that only seemed to intensify as her gaze landed on Blackwood.

Blackwood's newest team member was seated at the table across from her, hands folded in his lap. Blackwood suppressed a sigh as she brought her right fist to her left shoulder and stood at attention.

"Close the door, CSO Blackwood."

Blackwood lowered her fist and did so before turning back, standing stiff with hands at her sides.

"Apprentice Deckman Holland was found in an unauthorized area," said the captain. "Specifically, he was discovered in the lower flat beneath the solar power room."

Blackwood felt her stomach drop. That was where the new shrouding drive for the submarine had been installed. Blackwood could see the appeal to the young submariner – the bright glittering arphanium pipes, the crackling of the stored energy in the reservoirs, the hot steel smell that overpowered the stench of kaullix grease permeating the rest of the boat. Slipping behind the heated pipes to get some alone time, especially in the early hours before a precarious mission, would be almost irresistible to someone barely on the sane side of losing his mind.

Blackwood pursed her lips and glanced at Kyle Holland. The kid looked back just long enough to meet her eyes from behind wisps of black bangs, his face clean of any emotion. His skin, already almost as pale as a Dhavnak's, seemed even whiter in the solar lamps of the captain's stateroom. If he'd had light hair to go with that skin, the captain might have given him a full interrogation without ever calling Blackwood. The slight slant to Holland's dark eyes, giving him a hint of Criesucan blood, was a blessing with that washed-out complexion; most Belzene folks would see that first and think 'ally' rather than 'enemy.'

"Captain," Blackwood said, turning her attention back to the senior officer. "My apologies. I can assure you it won't happen again."

"This is the fourth new recruit that's landed here in the two days since we left port," Captain Rosen said. "I know there wasn't sufficient time for training, but I *don't* have time for this. If it happens again, I will hold you personally accountable. Is that understood?"

"Perfectly, ma'am."

"Good. Please go." The captain pulled a pile of papers from a drawer behind her. As Holland stood, she glanced up again. Her voice came out even harder than before.

"If you try sneaking off tonight, deckman, or any other time the sub shrouds, there could be far more dire consequences than this. Think long and hard about that before you give Chief Sea Officer Blackwood the slip again."

"Yes, ma'am. I understand that, ma'am." Holland's voice came out as cool and collected as ever, if a bit on the high side.

Blackwood sighed. Holland hadn't even been on her roster. It had originally been some fellow named Jeremiah Magnus. But Magnus hadn't shown up the morning of the mission, so Holland had been sent running from the academy practically as the gangway was rising. Blackwood was just glad to have gotten a replacement for her fifth torpedomate in time. A body fighting Dhavnakir was a body fighting Dhavnakir. Even if he was undertrained. Even if he was skittish as a weerbat in the daylight. Even if he was always awake when Blackwood left the compartment for the half-light watch, eyes staring into the bunk above as his lips moved in some silent comfort to himself.

Blackwood led Holland from the stateroom in silence. As they passed through the mess, she grabbed a mug of nettlebark tea and sprinkled some sugar in it. She blew on it on her way through the crew's quarters, squeezing past all the sailors who were climbing out of their bunks and zipping up brown-checkered coveralls for the day. In the solar power room beyond, the generators were running strong as cells just below the ocean waves absorbed as much sunlight as possible without reflecting the glare up toward potential Dhavnak spyplanes. Technicians hurried around them, adjusting and distributing the energy throughout the boat in preparation for the upcoming dive. It reminded Blackwood of how much work still had to be done in her own compartment. She swallowed a mouthful of tea, grateful for the slightly-sweetened but still acerbic taste of nettle to jolt her brain awake. She wouldn't be getting so much as a half-shift of sleep today, and she was already running on little more than naps as it was.

When Blackwood and Holland reached the maneuvering room, she took the young man by the elbow and guided him to the other side of the propulsion controls, away from the sailors fixing a pipe valve at the fore. Holland squared his shoulders and met her eyes calmly.

"Listen, Deckman Holland," said Blackwood. "Captain Rosen is right. This behavior has to stop. The only reason you haven't been called up on charges by now is because the captain doesn't know about the *last* two times you showed up somewhere you shouldn't have been. Next time you need to have a panic attack, or break down, or whatever it is you do, do it in your own bunk."

Holland glanced toward the hatch leading to the aft torpedo room, his eyebrows creased. Blackwood snapped her fingers in irritation, bringing Holland's gaze back to her.

"Don't worry what your crewmembers think," she said. "If you're the guy who can't listen to orders, or the guy who isn't there when we need him, that's worse. Those are serious offenses, Holland. Do you have any idea what people will think if you keep turning up in random corners of the boat?"

"No, ma'am."

"They'll think you're a Dhavvie spy."

The kid's face went white. "But–"

"Just stop hiding and stay where you're supposed to. This is life and death we're talking about."

Holland nodded, swallowing. "Yes, ma'am."

Blackwood started to turn away but paused. They'd been losing sailors to the war so fast that the whole boat had gone through three batches of new recruits over the last month, each one more raw than the one before. But the aft torpedo crew had been lucky, and Holland was the first one she'd personally trained – a replacement for Christa Thickrey, whom they'd lost to that last devastating shrouding accident. The accident that Holland had undoubtedly heard about by now. Every other department head was probably going through this same thing. She sighed and turned back to him.

"Look," she said. "I know the idea of shrouding terrifies you, deckman. It terrified me too when they first developed it. But I can promise you, it's actually safer in some ways than a regular patrol. There's less chance of being seen by a Dhavvie warplane since we don't have to travel through the whole ocean. They haven't figured out where we come out on the Dhavnak side, so we've never been ambushed either. And they don't have shrouding technology yet, so we don't have anything to fear *while* we're in the shrouding realm."

"Yes, ma'am," Holland said. "But…"

"But what? Go ahead."

"But they say sometimes people've disappeared when you come out on the Dhavnak side," Holland said in a rush. "They say there are *things* out there while you're shrouding. They say if you shroud without steel around you, you'll be ripped apart! They say even if *none* of those things happen, you have to stay completely still and quiet, or–"

Blackwood grabbed Holland's shoulder. The kid clammed up immediately, staring at her with wide eyes. "Who are they?" said Blackwood. "Who are the 'they's' who have been telling you these things?"

"Just… just heard it around, ma'am."

Blackwood felt a surge of anger and fought to keep it from her face. She settled with running a hand through her dark hair, tucking a stray curl back into her ponytail. "Deckman Dillon Vin. Right?"

Holland looked down.

"His sister was killed at the Battle of Riachmar," said Blackwood. "So, when he sees someone with pale skin, he can be more… judgmental than most. He was the same way with Deckwoman Strachan till he got to know her. He'll come around."

Holland shrugged, his gaze flicking around the small compartment. "But is any of it true about shrouding, ma'am? Or was he just… I mean, was it all just a way to scare me?"

"Something in the boat reacted badly with the dekatite vein we traveled through last time," said Blackwood. "That's it. It's been fixed. It won't happen again." She hoped Holland wouldn't realize that she hadn't answered his question.

"The dekatite vein?" Holland asked.

"Yes, the dekatite veins we use to enter and exit the shrouding realm. Like Kheppra Isle."

"But—"

Blackwood stopped him with a raised hand, her patience finally frayed to its end. "You've been through all the guidelines and precautions. You know about not wearing dekatite jewelry, and about what to expect when we shroud. And that is *all* you should be thinking about. Letting yourself be distracted by rumors is *dangerous* in this line of work. I don't want to hear about this again. Got it, deckman?"

"Of course, ma'am," said Holland hastily. A look of uncertainty flashed across his face, but it disappeared as quickly as it arrived. She knew what he was thinking. Yes, he'd been trained not to wear dekatite jewelry, but what did *that* have to do with shrouding?

He would just have to wonder. She wasn't about to tell him that a piece of dekatite was found on one of the bodies after the accident. It would lead to the *why* of the matter, and the veteran sailors knew full well not to mention that those things in the shrouding realm – those creatures, or whatever they were – were actually *drawn* to dekatite. They knew not to wear dekatite now. It wouldn't happen again. And that was the end of it.

Xeil's grace, let that be the end of it.

Blackwood turned and pushed open the hatch to the aft torpedo room. Mahanner, Vin, and Strachan were all at the other end by the torpedoes, deep in conversation. Vin sat at the edge of his bunk, his coveralls on his bottom half but the top unzipped and lying on the blankets. His hair hung in dark curls around his face, still mussed from sleep. Mahanner sat on the opposite bunk from Vin, pulling his long black hair back, and Strachan leaned against the lower starboard torpedo. When they noticed Blackwood, they came to their feet, fists to their shoulders. Blackwood gave a quick nod.

"Deckman Holland," she said, "help Deckman Mahanner finish the fuse sweep on the port side, and don't forget capacity checks on the last fuse replacements. Deckwoman Strachan, inventory the torpedoes and run the count by the forward torpedo room when you're done. Deckman Vin. Over here. Now."

"Yes, ma'am," Vin said, his words several seconds behind the other deckmates'. He pulled up the top half of his coveralls over his undershirt as he made his way over to her. Blackwood set her mug down on the locker by the hatch. She waited until the other sailors were absorbed in their duties before speaking.

"Stop with the stories about shrouding," she said.

Vin's lips twitched. "To Holland, ma'am? I'm just making sure he's prepared so he doesn't panic when the time comes. You know how that kid—"

"It never occurred to you that you're making it worse?" she cut in.

"No, ma'am." A light of defiance flashed through his eyes. "If he doesn't know what to expect, how can we trust him if it goes down again? It's hard enough to trust them as it is, that's all I'm sayin'."

"*Them*," Blackwood repeated. "Trust *them*."

"Anybody with…" Vin finished with a gesture toward his own dark-toned skin, in an obvious comparison to Holland's light shade.

Blackwood felt her anger creeping up again. She took three deep breaths before answering, "No, Vin. It is not hard to *trust* them."

"No, ma'am? Their entire *religion* is built around cutting out some woman's eye for stealing—"

"Vo Hina?" Blackwood broke in. "She's one of their goddesses, not 'some woman'. And she wasn't stealing, she was hoarding. Her eye was *shattered*, not cut out. Their main god, Shon Aha, was punishing her – that's why the Dhavnaks call the Shattered Moon 'Vo Hina'!" By the moons, his ignorance sometimes…

"Hoarding. Exactly," Vin said with a wave of his hand. "How dare anyone try to keep money for themselves in that forsaken country? And it's *always* women, right?" He stopped, narrowing his eyes. "Wait. You actually know the legend of how it happened?"

Blackwood let out a sigh through her teeth. "A Dhavnak family used to live in our neighborhood. Four years ago, just before Belzen was pulled into the war. My little brother was friends with their kid. I caught pieces of the stories he'd share with him."

"Your brother's cozy with a *Dhavvie?*" Vin said incredulously.

"It was when he was thirteen," Blackwood answered coldly. "Andrew's friend is long gone now."

"Thank Xeil for that, huh? Else you mighta gone home to find him a woman-beating, polytheistic, fair-skinned loving–"

Blackwood grabbed a fistful of Vin's coveralls and pulled him toward her. "I have a problem with their *politics*, Vin!" she hissed under her breath. "I have a problem with them attacking us and starting this stupid war. But I don't treat every light-skinned person like a sandbarb in my shoe. You focus on your damn job and mind your own affairs. Or I will *keelhaul* you myself, war or not."

Vin took a step back, raising his hands in placation. "Didn't mean anything by it, CSO," he said evenly.

Blackwood took a deep breath, then another. And a third. *Vin is not my enemy. My anger is the enemy.*

She shoved away from him and turned back to the rest of the room. Holland looked away quickly. Mahanner and Strachan were still hard at work, not wishing to get involved. Blackwood retrieved her mug and took a life-restoring swig, avoiding her crewmates' eyes as she appraised the compartment. The four brass torpedo tubes at the stern were loaded, and the reloads were stored on skids above the top bunk and below her own. Three of the twelve bunks were still folded out. Mahanner's was spread with books.

"You want to get some sleep, CSO, we'll finish up here," said Mahanner, as casually as if nothing had happened.

"No sleep," said Blackwood. "Just get that–"

The rest of her words were drowned out as the loud blat of the klaxon sounded, echoing through the small room. It rang out twice, and before the sound had faded from Blackwood's ears, the Chief of Boat's voice boomed throughout the sub.

"Dive, dive. Repeat. Dive, dive."

A Dhavnak spyplane. It had to be. Mahanner grabbed the books strewn on his bunk and swept them into his bag. Blackwood tossed back the rest of her tea, and threw the mug, along with Mahanner's bag, into the locker by the maneuvering hatch. By the time she'd finished, all the bunks were folded up against the walls, and the other sailors were finding handholds on the bulkheads. Blackwood scrambled up the ladder in the center of the compartment to ensure the hatch was tight and sealed. The boat was going quiet around them as the power draw was rerouted to the battery. Blackwood kept a tight hold on the ladder as the deck began to tilt slightly beneath her feet.

"Are we shrouding, ma'am?"

Blackwood looked over to see Holland watching her with wide eyes, both hands clutching the chain on one of the bunks.

"Not yet," she told him.

"Because we're not close enough to... to a dekatite source...?"

"The source is Kheppra Isle," she said, "and yes, we are. But we get more warning than this. Unless we're actually being pursued, or if a Dhavvie ship is using hydroacoustics to track us..."

She trailed off. *Unless we're actually being pursued.* With their boat out of commission for the few days following the accident, it was entirely possible a Dhavnak ship had gotten through the Qosmya Canal. And the last thing Captain Rosen would want was to inadvertently lead the enemy to the other side of the island, where all the research stations were. What better way to vanish without a trace than by diving under the waves and shrouding through the dekatite of Kheppra Isle?

"CSO?" said Holland. The kid's hand was to his chest, clutching a fistful of coverall.

"Don't skip out," said Blackwood tightly. "We need you here."

"I'm not going anywhere," Holland answered, sounding uncertain.

"You'll be fine. Remember, the accident was a freak incident."

Holland nodded, his breath coming fast and short.

With the solar motors off, the temperature was already rising. As the ocean around them grew colder, condensation formed on everything in the compartment. Within moments, sweat ran down Blackwood's body, stinging her eyes and wetting her palms against the metal of the ladder. Only red emergency lights lit the interior of the sub, as all extraneous energy had been powered down for the dive. Blackwood worked on keeping her breathing long and slow, but the tension in the compartment was palpable. Knowing their oxygen would get thinner the longer they were under was always at the back of everyone's mind. Knowing a potential enemy was overhead, tracking their every move and sound, was at the front.

The deck tilted again, steeper than usual, and Blackwood could tell by the tension on her arms that they were moving fast into the dark water. Any doubt had left her mind now. They were heading straight for the side of Kheppra Isle. Her feet slipped toward the maneuvering hatch. She looped her arm around the rung of the ladder, holding tight. On the other side of the ladder, Mahanner did the same.

A hollow click sounded throughout the bulkhead. The Chief of Boat wouldn't speak over the loud system now, but the click was all the warning Blackwood needed; they were getting ready to shroud. Only moments later, the walls seemed to dim around them. The red emergency lights blurred as if a cloud of smoke obscured them. The stifling air dampened and cooled. A heavy weight settled throughout the boat, pressing against Blackwood's skin.

"Stay still," she said, as a general reminder to everyone. She watched the hatch overhead, which was barely visible in the murky light. She'd gone through this process nine times now.

She couldn't shake the memory of that last time from her head, though. A huge jarring against the boat. Screams through the maneuvering hatch. The breach had been in the radio room. The galley, mess, and crew's quarters had been flooded before the rest of the boat was sealed off. Thirty-nine lives were lost. The bodies left behind were twisted, ripped apart, drowned, smothered. Some even had burns. It was thought to be linked to the dekatite ring found on a disembodied hand afterward, coupled with similar incidents involving a tank and an armored truck in recent days. Blackwood was sure they wouldn't have shrouded again so soon, except for the fact that every act of aggression kept Belzen one step ahead of being taken.

Desperate times required sacrifices. From them all.

The boat grew colder around them as they passed into the dekatite face of the island. Blackwood realized Holland was breathing in shallow gasps off to her left, every breath catching just short of a whimper. She reached across the narrow space between the ladder and bulkhead to wrap her hand around the young man's wrist. Holland jumped at the touch.

"Is it almost over?" he said in a shaky voice.

"Not yet," murmured Blackwood. "But while we're shrouding, we're safe from the Dhavnaks. See? It's a good thing."

Before she'd finished the sentence, something collided with the hull, explosively loud inside the small compartment. The submarine twisted to its side and the ladder jerked against Blackwood's arm as gravity suddenly shifted to her back. Above her, Mahanner gasped as his face smashed against the ladder. She looked up to see him covering his face with his hand, but not before she saw the blood pouring from his nose. It hit her forehead, hot and sticky. The convulsion of the boat shook Blackwood's grip. She tried to get her other arm around the rung, but Mahanner's blood had made the ladder slick, and her fingers slipped. She fell, crashing into the folded bunk on the wall. She heard a distinctive crack somewhere near the stern, and suddenly water was spraying into the aft torpedo room. The water was freezing, and thick with salt; not pipe water, but cold seawater never touched by the suns. The red emergency lights flickered and died.

Blackwood swallowed back a surge of nausea. It was the accident all over again. Except this time, it was their compartment that had been hit.

Chapter 2

KLARA YANA'S PENDANT

Klara Yana Hollanelea could feel her ama's dekatite pendant burning into her chest. The terror almost paralyzed her.

How could Cu Zanthus have missed that detail during his briefing? Maybe I should have told Blackwood when she mentioned it.

So the chief sea officer would have seen the Broken Eye? Surely she would have recognized it – she clearly had ample knowledge of Dhavnak culture, based on what she'd been telling Vin in the corner. What else would she have recognized? That Kyle Holland, with Vo Hina's symbol, could surely not be a male, either? Being Belzene, it probably wouldn't bother the senior officer, but even the thought of letting *that* secret out made Klara Yana sick with fear. If only she could have been a female for this mission... just this once.

If Cu Zanthus hadn't been watching when I boarded, maybe. Or if he'd given me more warning, instead of changing my assignment the moment I crossed the border...

But no. Anger at her boy of a kommandir would do no good now. She was Deckman Holland now, like it or not, and following the CSO's lead was her best hope of getting out of this alive.

"It's happening again. Xeil save us!"

Klara Yana thought that was the other woman, Strachan. Blackwood cut her off sharply.

"That's not helping! Shut it."

A light came to life, weak and murky, near where Blackwood had fallen. The deck lurched again, and Klara Yana clung to the bunk chain as water caught at her ankles. The light swung up. A torrential force of water was spraying into the compartment from above one of the torpedoes.

"Where *are* we?" Klara Yana said, staring in horror at the gushing water. "Inside the dekatite, or…?"

"We're in shrouding," Mahanner snapped.

"Like some sort of passage between the dekatite sources? Through the center of Mirrix?"

"We're dead, if you don't focus," said Blackwood. The light swung back toward the hatch behind Klara Yana, sweeping over the locker. "Damage control kit, Holland. Now!"

Klara Yana's eyes followed the light. A red canvas bag was stuffed under the locker, already half-submerged. She knelt in the cold water to pull the kit out, staggering on the slight angle of the deck.

"Mahanner!" barked Blackwood. "Seal the maneuvering room hatch."

"The hole's too big, ma'am!" Strachan shouted.

"For wedges, maybe, but not for shoring," said Blackwood.

"We need to evacuate before sealing the compartment!" Strachan insisted.

"And let in whatever it is that ripped us apart last time?" snarled Blackwood. "It's in our hands, Strachan. This doesn't end like that. Not on my watch."

"This is your fault, Holland!" someone else screamed. Klara Yana froze, the bag pulled out and clutched in her hands. "You have dekatite, don't you?"

Rot in solitude, hoarder! she almost spat back. She curbed the words just in time. Not a good Belzene answer, nor even a Dhavnak female's, but a typical young Dhavnak male's, ingrained in her over cycles of playing the part. Apprentice Deckman Kyle Holland would never talk that way to crewmates he'd barely met two days earlier, though, no matter how badly they'd been treating him.

"N- No," she made herself stammer. "I swear…"

"Vin!" CSO Blackwood exploded. "I will personally put my fist through your face if you don't get ahold of yourself. Mahanner, close the hatch before the rest of the boat floods! Vin, Strachan, find the rubber lungs and mouthpieces. Anyone not willing to help, get out now. I'm not dealing with it."

Anyone not willing to help? Is she serious? Surely, none of these sailors would walk away from a comrade in crisis. But what was she thinking? They were Belzene. Their sense of camaraderie seemed strained at the best of times.

Blackwood pulled something out from below one of the bunks – a long board covered in rubber or sealant. Klara Yana struggled back to her feet, hauling the bag with her. The water was just over her knees now. Her legs already felt frozen beneath the thin fabric of her coveralls.

As she got closer to the leak, where Blackwood was hauling herself up the sides of the torpedo tubes, it was harder to hear anything else. Someone shouted, but she couldn't make out the words. She did hear the creak of the wheel as one of her deckmates locked the hatch, and knew the five of them were cut off from the rest of the sub now.

"Holland!" Blackwood called.

"I'm here," she managed, sloshing up next to the senior officer. Blackwood's headlamp swung down in her direction, wavering in the thickly spraying water. This close, the water poured down on Klara Yana's head too, drenching her.

"Holland, I need a shole!"

What in Vo Hina's mercy is a shole? She opened the bag, holding it as far from the spray of water as she could, feeling the contents within by hand. A screwdriver? No, how would that help? There was some sort of axe… maybe… a roll of tape… *don't think so…*

"For Xeil's sake, Holland, some time *today!*" Blackwood erupted. "This hole's not gonna patch itself!"

A patch! She found it: a piece of metal wrapped in the same rubber gasket as the board, a little larger than a Synivistic Scripture. She held it up, choking as salt-saturated water poured into her face. Blackwood grabbed it.

"I need to drop the beam for a second. You have it?"

"We've got it!" someone answered from beside Klara Yana. She almost jumped at the heavy Qosmyan accent. Shameful for an agent. She blamed it on the fear still pulsing through her.

"Mahanner?" said Blackwood. "I thought you were still back by the hatch! Where did Vin–"

"He left, ma'am," the other sailor answered. "Him and Strachan both. *Abandoned* us."

"*What?*" Klara Yana said. Her voice came out sharper than she intended. *Miserable Belzene bastards!*

"Quiet!" Blackwood growled. "It doesn't matter now. See if you can find another light or two in there, will you?"

Klara Yana found a headlamp and strapped it around her head, then twisted the beam on. The light shone brightly, clearly designed to operate well even drenched in water. She watched as Blackwood looped her arm around a pipe and pulled herself up. Balancing herself, Blackwood pushed the shole upward to cover the hole. Klara Yana could tell the immense pressure of the water would be too much for the sea officer by herself. Freezing cold saltwater swirled at the level of Klara Yana's hips now. Blackwood turned her face away, coughing.

"I can't feel my fingers," she ground out. "We have to–"

"We can use the beam, ma'am," Mahanner broke in, holding up the board that Blackwood had pulled from under the bunk. "The two of us will push from below while you steady it."

Something banged against the boat, hard. A deep, deafening *whoomp* passed through the walls and into their rapidly-shrinking space, echoing off the steel bulkheads before being absorbed by the water. The impact sent the boat swaying to the left. The water filling the torpedo room churned like a violent river. Klara Yana lost her balance, going under for just a second, before resurfacing with a gasp. She looked around frantically, but everything seemed fuzzy. Something was in her eye. She dug the heels of her hands into her eye sockets until her vision cleared, not realizing until the last horrible second that she'd just scrubbed the colored optics for Kyle Holland's disguise right from her eyes. *Gods!* She looked down, straining to look for the tiny pieces of glass. All she saw was dark water lapping against her coveralls. *Get through this first! Then figure it out.*

"Holland!" Blackwood shouted raggedly. "Get back up here! We *have* to seal this! Now!"

"Coming, CSO!"

Klara Yana half-walked, half-swam toward the beam of Blackwood's headlamp, shoving through the water's resistance as quickly as possible. The submarine bucked again, but this time Klara Yana kept her feet. The water surged almost to her neck. The steady drone of water pouring into the compartment sent tremors of panic through her. After five cycles in the field, and being so close to the promotion that would help her track down her ama, *this* was how she'd die? Deep underwater in enemy territory, in some unknown part of the world, wearing a false identity and surrounded by strangers?

No. Think, *damnit!* What had Blackwood said right before they'd entered the compartment? *Something in the boat reacted badly with the dekatite vein.* She'd been lying. There was something out there. And, if Blackwood's and Vin's comments about having dekatite were true, it wanted Klara Yana's dekatite pendant. The one her ama had given her. Klara Yana reached into her shirt and pulled out her necklace, feeling the round shape of the Broken Eye within her palm.

If I can somehow get it off the boat… maybe it will let us live.

She pulled the long chain over her head, then clutched the pendant as she climbed up the pipes by the wall to join Blackwood. The officer held the shole and was shoving it toward the leak again. Klara Yana couldn't see the hole specifically, but it felt like the whole Trievanic Sea was pouring in from above. There was also, unmistakably, a deep, guttural howling that seemed to be coming in on the waves themselves, woven into the water as thickly as the salt. The boat shuddered again, and Klara Yana gripped the pipes, barely holding herself up.

"Hey!" Mahanner yelled from below. "I have the beam. You two press that shole up there, and we'll get it covered. We can do this!"

Klara Yana was already up by Blackwood, and she shoved her hands toward the shole, the necklace still tight in her palm. She had no idea how she could possibly get the pendant outside through the insane pressure of that water. But it was the only chance they had. She had to *try*.

"You take the left side," Blackwood grunted. "I'll take the right."

Mahanner's beam now pressed into the center, and slowly, the patch forced up against that unbearable pressure. On the spot directly over Klara Yana's head, the flow lessened. At her left hand, where she held the other end of the shole, water continued to spill in, increasing in pressure as the hole shrank. She shoved the pendant toward that gap, forcing herself to pry her fingers apart.

There was a growl above her, terrifyingly loud. Something grabbed her hand – something warmer than the freezing water, with a rough grip and a crushing hold. Klara Yana's fingers were forced closed around the pendant before she could release it. The hard edges of the dekatite bit into her palm. The entire hull seemed to flicker, so fast and bright that her eyes barely registered it behind the saltwater covering them. Pain flared in her left hand. The unseen force still held her fast; it felt like her hand was being ground between two boulders. She screamed, although the saltwater spilling in gagged her almost immediately. Out of the corner of her eye, she saw the flickering light dance over Blackwood's form, illuminating her like a lightning bolt. The senior officer fell.

Klara Yana spat out the water as best she could, violently coughing the silt from her lungs. Mahanner's beam was still steady, despite their loss of Blackwood's strength. Klara Yana yanked her closed fist back, pulling with every ounce of strength she had. After a heartbeat of agonizing pressure as the joints in her elbow and shoulder protested, she finally broke the creature's grip. Something hissed, almost at her ear. Her hand throbbed with pain, and she didn't know if she'd ever be able to force the fingers apart again, but she was free. She used the hand to redouble the force against the shole. The flow of water became a cascade... then a torrent... then suddenly, it ceased altogether. Outside, the unearthly howling went on, muted now.

"Holland!" yelled Mahanner. "Grab the beam. I need to dive under and get a wedge placed so it holds. *Don't* release it, whatever you do."

"I've got it!" she choked out.

Her fingers finally unfolded and the pendant fell free, dangling on the chain now looped around her wrist. She had no choice but to leave it there as she put all her strength on the beam. The dark gray of the dekatite sparkled in the light of her headlamp – not just the pendant, but the chain, too; tiny links of dekatite made up its entire long length. She gritted her teeth and turned her head to look for Blackwood, sweeping her light across a room of deep waves. She finally saw her body, floating back by the locker. Her heart stuttered. Out of everyone on this submarine, CSO Blackwood was the one who *didn't* deserve this. Unlike her comrades, she'd stayed and fought. And unlike Klara Yana, she'd done it *without* hiding her gender. *Someday,* Klara Yana thought, *maybe that could be me.*

Someday. When women were allowed to serve in Dhavnakir's military. When privileged positions, like her ama's former role as ambassador, were commonplace for females, rather than practically unheard of. But Klara Yana didn't have until 'someday.' Her ama was a political prisoner *now*, of one of the very countries she'd negotiated with, and the Dhavnak government either couldn't or wouldn't get her released. Klara Yana couldn't ask, not at her current rank. But just one more promotion – one more big mission – and she'd have access to those records.

So here she was. Half-drowned in an enemy submarine surrounded by monsters, missing a piece of her disguise, and holding incriminating evidence that she was responsible for the attack. But she'd gotten the intel she'd been sent for. The dekatite veins, the arphanium pipes, Kheppra Isle, all of it.

Now she just had to get out alive.

It felt like forever, but Mahanner finally surfaced again. Klara Yana immediately yelled, "Get CSO Blackwood, sir! She might still be alive!"

The dark man nodded and dove across the compartment, coming up right at Blackwood's side. Klara Yana released the board, relieved when it didn't budge. She swept up her necklace before Mahanner could turn and catch sight of it, and pulled the chain free of the pendant. She unzipped her coverall just long enough to stuff the pendant into the soaked fabric holding her breasts flat. The chain, she kept in her right hand.

"She's alive," Mahanner said, "but unconscious."

"Xeil be praised," said Klara Yana. She took off her headlamp. "Catch!"

Mahanner caught the light. "Get over here and help me get her out of the water."

"On my way."

She dove under, the same way Mahanner had, but hurriedly kicked toward the left wall – the portside bulkhead – as soon as she was submerged. She tried opening her eyes, but they burned in the salty, pitch-black water. So she did it by feel, brushing her aching palm over chains, metal frames, and vinyl mattresses with the threadbare sheets still on them. By the time she'd rid herself of the dekatite chain, her lungs were begging for air. She kicked herself back to the front of the compartment – *the fore* – and burst to the surface with stars spotting her vision.

"By the moons," she gasped.

"Get lost?"

"I must have gotten turned around! I couldn't even see your light."

"Calm down, kid. You're OK now. Help me with Blackwood."

Together, they managed to get Blackwood on top of the flat locker by the maneuvering hatch – normally taller than Klara Yana, but now only a half-hand above the lapping water.

"There's some sort of... injury... on her arm," grunted Mahanner. "What happened up there? It looked like some sort of energized shock or something. Was it that thing that kept hitting the boat? That... what was it?"

"No clue," said Klara Yana. A shiver shook her, rattling her words. Mahanner's mention of an injury reminded her of the sharp pangs still coursing over her own left palm, excruciating in the undercurrents of icy seawater. Was her blood leaking out in the water? She kept her fist submerged, not daring to look in front of the other sailor.

Klara Yana could just see Blackwood's wound beneath her shoved-up sleeve. It was on the bottom of her forearm and resembled a lightning bolt, etched in something much darker than blood. Something dark gray, almost metallic.

When Mahanner wasn't looking, Klara Yana opened her palm for a

19

quick glimpse of her own wound. Although it was slightly distorted by the tight grip she'd had on the pendant, the shape of the Broken Eye was unmistakable. Burned into her palm... with dekatite.

Chapter 3

BLACKWOOD'S MARK

Instinctively, as she forced the shole up to the overhead with all her strength, Blackwood knew she'd been here already, done this before. There'd been a monster just outside the hull, fighting its way in to rip the crew apart. She knew the lives of every sailor in the *Desert Crab* were in her hands. And that was why she pressed against the flooding water until her shoulders screamed with pain and her hands went numb.

But it wasn't a monster's growls that reached her ears from outside the submarine this time. It was Andrew Blackwood's terrified yells, and the sound of his fists banging against the hull.

Mila! Don't abandon me! Please!

Blackwood pushed harder. Their lives… her hands…

Mila! You abandoned me!

"No!" she shouted. "That's not how it was! You don't understand, you're just a kid–"

"You abandoned us!" That voice definitely wasn't her brother's; too deep and forceful for a fifteen year-old boy.

Blackwood's lips turned down, her eyes twitching behind her eyelids. No, not fifteen… he'd been fifteen when she left. How old now? *Seventeen. Right.* Plenty old enough to be on his own. Fifteen had been old enough. Stupid to keep having these dreams when there was so much else to worry about. Andrew was fine. Aside from Ellemko's air raids, and his own haunting grief, his self-imposed silences, his passive-aggressive moodiness…

"The compartment was *lost!*" someone yelled. "It was suicide to stay there! The CSO said as much when she let us go. If *she* wanted to sacrifice her life–"

"And you better be glad she did! If she and Holland hadn't gotten that breach sealed, this whole boat would be in shards by now, and *you'd* be a dismembered corpse at the bottom of the sea."

"Holland? Really? You're giving *him* credit? It's his fault! I bet my life he's carrying dekatite. *We* all knew better–"

"Deckman Vin!" Blackwood growled, forcing her eyes open. Harsh light greeted her, and her lids clamped shut again. She put a hand out, feeling a metal bunk rail against the mattress she laid on. Her forearm throbbed, the whole surface a strange combination of needles and numbness. The smell of antiseptics and bandages filled the air. "Deckman Mahanner," she added. Her voice was rough; she swore a layer of salt still coated the inside of her mouth. "Who else is here?"

"At the moment, no one, ma'am," said Mahanner. "How are you feeling, CSO?"

"Just the two of you then?" She pried her eyes open again, more successfully this time, and found herself, as she'd expected, in the sub's medbay. Mahanner and Vin were close to the hatch, an arm-span away from each other. The other two bunks in the space were empty. Blackwood glanced from the glass-fronted metal cabinet in one corner, filled with bandages, tools, and ointments, to the stainless steel sink bolted against the bulkhead at the other. Empty.

Mahanner came closer, leaving Vin at the door. "Do you remember anything, CSO?"

Struggling to seal the breach. A banging on the hull. Andrew screaming. *No.* A monster. She looked up.

"We succeeded?" she said. "We kept it out? We came out of shrouding OK? Did… did anyone die?"

His smile softened his whole face. "No, ma'am. We did it. You, me, and Holland."

She felt her own lips curve up. "Holland, huh?"

"Yes, ma'am."

"Spanking brand new recruit, barely trained, scared out of his mind… and he was up there with me, pushing that thing away from the boat. Wouldn't have guessed he had it in him."

Vin started forward, his face dark with anger. "It was probably guilt that put him up there in the first place, ma'am–"

"It's guilt making those accusations, deckman." Blackwood pushed herself to sitting on the little cot, swinging her legs over the unrailed side of the bunk. She was in dry coveralls, and her curls were unbound. She glared at Vin. "Deckman, go find Captain Rosen and inform her I need to speak with her at her earliest possible convenience."

"Ma'am, if this is about–"

"*Go*, deckman!"

With a sharp nod, Vin went. Blackwood turned to Mahanner. "Where is Deckman Holland?"

"With Captain Rosen, ma'am. Corpsmate Tolonen is with them, since she was the one who treated the marks. Holland has one, too. We've been informed to keep them as low profile as possible."

"Marks?" Blackwood followed Mahanner's gaze to her right arm – the same one that had been tingling since she woke. Her eyes widened.

"It's dekatite," she whispered.

Mahanner nodded. "Yes. The corpsmate and captain agree."

"But what do they–"

"Whatever was there at the hull by you and Holland left those marks. A creature of dekatite, or you scraping against the interior of the stone, no one knows. Holland has a round mark on his palm, right where he had it up at the breach. But you were shocked much worse than he was."

"*Shocked?*"

"That's what it looked like. From the outside, anyway. Given the shape of your mark, it's almost like a lightning bolt of dekatite traveled right down your arm. It's… it was…"

She held up a hand. "Where are we now? We *are* back on Mirrix, right?"

"Yes, but the captain turned us as soon as we were struck, and we came back out in our own waters. We're almost back to Belzen now."

"I didn't realize she could turn us during shrouding."

Mahanner shrugged. "To us, it's just hanging on till we get there. She's doing all the navigation."

Blackwood remembered Holland's question in the wake of the strike. *Where are we? Inside the dekatite? Through the center of Mirrix?* The answer was, no one knew. Anyone who'd ever tried to find out was dead. Her jaw clenched.

"Shrouding is too dangerous. We can't keep doing this."

"It's not our call, ma'am. You know that."

"And I'm not just talking about what goes on *inside* shrouding. It's the increased volcanic activity on Kheppra Isle. The more we use it to shroud through, the more unstable the whole island gets."

"That's true," Mahanner conceded. "But that just makes it a safer place for the research base. The Dhavvies would never suspect our scientists are working on the side of a semi-active volcano. And who'd guess we're using it to shroud through?"

Blackwood's lips thinned. "If this war hadn't rushed them into it, they would have taken the time to find somewhere safer. They would've figured out how to navigate that realm without us being attacked. But now they'll slap another shoddy repair on the *Desert Crab* like last time and we'll be shrouding again in three days, as if this accident never happened! They'll ignore every Xeil-cursed–"

The medbay door opened and Blackwood clamped her lips shut. Corpsmate Tolonen walked in, followed by Kyle Holland.

Tolonen gave a start to see Blackwood awake and sitting up. "CSO! Are you feeling alright, ma'am?"

"A bit of a headache and a stiff neck," said Blackwood. "Other than that, it's just this mark on my arm. It stings and tingles a bit. Do you have any idea what happened?"

"No, ma'am. The captain summoned Holland before I'd had much of a chance to look, and I went along in case I could help. From what we could tell…" she glanced down at Holland's hands, frowning, "…it *is* dekatite. Branded right into the skin."

Holland stood at Tolonen's shoulder, his hands pressed together and fingers tapping against each other. He probably meant the gesture to look nonchalant, but it came off as nervous. He caught Blackwood's gaze and his shoulders straightened, the tapping stopped. Blackwood was struck for the first time that it wasn't just a Criesucan slant to his eyes that set them apart – it was their color. Or, more specifically, *colors*. His irises were olive green with gold flecks. In dimmer confines, like the aft torpedo room, they'd swallowed the light and turned nearly black. But here, in the brighter lights of the medbay, the colors were obvious. It wasn't that it was *so* rare, but with his Criesucan features and pale skin...

"Ma'am? Is something wrong?" Holland said uncertainly.

"No, deckman," said Blackwood. "Just hadn't noticed your eyes before."

He seemed genuinely surprised for a moment, then a smile quirked his lip. "Well. They've been there, ma'am."

Blackwood dipped her head, acknowledging the point. "You really came through for us back there, Holland."

The smile broadened. "Thank you, CSO."

"So what about this mark we got? What do you think?"

The smile slowly faded again. "Don't know, ma'am. Something grabbed my hand, right before we got the hole sealed. That's when it happened, I think. That's when you fell."

That's right. She'd forgotten she fell. Holland really had saved their necks. If he hadn't been sent from the academy at the last minute, she would have been down a member during that accident. She'd be dead now. Very likely, they all would.

"Don't get up yet, CSO," said Tolonen. "You got hit a lot worse than Holland, and I want to give you a full examination before I send you out again. Give me a second to slap a bandage on Holland's hand."

"A bandage?"

"Captain wants these marks covered, and discreet. We'll get Holland some gloves, and you'll be OK in long sleeves, at least until..."

"Until what?"

"Sorry, ma'am. That's not for me to say." She ducked her head and walked around Blackwood's bunk to the aft, Holland in her wake.

Blackwood tried to catch a glimpse of Holland's mark, but the deckman had his hands in his pockets now, and his eyes were roaming over the medical bay rather than watching her. Blackwood turned back to Mahanner, but the door opened again. This time, Captain Rosen herself walked in. Blackwood began to push herself to her feet to salute, but Tolonen's voice stopped her.

"I said, don't get up, CSO."

Blackwood settled for saluting from her bunk, pushing her shoulders as straight as she could. "Sorry, captain. Corpsmate's orders."

"I understand," Rosen sighed, glancing around the room. "I guess I'll just have to speak with you here. Deckman Mahanner…"

"Say no more, captain. I'm on my way out," said Mahanner, pressing his fist to his shoulder.

Rosen nodded, and Mahanner let himself out. The captain spared a single glance for Tolonen and Holland, at the aft, but chose not to expel them. After saluting, the two had fallen into a quiet conversation, and paid them no mind. Rosen found a chair and pulled it to Blackwood's side.

"First of all, I want to commend you for your bravery in tackling a breach that anyone else would have given up as lost. You, Mahanner, and Holland showed great courage and admirable teamwork. That you did it during shrouding is even more impressive."

"Thank you, ma'am." It wasn't until Blackwood spoke that she realized how dry the inside of her mouth was. She swallowed, waiting.

"But," said Rosen, "there are mixed accounts of what happened in the aft torpedo room just before we shrouded. In fact, one of your crewmembers insists that someone is hiding dekatite."

"Let me guess," said Blackwood with a sigh. "Vin accusing Holland?"

"Do you believe it was him, CSO?" said Rosen, watching her closely.

"No, ma'am!" Anger made Blackwood want to raise her voice, but she forced herself to deliver the words quietly. "Not in the slightest. I'm sure he was briefed on the way over, and even if he wasn't, no one *wears* dekatite jewelry anymore. Most of it goes into tread for the tanks we don't use for shrouding, same as most of the arphanium has been repurposed for pipes we *do* use for shrouding. Besides, dekatite's always been associated with Dhavnak trinkets; it's hardly fashionable these days. The idea of him accidentally wearing something when he was called out of class is… outlandish, frankly."

Simultaneously, they turned to look at Holland. The kid was smiling at something Tolonen had said and shaking his head. Blackwood detected a hint of subtle flirting there.

"Did you ask him, ma'am?" she said, turning back to Rosen.

"Of course. I've asked every sailor in your department. Except you."

"Well, I don't have any."

"I know. Unless there's some hidden in the compartment somehow…"

"…Or unless dekatite's not the only thing that causes that reaction," added Blackwood. "This is still a raw science, after all."

"That's a good point," said Rosen, nodding. "However, I do need to talk with you about something else."

"Yes, captain?"

"I think there was a lack of clear leadership in that department."

Blackwood went cold. "Ma'am?"

"When firm orders aren't given, it creates division and conflicts within the department. In times of high stress or battle, soldiers need to be given orders that are easy to follow, without thinking, rather than being offered chances for second-guesses and doubts. But the way I understand it, you gave them a choice between staying or leaving."

A choice? She'd wanted to fix the damn breach – to save the *boat*, and all their lives – but Vin, with his constant insubordination, would've hampered her every step of the way. And he'd thought *Holland* would get them killed? It was just as good he'd left.

A voice spoke from behind Blackwood. "Captain?"

Rosen's eyes hardened, and her gaze snapped over Blackwood's shoulder. Blackwood turned slightly on the cot to see Holland coming forward, his wide-eyed gaze flickering between his two superior officers.

"What is it, deckman?" said Rosen, irritation creeping into her voice.

"It's just… CSO Blackwood *did* give a firm order, ma'am. 'Anyone not willing to help, get out now.' Couldn't have been more straightforward, if you ask me."

Rosen watched him for several moments, her lips pursed. "Thank you, deckman. Your observation is noted." She looked back to Blackwood, but the angle of her head kept Holland included this time. "In any case, the dispute will be put off for the time being. We'll have to review this in more detail before you'll lead your next command, CSO Blackwood."

Stripped of command. After she'd helped save the submarine. Her jaw clenched hard enough to send pain shooting through her face.

"Both you and Deckman Holland are being sent back to Ellemko," Captain Rosen continued. "Because of the dekatite now in your skin, shrouding is out of the question, obviously, and it's critical we get to the bottom of what happened. In short, you both need to be studied, to find out what effects this had on your bodies. It's the first time anything like this has ever happened, and we can't ignore it."

Blackwood heard a strangled gasp from Holland, and felt close to echoing the sound herself. Not just stripped of command, but sent to some laboratory at the capital? During wartime?

"But- but, captain," she finally got out, "you *need* me. And you need Holland! Without the two of us-"

"I understand," Rosen said. "The work you did will be put into both your records, I assure you. But this is more important. Criesuce is too wrapped up in their revolution to send aid anymore. Qosmya's doing what they can, but Dhavnakir's allied forces from both Narbona and Jasterus are battering *them*. And with Atrary's capital taken now, and Cardinia insisting on remaining neutral..." She grimaced. "As experimental as shrouding is, anything at all that helps us learn more about it is to our advantage – and to Dhavnakir's detriment. *Anything* we can learn may tip the scales back in our direction. There is nothing we won't do for that possibility."

Nothing. They wouldn't stop shrouding, despite the mounting dangers. They would continue their acts of sabotage, their futile stabs at the enemy's underbelly. They would cut her up if they had to – her and Holland both.

"You have family in Ellemko. Don't you, Blackwood?" Rosen was trying to soften the news. It wasn't helping.

"Yes, ma'am. A brother," Blackwood muttered.

"Younger or older?"

"Younger. By six and a half years."

"We might be able to spare you time to see him. Is he living with your parents?"

"Our parents died in a factory accident, ma'am. Five years ago."

"Scicorp Applications Industries? I remember that one." Rosen caught her breath. "Owen and Carrie Blackwood. They're your parents. Of course."

"Yes, ma'am."

"It's thanks to them we even have shrouding. If not for their early research…"

"Yes, ma'am."

"How is it *you* ended up working with shrouding? We don't have that many vehicles in the field yet using the technology."

"I requested it, ma'am. My parents died for this research. If not for Dhavnakir's aggression, they would never have been rerouted to making war weapons, and the accident would never have happened. So I vowed I'd do whatever it took to keep their legacy out of Dhavnak hands." She held Rosen's eyes. "It was supposed to be used for trading. It was never *meant* to be used as a weapon. It's getting more and more dangerous, and if Dhavnakir takes us–"

"I can't talk about this with you," Rosen broke in. "I'm sorry."

"If we don't destroy it soon–"

"I *can't*, Blackwood. It's above my station."

Blackwood looked away, struggling to keep the anger from her face. *Instead, you're sending me away.* She didn't like shrouding – she was starting to hate it, in fact – but if they were going to keep doing it, she *needed* to be part of it. How else could she know whether Belzen's largest warcraft outfitted with the technology remained safe from the Dhavnaks? It had been the one thing she felt she had control over, even if that control was more illusion than reality. *What else can I do? With this mark, they'll never let me shroud again!*

"The rest of your crew will be here shortly, along with Chief of Boat Ceresin," said Captain Rosen. "We're in the process of searching your compartment, but we also need to check everyone who was in there before it happened."

"That's fine, ma'am."

"And Chief Sea Officer Blackwood?"

Blackwood looked up at the captain's tone. "Ma'am?"

Rosen put a hand on her shoulder. "I commend your dedication to your parents, but sometimes you need to take the breaks that life offers you. If the army gives you a few weeks of boredom in some research chair at the lab, be grateful for it. Do some reading. Get some sleep. Try to spend time with your brother. The war isn't going anywhere."

Blackwood breathed out slowly as Rosen left the medbay. The reading and the sleep… yeah, that would be nice. But spending time with Andrew? That awful last visit, three months ago, was still vivid in her mind.

Right after their parents died, Blackwood had been given a key to a safety deposit box containing all their research from the last five years. She'd chosen to leave it at the counting firm, thinking it a safer place than their home. But after she'd left for the navy, Andrew had found the key in her room and retrieved the notes. She'd found two boxes stacked in their parents' closet. She'd told Andrew that, especially with the war on, the notes weren't safe there.

But when she'd grabbed the first box, Andrew had physically *attacked* her, kicking the bedroom door off its hinges in the process. Then he started screaming. Something about their goddess, Xeil, and how She'd never guided their parents' spirits to their loved ones after they died. Something about false promises. Not knowing how to answer, Blackwood had shouted back, "It's been five years! Let it go!" Andrew had shut down again as fast as he'd opened up. She couldn't remember if she'd spoken another word the whole time she'd been there. She was positive *he* hadn't. She was equally positive she hadn't gone near that closet again.

She winced. *I just wanted to call when we got back, give him the usual quick update before heading out again. I'm not ready to see him. And I know he doesn't want to see me.*

She was relieved when Holland came to stand by her bunk. The deckman's face was positively ashen.

"How long till we get back, do you think?" he said. "And to the – the laboratory?"

"We'll be docked by half-light tomorrow," said Blackwood. "Ellemko the day after that, if not earlier."

"OK," said Holland, swallowing.

"It *will* be OK," said Blackwood.

"I… I know." Holland put his hands over his stomach and swallowed again, closing his eyes. Blackwood frowned. After facing whatever had been outside during shrouding, *this* was getting to him? Maybe it was delayed adrenaline. Blackwood had heard some people completely lost it several hours after a crisis, especially if they'd never been in one before.

Corpsmate Tolonen came up with a medical bag and set it on the cot next to Blackwood. "This won't take long," she said.

Holland stepped back as Tolonen listened to Blackwood's heart and took her temperature. It was while the corpsmate was shining a bright light straight into her pupils that Blackwood heard the medbay door open again. There were several moments of silence before the newcomer spoke.

"You still have that dekatite on you? Or did you ditch it somewhere in the compartment before they drained it?"

Blackwood tensed.

"Why don't you shut up?" Holland answered, his voice tight.

Footsteps scuffed across the deck. Then Vin said, "Hey, where do you think you're going? The captain said to wait here."

Tolonen finally lowered the light. Blackwood blinked the strobing spots from her eyes.

"I'm not feeling well," said Holland. "I need to run to the head. Move."

"Oh no, you're not getting away that easy."

"*Move*, Vin."

Blackwood's vision finally cleared in time to see Holland try to shove past the other deckman. Vin grabbed him and pushed him back, hard.

"Hey!" Blackwood yelled, leaping to her feet.

Holland crashed backward into the bulkhead, shoved against it by Vin's greater weight. Vin pulled him up, then slammed him again. Holland went down with the second push. Halfway down, Vin's knee caught him in the face. He collapsed with a cry.

"Deckman Vin!" someone roared. By this time, Blackwood had reached Vin, and grabbed the back of his coveralls with both hands.

She yanked him away from Holland, who was staring up from the deck, his bloody hand clamped over his nose.

Blackwood pushed Vin against the adjoining wall, her hand tight around his neck and her knee shoved into his crotch. "We almost died in there, partly because you *left*, and you have the nerve—"

"CSO Blackwood! Stand *down!*"

For several moments, Blackwood kept her gaze locked on Vin's fuming face, fighting to keep from pummeling him through the wall. The tingling in her dekatite mark increased, as if in response to her anger.

"*Mila Blackwood!*"

Blackwood forced herself to step back. She turned toward the door to see the captain standing just inside the compartment. She straightened hurriedly and saluted. Behind her, Vin did the same, breathing in short, angry huffs. The captain looked from one of them to the other, her face furious. Her gaze settled on Blackwood first.

"Do you need to revisit the seminar again, CSO?"

"No, ma'am," said Blackwood stiffly. *Three deep breaths. Vin is not my enemy. My anger is the enemy.* The last thing she needed right now was to be forced into another forty-day anger rehabilitation symposium, where aging military specialists tied every moment of rage to her parents' deaths.

"Captain," Vin said, "I apologize. But Deckman Holland was trying to leave. You told us to wait in here until we were searched!"

"There's no longer any need for a search, Deckman Vin." Rosen held up a long dark chain. Links of dekatite glittered in the medbay lights. "This was found in your bunk during our last sweep. You're under arrest."

Chapter 4

ANDREW'S GUEST

A harsh trilling pierced the dark comfort of Andrew's unconscious, driving into his skull like a needle. He awoke with a gasp, blindly flinging a hand out. He hit something hard. Glass shattered, explosively loud. The trilling sounded again in its wake. He jerked the hand back to shield his face before blinking himself into the real world. His chest, pressed against the mattress beneath him, heaved in an effort to give him enough breath. His heart pounded a violent rhythm. He heard the trill again, but on this side of consciousness, it was comfortably distant, far off in the kitchen. He swallowed, pulling his hand slowly from his face. He didn't recall the dream. Only the terror. Staring at the teetering stacks of books against his wall, he found himself having trouble recalling anything at all. But he did remember he had a reason – a reason to get up. Couldn't remember the reason.

He pushed himself to his feet, allowing his mind to remain in that foggy state without pushing it. Whoever had called on the Wired Correspondence had given up for the moment, and only a familiar throbbing occupied his skull. He smelled alcohol in the air. He remembered the shattered glass only when his bare foot almost slipped in a puddle of liquid. He looked down, noticing the soaked Cordinian Coinavini label, half-torn in the dark red fluid. His brow furrowed. *Coinavini? How under the suns did I afford that?* He started toward his bedroom door, one hand balancing him with the bedpost, the other shaking out the twists in the open button-down shirt and undershorts he wore. Something bit into the side of his foot and he hissed, kicking the shard of broken glass away. *Coinavini*, he thought again. *How much did I waste? Where did I get it?* He laughed under his breath. He wasn't sure why, except that it seemed appropriate. There was an almost genuinely good memory there, hanging just out of reach. A reason to get up. *We were drinking…*

He pulled open his door. Without warning, the WiCorr sounded again. The noise sent a fresh wave of pulsing through his head. Andrew's lips thinned and he limped down the hall. A stab of pain shot through the bottom of his right foot with every step. He rounded the doorway into the kitchen, put one hand on the headset… then paused. Yes. He remembered now. The friend from his past. The drinking. Two days they'd been together, then five days of…

The WiCorr screeched again, insistently loud, vibrating beneath his palm. He snatched the headset from the base and jammed it over his ears one-handed, so the mouthpiece ended up skewed. He pulled it down hard, feeling new pain blossom as his nails dug into his cheek.

"Andrew?"

He kept his gaze on the hallway, eyes darting between the closed doors on either side. The galvanized bulbs had long since burned out, and the two arphanium-powered lanterns were empty now, their crystals sent off for war equipment. His eyes hurt just trying to penetrate the early morning shadows.

"Andrew!"

He winced. "Don't yell," he muttered into the mouthpiece.

"If you'd talk, I wouldn't have to," the voice answered tersely. Mila Blackwood. His sister. Who else would it be? The hallway doors remained closed. Andrew turned, sweeping his gaze over the kitchen. Soup cans were scattered across the floor, fallen during an air raid three days ago. Four. Something like that. A morning beam from the Main Sun illuminated a fine sheen of dust on the floor.

"Is everything OK with you?" Mila said.

"Fine."

"Listen. There's been an incident here. I'm coming back to Ellemko for a while."

"You already told me about the incident. When you called last week." He pulled the long cord from under the WiCorr's base until it trailed on the floor. He rounded the kitchen doorway and made his way toward the living area.

"There was another one," she said. "It's a long story, but I'm being sent back to help out from the capital. I'll probably be working out of the FCB. That's… the Federal Combat Base, obviously."

Andrew paused in his tracks. "You were wounded."

"Not badly."

Andrew nodded. He continued toward the living space, staying as light on his injured foot as he could.

"Are you…" he began.

"Yes?"

"…Planning to stay here?"

There was a pregnant pause before she answered, "I don't know yet. They'll probably choose to put me up at the barracks or something. I wouldn't want to… you know. Put you out."

"Right," he said. The couch came into view. He couldn't see over the arm from his angle, but he could see the large yellow duffel on the floor by the brick fireplace. He wet his dry lips, realizing his heart had begun racing again.

"But I might be able to stop by for a visit," she said. "If that's all right with you."

"Whatever you want."

"It's been over three months since I've seen you."

"I lost track."

"Yeah. But everything's been… you sure you're OK?"

"I told you. Fine."

"OK." Still, she didn't hang up. Andrew could picture his sister straining for something else to say, winding a dark ringlet around her finger, then letting it spring out before picking up another one, over and over again. One of the cushions on the couch moved and a foot came down from the side, swinging to touch the floor. Andrew thought of asking Mila how she'd been injured, but knew it would start a whole new round of her trying to fill awkward silences. So he stayed quiet.

"Well," she finally said, "see you soon."

"Yeah."

The line clicked dead and Andrew pulled off the headset. It dangled in one hand as he stared at the couch.

"You came back," he said.

Cu Zanthus Ayaterossi sat up on the couch, stretching his long arms overhead. He was dressed in a button-down with the sleeves rolled to his elbows. Suspenders hung at his waist over brown plaid trousers, checkered in typical Belzene style. He flashed a grin.

"I was only gone five days. Enough to throw 'em off my trail."

Andrew shook his head. "No one was *after* you. No one came here, Dhavnak soldier or otherwise."

"They were watching your place for draft-dodgers, Andy. Shon Aha save my soul if I'm lying."

"But you were only here for two days! And then Mila called, about that accident she'd been in, and you... you *ran*." Andrew's stomach lurched. That had been after the first accident. Surely, Cu Zanthus wouldn't leave after this one, too. Unless he was afraid of her coming home...

"It wasn't because of Mila!" Cu Zanthus said, as if he'd read Andrew's mind. "I had to make sure, OK? I *don't* want to be found and dragged back to Dhavnakir! I thought you'd understand. But if you want me to find somewhere else to stay–"

"No!" Andrew burst out.

Cu Zanthus frowned.

Andrew swallowed, closing his eyes briefly. "No," he repeated in a whisper. "Stay."

"If you're sure," Cu Zanthus said warily.

"I am. Just seeing you again..."

Escape. Escape from myself. Uncomfortable thoughts. As were the ones about the deep despair he'd fallen into after Cu Zanthus had left again. Though he'd been gone only five days, it was a hard crash from those two endless days of gambling, drinking, getting out of his dead parents' house, ducking into bomb shelters… The word *alive* came to mind. Cu Zanthus was just as thrilling as he'd been three and a half years ago, right before he'd had to move back home. Except now he was… more, somehow. More thrilling. More engaged. More grown up. Before his unexpected return, the only thing that pulled Andrew out of bed at all was the hundreds of pages of handwritten notes left behind by his parents. Dry stuff. Bleak stuff. But at least it was the ghost of a companion. *And Mila was going to take it away.* Anger flashed, hot and bright.

"Andy?"

Andrew looked up, blinking. The anger ebbed, edging back toward the feeling he'd woken up with. *A reason to get up.* "You brought the Coinavini?" he asked. His voice came out rough.

"Of course," said Cu Zanthus. "You remember anything of last night?"

Slowly, Andrew shook his head. "Not really."

"*You* recited the entire second episode of *Darrina Leal Hammers Steel.* In *Dhavvish.* By the gods, how do you know about *Darrina Leal?* You get Dhavnak radio here?"

Andrew huffed out a laugh. "I wouldn't know. Mila threw our radio across the room the same year our…" He shook his head with a violent jerk, stopping the thought dead. "No. I got the comics. Shortly after you moved. I wanted to… know you better. Your country, I mean."

"You read them in Dhavvish? But you don't speak–"

"*Tha, mia dennoch.*"

Cu Zanthus blinked, shocked into silence.

"I taught myself," Andrew added. "After you moved back to Dhavnakir, I…" He felt his face heating and looked down at the headset hanging from his fingers.

"None of your letters were in Dhavvish. You should have said something."

Andrew shrugged. "Wasn't a big deal."

"If you say so," said Cu Zanthus with a slight laugh. "So? Who called?"

"My sister."

"What did she want?"

"Please don't leave again." Andrew hated the words even as they left his mouth.

"What did she *say*, Andy?"

"She's coming home."

Something uneasy flitted across Cu Zanthus's eyes. "Another accident? On her ship?"

"Submarine. Yeah."

"Bad as the last one?"

"Don't know. She's OK, though."

"But they're sending her home?"

"It won't be an issue," said Andrew, his eyes flying up to meet Cu Zanthus's. "She says she'll be working on the base. She'll probably call in a few days and say she's too busy to come by. She doesn't *want* to see me. She just feels like she has to." It hurt more than he expected to say the simple truth out loud. He set his jaw, changing the subject before the anger threatened again. "If she stops by, we'll just explain. You're hiding from the draft. She's known you since you were fifteen, when your whole family lived here. She'll understand."

"I'm not so sure," Cu Zanthus said.

"But she won't stop by."

"Let's hunt up some breakfast. And find some trousers for you, huh?"

Andrew's face heated again. He managed a tight smile and limped back to put the headset on the base, then headed to his room. Cu Zanthus called after him.

"Why's all this blood on the floor?"

"Coinavini!" Andrew called back.

"You need help?"

"No! I'm fine."

Andrew found a pair of gray striped trousers and a clean shirt. His fine brown hair was hanging in his eyes again, though he could have sworn he'd just trimmed it; it had been right after Mila made such a big deal out of how ragged it was. *Three months ago. Right.* He headed to the washroom and relieved himself. Out of habit, he tried flushing, but there was no running water again. He'd gotten a few jugs the week before, with his ration card, but he was pretty sure those were dwindling, too. The money Mila sent home wasn't stretching nearly as far as it used to.

He didn't find any bandages, so he went back to his room to rip off a strip of sheet. The cut was on the outside bottom of his right foot, about as long as his thumb. Sitting on the edge of his mattress, he ran a finger along one side of it, noting the perfect slice the glass shard had made under the bright blood – as neat as the line of a razor. His eyes flitted over the room, picking out dozens of sharp points and broken edges strewn like shattered bone.

The door creaked behind him, and he flinched.

"You OK in here?"

"Fine."

"Let me help you with that." Cu Zanthus came and sat on the bed by Andrew, taking the torn sheet from his hands. "You really sliced this up."

Andrew shrugged. The soft linen sheet wrapped tight around his foot. Andrew kept his eyes on the broken glass. But the stiffness in his shoulders eased.

"Can't thank you enough for letting me stay here," Cu Zanthus said.

"We were friends," said Andrew quietly.

"You're not worried about being arrested for harboring an enemy?" said Cu Zanthus.

"There are other Dhavnaks in Belzen," Andrew answered.

"Naturalized citizens, though."

"The only Dhavnak that was ever killed here was that Onosylvani woman," said Andrew. "The one who requested amnesty. And one of *your* guys did that. An assassin. It set off the war!"

"Plenty of Dhavnaks are still killed here, believe me." Cu Zanthus tied the knot off, then brushed his straight hair from his eyes. It was much darker than Andrew remembered from when he was thirteen and Cu Zanthus fifteen. He must have dyed it to keep a low profile. Despite that, his skin was so pale, it almost shone like arphanium. He glanced around Andrew's bedroom in interest. Andrew tucked his wounded foot beneath his other leg, suddenly self-conscious.

"Living gods, you have a lot of books," Cu Zanthus finally said.

Andrew nervously followed his gaze to the various stacks around the room and on the broken dresser in the corner. *Now he probably thinks I have no life. By the moons, he's right.* His hands clenched in his lap.

Cu Zanthus stood and walked to the closest pile, running a thumb down the spines. "Synivism? You're studying Dhavnak religion?"

"I, um…"

"No, not just Synivism. *Back in Xeil's Arms: What Happens When the Goddess Can't Find a Living Loved One.*" He glanced back at Andrew, brow creased, before turning to the stack again. "*The Exodus of the Cardinian Deities. Survivors in the Stars. Infinite Spirit…* Gods, you even have atheist texts! What, did you get these straight from Qosmya?"

"No. The university," Andrew said faintly.

"Don't you believe in Xeil? Don't *all* Belzenes?"

"Do all Dhavnaks follow the brotherhood?" answered Andrew, his voice barely above a whisper.

"Most. Well, not the Vo Hina worshippers, obviously, or the women. But even they say the Synivistic Oaths every morning during the Bright Cycle…" He paused. "You know, between the rising of the two suns? Bitu Lan and Shon Aha?"

"Half-light."

"Yes. Even if they're not part of the brotherhood, they're still contributing to the commonwealth and well-being of the community. It's all part of…" He trailed to a stop, eyes narrowed. "You've distracted me. Why? What's going on with these books?"

"Nothing. Just… just a project."

"Is it about your parents?"

"It's stupid. Forget it."

"Andy. You can tell me."

Andrew lowered his gaze to the red alcohol-stained floorboards. "Vo Hina betrayed the other gods, right? Shon Aha, Bitu Lan, Luma Nala? With her hoarding?"

"Yes…"

"And after Shon Aha punished her by shattering her eye, there was an eternal darkness over the land. For something like two thousand years, right? Before the gods came back as the suns and moons, and made it light again?"

"The Age of Fallen Light," said Cu Zanthus, nodding. "One thousand, seven hundred, and sixteen cycles of darkness."

"Right. A darkness *caused* by Vo Hina's betrayal. But here's where it gets interesting. That 'fallen light'? It shows up in other religions, too. Even some atheist texts, as the trigger of a mass extinction. It's not just a Synivistic legend."

"Not *just* a Synivistic legend?" Cu Zanthus cut in.

Andrew held up his hands hurriedly. "That's not what I mean. I actually... I mean, through all my studying, that version *does* seem possible. But in our religion – in Xeil's, that is – it isn't mentioned. And I'm trying to figure out whether this darkness was a real actual phenomenon, or whether it was a metaphor that was expounded upon and adopted to fit each religion's demands."

He looked up. Cu Zanthus was staring at him, eyebrows drawn. *Stop,* a voice inside Andrew said. *Stop right now before he leaves, you idiot.* But his mouth kept moving, unheeding.

"So I'm trying to delve more into... you know... the why and how. If your gods – if *any* gods; if anything, period – killed off most of our world in one blow like that, what's to stop it happening again? What caused it the first time? Would we have any control over it in the future?"

"Wait," Cu Zanthus said. "Are you telling me you've been sitting alone in your house studying history and religious texts to try to prevent an ancient darkness from happening again someday? *That's* what you've been doing?"

"Well, if I can find the root cause..."

"But *why*, Andrew? It happened a hundred thousand cycles ago. Doesn't it seem a little crazy to think it'll suddenly–"

Andrew jerked back. "No! It's not crazy!"

"But it doesn't seem–"

"I *know*, OK? I told you it was stupid, I *told* you!" He pressed both hands over his eyes. *What is wrong with me? Why don't I ever keep my mouth shut?*

"I'm sorry. I can tell this is important to you." The mattress shifted as Cu Zanthus sat beside him. "Is it about your parents?" he asked again.

Andrew swallowed hard, struggling to get himself under control. "Why?" he forced out. "Why would you assume that?"

"Because I know how hard it was for you," said Cu Zanthus gently. "What happened to them. So… if you can prove the darkness didn't happen – because there's nothing in Xeil's legends – then maybe you think it proves Xeil is real after all. And that She really did deliver your parents' souls back to you, rather than…"

Andrew made a small noise in the back of his throat and Cu Zanthus trailed off.

"It's just… it's something I read," Andrew finally mumbled. He slowly lowered his hands, but couldn't bring himself to look Cu Zanthus in the eye. Instead, his gaze flicked over the stacks of books against the wall. Cu Zanthus would assume he meant in one of those books. He wouldn't think of his parents' notes… their research…

"Have you told your sister?" said Cu Zanthus.

"About my research? Are you kidding? She'd tell me what a waste of time it was! There's a *war* on, you know."

"But if it's important to you–"

"No," broke in Andrew desperately. "I don't even… I'm not… look, can we just forget it? Please?"

"Are you sure?" said Cu Zanthus. "You know I don't mind."

"Yeah. I'm sure."

Andrew closed his eyes again, trying to claw his way back to that headiness he'd felt upon waking. Fear still lurked, left over from several mornings ago when he'd awoken to find Cu Zanthus gone. It *had* been because of Mila's call, he was sure of it. Though why someone dying on Mila's crew should make him disappear for five days, he couldn't fathom. Cu Zanthus must have been afraid Mila would come back to the house. It was the only thing that made sense. But all that really mattered was the sense of self-hatred and betrayal he'd been left with.

"How long?" he made himself ask. It was a dangerous question, but the sooner he knew, the better he could brace himself for next time. "How long will you be here?"

Cu Zanthus blew his breath out. "Depends how long the war lasts. Dhavnakir will probably take Belzen in, what, the next half-cycle? Easily the next full one. Then Belzen will just become another Dhavnak territory."

Andrew opened his eyes, glancing uneasily at Cu Zanthus. "That wasn't what I…"

A Dhavnak territory? He knew the basics of Dhavnak government, and tried to think what that would mean for Belzen. Women staying home, obviously. The money problems would be better, right? He recalled there being more of an equality between the classes. The government took better care of their people, which couldn't be a bad thing; his own government had cut off the monthly pension Andrew and Mila received from their parents' death pretty abruptly two years before, when the war took a turn for the worst. Had Dhavnakir left its own war orphans in the lurch like that?

No, he realized. Because the kids wouldn't have been left alone in the first place under a Dhavnak government. His mother would have been home that day. *She would never have died.*

He sucked in his breath, a small sharp sound. Cu Zanthus ran a hand over the back of his neck, watching him. Probably still waiting for him to finish his thought.

"What about you?" Andrew asked. "Will you be imprisoned for dodging your draft? If we *are* taken, I mean?"

"I should be fine," said Cu Zanthus, with a reassuring smile. "There'll be more than enough jobs with the rebuilding afterward, and they won't want to lose the labor."

"And what about…"

"Yes?"

Andrew froze, suddenly terrified of the look on Cu Zanthus's face if he finished that question. *Us?* What us? *But as friends.* It was an innocent enough question. Would Cu Zanthus take it that way, though? Or would his conservative Dhavnak beliefs drive him from the house as fast as his feet could take him?

Cu Zanthus was still waiting, his brow furrowing slightly now.

"What about my sister?" Andrew managed. *Wimp.*

"Oh." Cu Zanthus grimaced. "It depends on her level of cooperation."

"You won't get it."

"I don't know, then. Most Belzene women will probably be married to Dhavnak men, to tie the future generations together. Foreigners will be sent back where they came from. The soldiers... I don't know. The women soldiers are even more complicated. If they don't cooperate..." He breathed out slowly. "Prison, maybe."

"Execution?"

"I don't know."

"Right."

Cu Zanthus looked at him closely. "How would you feel about that?"

"Well, of course I don't want Mila to die." Andrew shrugged uncomfortably. "But sometimes, I feel like she might as well be dead, for all the times she bothers calling."

"If you could go back, would you tell her to hide from her draft, too?"

"Mila wasn't drafted."

"She wasn't? Then why'd she..."

"Lots of reasons. The loss of our pension. Her anger at Dhavnakir for what happened to our parents. The fact that she... she didn't want to be a mother. She was gone the second she thought I was old enough to take care of myself. If I died, it'd be a load off her shoulders, and that's the truth."

As if her name had been a summons, the WiCorr jangled from the kitchen again. Andrew pushed himself to his feet. "If she says she has decided to stay here after all, I swear I'll snap that headset in half," he bit out as he headed for the door. Cu Zanthus followed him, leaning against the wall with folded arms and watching. Andrew slipped the headset on, hands holding it tight to his head.

"What?"

Several seconds of silence greeted him. Then, "Cu Zanthus?"

"Yeah. Hold on." He pulled the headset off, holding it out toward the Dhavnak. "It's for you. It sounds like a girl."

Cu Zanthus's face became guarded. "A girl? I haven't been giving your contact info to girls."

"I don't mind. Here." It was a lie. Andrew realized it was a lie as soon as he said it. Why *should* he care if Cu Zanthus had met some Belzene girl? Was he afraid he'd treat her the way Dhavnak men treated *their* women?

Cu Zanthus took the headset and put it cautiously over his ears. "Can I help you?" A couple moments later, a smile spread across his face and he laughed. He pulled the mouthpiece back. "It's not a girl, it's my buddy, Holland. You're quite the highland droll, Andy. Listen, you don't mind if I step into another room for this, right?"

"Of course not," Andrew managed. He waved to his bedroom door, close enough for the long Wired Correspondence cord to reach, barely. Cu Zanthus headed in and closed the door behind him.

Andrew stood in the hallway, staring at the door. Who was Holland? Belzene or Dhavnak? Was it a real name? *Was* it a girl, and Cu Zanthus was just hiding it? Why would he do that? *It's my buddy, Holland.* It felt like a violation, for some reason. *My home. My friend. We were talking, and* you *called and pulled him away.*

Holding his breath, Andrew pushed himself to the dusty wooden floor, putting his ear next to the too-wide gap at the bottom of the door. The smell of spilled Coinavini mingled with dust almost made him sneeze, but he forced it back. Cu Zanthus was right next to the door, an arm's length away. The cord wouldn't be long enough for him to even sit on the bed.

"This makes things easier," he was saying softly in Dhavvish. "I'll find you when you get here. Nothing's gonna happen. More importantly, did you get anything?" There were only a few seconds of silence before he said, "No, no… wait until I see you. Too much riding on this. But it's good news. It's great news."

Andrew heard a bump against the door and didn't dare wait a moment longer. He pushed himself up and scooted back to the kitchen. By the time Cu Zanthus came in, he was knocking dust from a can of sliced potatoes.

"Baked knish?" he said. He didn't have a clue how to make it – didn't remember the last time he'd cooked – but he remembered it as one of Mila's failed recipes, back when she bothered trying to cook for him.

Cu Zanthus eyed the can as he put the headset back on its base. "Wouldn't you need flour? Doubt your ration cards are covering it anymore."

"Flour. Yeah," Andrew muttered.

"I'll see what you've got," Cu Zanthus said, heading toward the pantry.

Andrew grabbed a knife and sawed a circle around the lid. His heart was pounding. He was positive; Cu Zanthus had a girl coming to town. And he'd had to reassure her nothing would happen. What did it mean? Was she Dhavnak? Was Cu Zanthus trying to get her to defect, the same way the Onosylvani woman had? A *war* had been sparked over that incident. Andrew wondered whether Cu Zanthus expected to hide Holland out at his house when she showed up.

But he was bothered more by the thought of sharing Cu Zanthus. Because Andrew had been through this before. When something better came along, he was pushed aside. Every time. His hand slipped and the knife missed the metal, gouging into the side of his finger instead. He threw both can and knife down on the counter and stalked to the washroom, slamming the door behind him.

"Andy?" Cu Zanthus called. "You OK?"

"I'm fine!" he yelled. He sat on the toilet and put his head in his hands, feeling blood flowing from his finger to forge a slow track down his face.

Chapter 5

KLARA YANA'S RENDEZVOUS

The northern border of Ellemko – and, Klara Yana suspected, every other border as well – was heavily guarded by Belzene troops outfitted in brown-checkered combat uniforms and bristling with firearms. Massive anti-tank guns were stationed on either side, and a triangular trench dug twice as wide as Klara Yana was tall, barred the road, wide cylinders filled with concrete waiting behind it. As the military truck from Marldox approached, the infantry guards threw down a thick wooden plank for it to drive over. On the Ellemko side, Klara Yana climbed from the truck, blinking weary eyes in the morning sunlight. The heat was coming in from both suns now – smaller Bitu Lan, straight overhead, and bigger Shon Aha, who'd just cleared the eastern horizon.

Klara Yana took stock of her surroundings. Fifty soldiers present, give or take, though sleek helio-celled Belzene trucks with those huge sand tires came and went frequently, both in and out of the city. The closest building was no more than a pile of rubble, pouring half into the street and forcing the vehicles to pass singly around it. A pair of men, stripped down to their shirtsleeves, loaded broken adobe bricks and steel rebar into carts. Next to that was a four-story structure, still standing but with its sun-baked surface blackened and broken, multiple windows busted out. One hulking monstrosity, just beyond it, was so wracked with gaping black holes that it seemed nothing had survived except the interior construction. The city smelled of lingering smoke and dust, with a subtle undertone that might have been decay.

Klara Yana took off her beret, shaking the wrinkles from it. She was in a full naval dress uniform now – silk neckerchief, black jacket, piping, and a sleeve patch with Belzen's blue and yellow moons symbol embroidered on a tiny flag. Her uniform differed from Blackwood's only by the thin pair of fingerless black gloves she wore, to hide the mark on her palm. They'd been given one night to clean up, rest, and change – in individual rooms rather than barracks, by Vo Hina's good grace. Klara Yana had been able to say the Synivistic Oaths with Bitu Lan's rising, instead of barely mouthing them in fear of the submariners hearing her. She'd been able to wash and dry her breast wrap, and move her dekatite pendant to an inner pocket of the uniform's jacket.

Should have gotten rid of it, she thought for the hundredth time. It had been too close a call. Captain Rosen getting ready to search the crew, Klara Yana faking illness so she could get out and flush it down the head, Vin stopping her... but Rosen had found the chain in time. In the *nick* of time. If that wasn't Vo Hina telling her to hold onto the Broken Eye, she'd be an axolot's lunch.

But she wasn't out yet. If the Belzene government discovered she was a female masquerading as a man, the first thing they'd think would be *Dhavnak*. The very thought of such a disguise would never even occur to a Belzene. With any luck, they'd just look at her hand. *With any luck, Cu Zanthus will extract me before I even get close.* She slipped the beret back onto her short black hair, pulling the brim low so she could peer through Ellemko's broken buildings circumspectly. *He'll get me out. He promised.*

The door of a nearby vehicle opened and a soldier jumped out, trotting over to meet them. He was about thirty cycles old, with a silver bar on his collar and a tobie clamped between his dark lips. "You must be the sailors," he said as he reached them. He pulled the tobie out as an afterthought, blowing smoke into the warm morning air. "Which one of you is Officer Blackwood?"

"I'm Chief Sea Officer Blackwood, sir." Blackwood stepped forward and put her fist to her chest in salute. Klara Yana did the same.

The soldier gave a quick nod. "I'm Lieutenant Nicholls. I'm here to bring you to Admiral Farring at the FCB." He turned and waved for them to follow. They fell in step behind him.

"Has there been a ground invasion yet, sir, or is this all just in preparation?" asked Blackwood.

"In preparation, thank the moons. The air raids are bad enough." Nicholls came to a stop at the back of his automobile. It was an open-topped vehicle with a long body and three axles. Its helio-cells were built into its sloped sides. The front section had room for a driver and passenger, and the back part had space for another six or so. A Kohut-something, Klara Yana recalled from her studies.

Nicholls turned and tossed something back. Blackwood caught it. A pack of tobies. "Help yourselves, sailors," he said. "I have to grab something, then we'll be on our way." He jogged toward the border.

Blackwood pulled one out and passed the packet to Klara Yana. "Need a light?"

"I got one, ma'am." Klara Yana pulled a lighter from her pocket. Authentic Belzene issue and everything. She pulled a tobie and put it on her lips, then passed the rumpled package back. She was grateful for the deadnettle-infused skijj, even sour and spiced as it was. She stuck her other hand in her pocket and relaxed her hips, letting a natural boredom take her body. With the hand holding the tobie, she rubbed her wrist across her forehead under the beret, wiping away a layer of sweat. Shon Aha even looked bigger up north from the equator. How did they stand the heat here?

"Got a question," said Blackwood.

"Go ahead, CSO."

"That mark of yours. Does it bother you?"

Klara Yana rubbed her fingertips over her palm within her pocket. She kept one eye on Nicholls, now chatting with a pair of soldiers by the anti-aircraft gun. "Still hurts, ma'am. Just a distant ache, though."

"Mine's tingling," said Blackwood. "Kind of numb. I don't like it. Bad enough there's a layer of *dekatite* in our skin. What in Xeil's name is it doing to our nerves? Our muscles? Our blood? With what we know about it now... what it can do in combination with arphanium... I'm not real comfortable with the idea of carrying that around in my body. You know?"

"I do, ma'am," Klara Yana muttered. The thing that had grabbed her hand from outside the submarine suddenly surfaced in her mind again, and she suppressed a shiver. "We're lucky we're alive. Let's just remember that." The mark *was* tingling; she didn't think it had been before, but now that Blackwood had brought it up, she couldn't think of anything else. She took another drag on the tobie, long and deep, grimacing slightly at the foreign taste.

What if Cu Zanthus gets me home and the Dhavnaks *want to study me? Maybe Cu Zanthus won't ask what's under the glove. Maybe I don't even mention it.* But then would he wonder why she'd been sent back to Ellemko for questioning in the first place?

She blew out the smoke slowly. *Just think about the promotion.* Her ama's face flashed vividly in her mind for a second. It was an image Klara Yana revisited often, because it was one of the few times she'd seen her smile. She'd just been chosen as part of Dhavnakir's initiative to employ more females in prestigious jobs. *This is a sure sign things are changing,* she'd said, her pale face flushed in excitement. *Someday,* all *women will be able to choose whether to work or stay home.*

I believe it, ama, Klara Yana thought. *But that's not what you should've been worried about.* Her ama had disappeared during a diplomatic mission outside of Dhavnakir less than a cycle later. Dhavnakir wasn't the enemy here. It was the countries hoarding resources from them and cutting off their trade. It was countries that would take innocent envoys as political prisoners. It was countries like Belzen.

"I never saw your mark," Blackwood said, oblivious to the dark turn her thoughts had taken. She looked at Klara Yana curiously as she put her dark ringlets up in a ponytail, completely unhindered by the tobie she held.

Klara Yana watched as some desert creature slithered under the tires of the Kohut – like a highland snake, but with claws and a sharp curving tail – and did her best not to cringe. She wrenched her gaze up to Nicholls instead, purposely taking as long as possible to blow out the smoke from her last drag. The lieutenant was on his way back, a couple rifles slung over his shoulder. He was on his own. It appeared it would be only the three of them for this trip back to the base.

Klara Yana waited until he'd almost reached them before answering Blackwood. "Yes, ma'am. I'm afraid it's not impressive compared to yours, though." She started to pull out her other hand, as if she intended to show Blackwood, but Nicholls arrived, interrupting the moment.

"Here you are, sailors," he said. "EMI rifles. Admiral's orders."

Blackwood dropped her tobie and ground it out with her heel before reaching to take the gun. "What for, sir?"

"On any given day," Nicholls said, "we might face planted explosives, snipers, deserters, you name it. There are already Dhavvies in Ellemko; they're just not advertisin' themselves yet. You need to be ready to take one out the second you see 'em. Things around here can go ass backwards faster than you can blink."

Klara Yana kept up a constant assessment of the city as the Kohut drove through its battered streets. It was bigger than she'd expected. The buildings were flat and wide, but they towered overhead to much the same height as the ones in Dhavnakir's capital. She knew the population to be only a little over half of Corvenyon, but the hulking structural style gave Ellemko a feel of massiveness… almost *heaviness*. They had as much steel as buildings back home did, but were designed with the old-fashioned adobe sand bricks as inspiration. If not for the jagged chunks out of them, the crumbling facades, the burned faces, the shattered windows, they might have held a touch of beauty, despite their broadness. But now they just felt confining, and all too capable of collapsing with a breath.

Klara Yana also studied the dark-skinned pedestrians. They favored patterned fabrics, with knee-length skirts for the women and button-downs or vests for the men. Most of the women wore their curls piled on top of their heads. The ones in nicer clothes often had wide-brimmed hats over the hairstyles, with satin coneflowers on their bands. Impossible not to notice how many of those women walked alone, or in pairs without men. Equally impossible not to notice how few people were around for such a big city in midmorning. Those she did see talked with heads huddled together, if they talked at all, and looked up at the sky often.

"When was the last air strike, sir?" Blackwood said. Her voice carried easily to the lieutenant over the vehicle's impossibly quiet motor, so different than the biodiesel engines in the Dhavnak rovers Klara Yana was used to. Belzen, she reflected, was the first place she'd ever been that seemed somehow *too* quiet to be at war.

"We were struck three days ago," Nicholls called back over his shoulder.

"Why are the streets so empty? Are folks hiding?"

"Everyone's been fleeing to the east or west. Trying to cross the borders into Criesuce or Sohos, while they still can. 'Course Criesuce's civil war's heated up to the point they're not sending aid anymore, and both Sohos and Descar have been part of Dhavnakir's empire for going on seventeen years now. Maybe folks think they can get to northern Atrary. Wouldn't count on it myself, though."

Klara Yana kept only half an ear on the conversation. She scanned every pedestrian she could – the sweeper in front of the shop, the man on a bench with a periodical, the couple sharing a smoke at a street corner – hoping she'd see Cu Zanthus look up and catch her eye. Folks did glance at them, from time to time, but their faces were exhausted – or worse, empty.

It was strikingly different from the atmosphere back home in Corvenyon. All the fallen buildings and broken streets would have been swarmed over with workers by now. There'd be an industry line of people stretching out of sight, a rollicking chant started to bump up cheer and productivity. There'd be women in that line. Children, too. And instead of despair, there'd be bolstered hope that they'd get through it together again, like they had once already. There was no hope here, no banding together, no sense of kinship at all. Just a depressing air of isolation. It made her ache for home in a way she hadn't in a long time. *Cu Zanthus, where are you?*

"You're not from Ellemko," said Blackwood. "Are you?"

"What?" Klara Yana returned her gaze to Blackwood. Nicholls, in the front, was speaking into a handheld radio now, and Blackwood was looking at her.

"The way you're gawking. It's like you've never seen it before."

"No, ma'am," said Klara Yana. "Artora. To the east. Small town."

"Near the border?"

"Yes, ma'am."

"Still doesn't explain the light skin. You *are* part-Dhavnak, right?"

Klara Yana flashed back on Vin punching her in the face. "My mother was from southern Descar," she said firmly. "*Not* Dhavnakir."

She caught the subtle relaxation of Blackwood's shoulders. The CSO had defended her well on the submarine, but there was still a part of her that felt uncomfortable associating with a Dhavnak. *I vowed I'd do whatever it took to keep their legacy out of Dhavnak hands,* she'd told Captain Rosen.

Klara Yana shook Blackwood's words from her head, annoyed with herself. *Lose the emotions. They've done the same thing to us. They sent a spy to rob the Synivistic Sacrarium, by Vo Hina's grace!*

"What about your father?" Blackwood asked. "Part-Criesucan, I'm guessing?"

"Oh. The eyes," said Klara Yana. "Yeah, I've heard that."

"It's not true?"

"I don't know, ma'am. Maybe. I never knew my real father. Disappeared when I was a baby."

"Oh." Blackwood's eyes crinkled in sympathy. "Sorry to hear that."

"It doesn't matter, ma'am. My mother... remarried. It was a long time ago." She tensed, hoping Blackwood wouldn't follow up with questions about the abusive husband her ama had been assigned.

But Blackwood went in a different direction. "So which one of them had that eye color?"

Klara Yana barely held back a flinch. Because there it was. It wasn't such a strange color that people stopped and stared – most of the time – but they did *notice*. And being noticed meant being remembered. How could a spy blend in and disappear if people *remembered* her?

"My mother, ma'am," she said with an offhand shrug. *Curse Cu Zanthus for not warning me I'd be swimming in the gods-damned ocean on this mission! I could've brought a backup pair of optics and avoided all this.* She cast about for a change in subject – how in Shon Aha's name had this conversation become about her, anyway? – when something glinted across the street, five stories up. She jerked her attention toward the building, pulling her rifle up.

"Holland?" said Blackwood.

Klara Yana caught sight of a shadow on the top floor only a split second before a gunshot sounded, its sharp crack echoing off the buildings around them. Blood sprayed as Nicholls took the shot in the head. Screaming filled the air as any pedestrians around cleared out, fast. The vehicle careened sideways, but another shot, right on the heels of the first, took out a tire and sent the Kohut lurching into the sidewalk hard enough to jar bones. Klara Yana, halfway on her feet already, grabbed the side before she was thrown into the front seat.

"Off the truck!" Blackwood yelled. She leaned over the front seat just long enough to snatch the radio from Nicholls's limp hand.

Klara Yana leapt from the open truck, putting it between her and the building, but her heart pounded with adrenaline. It was Cu Zanthus extracting her. She was positive. She put the EMI rifle to her shoulder and crept toward the back of the vehicle in a crouch. Blackwood landed behind her. Klara Yana heard her speak into the radio.

"Sniper firing on Belzene soldiers, old Highland Bank headquarters. One man down."

Klara Yana turned her head. "Cover me, CSO. I'm going after him."

"You're *what?*" Blackwood said incredulously.

But Klara Yana was already running, leaping over a crumbled sidewalk curb and into the awning of the building. She tried the handle on the steel door. Locked. She heard another shot, and looked back to see Blackwood stagger with a gasp of pain. She gritted her teeth. *She was supposed to* cover *me, not* follow *me!*

Blood stained the left sleeve of Blackwood's brown uniform, but she ran just as fast as before, her rifle clutched in her right hand.

"Wait there for *me*, Holland!" she snapped. "That's an order!"

Klara Yana caught sight of an object falling a split second before it hit the ground. "Blackwood! *Down!*" she screamed. She turned her own face just in time to shield her eyes from the shock grenade's impact, hands as tight over her ears as possible with the rifle still in her grip. The crash of noise still seemed to drown her, throwing off her balance and sending her stumbling against the steel door. But as she'd suspected, no shrapnel tore into her body; Cu Zanthus wouldn't have wanted to risk killing her. She pulled her hands down and bashed the stock of her rifle against the door handle, giving it three powerful strikes before the lock broke. She shoved the door open with her foot and bolted inside, rifle at her shoulder again. She could still hear somewhat, though even the clash of her rifle on the door had been muted. Someone yelled outside, but it was too soft to make out the words. Blackwood calling for her again, no doubt. She sped up into a quiet run, taking the first turn she saw and following a hallway deeper into the framework. *Stairs. Have to find stairs.*

Holes in the floor above let in only a small amount of light, and the blackened, peeling walls of the interior absorbed even that. Many of the doors on either side of the hallway were closed, but a few hung askew and others were gone. Smashed desks and upended bookcases were visible within, as well as what were unmistakably bodies, half-buried in the detritus.

A gunshot sounded up ahead. Klara Yana winced, hoping Cu Zanthus didn't kill Blackwood. Yes, it would make the best cover story – where would Blackwood think she'd disappeared to, otherwise? – but it was the first time she'd worked with a woman like her, and the thought of being responsible for her death pained her. Cu Zanthus would chastise her for getting too close to her mark if she brought it up, and it wouldn't be the first time, either

She cursed and increased her pace, finally stumbling across a stairwell that headed up to the right, scattered with broken wood and scorched pieces of wall from a jagged gap overhead. She had just hurtled up to the first landing and swung herself around to the next switchback when a black-clad figure charged into sight above.

Klara Yana stepped back, bracing herself against the wall as she pointed her rifle. She almost fired when she didn't see Cu Zanthus's familiar blond military haircut, but remembered just in time that his hair was dark with a straight part now. As always, she was jolted by his youth. She knew he'd been a spy since the tender age of fourteen; now, at nineteen, he still looked to her like he belonged with front line rank-and-files rather than as a kommandir deep in an operation. She knew nothing about the contact that had informed him of the open spot on the submarine, and could only guess the Dhavnak government had needed someone younger to get the intel. She'd seen first-hand how people automatically dismissed an insecure-looking youngster.

Cu Zanthus hurried down to her level, shoving the barrel of her gun aside and leaning close, gray eyes focused on hers.

"What do you have for me, Keiller Yano?" he said, addressing her by her male Dhavnak name. Though they'd worked together for two cycles now, he still didn't suspect her true gender.

"They're traveling through dekatite veins, using arphanium crystal pipes," she said. "Some other realm or reality, I don't know. It's dangerous. There are creatures."

"Creatures?" His brow furrowed. "Another *realm?*"

"I know. It sounds crazy. But I was there. That's how they're getting to us. From one dekatite vein to another."

"Which dekatite vein were they using?"

"Kheppra Isle. The whole island is made of dekatite."

"Wow," Cu Zanthus said. "OK. Anything else?"

"Go through surrounded by steel. That's the only safe way. Unless you're wearing dekatite. Whatever you do, don't bring dekatite when you're traveling through."

"Travel through dekatite, but not *carrying* dekatite. Arphanium pipes. Kheppra Isle. Got it." He took a deep breath. "Good work, Keiller Yano. Now here's an address for you. Twenty-eight Bellamy Road. It's near the Sandhill Primary School. Repeat it back."

"Twenty-eight Bellamy Road."

"Good. There's a loose brick on the front I'll use as a drop site if I have further instructions. Find your comrade and say you lost me. Apologize, blame it on your hotheadedness, say whatever you need to get back on her good side." He turned toward the broken window behind her, putting a foot on the sill.

"Wait!" Klara Yana held a hand out. "I thought you were going to extract me!"

"No. We want someone on the inside of the technology, at least until we get a foothold in using it ourselves. But your intel will move that forward faster. The more you can get, the better."

"But they're going to… the in-depth questioning, the…"

"Are they suspicious?" His gaze snapped back to her face, an underlying fury in his eyes.

"No. No! I swear!"

"Then get back out there before you ruin everything!" He grabbed her arm and shoved her toward the stairs. She stumbled down the first few steps, then grabbed the broken bannister, looking back.

"Cu Zanthus. My promotion."

His mouth twisted. "I'll check on it."

Then he pulled another shock grenade from his pocket, yanked the pin, and sent it across the floor, so quickly she didn't have time to look away. Searing, white light burned into her eyes, as excruciating as staring directly at Shon Aha. At the same time, a deafening bang hit her ears. The world disappeared as her senses went dead. Her body tilted, and she felt the sharp edges of the staircase jabbing into her shoulders, hips, and legs as she tumbled to the ground floor. She finally came to a stop, but could do no more than lay there with her gloved hands pressed to her eyes, as if she could even now protect them from the pain. The tingling Blackwood had mentioned had intensified, until her hand felt half-dead. Her heart hammered with a combination of anger and fear. She knew Cu Zanthus had done it to help the realism of her not catching him, but all she could think of was being left behind with the enemy. *It's my job. He did what he had to. And I'll do the same.*

She rolled to her stomach and tried to open her eyes, but couldn't manage more than slits before they teared up and closed again. Blindly, she groped her fingers over the filthy floor. Her rifle was nowhere to be found.

"Holland! Holland!" Blackwood's voice penetrated her ringing eardrums. Klara Yana got her hands under her and struggled to her knees. The world rocked beneath her. She finally forced her eyes open, though she had to stare through a blur of tears. Blackwood came into focus, kneeling in front of her.

"I lost him," she choked out.

"You're an idiot!" Blackwood shot back. "You could have been *killed*. What were you thinking?"

"I'm sorry, CSO. When Nicholls was shot, I... I didn't think. I just wanted to catch him. I–"

"You disobeyed a direct order! I thought you were smarter than that, Holland! For Xeil's sake, I've never been so–" Blackwood ended the thought with a snarl, fingers curling into fists. Klara Yana realized the CSO was fighting not to lash out at her the way she had at Vin in the medbay.

"I'm sorry," Klara Yana said again. "But after facing that... that thing during shrouding, it just seemed so *stupid*, hiding from some guy with a gun." She put a hint of rage in her voice there; men were ruled by their aggression, and that's exactly what would have driven young Deckman Holland to such a reckless action. "But you're right. I should have listened. I promise it won't happen again, ma'am."

Blackwood glared at her, pulling in long deep breaths through gritted teeth. Klara Yana had to close her eyes as another wave of dizziness washed over her. She hadn't been stunned by a shock grenade in a long time, not since her training with the NIC. She'd forgotten how miserably disorienting it was.

"What did he look like?" Blackwood finally said. "Get any details?"

"Black shirtsleeves and trousers. Tall boots. Had a hood pulled up."

Blackwood grunted. "It's not much. But more than I saw."

"Yes, CSO."

"Look at me, Holland." Blackwood waited until Klara Yana opened her eyes again before continuing. "I was shot. Do you know what that means? It means I was wounded because of *your* carelessness. You could face serious charges for this. You know that. Right?"

"Yes, CSO," Klara Yana said faintly.

Blackwood let out a sigh through her teeth. "But you saved my life on the boat, and I don't want to do that to you right at the start of your career. So grow up, for Xeil's sake, and *listen* to your commanding officer. No matter what. Not only can you land yourself in prison, you can get yourself and your entire team killed. *Do you understand me?*"

"Yes, CSO. I understand. It won't happen again."

Blackwood took Klara Yana's arm and helped her to her feet. Klara Yana took a shuddering breath, casting one last glance back at the stairwell. Then she followed Blackwood out of the building.

Chapter 6

BLACKWOOD AND THE SCIENTISTS

They were picked up by an APT Rambler – a vehicle so old, it still had a loudly rumbling engine from the days they'd used axolot biodiesel from Dhavnakir. The fact that they'd had to pull out war equipment from over ten years ago wasn't a good sign. Blackwood sat up front with the sergeant who'd collected them, holding her beret clamped over her aching gunshot wound. She just wanted to close her eyes, but the sergeant yelled over the roaring engine the whole way back, apologizing for taking so long to pick them up. He said they'd uprooted a cell of saboteurs the day before, planting explosives at infrastructure sites, and a brutal firefight had broken out. One of the bombs had gone off, taking out a water treatment plant and destroying half its supply. Added to the water shortages they always battled during dry season, panic had broken out; even now, soldiers were piling into transports to help quell the southwestern quadrant, which had been the first to have its rations cut.

Blackwood tuned him out and glanced back to check on Holland. The deckman had gone pale and silent, probably still shaken by either his encounter with the assassin or his reprimand from Blackwood. His eyes took in the damaged statue of a soldier half-obscured by fallen wreckage, the tank traps and anti-infantry barricades bristling with barbed wire in the FCB's plaza, the sliding iron gate with the sharply bent corner, the ragged brick wall and dark archways. That wide-eyed gaze, so similar to the one he'd had on the boat, reminded her that young and stupid was sometimes just young and scared out of your mind. His reckless behavior earlier that day didn't change that; everyone handled fear differently. At least he hadn't frozen or run away, the way she'd heard some new recruits did. But not obeying orders...

I have to get this kid straightened out, she thought. *If he does that again, we're gonna end up losing a good sailor.*

Between the lateness of the day, finding a medic to dress Blackwood's wound, and the general chaos in the wake of the rioting, Blackwood and Holland were given two cots in a cleared-out office and told to report to the underground lab first thing in the morning. They were also given two clean dark brown uniforms, infantry-style, along with a couple of barely-heated slivertail breast patties seasoned with snappy pepper, and a handful of freeze-dried vict bars. The bars were made of cactus mash and bean paste – a recent recipe Blackwood wished the military had never discovered, despite food shortages. Blackwood watched as Holland choked his way through the heavily spiced bird, taking gulps of tepid water often. Small town tastes, no doubt, unused to the spiciness of Ellemko's food. The vict bars were left untouched. Blackwood stuck them in her trouser pockets for later.

A soldier was posted outside the door, "just in case they needed anything." Blackwood privately wondered whether he was supposed to keep them in or others out. She was almost too tired to care. Although the Main Sun hadn't yet sunk, she collapsed onto the bunk, still fully clothed in her naval dress uniform, and passed out instantly. It seemed she'd only been asleep seconds before Andrew was banging on the outside of the submarine again.

Mila! Don't abandon me! Please!

She gasped, opening her eyes to blackness. The painkiller she'd been given had worn off, and the stab of pain in her bandaged bicep was excruciating. The dekatite brand, on her other arm, tingled as if it had cut off her blood flow. On the opposite side of the room, Holland slept, his breathing long and deep. Blackwood's ponytail was a hard knot under her head. She reached back and pulled the band out.

Despite her exhaustion, sleep didn't return. She found herself thinking of Vin, and the dekatite chain. What had he been thinking, to risk all their lives like that? The sergeant's news about saboteurs struck an uncomfortable chord there. Could Vin really be such a thing? He'd been with them for two years. But she supposed spies could be planted at any time, and could lie dormant as long as necessary. If it was true, he'd failed, and he'd pay for it.

She thought about Andrew, and mentally wrote the beginnings of conversations should she see him again. Most ended after a couple awkward moments with her saying she hoped he was well and she had to get back to the base. *I'm sure it'll be true, anyway.* The scientists' approaching tests seemed almost better than trying to fill his terrible silences. But then her mind turned to the scientists themselves. What *were* they going to do? She pictured them cutting the mark out of her arm, severing muscle and nerves, chopping off Holland's hand… She shivered. *If it'll help protect our parents' research, it's worth it.*

She realized Holland's breathing had changed and he'd shifted position on his cot. He was whispering, too quiet to make out any words, almost too quiet to hear at all, except for the abnormally quiet office space. Blackwood listened for a moment, but heard little more than the hitches in his breath. She turned to her side.

"Holland?"

He fell silent abruptly. "CSO," he finally said. "I hope I didn't wake you."

"No. I couldn't sleep. What were you saying just now?"

"Just… just talking to my mother. It's nothing."

"Your mother? You talk to her?"

"Sometimes."

"Is she still alive?"

"Don't know, ma'am."

Blackwood raised her eyebrows, surprised. "How long have you been on your own?"

"Um. A long time, CSO. At least ten – ten years."

"You were a child," Blackwood said softly.

"Yes, ma'am."

"Then you have something in common with my brother and I. We lost our parents at a young age, too. I was eighteen. Andrew was twelve. I raised him on my own for the next three years."

"Fifteen, ma'am?" said Holland after a few moments. "You left him when he was fifteen?"

"Yes, that's right."

"Did he have relatives staying with him?"

"N- No. He was old enough to take care of himself. I only made things worse by being there."

"Is he still around?" asked Holland.

"Yes. I told him I'd try to stop by. He lives here in Ellemko. Maybe I'll introduce you. You're almost the same age, you'd get along." Not likely. But who knew? He'd seemed to hit it off with that Dhavvie kid down the street four years back. Even with the increasing tensions between their countries, Blackwood had been sorry when the kid had to move back. He'd drawn Andrew out again when nothing else worked. *He's probably in the army now, fighting to take Belzen away from us. Maybe after they've taken us, he can get in touch with Andrew again.* She snorted under her breath.

"CSO?"

"I think you'd be good for him," she said. "Someone closer to his age, with a similar past. You can show him it's OK to move on. To live a life outside the shadow of grief."

"Sure, CSO," said Holland, his voice cautious. "I'd be happy to."

Blackwood sat up, wincing at the stab of pain in her bicep, and glanced at the dark sandpane in the far corner. "Bet it's right around half-light. I swear, that early morning shift is in my bones now."

"Could be, ma'am."

She found the infantry uniform on her cot, still folded. "You already changed?"

"Yes, ma'am."

"Well, let me get dressed, and we'll head down and get this over with."

"Ma'am?"

"We were told first thing in the morning. Come on, Holland. When things seem overwhelming, getting back in control is half the battle. You have the stones to chase a sniper into a building, you can handle some scientist looking at your hand."

"I… I guess you're right, ma'am."

"Stick by me," said Blackwood, pushing herself to her feet. "I won't let 'em hurt you."

She prayed to Xeil it was a promise she could keep.

"Well, I'll be sandblasted if you ain't the child of Carrie and Owen Blackwood!"

"Yes, ma'am. That's me." Blackwood did her best to extricate her hand from the overeager scientist who greeted her and Holland just inside the lab. Rows and rows of stone-varnished tables lined the room, glass vials stacked neatly in racks in each one's center. Each table had a faucet at the end opening over a tiny sink. Despite the earliness of the day, four students, barely out of secondary school, worked in aprons, pouring colored liquids into beakers or holding pots over small flames. The air smelled astringent and sour. The lab was lit with old galvanized power, old enough to hum loudly through the warm air.

"I'm Doctor Nadia Zurlig." The woman twisted her long, red hair into an impossibly neat chiffon on the back of her head in seconds flat. The broad smile hadn't left her freckled Atrarian face. "I *worked* with your parents, Mila! Fact, I met you when you were no taller than a pygmy poke. Back then, you were 'bout as prickly as one too, if I recall."

Blackwood smiled politely. "Sorry, ma'am, but I don't remember."

"Your parents were good folks, Mila, good as I've ever known. Only reason I wasn't with 'em the day they… well, you know the day… was that my own young one was sick at home. Timmon, you remember 'im?"

"Sorry, ma'am."

"He's workin' the train yard now, pulling all-night shifts. I bet he'd remember you. How's your brother?"

Blackwood cut a quick look to Holland. The other sailor was looking around the lab, head still but eyes moving to take in every detail, as if he'd be quizzed the second they left. Blackwood had never seen anyone as aware of his surroundings as this kid. She suppressed a sigh as she turned back to Zurlig.

"He's fine, ma'am, as far as I know. I don't get back to see him much." Gently, she tried to steer the conversation to their reason for coming. "Were you contacted about... our situation?"

"Of course. Follow me out this way and we'll grab Doctor Marson. We have a separate lab we use for–" she glanced back at the seemingly absorbed students as she headed out the door, "–the special projects." She whistled under her breath as they headed down the hall. "Just think. Your parents working with the early R&D for shrouding, and now here you are, six years later, with some trials of your own. 'Spect your parents would be proud."

She glanced back again, and then paused as she noticed Holland in Blackwood's wake. "This guy's with you, then?" she said with a jerk of her thumb.

"Yes, ma'am," said Blackwood. "Apprentice Deckman Holland. If not for his help, I'd be dead now."

Zurlig grunted. Her streak of friendliness was gone, as suddenly as that. She stopped at a door and pounded on it with her fist.

"Marson! Up and at 'em! The sailors are here, and there's a war on. No time to waste."

"Coming." A man pushed the door open, thinning hair brushed over his dark scalp. He pushed his spectacles up onto his head as he came out, pushing his neat hair strands into disarray. His eyes lit up at the sight of them. "Is it true? Dekatite? In your skin?"

"Marson," Zurlig growled, "save it for the lab."

Marson fell into step beside Blackwood as Zurlig led them the rest of the way down the hall. Dutifully, he kept his mouth shut until Zurlig had unlocked three sets of locks on an iron door at the end and thrown the light switch. They walked into a cavernous room, walls and ceiling covered in crisscrossed steel bars. The room was so long, Blackwood could barely see the other side. Although a combination of galvanized and arphanium lanterns lined the ceiling, the arphanium crystals were absent from the globes.

The galvanized light, though, gleamed off tanks, military trucks, a few small aircraft, and even a midget sub and a stack of torpedoes. The northern and eastern walls of the room, including the corner, were made up of rock, rather than steel. The lab had been built right up against a mountain, and the reason was obvious; swathes of dekatite had been uncovered, until monstrous expanses of the dark gray and silver stone sparkled in the artificial light. Blackwood realized they must shroud from one section to another during their experiments. Every vehicle in the room was probably outfitted with arphanium pipes. Blackwood couldn't help glancing at the torpedoes. She hadn't heard they were testing nonpiloted vessels yet. But the benefits were undeniable. Send one of those through and they wouldn't even need to risk a life.

Zurlig closed the door behind the four of them, locking it for good measure. "Let's see what you got."

Blackwood pulled the uniform's right sleeve up, exposing the lightning streak of dekatite branded into her arm. Beside her, Marson sucked in his breath. He put out a hand.

"May I?"

"Go ahead, sir," Blackwood said.

Marson ran his fingers over the thin strands of deep gray, sparkling metallically, that ran between her wrist and forearm. Blackwood didn't feel anything at all; it was like the dekatite wasn't even part of her skin. The tingling that plagued it hung deep underneath, in her nerves, too deep to be affected. Out of the corner of her eye, she saw Holland peeling off his left glove for Zurlig. She couldn't see anything from her angle, but Zurlig bent over it, eyebrows raised.

"They're quite different, aren't they?" she said. "Yours, Mila, looks like a streak of lightning came right out of the vein and into your skin. Your associate's, on the other hand... there's a circular design here, sort of, distorted a bit. Almost like they were different... creatures... that struck you. Or different phenomena." She held Holland's hand flat with both her own, splaying his fingers so wide that Holland grimaced. "Did you feel anything?" Zurlig asked him.

"Something grabbed my hand, ma'am," said Holland. "And then, right after, there was a shock. Energized, like a galvanized jolt. Blackwood was thrown. She lost consciousness."

"But not you?"

"No, ma'am."

"Has anything happened since then? Away from the shrouding?"

"Just a tingling," said Blackwood. "No pain. No… creatures, nothing like that."

"Tingling," said Marson. "Like an energized shock? Under the skin?"

"Maybe," said Blackwood.

Zurlig released Holland's hand. Holland quickly folded his hand back to his side, but not before Blackwood caught a glimpse of a curved dekatite line against his palm, a little thicker than hers. The shape of the boat itself, maybe? No. She could almost put her finger on it… but Zurlig broke in before she could follow the line of thought any further.

"Was there dekatite on the boat?"

"Yes, ma'am," said Blackwood. "One of my deckmen."

"With you at the time this happened?"

"At the time of the accident, yes. At the time of the markings, no."

"Was it someone you knew well?"

"I… I thought so."

Zurlig nodded. Her gaze lingered on Holland for several moments before she turned her attention back to Blackwood. "There was one experiment that resulted in a marking similar to yours."

Blackwood's heart leapt. "That means—"

"And in that one case, we were able to shroud the subject without any sort of protection afterward."

"No protection?" The bottom dropped from Blackwood's stomach. "But I'd heard *no one* had successfully shrouded without shielding and not been killed."

"That was the only time," Marson said from behind her. "We've tried replicating it other ways. Suits, for example, but we could never go that small with arphanium pipes. And simply holding arphanium resulted in horrendous deaths, even when we *did* put a suit of metal on individual soldiers. But sending soldiers through by themselves is something we've wanted to do for a long time."

"But what about the mark?" Blackwood asked. "How did it happen last time?"

"During shrouding," said Zurlig. "Same as you. The subject who received it was the only survivor in that group."

"And then afterward they were able to shroud... unshielded."

"Indeed."

"And then what? Where is this person now?"

"Gone," said Zurlig.

"You mean dead," said Blackwood.

"It wasn't connected to the mark. There were... other circumstances."

"You mean the factory accident? The one that killed my parents?"

Zurlig just stared at her, unblinking.

"How long after this experiment did *that* happen?" Blackwood said sharply.

"You know I can't talk about it."

"Just tell me if it was connected."

"Respectfully, Officer Blackwood, you need to stop asking. It is not within your authorization."

Blackwood's breath was speeding up. This was different than the building anger she was used to. There was a seed of real fear in there that she hardly recognized. She tried her breathing exercise anyway. *Three deep breaths. My anger is the enemy. Not...*

She couldn't stay focused. Her thoughts burst out before she could stop them. "This is insane! I was afraid of you cutting us up, but making us shroud without a *scrap* of protection? I saw the bodies in *Desert Crab*'s first accident – they were torn up, *mutilated*, like a nest of cleaving scorps had torn them apart!" She pointed at Holland, who stood frozen, watching. "If not for the two of us, every sailor on that submarine would be dead. And *this* is how you repay us? By *forcing* us into the shrouding realm unshielded?"

She hoped desperately she was wrong, and that she'd somehow, miraculously, jumped to the wrong conclusion. But Zurlig broke that hope with her next words.

"I'm sorry, Mila, but in these times, it's worth the risk. Those of us who worked with Scicorp Industries have reason to believe we can't leave marks like these uninvestigated. Please. Try to trust me."

"We'll give you a single crystal of arphanium," said Marson. "It should allow you to pass."

"But aren't those the times that resulted in horrendous deaths?" Blackwood protested.

"Not in people marked as you are."

"*One* person," said Blackwood. "You only mentioned one person. A person who died shortly afterward anyway. You don't actually *know* that we won't die."

"That's why they're called experiments," said Zurlig, an edge of impatience entering her voice. "Seeing whether you survive your first unshielded trip into the shrouding realm is only the first step. It'll just be long enough for you to give us a good report of your surroundings. To see if the dekatite mark draws any creatures, and whether they seem hostile. You'll be in and out before you know it."

Seeing whether you survive is only the first step. With those words, Blackwood realized the horrible truth. They didn't care. Despite Zurlig knowing her as a child, despite everything Blackwood had done for the Belzene military, they were more concerned with using those marks of theirs. Maybe they *wanted* them to survive the shrouding realm without protection – but they didn't necessarily *expect* them to. They were more interested in the outcome of the experiment than in keeping either of them alive.

And her duty, as an officer in the navy, was to offer up her body to those ends.

Zurlig, seeing the despair in her eyes, softened. "You don't have to walk into the dekatite right now, Mila. We can take this one step at a time."

Blackwood nodded, swallowing. "OK. Yes. What's the next step then?"

Zurlig turned toward Holland. "We'll see how it affects your colleague, and make adjustments from there."

Panic flashed across Holland's eyes. His gaze flitted from side to side as he took in the huge space. Trapped. Blackwood's fists clenched at her sides, and she started to speak. But Holland beat her there.

"What if I refuse?" he said, raising his chin. "Will you force me? Like a war prisoner?"

"Refuse to help your country, when you're given the means?" said Zurlig coolly. "I'd have every right. If you don't cooperate, it makes you either a coward or a traitor, and neither is something we need in our armed forces during wartime."

"I'll do it!" Blackwood spat. "You're not touching him."

Zurlig turned her head, a brittle smile on her face. "I have no doubts about *your* willingness, Mila. That's not the issue here. I want to know whether your *colleague* is willing to help."

"You're saying you don't trust him?"

"In past experiments, we had more luck with some people than others. Holland's experience during shrouding – then and now – may differ significantly from yours; and that will tell us something. If your experiences are similar, that tells us something, too. At the moment, I'm not speaking of trust. I am speaking of the willingness of each of you to help us. If you are willing and he is not... well, that tells us something, too."

Blackwood gritted her teeth. "Give me the arphanium crystal. I am Holland's commanding officer, and he's not doing anything without my permission. I'm taking point on this."

"I need to hear it from Holland," said Zurlig, still staring at the young man. "This is important. I need to know whether he's planning to refuse."

For several moments, Holland glared at the scientist. "Give me the crystal," he said.

"I won't allow it!" Blackwood said immediately.

But Marson had already gone to a table in the back and was bringing over a length of crystal pipe, sharply cut, hollow, and glowing with a faint, inner light. Marson held it out to Holland. Holland took it with his unmarked hand, hiding the marked one by his body. Blackwood stepped forward.

"Let him do it, Mila," Zurlig said.

Blackwood glanced in her direction – and froze. The scientist had a pistol trained on her. Blackwood had never even heard her pull it.

"You are soldiers," Zurlig said. "Your job is to do as you're told."

"I want to speak to Admiral Farring!" Blackwood demanded. "Before this goes any further!" There was a buzzing in her head, making everything feel surreal. The tingling in her skin had magnified, so her whole forearm seemed to vibrate with it.

"That's not an option," said Zurlig. "We've been given the go-ahead on this from a higher authority than your admiral."

"The go-ahead on killing us." In a sudden flash of clarity, Blackwood saw what was going on. "You think Holland is a traitor. You think he was responsible for what happened. That's why you feel OK about experimenting on him. Why you'd force him into it."

"I don't know that Holland was the traitor. But I do know a traitor was involved. Given everything you've told me, he is a very likely suspect."

"That's a load of kaullix shit!" Blackwood bit out. "He *stood* by Mahanner and I when we fixed that breach. He was up there with me! He—"

"He was holding something," Zurlig cut in, "in his hand. Most likely dekatite."

"I told you, it wasn't him with the dekatite! Are you going to accuse me of having dekatite, too?"

"Mila, think about this reasonably…"

Pins and needles shot through the mark in Blackwood's arm. She felt heady from trying to make sense of everything, and the weight of her responsibility for Holland was overwhelming. They hadn't been there; they hadn't been drowning in a freezing torrent of water, holding up a patch keeping the entire ocean and Xeil knew how many otherworldly monsters from breaking through, and knowing that without Holland's help, their strength would fail and the whole crew would be killed. They hadn't been through the first accident. They didn't *know*.

Breathe! Keep it together! One deep breath. *If they kill Holland…* Another. *Nadia Zurlig is not my…* But she was. Holland was going to *die*, and it was her fault.

Blackwood's third breath faltered in the same moment that a bolt of lightning shot from overhead, searing her eyes and sending a surge of scalding heat through the room. Blackwood only realized what happened because she was watching Zurlig, and she saw the scientist crumple. Thunder erupted through the lab, so loud that glass shattered. Other bolts hit too, lighting up the room around her. The flashes seared through her retinas, blinding her. Blackwood was barely conscious of her body tipping in disorientation. She felt the rough surface of the laboratory floor slam against her right side. The scent of burning and sulfur was so overpowering, it almost made her sick.

When her vision broke through again, in patchy flashes of strangely lit shapes, the first thing she saw was a jagged scar of broken concrete, zagging out from between her hands.

What? Lightning hit us? How in the...?

"Mila!" someone called feebly.

Zurlig. Still alive. Blackwood looked up, pushing herself to hands and knees. She crawled, though her elbows threatened to give out every time she put weight on them. She was shivering violently, mostly from adrenaline. She wondered if she were injured somehow, but except for the gunshot wound, she didn't feel pain. Just a hammering heart and a shaking body; a head so light, it felt it might drift away at any moment. Not far from losing consciousness, she thought. *Fight it.* Where was Holland? She tried to call out, but her voice didn't come.

"Mila..."

Through the smoke, she saw the scientist. The woman's eyes were closed, the skin around them blackened, even gone in some places. Bone showed through over her right cheekbone. Blackwood felt nausea collecting in her throat, and choked back the urge to retch. But she didn't stop until she was at Zurlig's side. She sat back on her knees, putting her hand on the woman's tattered sleeve.

Zurlig moved at her touch. "Mila?"

"Yes." Blackwood's voice came out hoarse, barely audible.

"This happened before," Zurlig gasped out. "Your parents... the factory..."

Blackwood sucked in her breath. "The accident? It was... lightning? Like this?"

"Yes. But I thought... circumstances different. From the wall... but no. Her."

72

"Her? Her who?"

"Idyna Larine Onosylvani."

"Onosylvani? The Dhavvie woman who requested amnesty?"

"Yes. President Wixxer gave her to SAI, for studying. It was because of her…"

"The lightning?" Blackwood said when she didn't continue. "Because of her?"

"Yes." Zurlig's voice was softer now, so she barely breathed the words. "Because… Dhavnak… the monsters… it was key. But the assassin… that Dhavnak assassin…"

"At the lab? That's where it happened? But I always thought…"

"Yes. As you were meant to." Zurlig looked up at Blackwood with her closed eyes. She tried to speak three times before she got the words out. "She was Dhavnak."

"Yes. I know."

"The monsters…" She shuddered again, gasping. Her breath came out in a rattle, and was never drawn back in. Zurlig was gone.

Blackwood sat back, feeling ill. Her own government had experimented on the Dhavnak woman who had come to them for protection. This was the big secret Zurlig had held back from telling her. But it hadn't been what she was trying to reveal at the end. It was very important to her that the lab subject was Dhavvie. What did it mean?

"CSO?"

"Holland!" Blackwood looked up. Only a single overhead light still shone, and even that flickered erratically. An overturned table toppled to the floor as Holland pushed it off. His face was blackened along one side, with the bloody edges of a scrape showing beneath it. He looked at Blackwood with wild eyes.

"Marson's dead," he said. "And that – whatever that was – it wasn't an air raid. The scientists were struck. *Targeted.*"

"Targeted?" Blackwood said. "What do you mean?"

"The way they were pushing you, you trying to protect me, them alone being struck, the… the tingling…" Holland swallowed, his eyes pinned on Blackwood's. "I know it sounds crazy. But I think you did it."

Chapter 7

ANDREW'S ENCOUNTER

The day after Cu Zanthus got the call from Holland, he left the house so early in the morning that Andrew never saw him. He returned just after midday. Looking for work, he explained. Might have found a job as a fire watcher at a clothing factory, keeping an eye out for incendiary bombs on the overnight shift. He told Andrew he was going by Zane, keeping his true origins toned down. The only danger, he added with a laugh, was getting snared by Belzen's draft.

"I've been limping," he said, his lip quirking up. "Got the idea from you."

"Wouldn't be so funny if your foot hurt like mine," Andrew grumbled.

He swept the shards of glass in his room into a cookie sheet, not particularly carefully. The day before had passed in a blur – coffee at the intermittently operating Willow Cafe, gambling with Cu Zanthus and a couple other draft-dodgers down at the trainyard, then more alcohol – and he'd never gotten around to cleaning up the mess.

Andrew's head was still fuzzy. He wasn't in as good a place as he'd been the day before – or the previous night, for that matter. If Cu Zanthus weren't here, he'd leave the mess and crawl back into bed. Or maybe he'd lay on the couch and look up at the family photos that had never been taken down, staring at that picture of himself grinning as a toddler in his mother's arms. Maybe he'd go back to his parents' notes and while away the next three days, without food, without sleep. The mere thought pulled at him, even now. Three more days to put behind him, instead of ahead. Days where he could analyze the swoop of Mother's cursive letters, or watch Father's words squeeze closer and closer together as his ideas ran faster than his fingers. His favorite parts were when his parents were working together and their handwriting shared a page, creating a back and forth of ideas that was almost like hearing them speak. *We lost another two subjects today,* Father would say, and Mother would add, *But learned three important directions for next time, dear, don't lose hope yet.*

Cu Zanthus, in his bedroom doorway, pulled something out from behind his back. "Got more Coinavini!" he said with a grin.

Andrew groaned. *Does he never want me to think straight again?* He got slowly to his feet, holding the cookie sheet as straight as possible. He blinked lingering sleep from his eyes, and looked blearily at the Dhavnak.

"What's with the outfit?" he mumbled. "Does wearing all black make you a better job candidate or something?"

"Based on my luck," said Cu Zanthus, "it seems to."

He looked good in the short, collared jacket and high boots. Too good. He'd probably been meeting Holland. *I'll find you when you get here.* Andrew winced at a fresh stab in his head. *None of my business.* He limped past Cu Zanthus to empty the shards in the kitchen wastebin. He sat on the couch afterward, laying his head back and waiting for the throbbing to subside.

"Do you still go sledding on the sand dunes?" Cu Zanthus asked as he sat beside him.

Andrew shrugged a shoulder. If Cu Zanthus, as an eager child, hadn't dragged him from his house, or if Mila hadn't left him alone to go out with friends like she always did, he would never have done it then. "I'm a little old now," was all he said.

"What about the trackline tunnels we used to play in?"

"Closed off now. Years ago."

"Come on, Andy," said Cu Zanthus. "What do you do with your time? Now, I mean? School?"

"I stopped going. Long time ago."

"Why?"

"It was boring. Mind-numbingly boring. And besides, it just gave the other kids excuses to call me…"

"Call you what?"

His face burned with embarrassment. "Sensitive. Emotional. Stupid things kids say."

"They were mean to you?" said Cu Zanthus.

Please. Don't talk about this.

"They didn't hurt you, did they?"

Andrew tried to keep his breathing steady, but it was no use. All the fear and helplessness from the last few years was flooding back.

"Have you told anyone?" said Cu Zanthus, an edge entering his voice now. "Have you told Mila?"

"It wouldn't matter!" Andrew burst out. "No one's *ever* helped! Not Mila, not Father, not anyone! Mother *tried*, but she was always saying, just stand up for yourself, Andrew, look at your sister, but… but Mila's always had friends, she's never been alone in her life, it's only stupid broken people like me–"

"Andrew! You're not broken!" Cu Zanthus wrapped a hand around his wrist. Andrew stared down at it, his breath coming fast. *He thinks it, too. Overly emotional Andrew. Why can't I ever just stay quiet?* He closed his eyes, clamping his teeth tight over the words that still tried to pour out. A small keening broke through. It was the most pathetic sound he'd ever heard.

"I'll make us some tea," said Cu Zanthus. "Just breathe. You're fine."

Andrew managed a jerky nod. He let his eyes drift open just enough to watch Cu Zanthus build a small fire in the hearth and bring in a half-jug of the weekly water ration to fill a pot over the flames. When the nettlebark tea was ready, Cu Zanthus filled two mugs and set them on the small table in front of the couch. By the time he sat down again, Andrew was staring at his folded hands, deep in regret.

"The brotherhood wouldn't have let anyone treat you like that," Cu Zanthus said quietly.

Andrew blinked, looking up. "The... the Synivistic brotherhood, you mean?"

Cu Zanthus nodded. "We understand that everyone has a place in the community, and it's our job to make sure each person is placed to best utilize their strengths. You wouldn't have been left *alone* here, that's for sure. You would have gone in for an analysis – several cycles ago, with updates done every cycle – and given a list of careers best suited to your personality. You would have joined a syndicate by now. And the workers on a syndicate *look out* for each other. As long as folks know you're part of the brotherhood, they'll defend you till their last breath."

Andrew swallowed. "Sounds nice."

"You never thought about getting a job here?"

"I've been... busy. My books."

"Your books are not enough, Andy. There's no sense of camaraderie here. Loners like you get left behind. It's not healthy." He put his mug down and turned toward Andrew. "Here. I'll try to make you understand."

"How?" said Andrew cautiously.

"Have you ever said the Synivistic Oaths? Like we do during the Bright Cycle?"

"I've read them–"

"It's not the same. Give me your hands. I'll show you."

Andrew set his tea down. His hands trembled as he held them out. Cu Zanthus took them in his own. He had cool skin. Long fingers. A strong grip. When he bowed his head, Andrew followed suit. Cu Zanthus recited the words in Dhavvish.

"*May Bitu Lan, the Combatant, always guide my spear. May Luma Nala, the Gatherer, give bounty far and near. May Shon Aha, the Marshal, keep our enemies subdued. May Vo Hina, the Informer, remain in solitude. Bring justice to the righteous, and fortune to the bold; bring justice to our enemies, and judgment to their souls.*" He released his grip and passed a hand over his eyes, then his mouth, then folded them both over his heart.

"Every morning," he said, "you hold hands with whoever's around you and say the oaths. It reminds you that you're never alone. Even now, I know my countrymen are out there, saying them along with me every Bright Cycle. Does that make sense?"

Andrew nodded, his throat tight.

"Do you want me to tell you more?"

"Yes," Andrew whispered. "Please."

So Cu Zanthus talked. About Bitu Lan's double-bladed saber, that could slice through any material; and Luma Nala's fields of wheat, that grew even in the darkest depths of winter; and Shon Aha shattering Vo Hina's eye like glass when she was caught hoarding "the black and white gems of the valleys and mountains."

"We think that might have been referring to dekatite and arphanium," Cu Zanthus explained, "long before either was discovered."

The day went from full of sharp edges to a soft, muted glow, and Andrew felt close to sane again by the time the Early Sun had gone down.

But he didn't touch Cu Zanthus's Coinavini. He took an early bedtime instead, venturing out a fair time later to check on the Dhavnak. Cu Zanthus was asleep on the couch, the fire still burning in the hearth beside him. Once again, Andrew heard his words to Holland on the WiCorr. *I'll find you when you get here.*

Andrew crept back to his parents' room and eased open the door, holding it up so it didn't drag from the broken hinge. His parents' notes were in boxes on the closet floor. He gave them a cursory glance, only long enough to make sure they hadn't been disturbed since Mila's intrusion. He took his father's old coneflower-spun jacket, with the woven fibers and belted waist. The matching brimmed cap was on the same hanger. Andrew snuck back to his room and chose a nondescript button-down and trousers, then stashed the whole outfit beneath his pillow.

He slept fitfully, and was wide awake when he heard Cu Zanthus pray at half-light. Still he waited, slipping on the clothes as quietly as possible beneath his blanket. It was just before the Main Sun rose that he heard the soft thump of the front door. He sat up, slipped on a pair of scuffed kaullix leather boots, and stuck the cap over his ragged hair. The whole time, a distant litany played through his mind. *None of my business. None of my business.*

But he had to see who Cu Zanthus was meeting. He *had* to. It would kill him if he didn't.

Half a block away from his house, Andrew realized he couldn't remember the last time he'd been outside alone. He'd been with Cu Zanthus the last several times, and hadn't paid much attention to anything else. The air, already heating up for the day, had felt refreshing for just a second, but it didn't last. The slowly brightening sky seemed even bigger than usual. If Andrew glanced up for more than a moment, he felt its weight pulling at him, like it was a vast ocean he might fall into. He quickly jerked his eyes away and huddled into his father's coat, feeling nauseous and dizzy at the sight. He imagined the Dhavnak warplanes that might send the air raid sirens wailing at any moment, and felt horribly vulnerable under that huge, open sky. Twice he faltered in his steps, half-turning to see the rapidly dwindling shape of his house – a safe haven he was leaving behind. But Cu Zanthus's form walked swiftly ahead, his faint double-shadow blending into the long ones thrown by the gradually emerging Main Sun. Andrew sped up his pace. Pain lanced through his right foot, even protected as it was by the bandage and boot together.

Cu Zanthus left Andrew's well-off district and headed south toward the heart of Ellemko, with a western slant that almost assured he aimed for the industrial parts. Maybe he was looking for a job after all. Andrew's breath came easier. But he still ducked behind parked or broken mobies lining the curbs whenever his friend turned his head, or took shelter in the tattered wrecks of bombed buildings.

Everything seemed dirtier than Andrew remembered: chunks of stones lying in the pathways, blackened concrete walls, shredded paper coasting down the streets, rodents at the corners of his vision, people in layers of coats despite the warmth of both suns, hauling bags, hauling weary children, hanging tight to another's hand or elbow. Andrew couldn't help eyeing them as he passed. Exhausted, homeless, but together. He had a house, but they had love. Which was better? He watched one couple with a young boy and girl so long that the father turned and narrowed his eyes. Andrew ducked his head and hugged the wall of a boarded-up storefront, feeling his cheeks heat.

"Boy!" the man called.

Andrew turned his head. The man walked back a couple steps and held out a handful of dried apples. Andrew's eyes widened. He shook his head.

"You may've got yourself a fancy coat," the man said gruffly, "but it's clear you're starvin' to death. Take it. It's the least I can do."

"No," Andrew said, "I'm not–"

But the man stepped forward and stuck them in his jacket pocket, then hurried back to his family, who were now crossing the street. Andrew started to follow, but a military truck drove up at that moment, parking with one wide tire on the curb. Andrew thought about running around the truck to grab the man, but Cu Zanthus was disappearing off to his left. Andrew gritted his teeth in frustration and headed left instead. *Great. Now I'm getting handouts from homeless folks. Maybe it wouldn't kill me to eat a meal once in a while.* It sounded like more trouble than it was worth.

By the time the Main Sun had cleared the distant eastern dunes, Cu Zanthus had cut through the old metal scrapyards downtown and ventured into the huge back lot of a shipping center, far from the residential or commercial spaces. Andrew's foot was hurting worse than ever, and he could barely keep Cu Zanthus in sight as he lagged farther behind. He took shelter behind a stack of ironwood crates to catch his breath. He finally admitted it to himself: his hunch had been wrong. Cu Zanthus would never have come to meet a girl in a place like this. He was doing exactly what he'd told Andrew – pursuing a job. And Holland was probably just the buddy helping him find one.

Andrew swallowed back a wave of dizziness. The side of his right foot ached with a stabbing pulse that made him want to scream. Even the gash on his forefinger had started to throb. He had no idea how far he'd walked, and couldn't begin to fathom the thought of going back. He took one of the man's apple slices from his pocket and nibbled off a chunk of the rubbery flesh. It was sweeter than he expected and Andrew chewed it for several moments before swallowing it down. It left a pleasant spice in his mouth. He ate the other half of the slice, feeling a twinge of guilt when he pictured the man's young kids. The snack didn't exactly give him the energy to go home, but it did give him the mental clarity to stagger back to his feet.

When he left his hiding place, Cu Zanthus was nowhere in sight. Because it seemed easier than starting that long, dreary walk home,

Andrew headed toward where he'd seen him last. He didn't want to bother him, especially if he was meeting with the proprietor or something, but he didn't think a glimpse at the new workplace would hurt anything.

He was just passing the loading dock of the huge factory, still quiet despite the big truck sitting at the back, when he heard voices somewhere ahead. He walked down the side of the truck, running one hand along the solar cells on its side, toward the narrow alley that ran between the shipping building and the next warehouse over. That was where the voices came from.

"…The missing link then," a man was saying in Dhavvish. "But Lyanirus will want to know what he meant about the dekatite. About not bringing it through. How did he know? What did he do?"

"Nothing, I'm sure." The second man's voice was cold. "Maybe he was told."

Andrew stopped, turning his head. That last voice had been Cu Zanthus's.

"Really? Despite getting sent back here?" This voice, though, was deeper. Definitely not the same voice from the WiCorr.

"He knows what he's doing," said Cu Zanthus. "I trust him."

There was a rustling sound, the crinkling of paper, and then the scratch of a nib against it. "Here," said the other man. "Get this to him. As soon as you can."

After a moment, Cu Zanthus said, "Are you–"

"I'm taking initiative, yes. There are too many variables here."

"I understand." Cu Zanthus's voice sounded more subdued than before. "One more thing. He wanted me to ask about a promotion."

The other man paused. "You want me to pass that on? Seriously?"

"It's important to him."

"It's important to me that I take a shit every day, but you don't see me writing a memo on it. And you can pass that back." Footsteps sounded then, fading in the other direction.

Andrew, flat against the truck's side, started to slide back, but Cu Zanthus came out of the alley at that moment, sticking something into his jacket pocket. His eyes landed on Andrew. He stopped dead.

"What are you doing here?" he said.

"I… I followed you," said Andrew. "I thought…"

"Thought what?"

"A girl. I thought you were meeting a girl."

Cu Zanthus's brow furrowed.

"I was worried," said Andrew faintly, "that you wouldn't treat her… I mean, you being from Dhavnakir…"

"How long have you been there?"

A transparent question, if Andrew had ever heard one. *How much did you hear?* Andrew barely knew where to start. He had no idea what to think.

"Was it about your friend Holland?" he finally said. "A promotion? If he recruits more employees? That sort of thing?" *But why the secrecy?*

Cu Zanthus came closer, putting one hand against the truck by Andrew's shoulder. Andrew's heart was beating hard now, but he didn't know if it was from fear or from something else entirely.

"I told you I was being considered for a job," said Cu Zanthus, his eyes boring into Andrew's. "But the truth is, my buddy Holland and I are already working for some chop shop scum that steals mobies and guts 'em to sell for parts. Holland recently came back with a captured Dhavnak transport – a real gem. It'll make us rich. But I was ashamed to tell you. I wanted you to think I'd find a real job. The pale skin, though… folks aren't so forgiving as they used to be. And at least this'll keep us – you and I – with food and beds till the end of the war. You're having such a tough time of it without that on your shoulders. You know?"

It took several moments for Andrew to find his voice. "A captured transport? That's serious business."

"Don't tell anyone."

"Of course not. I just can't believe you didn't tell me. I'm not exactly…"

"Your sister's in the military. I thought you might feel obligated to say something."

Andrew shook his head vigorously. "I'm not."

"Good."

"But what was he asking you about deka–" Andrew began.

He stuttered to a stop as Cu Zanthus leaned his head in closer. Andrew swallowed, sure he was about to breathe out some threat should

Andrew fail to keep his secret. But instead, Cu Zanthus lowered his lips onto Andrew's. Andrew blinked, startled, as Cu Zanthus pressed his head back against the truck and deepened the kiss, his lips firm and confident. Andrew finally found his breath and responded, feeling his body melt with the sudden warmth that flooded it. For several long moments, he left the perpetual self-loathing behind, and floated far, far above it, untouchable, unbreakable. When Cu Zanthus pulled away, he drew in a breath so ragged, it was almost a gulp. Cu Zanthus took a small step back.

"I'm sorry," he said softly, his head bowed. "I've wanted to do that since... well, ever since I got back."

"I wish I'd known," Andrew managed.

"You don't mind?"

"No! No. I don't mind." He licked his lips, relishing the new feel of them. "So that's all it ever was? You and Holland? The job? There's no girl?"

"There's no girl."

"Have you always been... I mean, this isn't the sort of thing you'd do in Dhavnakir. Right?"

Cu Zanthus laughed. "Living gods, no. I'd be beaten to death for the thought. But here, with you," he shrugged, "I'll take every moment I can get. As long as I've got you, it's enough."

Andrew couldn't remember the last time he'd smiled. But it came back as if he'd never stopped. It felt like the world grew bigger. Like he could find his place in it again.

Like it was possible to be loved.

Chapter 8

KLARA YANA'S
CONFESSION

Blackwood had Klara Yana's wrist and was pulling her through the corridors of the underground labs before Klara Yana could so much as raise a protest. It wasn't until Blackwood took turns to avoid two different scientists, running through crossing hallways and diving through a back emergency exit, that Klara Yana realized her commanding officer had no intention of reporting the incident. Blackwood pulled her up a narrow stairway, practically a tunnel, and out onto street level. There, she dropped Klara Yana's hand and leaned over, gasping for breath. Klara Yana, nowhere near as winded, checked their surroundings. The FCB headquarters weren't far behind them, and ahead was a series of long one-story buildings that might have been offices or barracks. Soldiers were running wild in every direction, rifles in hand. Even if they hadn't been down below for the lightning, the unexpected thunder had probably been loud enough to cause a state of panic.

"This way," Blackwood got out, waving her hand ahead and to the left. "Past the officers' quarters and through the tank yard. There's a back gate." She straightened, wincing as she moved her arm.

"Are you all right, ma'am?" said Klara Yana.

"That storm in there messed with me somehow. I'm weak. Cold. But we can discuss that later." She started forward, her gait considerably slower now. "If anyone asks, we're running an errand. Don't walk too fast, or too slow. And don't look around too much."

"Yes, CSO." Klara Yana stuck close to Blackwood's shoulder. She pulled her fingerless gloves from her pocket and slid them back on as she walked. She didn't check the gun she'd discreetly nabbed from Doctor Zurlig, while Blackwood was looking the other way, but she could feel its comforting bulk at the small of her back, beneath the thigh-length uniform jacket. It wasn't until they'd passed the officers' quarters and were heading past a metal warehouse that the sounds of pandemonium behind them dimmed, and Klara Yana dared to talk. Even then, she kept her voice as quiet as possible.

"What's the plan, CSO? You're running?"

Blackwood glared ahead like she intended to charge through the distant wall without stopping. "What happens if I stay, Holland?" she said, her lips barely moving. "You saw what they wanted to do. Now, after this… it'll only get worse. *They* don't have answers. And Zurlig – the things she told me – that's not something I can ask about. There's only one place we can hope to figure this mess out."

"Where's that, ma'am?"

"My parents. They left a couple boxes of notes behind. Zurlig mentioned a connection. There *has* to be something there. I'll never get a chance to lay eyes on them if I report in now. I don't like it, but this is the way things are."

They were experimenting on Onosylvani. Klara Yana had heard that much. She had also heard Zurlig's dying warning. *She was Dhavnak.* Even if Blackwood hadn't gotten the hint yet, it was clear as the wind to Klara Yana. Whatever had happened in that Belzene lab had happened *because* there had been a Dhavnak present. And Zurlig believed a Dhavnak was connected to their current situation as well. Was it true? Would Blackwood never have – what? Been given strange powers otherwise? *If* that's what had happened? *And what about me?* Though her palm tingled with an almost painful self-consciousness now, pulling lightning from thin air seemed impossible. But Klara Yana had seen it. Blackwood's mounting anger, the tightening of her fists, her unbridled focus. And now there was her unexplained weakness, as if the very act had taken more energy than she had to give. That mark *was* connected somehow.

A human weapon. Something the Dhavnaks would be overjoyed to have. But the thought of telling them what she *might* be able to do filled her with as much dread as it did Blackwood. More.

And there was another issue, even more uncomfortable. Blackwood had done it for *her*. If those scientists hadn't been ready to sacrifice Klara Yana to their experiments, Blackwood might very well have cooperated. Now... it was a debt. And Klara Yana wasn't in a great position to be indebted to a Belzene. *It's part of my job. Whether she saved my life or not. No such thing as debt when you're gathering intel.* She'd been doing the job a long time. The old words helped. Not a lot. But some.

"You don't have to come, Holland," said Blackwood.

Klara Yana suppressed a sigh. There it was again, that strange tendency of Belzenes to discard their comrades and strike out on their own. Where was the loyalty, the camaraderie? "I have a mark too, ma'am," was all she said.

"I could get in a lot of trouble for this. It'd be a shame to drag you down, too."

"I'm sticking by you, CSO."

Blackwood glanced at her, eyes flashing. Klara Yana knew she was remembering Zurlig's accusation of her holding dekatite during the submarine accident. She would have to address it, and soon. But it wasn't worth losing this chance to look at old pre-shrouding research – or letting Blackwood out of her sight.

They passed into a yard of tanks, all of which were torn apart or damaged almost beyond repair; a tank graveyard, filled up before its time during the frequent invasions. Tracks with missing links dangled heavily over metal wheels. Turrets sat precariously unattached to the bodies, taken apart and left in disrepair. Armored plates were blown free and blackened, leaving motor compartments exposed. The reinforced heliocells, normally shielded during combat but exposed now, hung skewed or detached, though very few had shattered. Bullet holes riddled the steel around them, though – huge, jagged tears as big around as Klara Yana's fist. Most of them were of a height with her, or a little taller, with the bodies of the tanks at shoulder level. Blackwood strode around the broken tracks and side skirts with confidence, for all the world as if they had a right to be there. Her breathing seemed to have recovered, at least to Klara Yana's ears. Maybe her mission had given her purpose.

The back gate Blackwood had mentioned was in the far south wall. There was a single pair of guards on it – one Belzene, and the other, Klara Yana noticed with a start, Dhavnak. Well, Dhavnak-Belzene, no doubt. Klara Yana wondered if he'd been treated as badly as she had by people like Vin and Zurlig, or if he'd been employed long enough that folks had stopped noticing his pale skin and light hair. Maybe Belzen was diverse enough that they'd barely noticed to begin with. But somehow, she doubted it.

The Belzene guard touched a radio at his belt as Blackwood and Klara Yana approached. Blackwood stopped and pressed her right fist to her left shoulder.

"We were sent in response to the ongoing riots, sir," she said. "Apparently, there's another rise-up a couple blocks from here."

"Without weapons?" the guard said, a frown creasing his narrow face.

"We're meeting a team there. Please, sir. Time is of the essence."

"Who sent you?"

"Sergeant Lerner," said Klara Yana quickly, stepping forward. "He's busy dealing with whatever happened at the complex this morning, but said he'd send someone."

"What happened at the complex?"

"I don't know, sir. But it's chaos that way. Far easier to head out here."

The two guards looked at each other. One picked up his radio. The other opened the gate and waved Klara Yana and Blackwood through.

"That thunder, I told you," she heard the Dhavnak say. Unlike her, he had an accent, giving a melodic hint to the staccato Belzene language. For just a second, Klara Yana's step faltered. She almost turned back just to hear more. But the gate closed behind them, and his voice was gone.

Blackwood immediately turned to the left, hands deep in her uniform pockets. "Who's Sergeant Lerner?" she asked.

"The one who drove us here yesterday, ma'am. The one who wouldn't stop talking."

"He gave us his name?"

"It was on his uniform."

"Huh. Good eye there, Holland."

Shon Aha was straight overhead now, and Bitu Lan an echoing sphere off to his right. Not a cloud to be seen, and hotter than her home country of Dhavnakir had been in its entire history. Klara Yana resisted the urge to fan her face; Blackwood seemed perfectly fine, as did every pedestrian they passed. Less mobies were out than the day before, despite it being midday. A pair of planes droned by overhead. People stopped to watch them, faces apprehensive, but Klara Yana knew by the quieter rumble that they were helio-powered Belzene models, rather than Dhavnak.

She didn't even glance up. She kept her eyes straight ahead, focused single-mindedly on fleshing out Deckman Kyle Holland's character. Saying anything at all about the dekatite would be a huge risk. But if she didn't, Blackwood would wonder from then on out if she was hiding something. Klara Yana knew she had to nip this doubt before it grew, or the operation would be tanked. *Young and unsure of myself. Thrown in over my head. But with a dark secret.*

The sound of the planes receded to the south. Klara Yana walked with her left hand clamped around her right wrist behind her back. It would take her half a second to twitch the long coat aside and pull the pistol should the need arise.

"CSO," she said, and her voice came out steady, if a bit too breathy. Perfect. "I made a mistake. A big one."

Blackwood looked at her now – not just a glance, but a searching stare, as if her dark eyes could penetrate her.

"I was hoping you wouldn't make me ask," she said with a small nod. "Please. Continue."

"I was thirteen. I woke up in the middle of the night and heard my mother…" she swallowed, "…screaming. Crying. Fighting someone. I got up. Ran into her bedroom. There were two men in there with her. Pale skin, light hair. She was naked. Bleeding. She yelled at me, 'Kyle, go back to your room. Now!' But there was no one else there to help. I pulled a big framed picture off the wall – wide as my outstretched arms – and smashed it over the closer guy's head. He didn't fall. Just got mad. He shoved me back into the wall. Mother screamed again. I didn't see much. I fell, and there was a big shard of glass by me. I grabbed it up, slashed at the guy's throat. Blood sprayed. He hit me again, hard. And I… that was it. It went black. When I woke up again…"

She allowed her voice to falter, but the set of her jaw was real. Parts of the story were true, but not all. She had never run in to try to stop her step-apa's brutality. Instead, she'd lain in bed, hands tight over her ears and sobs wracking her body. She'd been much younger than thirteen.

Blackwood was still watching her, but a slight crease of her brow betrayed an emotion lurking beneath. Sorrow? Anger? Revulsion? Klara Yana wasn't sure. She kept her own face as hard as possible, the way a man would if he was forced to share a childhood story like this.

"When I woke up again, my mother was gone. All that was left was blood. Hers. Theirs. And – and one other thing. A necklace. The string was severed, cut when I sliced the Dhavvie's throat. I took off the pendant. I've kept it with me ever since. To remind me of what they took. What they're capable of." She thinned her lips. "What I'm fighting for."

"And the pendant is dekatite," Blackwood finished.

"Y- Yes, ma'am."

"You were told before you got on the submarine, weren't you?"

"I…"

"*Weren't* you, Holland?"

Klara Yana, expecting this, made herself flinch. "I knew the rules. But I kept it with me at the academy, and I always thought if I got assigned to a shrouding submarine, I'd have time to find somewhere for it. But that morning, with everything so crazy, it completely slipped my mind. It wasn't until you mentioned it just before the attack that I remembered."

"And what, *exactly*, stopped you from saying something then?"

"I'm sorry," Klara Yana said. "I was afraid I'd be expelled from the navy. I thought…"

"You could have killed the entire crew!" Blackwood's face was reddening with anger now, her jaw tightening. Klara Yana couldn't help but remember the way she'd slammed Vin against the submarine wall. And Vo Hina's mercy, what about that lightning? If she could strike Doctor Zurlig on a whim…!

She held a handful of fabric between her finger and thumb, right hand half-open to grab for that gun.

"I'm sorry, CSO," she said again. "I am so sorry."

Blackwood didn't answer right away, just stared straight ahead as she walked, drawing in a series of deep breaths. Her lips moved around her clenched teeth. Klara Yana pretended to watch her feet, but was very careful not to look away.

"What about Vin's chain?" Blackwood finally said.

"I don't know the first thing about Vin's chain. I've never put the pendant on a chain or cord of any kind."

"But you were happy to let him take the fall."

"I'm not proud of it, CSO."

"And you were holding the pendant in your hand? Why?"

Finally. A truth. "I thought to somehow get it off the boat. To appease the monsters before they killed us."

"Were you successful? Is that why we were left alone?"

"No, CSO. I still have it."

"Show it to me."

Klara Yana forced herself to unclench her hands and bring them to her front. Blackwood stopped in the road and let a bicycle maneuver around them. She held out her hand. Klara Yana reached into the inside pocket of the uniform jacket and pulled the pendant out. With great reluctance, she laid it in Blackwood's palm.

Blackwood looked for a long time at the shape of the eye inside the glittering circle, with its pupil shattered into sharp edges. Klara Yana stood stiffly in front of her, fingers twitching with the effort not to snatch it back. She was fully aware Blackwood might confiscate it. Might hold it until Klara Yana faced trial. It would be used as evidence, kept in some Belzene officer's desk alongside his old paperclips and ration cards.

"The Broken Eye," said Blackwood softly. "Your mother's attacker worshipped Vo Hina, the Informer. I can't quite fathom that."

"Isn't Vo Hina their… their evil god? So maybe, I don't know, some sort of cult worshipper?"

"It's not that easy," said Blackwood. "I've long assumed that any Vo Hina worshippers would have to be female, since very few Dhavnak men would look up to a woman, divine or otherwise. And a rapist would clearly not fall into that 'very few' category."

"Maybe he stole it from another victim of his?" Klara Yana said.

"And wore it around his neck?" Blackwood handed it back, her face tight. "The way Dhavnak men are… Guess you never know," she said, a slight hint of disgust to her voice.

Klara Yana felt a surge of irritation to hear all Dhavnaks lumped together so casually. Yes, men like her step-apa were bad, but surely there were men like that in Belzen, too. Every country had them. Dhavnakir had plenty of *good* men as well. Foreigners like Blackwood just assumed all women were miserable there. They didn't see how integral a part Dhavnak women played in raising and educating the next generation, or how in Dhavnak society, a child would never have been left to raise himself at the age of *fifteen*. They didn't see how those solid communal foundations had made them stronger as a country. They only saw what they wanted to. Enemies and persecutors.

Klara Yana took the pendant and tucked it back in her jacket. Blackwood resumed walking, and Klara Yana joined her. Several long moments passed before the chief sea officer spoke again.

"Your story," she said. "It doesn't add up."

Klara Yana's heart jumped. *I really am going to have to kill her.*

"You told me this morning that at least ten years had passed since your mother disappeared. So how old were you really when you cut that man's throat?"

Right. Blackwood probably had her pegged as a boy of twenty-one cycles, if not younger. "Nine," she said.

"Xeil's grace," muttered Blackwood. "Well, I guess this explains why you were so adamant that your mother wasn't from Dhavnakir. And why you were willing to chase a Dhavnak sniper into a dark building."

"Yes, CSO."

"I won't report this, Holland. But I am putting in your record, as soon as I get the chance, that you are unfit to shroud, ever again. Do you understand me?"

"Yes, CSO. Clearly."

"And if anyone had died on that boat, you better believe I'd be hauling you in this second."

"Yes, ma'am. If anyone had died, I'd have brought myself in by now."

Neither of them mentioned the scientists. It was a connection they weren't openly acknowledging yet. Klara Yana finally allowed her breath to come easy again. She had gambled, and it had paid off.

Silence hung heavy between them until they turned onto a side street a good hour's walk from where they'd started. Klara Yana blinked in surprise to see the street name on the skewed plate at the corner. *Bellamy Road.* They were close to Cu Zanthus's drop site. Very close.

Blackwood stopped at a brick townhouse with five concrete steps leading up to a green-painted door. Both steps and paint were in poor repair, though the house itself was a nice one, judging by the scrollwork on the steel railings and fancy ironwood shutters.

Klara Yana started to follow Blackwood up. Blackwood turned.

"Wait out here."

"Ma'am?"

"My brother and I aren't on great terms. And he has a weird attachment to these notes. I'm not sure yet how this'll go."

"Didn't you say you wanted me to meet him?"

"Yes… maybe. But not like this."

"OK, ma'am," said Klara Yana, backing down the steps. "How long should I give you?"

Blackwood glanced at the front door again, and Klara Yana saw how much she was dreading the coming encounter. "No idea. If everything goes well, we can both stay here a few days while I search 'em through. But if Andrew gets unreasonable…" She shook her head, chuckling humorlessly under her breath. "*If.* Ha." She turned back toward the door, waving her other hand to the side of the steps. "Just hunker down, Holland. I'll let you know soon enough."

"Right, CSO." Klara Yana retreated to the side of the house and lowered herself to a crouch under the embossed number twenty-three. She peered up, watching Blackwood pound on the door with her fist.

"Andrew! It's me!" Blackwood called.

There was no immediate answer. Klara Yana allowed her eyes to scan the other houses in the neighborhood. *Twenty-eight, twenty-eight…* The one half-fallen across the street had a twenty-nine. She frowned.

"I'm coming in, Andrew, like it or not!" Blackwood pulled a key from her pocket and let herself in. The door thumped closed behind her. Klara Yana slowly stood, looking again at that number twenty-three an arm's-length above her head. No. Not twenty-three. Now that she was looking, she saw the flecks of black paint that had once turned the three into an eight; the pale shape of the missing number was still visible from up close. Brow furrowed, Klara Yana felt the bricks beneath it. And sure enough, there was a loose one by her elbow. She wriggled it out and saw nothing but darkness behind it. She slid it back in, her mind racing.

It doesn't mean anything. It was just a convenient place for Cu Zanthus to leave his messages. The contact he's staying with… She searched her memory for what she knew. It wasn't much. A longtime friend, he'd said, and she'd heard genuine warmth in his voice when he talked about catching up. A willing collaborator – Cu Zanthus had told her to ask for him by name on the WiCorr, after all. The only other thing she *knew* about his contact was that he or she somehow had access to the submarine records, at least enough to know when a spot opened up for Cu Zanthus to slip his partner into. Klara Yana had assumed it was someone who worked at naval headquarters, or maybe dealt with fatality reports.

Never, in her wildest imaginings, had she pictured it being an officer's kid sibling.

Why couldn't you go? Klara Yana had asked Cu Zanthus, as he drove her through the Belzene countryside just before the mission. *If you've already had the naval training–*

No, he'd answered. *There are complications with this one.*

And Blackwood, to Deckman Vin on the submarine:

A Dhavnak family used to live in our neighborhood. My little brother was friends with their kid.

Probably when Cu Zanthus was around the tender age of fourteen.

"Bitu Lan's balls," she said under her breath. She didn't know which was worse: that her commander's teenage brother was a Dhavnak collaborator, or that Blackwood would recognize Cu Zanthus if he was in there.

She glanced anxiously at the front door. There was no sound from within. She crept forward, putting a foot on the first step. Then a pair of people materialized at the end of the block, heading toward her.

Cu Zanthus. She could tell by his height, his casual gait. She thought about running out to him and his companion, and warning them that Blackwood was inside. But she knew instantly that was a bad idea. Speculate as she might, she had no real inkling of the situation here. Approaching him now would blow his cover wide open if she was wrong. So instead, she crouched and ran to the side of the house. She sat with her back to the brick wall, turning her face to look around the corner.

Cu Zanthus stopped in front of the steps, one hand on the boy's shoulder. And he *was* a boy. The cap on his head was tipped back, revealing wisps of dark hair hanging into eyes sunken with fatigue or dehydration. He was painfully thin, as if he'd been battling illness and losing. But he looked at Cu Zanthus with pure trust, his eyes wide and hopeful.

Klara Yana watched, heart pounding, as her partner leaned down and kissed him, long and deep.

Vo Hina, help me. I've misjudged this entire situation.

She turned away, hands around her knees. How could he seduce someone so *young*? So obviously vulnerable? Wasn't there some limit on how juvenile their marks could be?

If Blackwood's brother had grown up in Dhavnakir, she reflected, this would never have worked out. His ama would have stayed home with him. If something had happened to her, his older sister and her husband would have raised him to adulthood. And even if they hadn't, other women would have been there to take him in. That network of connections was what made their community so solid. But in Belzen, he'd been left alone, as if a child of their future meant nothing to them.

And here was her own partner, taking advantage of this failing in Belzene society. It didn't sit right with her that Dhavnakir would use a kid this way, no matter how young an agent they sent. It had to have been for those notes – the same ones Blackwood was going through right that moment.

"Head on in," Cu Zanthus said. "I have somewhere to be. But I'll be back by tonight. I'll make us dinner."

"OK," Andrew said. "I'll be here."

She heard the scrape of his feet against the concrete steps, then the opening and closing of the door. Klara Yana dared to peer around the base of the house again. Cu Zanthus was pulling the brick at the front of the house free, so carefully it didn't make a sound. He stuck a piece of paper behind it before reinserting it.

She ought to say something, let him know she was down there. But she knew what would happen if she did. Not only would he be furious she'd seen the kiss, but he'd know straightaway that Blackwood was inside. He'd go in after Andrew. And Blackwood would be killed. *We might still need her. I can't blow this operation yet.* So Klara Yana stayed quiet, hoping he'd leave without checking on Andrew again.

Cu Zanthus muttered something under his breath – Klara Yana was almost sure she heard her own name, 'Keiller Yano,' in there – then her partner headed back to the street and disappeared within moments toward the west. She wondered if he was planning to find her. If whatever he'd left was important enough, he might not want to risk her missing it.

Klara Yana came out from her cover, diving toward the loose brick. She wriggled it out and snatched the folded piece of paper inside, put the brick back, and ducked down again to read the note. The message was scrawled in fine cursive:

Leuftkernel Lyanirus to meet with Agent Hollanelea. Underneath L.T. Karlan Theater. Tonight.

Lyanirus? She choked on her next breath. She'd never met Larin Vron Lyanirus in person, but his name was famous in the Dhavnak military.

The rumors said he'd failed to father a child after three wives, and that he'd become convinced it was due to a gradual progression toward liberalism that was corrupting the entire gender. It was assumed he'd murdered those three wives. It was assumed he'd murdered others. The men she worked with spoke of it with horror – the wasting of those future generations, the lack of faith in one mate, even the *levels* of his hatred and violence.

He was an operative, like her, but as far as Klara Yana knew, he worked in much higher circles – embassies, security councils, trade associations, armament foundations. What was he doing here, in Belzen?

A sick feeling formed in her gut as comprehension dawned. Dhavnakir was on the brink of taking Belzen, and Klara Yana was the agent with the very information that could make that possible. The whole reason she'd requested Belzen was that she'd *known* information on their shrouding missions would lead to that promotion. She just hadn't stopped to consider who she'd have to report to in order to get it.

Klara Yana put a hand to her mouth, that sick feeling giving way to full-blown nausea. Not showing up wasn't an option, especially after her last mission; she'd be hunted and killed as a traitor. But if Leuftkernel Lyanirus got even a hint that she was a woman, she'd never walk out of that meeting alive.

Chapter 9

BLACKWOOD'S CONFRONTATION

Blackwood walked into a quiet house. Drawn shutters cast the inside into semi-darkness. The family room opened up on her right. A blue sofa stood against the back wall and a cold fireplace adorned the far right corner. A half-full bottle of red alcohol stood on the small table before the couch, along with a pair of mugs. Blackwood's brow furrowed at the label. *Coinavini? Since when...* Her gaze fell on a yellow duffel at the other side of the sofa, against the wall. Her lips parted and she took a couple steps forward, noticing the two folded blankets on a cushion. She blinked, having trouble processing the information.

Someone staying with her brother? It made no sense. Andrew was the most hostile person she'd ever met. Who on Mirrix would stay with him? Who would he *let* stay with him? Andrew loved his space. He resented every second she was home; she was surprised he hadn't changed the locks.

A lover? He was seventeen, after all, and probably starting to look. But even if he'd met someone, wouldn't he or she be sleeping on his bed, instead of the couch? Blackwood's eyes fell again on the alcohol. She tried to picture Andrew drinking with another person, laughing, kissing. All she could envision was him scowling and looking away the second he was asked about himself. *Small wonder there are blankets on the couch.*

She admonished herself the moment she thought it. Of course Andrew showed a different side of himself to others. Having company was a good thing. Maybe he was finally opening up. Maybe, someday, she'd see that side of him again herself.

Whatever it meant, Andrew was out of the house now, which was much better than she'd anticipated. She had no intention of robbing Andrew of whatever new romance or friendship he was developing. She'd find a bag, grab the notes, and leave him alone. Clean and easy. No fights, no obligations, no hurt feelings. He probably wouldn't even notice the notes were gone.

She jogged past the family room and through the hallway, to the broken door at the end. The two boxes of notes were still on the floor of the closet, exactly as she remembered. The skin on her right arm started crawling again. A finger of cold passed through her. She looked at the ceiling, half-expecting lightning to strike again, as if a simple chill would cause it. It was in her bones now; the cold, the tingling, the fear. At least the weakness seemed to have passed. Nevertheless, she felt the dekatite eating into her skin like a timed explosive.

She knelt and picked up the first several papers in the closer box. There was some typeset on them, but a majority of what she saw was handwritten, words crowded between and around the typed words in both her mother's and father's hands. Each page was so crammed, it was hard to know where to look first. She glanced through the first few anyway, hoping something would jump out – *lightning* or *Dhavnak* or *Onosylvani*. *Shrouding* wouldn't be used yet, that term had come later. But the things Zurlig had mentioned...

Something caught her eye, near the end of the top page. *"...dekatite mines in north central Ellemko not to be used. The risk to civilians, should the borders be breached, is too high."* The mines referenced here had been closed down five years earlier, and the FCB built on top of them. It had happened after her parents died – and therefore, after this note had been written. Clearly the dekatite veins were used *now*, for research and development, if nothing else. Were they no longer worried about the risk to civilians? Blackwood wondered. Or had the need simply outweighed the danger since then? And exactly what risk were they referring to here? Dhavvies? Monsters? Or something else? *This happened before,* Zurlig had said. *Your parents… the factory…*

"So you'll come by for the research, but not for me?" said a voice to her right.

Blackwood jerked her head up. She'd forgotten how quietly her brother moved. Andrew stood in the doorway, dressed in their father's old coat and hat. The belted coat was huge on his slender frame. Blackwood didn't know if it was the contrast that made him look so frail, or if he'd gotten worse since the last time she saw him. Did he even eat when she wasn't home? She put the notes down and rose to her feet.

"Andrew. I was just looking through these while I waited for you. Where have you been? Were you out with someone?"

He ignored the questions, his eyes tracking down to the notes. "Trying to get rid of them again?"

"No. Nothing like that."

"Why are you dressed that way?"

She looked down at her infantry uniform, and back again. "Told you. Working at the FCB now. Do you want to head back to the kitchen? I can make us lunch." It was a challenge to keep her tone so casual, but if she brought up needing the notes now, he might start screaming again. She took a step toward him, one hand out. "What would you like me to make?"

"Nothing. I'm fine."

She sighed through her teeth. "Then maybe we can sit on the couch? Catch up?"

"Why are you here?"

"To see you."

"You never wear a uniform when you're off duty. Try again."

She took a moment to choose her words. "I need to look through Mother and Father's notes. It's for work. I'm not going to destroy them. Just look at them."

His shoulders straightened, his eyes widening. "They want them? Now? Why now?"

"It's nothing. I promise. It's not even about the research. There was an old colleague they worked with; I'm just looking for a name. It's low priority – busy work really – until they find something better for me to do."

"They need a name?" he said, his voice hard. "What name?"

"I can't talk about this."

"How big of a secret can it be? I've read the notes!"

Small surprise there, after the way he'd acted last time. But the thought still made her tense. "That's not the point. You don't work for the government. You don't have the authorization to–"

"To what? Know about them experimenting on civilians? Against their will?"

The words she'd been preparing froze in her throat. "What do you know about that?" she said slowly.

"What I know," he said, his eyes boring into hers, "is that you all make such a big deal about the *Dhavnaks* being monsters while our own government is treating *them* like animals. That's what this is all about, isn't it? Erasing the evidence?"

Her breath hitched. "Xeil's grace, Andrew, you should *not* have read that!"

His eyes narrowed. "You knew?"

"Not exactly, but–"

"So that *is* why you tried to take them!"

"No!" she shot back. "I told you, I have no intention of destroying the notes."

He pulled the bedroom door open and stood pointedly to the side. "Get out."

Blackwood gritted her teeth. He was *impossible* to talk to. *Stay calm. Deep breath.* "Andrew. What I'm doing is more important than…" *Laying around at home all day. Sleeping. Reading. Drinking,* "…than you realize. I need these notes. Either you let me and my associate stay here and look at these, or I will take them. Am I clear?"

Andrew's face darkened. But before he could answer, a low-pitched wail sounded from all around them – a continuous tone, rising and falling at regular intervals. Blackwood's gaze shot to the shuttered sandpane.

Air raid siren.

She cursed and turned back toward the closet, looking into the dark corners. No bag. She strode past Andrew and threw open the door across the hallway, sticking her head into the bedroom that used to be hers. Nothing in that closet but a small handbag, suitable for no more than draftnotes and coins.

"What are you doing?" Andrew yelled.

She came back out to the hallway, snarling her answer as she headed into his room. "Looking for a pack."

"You're not taking the notes!" he answered.

His room was a mess. Red-stained floor, collapsing piles of books against the walls, blankets bunched at the foot of the bed, glass bottles... everywhere. It smelled strongly of alcohol, and faintly of mold. She tore open his closet door. Mostly empty, except for holes in the back wall and piles of trash. She slammed the door again in disgust. The drone of the air raid siren cut into her skull like a cleaver. She *hated* it. She'd forgotten how much. It made it hard to think straight. She marched back into the hallway. Andrew was still standing in the doorway of their parents' room, like he thought he could keep her out.

"Don't you have a bomb shelter to get to?" she growled.

"Where are *you* going?" he retorted.

"Holland and I have to get back on base. What do you think?" Not likely, but she wasn't about to tell Andrew that.

It hit her. Andrew's friend's bag. She turned and dashed back to the main room.

"Wait. *Who?*" Andrew called sharply.

"I told you, I'm here with a colleague," she said, raising her voice over the siren. "Are you gonna make me stuff you in a bunker on my way out? I'm not leaving without those notes, so you're wasting your time staying."

She leaned over the couch to grab the duffel from behind it, then ripped the straps from the clasps. Andrew skidded to a halt just inside the family room, his expression stunned. He started to say something, then noticed what she was doing.

"No! Not—"

She grabbed the bag by the bottom seams and upended the whole thing. A tightly netted bag of clothing thumped from the couch to the floor. A couple books followed, along with a palm-sized star of some kind, dark and heavy. A single piece of paper fluttered out last, drifting to the other side of the couch.

For a moment, the air raid siren was a distant drone, barely touching her. She stared at the paperback on the couch, at the curling black cover with silver-embossed letters. *Caertoas An Ugdanarian Rin TaSarrah.* The star laying next to it… a sun, its rays fragile and spindly. A sun made of dekatite.

She looked up at Andrew, her breath catching. "A *Dhavvie's* staying here?"

Andrew didn't answer. He was staring down at the paper on the couch. It looked to be a graphite drawing, rough and amateur, of a man with fire instead of hair, wielding a lightning bolt over his head. *Their god,* she realized with a chill. *The Marshal.*

Pieces started clicking into place, and she didn't like the way they were falling. She grabbed the book and flipped through it, stopping on the last page. And there was the name she remembered from four years before, written in black ballpoint. *Cu Zanthus Ayaterossi.* Stamped underneath it was a square of hands, each one grasping the wrist of the next, and the words *Arm Naa Bratheann.* She'd seen that logo on uniforms before. On equipment. *Army of the Brotherhood.* It wasn't just a Dhavnak book. It was a *military-issue* Dhavnak book. Her mouth went dry.

"Andrew!" she said.

His head shot up, his eyes wide and panicked. She stepped closer so he could hear her over the siren.

"What is he doing here? What is *Cu Zanthus* doing here?"

"He's hiding from his draft," he managed. "It's just till the war's over."

"Just till the war's over? He's *here* for the damn war! Look!" She thrust the book out before her, holding open the page to the stamp. Andrew only glanced at it a second before looking back at her.

"So?"

"So he's not hiding from a draft! He's *in* the army!"

"He could have gotten that book anywhere. A secondhand store. A friend. I don't know."

She threw the book down with a snarl. "Grow up, Andrew! Don't you see what you've *done?*"

"Nothing! I haven't done anything!"

"Nothing? You let a *Dhavnak* into our house! You let a *Dhavnak* see our parents' notes!"

"That's not true!" he said, his voice rising.

Should she just grab the notes and go? It was too late to change what Cu Zanthus had already seen, but if there was a chance he hadn't been through all of them yet...

She felt faintly nauseous. Then he wouldn't need Andrew anymore. If she was right about him – and maybe she wasn't, she could admit that much – but if she was, then who knew what he'd do to Andrew if he returned to find the notes gone? The risk was too great. If he got even a hint that Andrew suspected something, he'd be better off shooting him than letting him live. He probably wouldn't even hesitate.

"You have to come with me," she said.

"What are you talking about? No, I don't!"

"Cu Zanthus might hurt you. It's too dangerous."

"He's not *dangerous!*"

"Andrew, what do you think he'll do to you when he's done? When he doesn't need you anymore?"

For a moment, Andrew just stared at her, breathing so fast she knew he was on the verge of a panic attack. Then he turned and ran back down the hallway. A door slammed.

"Andrew! No!" She ran after him, skidding to a halt in front of his closed bedroom door. She tried the knob. Locked. She banged on it. "Come out! I'm trying to *help!*"

"Go away!" he screamed.

She stepped back, lifting her foot – and bumped into something. She spun, fist raised to put through Cu Zanthus's face if it was him.

But it was Holland, his hands raised in defense. "Ma'am, I'm sorry, but when you didn't–"

"Deckman, go grab that yellow bag and load up as many notes as will fit from the closet in the back bedroom. I have to get my brother."

"What's going on?"

"He… he's not safe here. I'll explain later."

"OK, ma'am."

Holland disappeared again. Blackwood leveled her foot and kicked as hard as she could, driving her heavy army boot between the knob and the latch. It gave on the second kick. Andrew was against the opposite wall, a big hardback book clutched in his hands.

"You don't *care* about me!" he yelled. "This isn't about keeping me safe! It's about wanting to be a hero for your army, taking the notes, taking Cu Zanthus, proving to them you're still *useful–*"

"Andrew, be quiet! We don't have time for this!"

She strode up to him and tried to take the book. He brought it down hard, hitting her hands when she reached out. She jerked them back, cursing. A spike of anger shot through her. She lunged for him and wrenched the book from his hands before he could swing it again. When he saw the look in her eyes, he turned quickly – maybe to try to escape out the sandpane, maybe to snatch another book – but before he could do either, she dove forward and latched her arm around his neck. A loose book slipped under his foot, and they both fell forward. His face smacked against the sill of the sandpane. Her heart jumped. He slid to the floor beneath it, motionless.

"CSO?"

Blackwood looked back. Holland was standing in the doorway, watching in horror.

"What are you – did you – is he–"

Blackwood still had her arm around Andrew's neck. It must look to Holland as if she'd shoved his face right into the pane. She hurriedly scrambled off him and rolled him over. He let out a moan. He had a nasty gash on his cheekbone from the sharp ledge and he was unconscious, but he was breathing. *Xeil be praised.*

"Were you *choking* him?" said Holland.

"No! I mean… I couldn't *force* him, not fighting the whole way, so I–"

"Knocked him out."

"I- I didn't mean to. Not like that, anyway. It wasn't out of anger. If that's what you're thinking."

Was it? No. She *had* been angry, but not out of control. *I was trying to help him. Why wouldn't he listen?* But there was Vin. There was Zurlig. A flash of fear numbed her for a moment. *I could have hurt him.* Really *hurt him.*

Three deep breaths. Andrew was not her enemy. But he was a young and naive adolescent who wouldn't listen to a word she said.

She didn't know which was worse.

They'd waited too long. She knew it the second they walked out of the door. Planes rumbled overhead, so loud they completely drowned out the air raid siren – if it was even still sounding. The low booms of explosions carried through the air. Blackwood jogged to the bottom of the steps, Andrew slung over one shoulder. Holland came right on her heels, the hefty duffel slung across his hip.

"Wouldn't it be safer to stay indoors at this point?" he yelled in Blackwood's ear.

"I don't know when Cu Zanthus will be back!" Blackwood answered.

"Who?"

"The Dhavvie who's been staying with him. Once he finds out Andrew's been compromised, he'll kill us all."

"*Kill* us, ma'am?"

"I'll explain later. But we can't take the risk." Blackwood swore under her breath. The situation had gotten way too complicated. "The Sandhill Primary School. There's a bomb shelter there. It's not far."

She swung Andrew's body so he straddled both shoulders and took off at a run. The incessant drone of the planes vibrated through her body until she was nearly numb. She couldn't help glancing overhead, tracking what seemed like hundreds of black shapes across the sky. She could even see the clusters of bombs falling from their bottoms, in every direction. Bile rose in her throat. The explosions sounded closer by the second; the blast from one washed past them in a cloud of dust and smoke, making the very ground shake. The streets were empty of people, and Blackwood felt like she and Holland were the last survivors at the end of the world.

The more the explosions rattled her brain, the more her dekatite mark hummed like a live wire. The tingling became harder and harder to ignore, tipping from discomfort into pain. Her fear. Her fear was making it worse. She struggled with Andrew's weight. His body felt like it slipped with every stumble, and she was afraid she'd drop him. The gunshot wound in her arm screamed in pain again too, delivering a sharp jab with every step. Nausea rose in her, sudden and unexpected, and she stopped, gasping for breath. Dust filled her lungs. She hacked to get it out. Holland stumbled to a stop beside her, his breath coming ragged. She saw him wince, pulling at the strap on his shoulder. All that paperwork wouldn't be a light burden.

They were in front of a physician's office, though the boarded entrance and shredded awning suggested the place had been long closed, maybe even since before the war. They were about halfway to the school, maybe less. It was farther than Blackwood remembered. She stooped, lowering her brother to the sidewalk. Just long enough to get a better grip, she told herself. That tingling was eating into her skin. If only that would stop, she could think straight. Was it just her? she wondered. Or was Holland's acting the same way?

"Holland!" she barked.

He looked at her, his pale face coated in dust, and shouted something back. She couldn't make out his words over the blasts from all around them. She held up her left hand and stabbed a finger at her palm. He shook his head and pointed the other direction: *Keep going!* She started to step closer, so she could shout her question in his ear, but at that moment, the sidewalk around them darkened. She looked up. Her stomach churned as she saw a black Dhavvie warplane swooping so low, she could actually make out the symbols on the bottoms of its wings – spirals in bright white. It barely cleared the twenty-story building across the street. As she watched, a shape detached from its undercarriage.

She threw out her right arm. The mark on her arm twinged, hard and sharp. A white, jagged slash rent the air, crackling with a terrible sizzle. The bright flare seared her eyes and heated her skin. It ripped through the fuselage of the plane. Another branch split from it, striking a direct hit on the falling bomb.

The force of the resulting explosion threw Blackwood against the wall of the office behind her. Pain shot through her left shoulder blade before she crumpled to the stone landing. Shocks rippled through her in quick succession. She curled on the stone sidewalk, hands clenched into tight fists at her midsection that she couldn't unfold if she tried. Though her eyes were open, all she saw was smoke and the ghostly afterimages of the lightning bolt – a barbed incandescent streak driving down again and again in an unchanging pattern. Thunder crashed around her, almost as loud as the bomb had been.

Seconds later, the plane fell, wings and tail burning as it ripped down the side of a building a half-block away. Chunks of steel and glass shot through the air, along with billowing smoke smelling of gunpowder and hot metal.

Blackwood struggled to move, to get up, but her muscles clenched tightly back toward her body as if they had a will of their own. She trembled. She turned toward the wall instead and used her cramping fists to stabilize her body before forcing her legs underneath her, bringing her up as far as her knees. She didn't know if the spasms wracking her were persisting shocks or uncontrollable shivers. She pressed her cheek to the wall, trying to muster the energy to pull herself up the rest of the way.

"Blackwood! I'm here." Holland ducked low to get an arm around her back and pull her up. The pain in her shoulder blade made her gasp, but she pushed through it and kept her feet, though only with the support of Holland on one side and the wall on the other. She could hear the bombing again, breaking through the fading echo of the thunder.

"Are you hurt? How bad?" Half of Holland's face was covered in blood. The gash was on his right temple; if the flying shrapnel had been a touch to the left, he would have lost the eye.

"No, I'm f- fine." It was hard to talk for the chattering of her teeth.

"You're cold?"

"J- Just shock. Andrew?"

"Yeah." Holland started out from under the awning, trying to pull Blackwood along. Blackwood shook her head.

"Don't think I c- can walk yet. Make sure he's OK. Come back."

Holland nodded and ran to the sidewalk. Blackwood closed her eyes and forced herself to breathe in and out deeply, to calm her racing heart. Every breath threatened to pull her from consciousness. *Holland was right. It was me. I took out that plane. That bomb… if I hadn't set it off so high in the air, it would have…*

"Blackwood!" The next thing she knew, Holland was holding her up, hands pinning her shoulders against the wall. She realized he'd caught her from falling. "Andrew's alive. But, Blackwood – you – what you did–"

She nodded, and her head swam.

Holland stared at her, his expression stricken. "You almost killed yourself, CSO! You can barely move."

"I'm OK." She shoved away from the wall. Her surroundings spun sickeningly. Holland caught her just before she went down again. Another explosion sounded, its report echoing off the buildings around them.

"CSO, no way are we gonna make that bomb shelter."

Blackwood grimaced, but the kid was right. "Get us in there," she said, jerking her head at the building behind them. "It's better than nothing."

She crawled back to the wall as Holland ripped a handful of boards off the front door, near the bottom. She listened to the low thrum of concussions in the distance as wind whipped the heat of burning buildings across her face. She could hear a subtle difference in the reports now. *Belzene planes fighting back*, she thought at first. But no. Something deep in her stomach clenched. Artillery. Tanks. It wasn't a good sign.

She watched Holland drag Andrew's limp body inside, then the duffel full of research. The next thing she knew, he was shaking her again. Blackwood drew in her breath, inhaling another lungful of smoke and dust.

"There's a basement!" Holland shouted. "Nothing big, just something they used for medical supplies, but we should be safer there."

Blackwood nodded. "You think this is the one?" she asked as she struggled toward the door.

"What one?"

The attack that captures the capital. But she kept herself from saying it at the last moment. No need to *plant* those thoughts, if Holland wasn't having them already.

She couldn't help casting one more glance overhead before heading inside. If Ellemko was taken... would she always wonder if she could have used this new power to save it?

Chapter 10

ANDREW'S BARGAIN

The deep thumps of explosions sounded somewhere just outside his awareness. Andrew was conscious only of fleeing down the hallway, his throat constricting painfully as smoke enveloped him. He was already burning from the bomb that had come through the roof, but if he could reach his parents, he could get them out in time. When he reached their doorway, though, someone was blocking it. Mila, her long curls blowing in the inferno.

"Let me through!" he yelled.

She shrugged, smirking, and stepped aside. Beyond her, he saw only charred skeletons in the bed. He rushed inside and fell to his knees at the bedside.

"Don't leave me!" he pleaded. "You're all I have."

From overhead, a weight descended. He looked up and saw not the gray-feathered form of Xeil, smiling in grace, but a man with fire burning on his head. The man cupped his hands, and Mother and Father's spirits drifted up into them. Andrew struggled to his feet, holding out his hands. The sun god started to pass the spirits over, but then hesitated, and changed course toward Mila instead. Andrew turned in horror, seeing Mila waiting with a grin. She offered her own hand. But then the sun god took the spirits and rose, disappearing into the ceiling. Andrew stared after him. A vast emptiness consumed him, so immense he felt he would die. He turned toward Mila, but she was gone, too.

Alone. He was alone. He screamed, turning in a circle, looking for someone, *anyone*. But all he heard were explosions destroying his world.

There's the brotherhood. The voice was distant, but it was there.

"Where?" he cried. "Tell me!"

All around you.

"I don't see them! Please! Help me!" He ran back to the doorway, to face the continuous ball of fire roiling in the hallway. The explosions shook the house around him. But as he stood gasping for breath, he heard another voice at the other end of the hall.

"…Put some sort of power in my *skin?*"

Mila. The flames still roared between them. He couldn't get through. He knew she would leave soon, but he couldn't get through to stop her. He closed his eyes. He had to face the fire. He had to reach her, no matter what it took.

"…Something not of this world, anyway. Nobody knows where we *were*, ma'am. There's no saying what sort of… magic, or science, or… or *what* they have in that realm. Maybe they…"

That voice. His eyes fluttered open again. It was *her*. The voice from the WiCorr. She'd taken something from him. What had she taken? *The brotherhood.* No. That didn't make sense. He looked up again, toward the vanished sun god.

"But why give the power to me, when they've only ever killed us before? What's changed? It couldn't have been the dekatite."

He had to reach them before they left. Andrew started to lunge from the doorway, but something held his arms tight. He pulled harder, straining. The flames were diminishing. He'd be able to reach her, if only…

"You're saying you don't feel anything at all?"

Other sensations were breaking through. Something hard directly behind him, like concrete. Cords biting into his wrists. *Cords?* He stopped struggling, noticing a new pain pulsing at his left cheekbone.

"The tingling, yes. It's still there. Doesn't sound as bad as what you describe, though."

"I got hit by something different. Must have been. Yours was marked by what you were holding, whereas mine was…"

"Lightning thrown by a monster?"

Andrew frowned, his closed eyes twitching, and pain traveled in waves across the left side of his face. *What on Mirrix are they talking about?* The noise of the bombs still broke through, safely distant at the moment, and he realized for the first time they weren't part of his dream. He started to push himself up. Something popped in his right shoulder blade when his hands refused to move, and he gasped. His hands were bound. His teeth ground together as memories sparked to life. *Mila.*

"Ssh! Andrew's waking up."

He opened his eyes, blinking in the erratically flickering light. He saw a long, narrow space lined with shelves. He sat on the hard floor at the back of it, his legs sprawled before him, his hands above him, wrists lashed to a pipe or some other fixture in the wall. There were two lanterns, one on each side of the space powered by kaullix grease and sinew. The air already carried a faint smokiness and odor from the flames.

Mila stood over him, arms crossed, just far enough away that he wouldn't be able to reach her with a kick. Her companion stood farther back, leaning against a shelf filled with dusty glass jars, broken syringes, and pestles and mortars. The young man's hands were in his pockets, his glance traveling between Andrew and the stairway at the other end. Three strips of medical tape held together a wound next to his right eye. His short hair was pure black, unnaturally straight strands sticking up in all directions. Andrew stared at him, trying to sort through the mess of his memories and dreams.

"Andrew." Mila knelt down so she was level with him. Andrew slowly transferred his gaze to her. Despite the pain in his face, he refused to let any expression show.

"How do you feel?" she asked.

"You attacked me," he said hoarsely. "And now you…"

"Andrew, it wasn't like that. It's *not* like that. I admit things got out of control back there, and that's exactly why I secured you. So we could talk. Without you attacking me."

He shook his head, and pain lanced through his cheek again. What had happened? Her face had contorted in anger, he'd tried to get away, and then… nothing. Had she hit him? Purposely knocked him out when he refused to leave? And now… now she'd tied him up in a cellar somewhere. Why not a bomb shelter? He tried to ignore the chill crawling up his spine.

His eyes slid back to the other soldier. "You. Who are you?"

"Me?" The soldier raised his eyebrows, glancing at Mila. He waited for her curt nod before answering, "Apprentice Deckman Kyle Holland. I work with CSO Blackwood."

Holland. It wasn't just the name. It was the voice. Unmistakable. He'd only heard that one phrase spoken – *Cu Zanthus?* – but it had the same resonance to it. A careful consideration before speaking; a low pitch that sounded almost practiced. He couldn't shake his first impression of it. *It sounds like a girl.* If he hadn't heard it on the WiCorr first, it would never have occurred to him. Nothing about it made sense. *Why under the moons would Cu Zanthus be in contact with a Belzene submariner?*

"Andrew. Look at me."

He turned his attention back to Mila.

"Tell me about Cu Zanthus. When did he come back? Have you stayed in contact with him for the last three years?"

"How dare you treat me like an enemy!" he said.

"You have jeopardized our country," she said evenly. "You better believe that makes you an enemy."

Andrew didn't know what he'd expected her to say, but it wasn't that. A sliver of fear ran through him. "I told you, Cu Zanthus is hiding from his draft! There's nothing criminal about it."

"Come on. You don't believe that. Do you?"

"I've known him since we were *kids*, Mila! He wouldn't do that to me!"

He was in contact with a Belzene submariner. A pale-skinned one at that. Andrew glanced at Holland again. The young man was rubbing his gloved palms together looking up at the ceiling. Toward the sound of the bombs and the spattering sound of gunfire. That was a serious attack going on out there. He tried to push himself straighter, to test his bonds – what had they used? Some sort of tape? – but the angle was bad, and he only succeeded in sending another pang through his shoulder.

"His government could have recruited him any time during the last three years," Mila insisted. "They might have even chosen him because of the connection with our parents! Have you stayed in touch with him ever since he left? Did you happen to tell him when you got our parents' notes out of the counting firm, and brought them home?"

He was in contact with... Andrew shook his head, shutting his eyes against the pulsing pain at his cheek. "You're *wrong!*"

"He seduced you, didn't he?"

"Shut up, Mila. Just *shut up!*"

"For Xeil's sake, Andrew, I'm just trying to–"

Andrew's eyes shot open. "I want to talk to your partner. Alone."

Mila halted mid-word. Her eyebrows drew down and she looked toward Holland. The other soldier straightened, frowning.

"Why?" Mila said.

"Because I trust he won't try to *kill* me, that's why."

Mila's hands tightened into fists at her sides. "That is *not* what happened! If you would just talk to me–"

"No. I'm done talking to you." He closed his eyes again, wishing he were anywhere but here. The lies. The talks. The kiss. He clung to the memories, desperate.

The picture. He saw it again, fluttering to the couch in front of him. Andrew had drawn it four years ago, and given it to Cu Zanthus before he moved back to Dhavnakir. Mila had just signed her contract with the Belzene Naval Academy. Investigations into Onosylvani's assassination were still ongoing, but warplanes already peppered the sky, and the official declaration of war was imminent. Andrew remembered the fear, the despair of knowing Mila would be leaving, the anger when he tried to talk to her and she brushed him off. He also remembered the small ray of hope he'd held when he'd drawn that picture. It had been the simple hope that Cu Zanthus would remember him. But the realization that Cu Zanthus had actually carried it around with him for all these years... Andrew felt short of breath even thinking about it. *I mattered to someone. I mattered to* him.

"See what he wants," he heard Mila mutter. "I'll try to see what's going on out there. Don't untie him, no matter what he says. His current situation aside, he's an uncannily smart kid, and he may get some ideas."

"Understood, CSO," Holland said. "No... funny business up there. Right?"

"Not planning on it," said Mila.

Just what did *that* mean? He kept his eyes shut, waiting for Mila to be gone. He couldn't believe he'd forgotten the extent of her anger issues; they'd flared up bad after their parents died. Slammed doors, holes punched in walls, screaming. Very rarely had she come after him – but she'd never really had reason to. If she'd decided to see him as an enemy now rather than a family member, that would change everything. *Maybe we've always been headed here.* It should have felt like a loss, but it had been so long now, he could hardly remember what they'd had. The whole thing just felt... inevitable.

"Hey, kid."

He opened his eyes. Holland had lowered himself to a crouch, closer than Mila had. The young soldier attempted a reassuring smile.

"Listen," he said, "I don't know anything about this, but I know you're scared. It's OK. We all are."

Andrew scanned the small room and made sure Mila had really stepped out. Then he took a moment just to study Holland, now that he was closer. If he hadn't been looking, would he have noticed the smoothness of Holland's cheeks? The prominence of his cheekbones? The delicacy of his eyebrows over his striking olive-colored eyes? Maybe. Male or female, he was definitely attractive.

"Is it true?" he said, looking Holland straight in the eye. "About Cu Zanthus?"

The smile slowly faded from the young soldier's face. "How would I–"

"I answered the WiCorr when you called. Don't you remember?"

His eyes widened, just slightly. "I don't know what you're talking about."

"Yes, you do."

"You're crazy." Holland started to stand.

"What would your government do if they found out you were a woman?"

If Holland had been pale before, she went absolutely white now. Her hand found a shelf and she lowered herself back to her former position, as if her legs wouldn't support her.

"Why would you say that?" she hissed.

"I could have said something when Mila was here," Andrew said. "I didn't. I just want answers, OK?"

"But to accuse me of…"

"I thought you were a woman when you called. I never would have thought it otherwise. Is that what you're asking?"

"Not just that. No." Holland put her hands over her knees, digging in her fingers. "You… you're saying you think your friend Cu Zanthus…"

"Is your partner? Seems likely. He targeted me, you targeted my sister. I get it."

"Well, I don't!" Holland whispered harshly. "Why did you send out the CSO? Are you trying to blackmail me? Frame me?"

"I want answers," he repeated.

"Seems like you've already come up with your own. Doesn't matter what I say."

"Mila will be back before long," Andrew said. "If you don't tell me everything, I'll tell her you're a woman. I can't prove you're Dhavnak, but she'll know you wouldn't have dressed like a man for *our* military."

"You can't prove I'm female, either!"

"Don't you think once she starts looking, she'll see it for herself?"

Holland reached behind her, and the next thing Andrew knew, she had a pistol leveled at his face. His heart seized but he breathed through it, forcing his face and muscles to betray nothing.

"Don't do it," he said. "Mila hears a gunshot, and you'll never get out of here alive."

"You don't think so? She'd barely hear it over everything else."

"But you'd be forced to kill her too. That can't be what your superiors want."

"What exactly did you expect to happen here? That you would force my hand? You know full well I can't let you live. Not with what you know."

"I do know that." Andrew's voice stayed amazingly steady. Maybe it was the result of giving up years ago, but his heartbeat had already slowed. Everything came back into focus, clear as glass. "And you know I would never have sent Mila from the room if I wasn't willing to take that risk."

She lowered the gun, just enough so he could see her eyes, narrowed and hard.

"Kill me if you have to," said Andrew. "But talk to me first."

Holland's expression didn't change but the gun lowered another handspan.

"Just tell me," he said. "How long? How long have I been... a project to him?"

Holland's jaw slowly unclenched. After what felt like an eternity, she shook her head. "You're not a *project* to him."

"Tell me the truth. I can handle it."

"No. I'm serious." The gun finally came all the way down, to rest in her lap. "You want to know what he says to me, before missions? 'I have a mark in Jasterus.' 'I'm shadowing a target in Descar.' 'Got an objective in Criesuce.' But when he told me about this assignment? 'I have an old friend in Ellemko. It's been too long.'" She brushed a hand over her eyes, then her lips. Andrew recognized the gesture from the Synivistic Oaths. "By the gods. His exact words."

"You're probably trained to say stuff like that," Andrew said after a few moments.

"No, I'm trained to shoot anyone who asks this many questions."

"Right," said Andrew. "So, um. How long?"

"All I know is he was recruited young. At the age of fourteen, is what I've heard."

He'd been fifteen when they'd met. A slow wave of nausea churned through Andrew's stomach.

"And it was always about the notes? Our parents?"

"I don't know, Andrew. I never knew about the notes till Blackwood brought it up on the way over."

"Mila was right. I mentioned bringing them home. In a letter I wrote him, about four months ago. I can't believe..." He slumped in his bonds, looking up toward the sounds of war above. "What would have happened if I *hadn't* let him stay? Would he have killed me?"

"We don't make it a habit to kill kids," Holland said, a slight growl to her words. "He would have found another way. Especially when it came to you. I firmly believe that."

Andrew took a long shuddering breath, letting her words sink in. "How long have you worked with him?"

"A couple cycles now. Why?"

"Does he know about you?"

"Are you threatening me?" said Holland, her voice cold.

"No," said Andrew hastily. "I'm just curious. Why do this for them, when they… treat women like they do?"

A look of disgust crossed her face. "That's all any of you see when you look at Dhavnakir. You assume all women are helpless victims, imprisoned in our homes and powerless to do anything on our own. But look how *lonely* your country is! Your community is fractured, your families broken, your children abandoned. It's because of our women that *we're* not like that."

"Then why the disguise?" he asked.

Her face tightened again. "I don't know what you're expecting to do here. Change my mind? Get me to want to escape and live in *Belzen?*"

"Are you *trying* to escape?" he said hesitantly.

"No! I just bent the rules a little to get information that women can't get. *Yet.* But things have been changing for a long time, and it's not… it's not the place you all seem to think it is. I couldn't *expect* you to understand that, though." She gritted her teeth and pushed herself to her feet, raising the gun again. "I wish you'd kept your mouth shut."

"If it makes any difference," said Andrew quietly, "that's not what I think when I look at Dhavnakir."

She looked back at him, her eyebrows drawn in suspicion. "No?"

"No. And just so you know, I wouldn't have said anything about you. To either Mila or Cu Zanthus."

"Why should I believe that?"

He let out a short, harsh laugh. "You saw what Mila did to me! The only thing that could make my situation any worse is telling her she's *right*! She's let me live only because there's a slight chance she's wrong."

"She wouldn't really kill you–" Holland began.

"She has anger issues. Always has. She won't mean to, but… No. I have nothing to gain by telling her. Trust me."

"Then what? You just stay quiet? Keep lying to her?"

He looked up, feeling that tiny spark of hope ignite again deep inside. "Help me escape."

Holland looked taken aback. "I – I can't! I'd lose any amount of trust Blackwood has left in me. I'd lose the assignment! And if that happens…" She winced, cursing. "I'm dead anyway, if I don't…"

"Don't what?"

She stared down at him, her lips thinning. "I have a meeting," she said reluctantly.

"When? Where?"

"Tonight. L.T. Karlan Theater." She looked behind her, toward the exit. For the first time, Andrew saw real fear in her eyes. No wonder she'd looked so distracted from the second he woke. "I'm probably already too late," she muttered, half to herself.

"Will Cu Zanthus be there?" Andrew said.

"Most likely."

"Then you have to go! You have to tell him where I am! Then it won't be on *your* head if he comes for me."

"But…" She turned back to him, her eyes wide. "Andrew, do you realize what you're…"

"Let's just say I feel safer with him than my sister."

"You're sure?"

Andrew nodded.

"Where is the theater?" Holland asked. "Do you know?"

"Ninety-fourth and Sterlington."

"OK." Holland swallowed, glancing toward the narrow stairs as she tucked the gun back in her waistband, behind her coat. Then she reached down and grabbed a handful of his fine hair. Andrew gasped in surprise as she wrenched his head back. "Scream," she said. "Loud as you can."

Andrew did. It was strangely liberating to let his anger and despair out in one long cry instead of holding it in. Holland pulled her other fist back. But just before she let the blow fall, Mila came running down the stairs, yelling,

"Holland, for Xeil's sake, *stop!*"

Andrew let his head remain pushed to the side, breathing the short, scared breaths of anyone bound and unable to protect himself.

"He won't talk, CSO," he heard Holland say, her voice rough. "Just insists his precious Zanthus ain't like other Dhavvies. When you and I both know he's prob'ly out there beatin' some Belzene woman to death right this second. Your brother's helping, if only by letting him stay. I *will not* let him get away with it." She jerked Andrew's head to the side so he was forced to look at her. He had no trouble feigning the flash of fear on his face. Her out-of-control fury was convincing, right down to the slipping of her perfect speech patterns.

"Step away, Holland."

"I can make him talk. I know I can!"

"That's my brother you're talking about! Get your hands off him!"

Holland finally released him with a hard shove. "Thought you'd be OK with this, CSO," she bit out. "Seeing as how you–"

"No, I'm not OK with it! This isn't – we're not–" She took a deep breath, glaring at both of them in turn. "Holland. Go up top. Take a few minutes to get ahold of yourself. As long as you need. It was recommended to me when…" Her cheek twitched as she stopped herself. "It helps. And Andrew… you need a second to breathe. This was never meant to be a… you know. An interrogation. I apologize."

Holland turned and stormed out, slamming a shelf with her fist on the way up the stairs. Right before she disappeared, she clasped her hands together behind her, looking back just long enough to catch Andrew's eye. Andrew dipped his chin in a barely discernible nod, his heart pounding. The clenched fists. The sign of the Synivistic brotherhood.

What am I doing? he thought.

The answer came easily. *I'm giving myself a future.* Belzen would be conquered with or without his help, but Cu Zanthus and Holland represented a change to his hated life. They'd both listened to him. They needed him. They might someday be real friends. He could take the chance or he could throw it away. He already knew what a future with Mila held. Loneliness. Uselessness. Fading away. When he looked at it like that, it wasn't even worth thinking about.

Maybe we've always been headed here.

Chapter 11

KLARA YANA'S DEBRIEFING

Deep in the cover of night, Klara Yana ran. Low booms and gunshots rang out in the distance. Buildings burned throughout the city, causing a perpetual haze of smoke in the air. Uniformed bodies littered the streets, bleeding out onto concrete and stone. Troops ran behind them, over the bodies of their former comrades. Belzene army trucks ripped down the roads. At an intersection a good distance away, Klara Yana saw the shape of a tank driving past.

The air raid siren had gone off some twelve hours ago now. Andrew had slept hard for a long time before even starting to surface. The kid was in bad shape, though whether it was from drugs, starvation, or sleep deprivation, she didn't know. Klara Yana had spent part of that time sleeping while Blackwood kept watch, and part of it keeping watch and hoping Blackwood would return the favor so she could escape to her rendezvous. But Blackwood had paced like a caged animal, too agitated to sleep or even go through that bag of notes she'd stolen. She'd just kept insisting she could get out there and *help*. She meant that power. That weapon. But Klara Yana had convinced her she was just as likely to hurt their own people as she was the Dhavnaks – she had no idea how to control it. Whatever it was. *This is something bigger. Bigger than the shrouding. This is at the heart of it somehow. And Blackwood and I...*

She cut the thoughts off brutally. As crazy as it was, Blackwood's unexplained power wasn't her biggest problem at the moment. Nor, amazingly, was her decision to leave Andrew Blackwood alive. With the attack going on, she had no idea whether Leuftkernel Lyanirus would still be at the meeting site. Still, she had to show up ready to face him.

As she reached the L.T. Karlan Theater, a dark form detached itself from the gaudy gilt framing the old building and ran toward her. Cu Zanthus was dressed in a long ragged coat, maybe trying to appear as some vagabond with nowhere to go during the raging battle. His usually perfect hair was mussed. He grabbed her by the arm.

"Where in Vo Hina's *slag* have you been?" he hissed.

"Got caught up."

"*Got caught up?* It's almost the Bright Cycle! By Shon Aha's justice, the *leuftkernel* is here! Come on!" Cursing, he pulled her through the battered front door and into a dingy lobby hanging with posters barely reflecting the light of outside fires.

Normally Cu Zanthus wouldn't have been this upset. He would have understood that escaping for a rendezvous was sometimes beyond their control. Normally, she would have been irritated he hadn't asked about the in-depth questioning he'd forced her to face. But they both knew that getting on Leuftkernel Lyanirus's bad side wasn't only career suicide, but quite possibly *real* suicide. If he decided her intel wasn't reliable, or that they were doing their jobs wrong, he'd pull them from the field in a second. And unreliable spies weren't sent back home, or even to labor camps. They were shot. *And that's if I'm lucky enough not to be discovered as a woman first.*

Cu Zanthus dragged her down two flights of stairs and through a hallway lit by dim, galvanized bulbs, though the empty arphanium globes around them were in decent condition. The whole place stank of mold and smoke. They stepped around bodies shoved against the walls. Probably people who'd tried to shelter in the wrong building when the air strike hit.

Her partner stopped before a closed door and paused to glare at her. "Stand up straighter. And wipe that dirt off your face."

"I went through an air raid," she said tightly. "He'll understand."

Cu Zanthus gave her a sharp look. He'd told her long ago to ditch the 'sirs' and treat him as a partner rather than a superior, but he clearly wasn't in the mood for informality right now.

Klara Yana grimaced, swiping a hand halfheartedly across her face. "Sorry. I just need to get back. I'm pushing my luck being gone even this long."

He nodded, his face still pinched in displeasure, and pushed open the door. Klara Yana strode in. Her eyes flicked over the large underground room, the mirrors bordered by dark bulbs, the racks of costumes, the trunks and stand lamps. It didn't take her long to spot the waiting team.

There were three of them. A heavyset man, a woman – *a woman?* – and… Her stomach heaved as she laid eyes on the infamous leuftkernel. He sat at a round table shoved to the back of the room. His wavy hair had been dyed almost as dark as hers, and he wore plain clothes rather than the uniform, medals, and gold shoulder cord she'd once seen him in from afar, but there was no mistaking his self-assured posture or severe profile. He held a leatherbound book, and was tapping at it as he talked to the man seated across the table.

The woman sat on a chair nearby, pretending to knit a hat. It was obvious she was pretending, because her eyes were on Lyanirus's book more than on her work, and she looked up at Klara Yana's approach before anyone else. They locked eyes. Larin Vron Lyanirus looked up, and Klara Yana pulled herself quickly to attention, breaking the woman's gaze. She loosely clasped her gloved hands and touched them to her eyes, mouth, and heart.

He smiled, not at all warmly. "You must be Leuftent Hollanelea."

"I apologize for the delay, sir. I don't know if Kommandir Ayaterossi mentioned the–"

Lyanirus held up a hand. "Stop talking."

"Right, sir." She almost apologized again, but no; Leuftent Hollanelea wasn't nervous. He was confident, maybe even a little impatient. He was here to make his report and get back to his mission as quickly as possible.

"Take a seat." Lyanirus gestured to a chair behind her.

"Thank you, sir." She pulled the chair forward and sat, her elbows on her knees and her hands clasped before her.

Lyanirus took his time closing the book and tucking it into a pocket. Then he sat back, studying her for several long moments. His gaze lingered briefly on her eyes. She had to resist the sudden urge to look down and hide her face. But that was something a woman would do, not a soldier. Out of the corner of her eye, she saw Cu Zanthus watching, his arms folded in front of him. The heavyset man Lyanirus had been talking to had his chin in one hand and a scowl on his face. The woman's gaze darted between all of them, like she didn't know who would move next. The distant sounds of warfare were the only intrusion in the suddenly quiet room.

Lyanirus leaned forward in his seat and, before she could react, backhanded her across the face. She rocked from the force of it, and barely caught herself before falling to the floor. Warm blood streamed down her cheekbone as the gash at her temple opened up and soaked the bandage. Her vision blurred. She forgot to breathe.

"That's for looking at my wife," said Lyanirus.

His *wife*? She'd never heard of an officer taking his wife into the field. Was this related to those rumors? Did he want a child so badly he didn't want to leave her at home? Was it a trust thing, to keep her in line? *Stop. All that matters right now is that a regular soldier wouldn't have been caught dead staring at an officer's wife. Stupid. Stupid!*

She caught a glimpse of Cu Zanthus standing with his hand over his eyes, as if too ashamed of her to watch. She let her breath out slowly, then clenched her jaw to harden her face before looking up. Not flustered. Not scared. Just a soldier put in his place.

"Nothing meant by it, sir," she said.

"As long as we're understood." Lyanirus settled back in his chair, crossing his arms. "I got your intel from the *Desert Crab*."

"Glad it reached you, sir," she said. "I hope it was helpful?"

"Very, as a matter of fact. Your discovery of arphanium as a driving factor for the way they travel has been, frankly, revolutionary. The dekatite we'd started to figure out, but we hadn't connected the gutting of arphanium to the enhancement of war technology. Everything we've attempted to capture on our side has been rigged with suicide explosives."

"As it happens," Klara Yana said, "that's the first thing I took care of."

Lyanirus's eyes narrowed. "You what?"

She knew immediately she'd said something wrong. She hastened to explain.

"Sabotaged the self-destruct system, sir," she said, keeping her eyebrows slightly raised and her voice steady. "But I made it look like a frayed wire had snapped, rather than been cut. And I didn't do it from the control room, where I would have been noticed. I went down to where the explosives were connected, in the lower power flats."

"Do you know how *careless* that was?" Lyanirus said, his voice edged in steel. "Your *only* job was to observe! What if you'd been discovered?"

Klara Yana barely held back a cringe. The damnedest thing was, he had a point. That last time, when she'd been brought to the captain's office, had been too close a call. But still. She was confident she'd made the right decision, if he would just hear her out.

"A valid concern, sir," she said. "But I knew it was a risk worth taking, since there might never be another chance–"

Lyanirus shot to his feet and wrapped a hand around her throat. She gasped as he hauled her out of her chair. "Since when do *you* decide what risks are worth taking?" he said sharply. "Do you make it a *habit* to show off by doing more than you're ordered to? Because it sounds like a pretty damn big liability to me!"

She tried to choke out an answer, but he'd completely cut off her airway. Silver stars exploded at the edges of her vision. She clutched Lyanirus's arm. Her toes scraped at the floor, trying desperately to find solid ground again.

The bigger soldier came up alongside Lyanirus. He jerked his head toward her. "Could be worth using, sir."

"*What* could, Telchimaris?" Lyanirus growled, tightening his grip.

"The incapacitated self-destruct, sir. We could pass it along to Captain Jerleromens."

Dark spots were bleeding into Klara Yana's vision now. She hissed

through her teeth, frantic for air. Any moment now, he'd let her go...
Gods, he'd made his point...!

"Which one is he again?" said Lyanirus.

"*Combatant's Carnage*, sir. The submarine patrolling the stretch between
Kheppra Isle and Qosmya Canal."

Sheer panic pulsed through Klara Yana's oxygen-deprived brain as
she realized Lyanirus had no intention of letting go. The rumors of
him murdering those wives ran through her head, and she wished she
could scream. But no. Impossible without air. Her fingers faltered and
lost their grip on his arm. Her eyelids fluttered. The room was going
black around her.

She barely heard Telchimaris's gruff voice. "You know you haven't
debriefed him yet, sir."

Lyanirus made a noise of disgust. Abruptly, Klara Yana landed
hard in her chair, nauseous and dizzy as oxygen suddenly rushed back
into her brain. She would have fallen if a hand hadn't steadied her
shoulder at the last moment. She gasped in huge lungfuls of air, her
head spinning with fear and disorientation. A split second. That's all
it had taken. A *second*. She'd never felt so completely powerless in her
life.

Lyanirus's voice was a far-off echo. "Is that the same submarine that's
been intercepting communications between the Kheppra Isle research
station and the Marldox Base?"

"Yes, sir," Telchimaris answered. "As of yesterday, there was still no
sign the Belzenes knew the research station had been compromised."

Compromised? The Dhavnaks had taken Kheppra Isle? Her half-
fogged brain grabbed on to the intel, as if she could restore control
of this situation by falling back on routines. But it was hard to focus
beyond the pounding in her head and the wheezing of her breath.

"Good," said Lyanirus. "Yes, mayora. Get this information about
the self-destruct to Captain Jerleromens as soon as possible."

"Yes, sir." Telchimaris walked back into the shadows, where Klara
Yana could just make out a radio set up on a small table.

Klara Yana could hear Cu Zanthus breathing unevenly behind her.
Lyanirus's sudden assault had rattled him too. He had let go of her

shoulder, but she didn't dare look back to thank him. Instead, she looked straight ahead, painfully conscious of her heaving chest as she got air back into her lungs. She had to fight the urge to snatch her concealed pistol and kill the leuftkernel, before he *ever* touched her again.

But doing so would wipe out everything she'd worked so hard for. It wasn't an option. No matter how bad this got.

Lyanirus settled back into his seat, contemplating her with thinned lips and a lingering glint of anger in his eyes. "As far as we know, you're the only Dhavnak who's been inside this... this form of travel." He paused. "Do the Belzenes have a name for it?"

"Yes, sir." Her voice came out hoarse, but she forced the words through it. "They call it shrouding, sir."

"You mentioned creatures," said Lyanirus.

"Sir. I don't know whether the dekatite mines lead through the center of the planet or go through another dimension entirely, but *something* lives there." She couldn't help it; she had to stop and cough harshly into the crook of her elbow. Her throat burned like fury.

Lyanirus's lip curled, and he turned his head. "Dela Savene!" he barked. "Water!"

The woman stood, gave a quick curtsy, and hurried away.

Lyanirus turned back to Klara Yana. "You reported that, under no circumstances, should one attempt to travel through carrying dekatite."

"Sir."

"Why not?"

"The creatures are drawn to dekatite, sir."

"And you know this how?"

"We were attacked by one."

He blinked, leaning forward in sudden interest. It was all she could do not to shove her chair back, where he couldn't reach her again. "And you didn't put that in your report?"

"There hasn't been time for a report, sir. I've hardly been free of CSO Blackwood since it happened. Even now, she's waiting on me."

"So if the crew already knew the dangers of carrying dekatite," Lyanirus said, "who brought it onboard? Was it you? Was it another *risk* you considered worth taking?"

She coughed again, panic fluttering through her breast. "I had been insufficiently briefed beforehand," she answered, "because the intel wasn't available at that point. I would never have brought it on if I'd known."

"Do your Belzene comrades know it was you?"

"No, sir. I planted the item on another sailor. He was arrested shortly afterward."

His jaw tightened. "Tell me about the attack."

She twitched her shoulders in a shrug. "I never even saw the creature. But it tore a hole through the submarine. We fixed it and got back to shore without casualties. The mission was aborted."

Lyanirus pursed his lips thoughtfully. Dela Savene returned, and lowered her head as she offered a tin cup of water to Klara Yana. Klara Yana took it, keeping her eyes straight ahead. She was just raising the cup to drink when Lyanirus spoke again.

"Is there any relationship between their shrouding technology and the freak lightning attack that struck our plane from the air last night?"

Klara Yana blinked, her lips frozen on the rim of the cup. She hadn't expected him to make the connection, and hadn't even considered what she might share of it. If anything. *The creature left a mark on my CSO. It left the Broken Eye burned into my palm. It might have given us strange powers.* She knew kidnapping Blackwood might very well be the next step of this operation. If she gave the word, Cu Zanthus would follow her back that second.

But Blackwood, under question, would divulge Klara Yana's own mark. And the last thing Klara Yana wanted was to be an object of interest to Lyanirus, in *any* capacity. No. Safer to play this out as an intelligence gatherer rather than a scientific experiment, as Blackwood's own government had proven.

She took a long gulp of the stale water, hoping the action would cover her initial delay. The liquid burned going down. She drained the cup anyway, then set it on the floor by her chair.

"Complicated," she answered. "The short answer is, maybe. But I can't back that up yet."

Lyanirus frowned. "Give me what you have, then."

"There was something about unnatural lightning in the early testing phases of shrouding. As far as I know, it never happened again until yesterday."

"If this is the next step of their technology," said Lyanirus, "it could bode even worse for us than the shrouding. Are you in a position to learn more about it?"

"Yes, sir. Blackwood and I are working with a team." At least, they had been.

"Good." Lyanirus glanced to his right as Telchimaris came back from the radio.

"I've passed the word, sir," said the large soldier. "I told him to capture the *Desert Crab*'s crew alive, if at all possible."

"Very good." Lyanirus rolled his neck, stretching it. He pinned his gaze on Klara Yana again as she prepared to get up. "Hollanelea, have we worked together before?"

She paused halfway out of her chair. "No, sir. Never."

"You look familiar."

She finished standing, but her heart was pounding fiercely again. What was he thinking? One of his former wives, maybe? Or was it just the familiarity of a female in a man's outfit that was bothering him?

"I know what it is," Telchimaris rumbled. "Resemblance to Ambassador Talgeron."

Lyanirus studied her for several moments. "You're right. The eyes."

Vo Hina's mercy! He'd connected her to her ama. If he got it in his head they were related, and knew she'd never had a son... *No.* Her eyes might be memorable, but that didn't make them completely unique. *Read his cues! Adjust my character.*

"Ambassador?" She forced a laugh through her raw throat. "Hardly. More like Terana Perro, I always thought."

Lyanirus raised an eyebrow. "The ice diver?"

"Same shade, sir. Gold flecks and all."

"I wasn't aware." A small smile quirked Lyanirus's lips. "A sports fan, huh, Hollanelea? Never would've guessed."

"Oh yes, sir. I follow most of 'em."

But her mouth was dry. Lyanirus had known her ama. What else did he know? Was he one of the ones responsible for not negotiating her release? Did he know which country had her? Saying anything was a risk, but regardless of what Lyanirus thought, some risks *had* to be taken. *Intelligence not seized in the moment might never be offered again.*

As casually as possible, she said, "Which ambassador was that again, sir?"

"Talgeron." Just like that, the smile was gone from Lyanirus's face. "Have you heard of her, leuftent?"

"I think so, sir. Before her disappearance, she helped negotiate the treaty with Jasterus, right?"

"Look at that. The soldier's done his research," said Lyanirus. "Yes, Hollanelea, she *helped* with Jasterus. But compared to some of the other countries she *helped* with, it was hardly enough to redeem her."

Klara Yana blinked uncertainly. Before she could answer, Telchimaris spoke up behind her, his deep voice resonating throughout the large space.

"She would have bled out the entire system if we hadn't stopped her, leuftkernel."

Lyanirus nodded grimly. "She's a classic example of what happens when you give a woman too much freedom. The problem is they can't *help* it, the wretched souls. They're all Vo Hina-cursed, every last one. Driven by greed. Greed for power, wealth, equality. But that greed drives them to take unnecessary risks. If a woman is killed doing a man's work, she doesn't just take her own life, but those of her potential offspring, and those of *their* potential offspring. Countless lives that could have contributed to our efforts, wasted on one foolish woman's whim. If not for us, they would throw away Dhavnakir's entire future." He cast a look at the woman who'd gone quietly back to her chair. "Dela Savene. Even with me watching, you still feel Vo Hina's curse, don't you? The drive toward greed?"

The woman's eyes flicked among all the men present, ending on Klara Yana. Dark bruises highlighted her face in the low light. "You keep it tamped down, sir, and thank the gods for that," she said softly.

"Speaking of thanking the gods," Lyanirus said abruptly, "Synivistic Oaths. Now. Hollanelea needs to get back." He stood, holding out both hands.

For a moment, Klara Yana just stared. A chill had infiltrated her entire body, seeping deep into her bones. *If we hadn't stopped her,* Telchimaris had said. We. We. If *we* hadn't stopped her.

"Keiller Yano," someone said.

She looked up. Cu Zanthus was holding his hand out to pull her into the circle. She joined him, feeling unsteady. Lyanirus took her other hand and they bowed their heads. She should have been relaxing now into the comfort of the brotherhood. The meeting was over, the tense atmosphere dissipated, the bonds of kinship being strengthened again as they were every Bright Cycle.

But unlike Cu Zanthus, Lyanirus and Telchimaris were no brothers of hers. That chill crept deeper, until it seemed to be squeezing her lungs shut.

If we hadn't stopped her.

They finally released their grips, then passed a hand over eyes and mouth, ending with both over their hearts. They kept their heads bowed for several heartbeats, eyes closed.

"Go, Hollanelea," said Lyanirus afterward. "Stay on top of that lead. Ayaterossi will reconnect with you soon. And by the gods' mercy... don't stray from your orders again, or there *will* be consequences. Is that understood?"

"Yes, sir," she managed.

Cu Zanthus walked her out of the building. The noise of the battle, which had begun to sound softer, flared up again as they reached the ground floor. Klara Yana rubbed her right hand compulsively over her tingling left palm.

"I thought he was gonna kill you," Cu Zanthus muttered as they reached the large double doors at the front.

Klara Yana barely kept her hand from going to her throat. *I think he almost did.*

"And what was that about your eyes? I've *told* you your natural shade is too conspicuous, haven't I?"

Her cheek twitched. She kept her eyes on the distant flashes outside. "Yes, sir. It happened during the attack. I'm sorry."

He sighed. "For what it's worth, I think you did the right thing, sabotaging that submarine. Making your own decisions in the field can make the difference between a successful mission and a failed one. Any other commander would've at least given you…" He shook his head, closing his eyes for a second. "It doesn't matter now. Just be careful, huh? And rub some dirt on your neck on the way back, to hide that…"

"Yes. I will, sir."

Cu Zanthus nodded. "By the way, did you hear we've taken Fort Grenard Base?"

She looked away from the window. "Really? Does that mean Ellemko's fallen?"

"Not yet. We're hammering away at Lemain Airfield, and we haven't broken through to northern Ellemko yet, where their combat base is. But if they can't pry our forces out by Shon Aha's setting tomorrow, it'll be a promising sign."

"That's good news." She hesitated. Here was the moment she should mention what had happened with Andrew. Andrew had practically begged her to. But she'd have to confess that her cover had been compromised. With Lyanirus just downstairs, she didn't dare admit to it now. "Will you still be at the same place?" she asked instead. "If I need to get in touch?"

"Yes. I'm heading back there now." Cu Zanthus licked his lips. "My, uh, contact is missing."

"Is that a problem?"

"I don't know yet. I've checked all the nearby bomb shelters and no sign. It's a little strange. He's not in a position to…" He waved a hand. "I won't bore you. Thanks for reporting tonight. It was on my ass if you didn't."

"Understood, sir." She paused. But she couldn't leave without asking, "Do you know what the mayora meant about the ambassador? Bleeding out the system?"

Cu Zanthus's brow furrowed at the question. "I'm not sure," he said. "But I've run across at least one account that has Talgeron speaking out on women's rights. It must be connected. Why do you ask?"

"No reason. His comment on her eyes piqued my curiosity, that's all."

She saluted and let herself out into the heavily smoke-scented air. That cold feeling had worked its way into her heart. Women's rights.

She would have bled out the entire system if we hadn't stopped her. There was only one thing Telchimaris could have meant by that.

Her ama hadn't been taken by a foreign government. She'd been arrested by her own.

Chapter 12

BLACKWOOD'S QUANDARY

Blackwood jerked awake into darkness heavy with smoke, the blast of a particularly close bomb ringing in her ears. The whole cellar seemed to vibrate from the force of it. The rough fabric of the duffel creased the side of her face. She hurt everywhere; pounding head, aching bicep, numb forearm, sore muscles. She fought through a wave of disorientation. She'd told Andrew they'd take a little time to cool off before talking again, then she'd headed back to the bag to look through those notes; and she'd been looking through that first page again – *dekatite mines in north central Ellemko* – when the words had blurred as several nearly sleepless nights in a row caught up and pulled her down hard. The last thing she remembered was running that line through her head over and over... the laboratory, the possibility of shrouding... but whatever she'd been grasping at had drifted away as fully as her consciousness.

How long had she been out? Long enough for the grease lamps to spend their fuel. She couldn't believe the attack was still raging outside. She hadn't expected to spend the whole afternoon and night down here, much less longer. This whole hiding business filled her with shame. If not for her brother...

Blackwood rubbed the underside of her arm, where the dekatite mark was. Could she be out there making a difference? If she actually tried to use the mark as a weapon, would she be able to *control* that lightning?

She sent the barest surge of awareness toward the mark, exploring the possibility of forcing something from it herself. The tingling was gentle rather than painful, at the moment, like the teasing touch of someone's fingertips. But as she focused on it, the soft tingle became a low vibration up and down her arm. The continuous bombing faded to background noise. She felt fuzzy, as if with excessive fatigue or low blood sugar – or maybe it was more like the buzz of too much alcohol. Disconnected, but still aware of the world around her. A feeling of cold crept over her in increments, inching outward from the mark toward the crook of her elbow and the palm of her hand.

Her right hand sparked, and a small bolt of lightning arced through the air, lighting up the whole shelter for a split second. It was there and gone so fast, she didn't even have time to see where it had come from and where it had gone. She was left with the pain in her retinas, the shortness of her breath, and a sudden wash of fatigue that left her momentarily too weak to move. She lay still, breathing as deeply as possible. *What am I doing?* she thought. *I could have killed Andrew, or Holland. I can't just…* But how else was she supposed to learn? *Learn? It's a freak accident! Don't even think that way!*

With effort, she pulled herself from the thoughts and forced them toward the things she could control. By now, the break she'd promised Andrew was long over. And where was Holland? She sat up, although her body screamed at her to rest longer. Andrew. Why hadn't he made a single noise at that bright flash of light?

"Andrew?" she said.

She heard a small exhalation from her left. She crawled in that direction. She found him slumped against the back wall, hands still tied. She shook him. He grunted. She felt the strips of medical tape on his cheek that covered the laceration from the sill – still secure – then let her hand linger on his brow. No fever, thank the goddess. He'd probably been sleeping like her.

"How long was I out?" she asked him.

He mumbled something, too soft to make out.

"Are you OK?"

"Fine."

"Of course. You're always 'fine'," she said, rolling her eyes. "Hey, has Holland been back?"

He waited several moments before saying, "Tried to. Told him to get out."

"I should go grab him," said Blackwood. "It sounds like it's getting worse out there."

She stood and groped around in the dark until she found the lamps. She lowered herself to her knees and unscrewed the glass tops, then combined the dregs of kaullix grease remaining in the bottom of each into one base. She finally got it lit again. *Probably won't even last till the Main Sun comes up.* Andrew ghosted into view, his eyes squinting against the dim light. She was struck once again by how fragile he looked, and felt a pang of guilt so strong it robbed her of breath for a second. She reached into a pocket and pulled out one of the disgusting vict bars she'd gotten from the FCB. She approached him, unwrapping it and holding it in front of his face. He pulled his head back, his lip curling.

"Take a bite," she said.

"What is it?"

"Vict bar. Army issue. Protein, carbos, lots of calories."

"I'll pass."

"It wasn't a request," she said. "Do you have any idea what you look like?"

"What do you mean?"

"You're not taking care of yourself. I know it's not a money issue; you had a bottle of *Coinavini* at your house, for Xeil's sake!"

Andrew grimaced, as if the very word pained him. Blackwood shook her head in disgust.

"Take a bite," she repeated.

"I'm not eating from your hand. Untie me."

"I'll untie one hand. I'm not letting you free completely until you've talked to me about Cu Zanthus. In a rational manner."

"You have the notes now," he said. "What are you still afraid of?"

"I'm afraid you won't believe me, you'll run back to him and bring it up, and he'll kill you." She stood, working out the knots in the linen bandages they'd used to constrain him.

"You're afraid of me being hurt," said Andrew flatly, watching her. "That's funny, 'cause last I heard you were ready to arrest me."

"It all depends on your involvement, Andrew. If you just talk to me, we can figure this out."

She finally got his right hand free. Andrew hissed in pain as she lowered it to his side. She noted the stripes it had made across his wrist, along with the redness of his hand, particularly around a fresh-looking gash on his forefinger. She sighed and started working the other hand free too.

"So he told you he was hiding from his draft?" she said.

"He *is* hiding from his draft."

"Why come all the way to Belzen? Dhavnakir's a big country."

"Yeah, and he wanted to get *away* from Dhavnakir. That's how dodging a draft works."

She got his other hand free, then knelt in front of him again. Another low boom shook their shelter and sent a powder of dust cascading from the ceiling. Andrew pulled his arms slowly into his lap, wincing as if they hurt to move.

Blackwood glanced at the stairs, wondering where Holland was. Probably waiting for her to come get him. But for the first time, Andrew was *talking* to her – kind of – and she didn't want to shut him down again. She held out the vict bar. Andrew took it, though his gaze stayed on her face, wary as a cornered dune snake.

"What if I got you back to the base?" she said. "Into some sort of protection? We can look into Cu Zanthus, make sure everything's safe before releasing you."

"Protection?" he repeated incredulously. "The only one I need protection from is you!"

Her anger flared. "I'm trying to help you!"

"*Help*? Is that what you call tying me up like an animal?"

She couldn't hold back a flinch. "I'm... I'm sorry about that. But you don't understand, Andrew. This isn't a game. You could be in a huge amount of danger!"

"No, *you* don't understand!" he said, his voice rising. "Cu Zanthus cares about me. He's the *only* one who cares about me. But because he's Dhavnak, you've decided that *I* can't be with him! What gives you the *right*? You don't know what it's like being alone, you've always had someone–"

"Andrew, stop!" He was spinning out of control again, just like that day she'd gone after the notes. She tried to take his hands and calm him down.

He dropped the bar and squeezed farther back against the wall, his teeth bared. "Don't touch me!"

"Then stop yelling and *listen* to me!" Her voice shook with anger. She fought to steady it, for Andrew's sake. Andrew's eyes flashed, but she forged ahead before he could speak. "You're not alone, and Cu Zanthus isn't the only one who cares about you! I know I'm not always there, but I *will* help you when you need it. And when you can't reach me, remember our parents. Remember their spirits inside us, helping us to be strong. Remember that Xeil gave their spirits to us for that very reason, for when times are hard and we feel alone and we don't know right from wrong…" She trailed off as she saw a single tear, glistening in the low lantern light, trail down his cheek. He still glared at her as hatefully as ever, but that tear…

"Andrew?" she said hesitantly.

"They're gone," he said roughly. "They're gone, you're gone, and I'm *alone*, Mila. Your stupid guilt won't change that."

The word *guilt* was a knife in her gut. She couldn't believe he'd seen it. "But they're *not* gone, Andrew. That's what I'm trying–"

"They're gone," he said again. "Xeil isn't real, and our parents are gone."

"Xeil not…?" she stuttered. "Andrew, why would you *say* that? You've never in your life…" She stopped, her breath catching. "Cu Zanthus. This is about him. He's poisoned your mind."

"I didn't *get* this from Cu Zanthus!" he said sharply. "I got it from Mother."

"What in Xeil's name are you talking about?"

Andrew's eyes burned with resentment, even as more tears ran down his cheeks. "The Synivistic gods are real, and Xeil isn't. That's what their research is about! It's about the Dhavnak gods and the eternal darkness after Vo Hina's betrayal, and how it might happen again! It's all there in those notes you stole. I don't have our parents' spirits, and I'm sick of being alone! At least the Dhavnaks–"

"Stop! Just stop!" Her fingers curled into fists. "So help me, Andrew, you better *watch* where you go with that thought!"

He slowly closed his mouth, still glaring murderously at her. She held his gaze, forcing her breath in and out as evenly as she could. *Andrew is not my enemy. Andrew is not my enemy.* Another explosion crashed through the small space, close enough to rattle the grease lamp and send shadows dancing throughout the storeroom.

As calmly as possible, she said, "Is Cu Zanthus the one who… who *interpreted* that research for you?"

"*No!* I saw it with my own eyes!"

"Well, our parents weren't researching religion. That's just – it's crazy. And you can't *disprove* the existence of Xeil. You can't just say our parents' spirits are gone. That there's nothing left of them. Even if our parents had wanted to, how could they confirm it? And as for the Dhavvie gods being real…" She cringed, feeling that guilt pulsing worse than ever. "The only reason you'd come to that conclusion is because you've *made* yourself believe it. Because of *him*. This is so much worse than I thought."

"No! I'm not crazy, and I'm not *lying* to myself! Don't you even–"

"Our parents worked at a lab, Andrew. They were scientists. They didn't work with mythology, or religion, or – or spiritual *anything*. They worked with… geology. Mines. With underground…"

Oh, Xeil's grace. Dekatite mines in north central Ellemko. The page had been right at the top. She'd picked up the papers and they'd been out of order and they'd started in the middle of a sentence and she hadn't thought anything of it; but now she *knew* why it had been on top.

"That's where they'll come through," she said, staring at Andrew in horror.

"W- What? Who? The gods?"

140

"No, not the gods! The *Dhavvies*! Right into the center of Ellemko. Cu Zanthus… he would have told them by now. How much did he know? Did he know how to get through? Was it in the notes?"

"Get through?" Andrew repeated.

"Did he know about *shrouding?*" she said impatiently.

"What in damnation is shrouding?"

"Never mind! I have to get out there! I–" She looked back for Holland, hissing through her teeth. She pushed herself to her feet. "You wait here. I have to find Holland. Don't move!"

He scrambled up and followed her toward the stairs. "Don't *move?*" he said hotly. "I'm not your *prisoner*, Mila!"

Her anger, barely hanging on by a thread as it was, finally snapped. She turned, grabbed Andrew's jacket, and shoved him backward. Shelves cracked and broke free as he crashed against them. He let out a panicked yell. She pulled him forward so their faces were only a handspan apart.

"If the Dhavnaks come through that vein, Andrew, that is your fault! Me and my sailors are out there *every day* risking our lives for people like you, and you're back here letting a Xeil-cursed Dhavvie take away everything I've worked so *damned* hard to protect. And all you can say is–"

She abruptly became aware that the dekatite mark on her arm was tingling furiously. The image of the lightning bolt that had killed Zurlig shot through her mind, and she backed away from Andrew with a gasp.

"No, no, no," she muttered under her breath. "Andrew is not my enemy. My anger. My anger is the enemy." Her vision flashed red. She shook her head violently, biting down on her lip. *I'm not angry. I'm not!* She fought to slow her agitated breathing.

Andrew bolted for the stairs. She half-raised an arm to stop him, but Holland burst through the door right at that moment and rushed down the steps. Andrew pulled up short just before crashing into him.

"CSO!" Holland bent over his knees, catching his breath. "I'm sorry…"

"Where have you been?" Blackwood snapped.

"There was a… Belzene squad a few streets over… I caught up to ask if they knew…"

"And?"

"Dhavnaks in the city. Broke in at the southeastern corner. They've taken Fort Grenard Base. We're holding 'em off at Lemain… for now…" Holland paused to let out a winded cough. His voice was hoarse, as if he'd run himself ragged getting back. "But they're heavily shelling the whole northern half of the city," he finally got out. "Our aerial forces have taken devastating losses, and unless we can get backup from, I don't know, Marldox or… or Criesuce? Do you think–?"

"Nothing about the Federal Combat Base?" said Blackwood. "The labs?"

"N- No, ma'am. As far as I know, anyway."

So if they were planning on coming through the dekatite mines, they hadn't *yet*. That was something. She put her left hand to her arm; the tingling had subsided to a mild buzzing. She let out a slow sigh, turning back to Andrew. Her brother was looking back and forth between the two of them, his breath uneven.

"What's going on down here?" said Holland, noticing their postures for the first time.

"We have a situation," Blackwood said. "I have to get to the base. As soon as possible."

"What situation?"

Blackwood started to answer, but at that moment, a boom that drowned out any of the previous ones enveloped them, so loud and overwhelming that Blackwood's ears barely registered it. The next thing she knew, a heavy weight slammed into her shoulders. Pain shot across her back, and then into the side of her head as she fell and hit a shelf. She screamed as something else crashed onto her legs. The ceiling was coming down. The blast still throbbed in her ears, even though she couldn't hear it as an actual sound – more of a crushing pressure around her head. She tried to shove herself forward, found she couldn't move, opened her mouth to yell… and then spun into darkness as something struck her across the head.

Chapter 13

ANDREW'S ESCAPE

The first sound Andrew became aware of was his own coughing. The pain in his ribs told him he'd been doing it a while. The second thing he noticed was the dust surrounding him on every side, hanging too thick to see through. He remembered every second of the devastating wash of noise and the feeling of the whole world caving in around him. He remembered falling to his knees, pressing himself against the wall and covering his head. Then his senses blurred, leaving him barely aware of anything at all for several terrifying seconds.

His constant hacking wasn't allowing him the air to breathe. He forced himself to stop and take in a deep breath instead. The air was stale and left dirt in his teeth, but it was something. He used the foundation to pull himself up, blinking particles of grit from under his stinging eyelids.

The wall had been his saving grace. The rest of the shelter had collapsed. Wooden boards and metal siding jutted from the underground space. A gap just over him was open to the sky, but all he could really see was dust, smoke, and the occasional orange flash as another bomb hit the city, sending the echoing concussion through his ringing ears. The Early Sun was up somewhere to the east, giving everything a grainy pall that was more irritating on the eyes than pure blackness. It was barely enough to paint the idea of shapes around him.

He knelt, knowing Mila hadn't been far from him. He found her an arm's span to his right, sprawled on her stomach beneath a large beam. She had a lump near the top of her head, but her breathing was steady. Andrew ran his hands over her body, making sure there were no gaping wounds or puddles of blood. He thought she'd be OK, as long as that beam hadn't snapped her spine. Would she be breathing so well if it had? He picked up one end of the beam and slanted it off to the side. He ran his fingers down her backbone. It all felt whole, as near as he could tell.

He left her, and started shifting through the detritus on his way toward the stairs. Holland was crumpled at the bottom of the steps. She was breathing too, though not quite as solidly as Mila. She was kind of whimpering beneath her breath, as if in the throes of a bad dream. There *was* a gash on her head; blood matted her shorn hair where her skull had connected with the bottom step's corner.

Andrew squatted at her side and brought his mouth to her ear. "Holland!" he whispered, giving her a shake.

He got no reaction – not so much as a break in her mumbles. He looked up the stairs, then back toward the other end of the cellar, his eyes straining in the dark. Before he could move, though, a low groan came from the other side of the room. Andrew froze. For just a moment he pictured going over there, helping Mila up… but she'd still be bent on reaching that base of hers, she'd still see him as a burden, she *still* wouldn't believe the things she didn't want to hear. *The one time I try to tell her something…* He hadn't thought Mila would believe him about the Dhavnak gods, necessarily, but he'd at least thought she'd *be* there for him, to tell him their parents still–

It didn't matter now. They had been stupid thoughts. Secrets were secrets for a reason; they weren't *meant* to be shared. *Never again.* His fingers twitched. If he tried to grab the bag of notes back now, he wouldn't make it out before she saw him. Digging his teeth into his lip, he turned the other way. As quietly as possible, he crept up the stairs, squeezing around the fallen debris.

The early morning haze, coupled with distant salvos and explosions, disoriented Andrew completely upon reaching ground level. He'd gone two blocks before he realized where he was. The feeling of nausea under the wide-open sky returned, but a thousand times worse; in the dark and the smoke, he felt like guns were pointed at him from every direction. His recent discussion with Holland left him feeling unmoored – equally likely to be picked off by either Belzene or Dhavnak, and rightly so. The sense of isolation was familiar, and not entirely unwelcome, but the feeling of naked exposure left him sick and unsettled.

He turned back toward his house, the complete opposite direction from the one he'd been going. Before he knew it, he was running, his hands over his ears, single-mindedly focused on the need to be back in his haven. Nothing else mattered.

The door had been left unlocked. He shoved his weight against it and spilled into the entryway, then scrambled in and kicked it shut behind him. He started coughing again, tasting particles of dust coming up from his throat. He had a compulsive need to get to his bed and crawl beneath the covers, and proceed to block out everything – the war, the loss of the notes, the bomb that had almost killed him, the things he'd told Mila…

"Andy! By the gods, you're alive!"

Andrew tried to answer, but couldn't catch his breath. He was only vaguely aware of Cu Zanthus running to the kitchen and returning moments later with a glass of water. Andrew accepted it gratefully, as much for the chance to collect himself as for the badly needed moisture. As he drank mouthful after mouthful, he kept a close eye on Cu Zanthus. The man was more disheveled than usual. He stared anxiously at Andrew, deep concern in his eyes. Real? If it wasn't…

What do I have left? I could stay quiet and pretend not to know, but I'd never be sure. Not like I was yesterday.

Andrew lowered the empty glass and leaned back against the wall, filling his lungs with air blessedly free of dust and smoke.

"Where did you go?" Cu Zanthus said. "And what under the gods happened to your face?"

Andrew put a hand to his left cheekbone. He felt the strips of medical tape there that had half-fallen off, and the crusted blood beneath it. Would her knuckles have done that? *Why can't I remember?*

"Mila was here," he said.

Cu Zanthus's face went still. "My stuff. Dumped out on the couch."

Andrew thinned his lips and nodded.

"What did she say? Anything? Did she know it was me?"

"She figured it out."

Anger flashed across Cu Zanthus's face. "And tried to kill you, by the look of it!"

"We need to talk," Andrew said. "But we can't stay. She might come back. She's still looking for me." By the moons, how he wished he could stay. Just crawl into bed…

Cu Zanthus nodded, his jaw tight. "The house two doors down. They've been gone for days."

Andrew struggled to his feet. His head spun. "Good. Let's go."

After running back home, Andrew's foot was hurting again, but he limped as quickly as he could bear. He kept his eyes on the ground this time, not willing to reintroduce the nausea that had plagued him on the way back. The sounds of distant gunfire and explosions were too loud and he jumped at every one. They reached the top of the steps after what felt like years. Cu Zanthus busted the lock, then led them in.

"When's the last time you ate?" Cu Zanthus said.

The dried apple the day before, the coffee that morning and the Coinavini… Wearily, Andrew just shook his head.

"Here." Cu Zanthus pulled a round tin from his pocket and handed it to him. The image on the front depicted a double-winged airplane swooping through a cloudless sky. A Belzene plane, Andrew thought, but he couldn't say for sure. He pried it open, and found a medley of dried meats, fruits, and nuts inside. He took a handful of the mix and chewed it as Cu Zanthus shut the door and slid a chair over to secure it. The meat was kaullix, tough and bland, with no spice to speak of – flavorless Dhavnak food – but chewing it helped steady him a little.

He drifted into the kitchen. A jewelry box lay in the sink, lid open and jewels gone. Dirty dishes crowded the counters, mouse droppings scattered the floor. It smelled of mold and dirt. Andrew walked across the room to peer out the sandpane. In the Early Sun's light, he could barely make out a broken playset in the rock and dirt yard.

"Andy? Tell me where she went."

Andrew turned around, swallowing the last bit of food in his mouth. Cu Zanthus stood in the doorway to the kitchen, blocking any possible way out. His face was deadly serious, like he'd go out and find Mila that second if Andrew asked him to. Andrew wanted to believe it.

But only if it was real.

He locked eyes with Cu Zanthus as he snapped the lid back on the tin and slid it into his jacket pocket. "Holland told me everything," he said.

Cu Zanthus opened his mouth, but no sound came out for several moments. "Holland?" he finally said. "The same Holland…"

"That you were in touch with? Yes. That one."

"How did you–"

"Mila's partner," said Andrew.

Cu Zanthus crossed his arms over his chest, his eyes narrowed. "What, exactly, do you mean by 'told you everything'?"

"I know why you're here," said Andrew. "What the two of you are doing for… for Dhavnakir."

"You're calling me a spy?"

Andrew gave a slight nod.

"Did you just hear the same name and jump to conclusions?" Cu Zanthus's voice was soft, his eyes drilling into Andrew's. Almost as if he were offering him a way out.

But Andrew shook his head. "No. I recognized the… the voice." *Not* her *voice*, he reminded himself just in time. Holland didn't wear a disguise in order to fool Belzenes. "So I asked him, when we had a moment alone."

"And he just…?" Cu Zanthus spread his hands.

Andrew shrugged.

"I'm going to kill him," Cu Zanthus said after a long pause. "I'm going to snap every bone in his body, ending with his neck."

Andrew's eyes widened. "No. No, no. It wasn't like that." *I threatened to expose her as a woman? She had no choice?* "It's OK. We… we bonded. Mila attacked me, but Holland–"

"So she *did* hurt you," Cu Zanthus interrupted sharply.

"When she realized you'd been staying," Andrew said, nodding.

"Does *she* know?"

"No, she doesn't know. She… suspects. But only because she's naturally suspicious."

Cu Zanthus's hands balled into fists. "This is a Vo Hina-cursed *nightmare*. I can't believe I just *saw* Holland, he looked me right in the face…" He ended with a growl so feral, it made Andrew shiver.

Holland never said anything to Cu Zanthus about me, he realized. What did it mean? That she'd never gotten the chance? That she'd never had any intention of getting him away from Mila? Or that she feared what Cu Zanthus would do if she told him – to either Andrew or her?

He took a deep breath. "Well, if you were staying for the notes, they're gone. Mila took them."

Cu Zanthus's eyes snapped up. "What?"

"It wasn't because of you," Andrew said quickly. "She needs them for her job. I don't know."

"I wasn't *done* with those! I hadn't finished copying the subjects' profiles, the list of samples, the gods-forsaken *map*…" He made a fist and ground it into his palm, glaring at the opposite wall. He made no move to open an exit for Andrew.

I'm afraid you won't believe me, Mila had said. *You'll run back to him and bring it up, and he'll kill you.* Andrew tried to picture how it would happen. A knife? A gun? Would he just hold him down and choke him to death? But none of the thoughts managed to scare him. All he felt was gratitude that he wasn't down in that cellar with Mila anymore. The way she'd grabbed him and shoved him into the wall… *Never again.*

"How many soldiers did you tell about me on your way back?" said Cu Zanthus abruptly. Andrew's heart fluttered with the first hint of fear. Cu Zanthus's thoughts had likely been going down the same tracks as his own.

"I didn't tell anyone," he said.

"You're telling me you figured this out and just *accepted* it?"

"Are you going to kill me?"

"No. I'm not. It hadn't crossed my mind."

Andrew almost laughed. "Of course it did."

"Andy…" Cu Zanthus walked over to the scarred kitchen table and sat in one of the rickety chairs. The brief flash of anger had faded from his face. "Half the time, it's hard to get more than a few words at a time out of you. The other half, you get so agitated, you come off as paranoid or self-destructive. And this isn't just with your sister. It's with *everyone*. Not only does it make you difficult to talk to, but it makes you appear… unreliable. Unbalanced. To put it bluntly, you're not a risk."

He held up a finger when Andrew opened his mouth. "However, you're crazy smart. And *that's* where I slipped up. People underestimate you. To them, you're just a seventeen cycle-old kid who hates the world. And that dichotomy? That's what allows folks like Holland to slip in under people's noses and use their assumptions against them. I would never throw away someone like that. I'd never throw away someone like *you*."

"What game are you playing at, to tell me this?" Andrew said uneasily.

"No game. I'm just laying it out. If I have to do something, I will. But killing you was never part of it."

So Holland had been right about him. *He would have found another way. Especially when it came to you.*

"*If* you have to do something," Andrew repeated.

"Like I said, you're smart. You wouldn't have come back here and told me unless you had a good reason. Not unless you're suicidal." He leaned forward, frowning. "That's not what this is, is it?"

It was undoubtedly the strangest conversation Andrew had ever had. Much stranger than the one with Holland. Threatening to kill him, he understood. But this? Cu Zanthus was opening it to discussion, considering his options, checking Andrew's opinion. Treating him like a *person*.

Slowly, Andrew walked forward and sat in the other chair. "Mila is on her way to the Federal Combat Base. She read something about dekatite, and mentioned the labs to Holland. She thinks Dhavnak forces will come through there."

Cu Zanthus blinked, his mouth opening slightly. "Did you just…"

"I did."

Cu Zanthus closed his mouth, staring at Andrew as if he'd never seen him before.

"I can't go on like this," said Andrew. "Not when there are other options."

"I thought – I had *hoped* – that you wouldn't report me. But to actually…" Cu Zanthus shook his head, his eyes never leaving Andrew's. "Have you thought this through?"

"You and Holland… you're the only two people who've ever *listened* to me. Mila, she – she attacks me, she ties me up, she won't even…" Andrew took a deep breath. His hands were shaking. Anger. Fear. Anticipation. "Yes. I want to help."

Cu Zanthus reached a hand onto the table and wrapped it around Andrew's. He ran his thumb over the inside of Andrew's wrist, and the touch was so intimate that it sent a tingle through Andrew's entire body. Cu Zanthus smiled at him – a heartbreakingly relieved smile – that dissolved any trace of doubt Andrew still held. Outside, the bombs fell, and Mila raged, and people died; but in here, he was safe and he *mattered*.

"We knew about the dekatite mines in the city," said Cu Zanthus. "But we had no idea they were under the Federal Combat Base."

"My parents mentioned some sort of realm in their notes," said Andrew. "Are you saying the… the Belzenes have been using it to–"

"Travel to Dhavnakir. Yes," said Cu Zanthus. "Acts of sabotage and underbelly assaults. And not just attacks on the troops, Andy. Countryside towns. Civilians. Children, even. And that's not all." His face tightened in anger. "About a cycle ago, they broke into the Synivistic Sacrarium and took some of our most sacred religious artifacts, like a piece of fulgurized land from Shon Aha and Vo Hina's battle, and the map Galene Marduc made of the Aphotic Fields. What use could any of that have to Belzenes? I mean, who *does* that?"

The Aphotic Fields, Andrew recalled, was the place Synivists went after they died – an eternal community of remembrance and kinship. *The map of the Aphotic Fields…* He frowned, filing the fact away for later. But his main thoughts lay elsewhere.

"So if you did read the notes," he said, "then you *know* why I've been researching the Age of Fallen Light. My parents thought it might happen again. Because of their research or something."

Cu Zanthus blinked, his face sliding back into a neutral expression. He took several moments to choose his words. "Yes. Your parents… definitely saw some things that shook their faith. But the idea of the darkness coming back someday is nothing new to Synivists. We believe it will be triggered by a great betrayal, so these things are always mentioned in times of war. Believe it or not, it's hardly the first time it's cropped up in some foreign document."

"So you're saying I've been… overreacting?" said Andrew. "By thinking it's imminent?"

"Probably. But I figured – like I told you – that you needed a distraction from the *other* things your parents wrote."

"You mean about Xeil not being real," said Andrew.

"Yes."

"And that you *do* believe?"

"I'm a Synivist, Andrew. It wasn't news to me."

"R- Right." Andrew looked down at his own slender wrist still encased in Cu Zanthus's palm. "So… so if you knew about this realm already, what was Holland doing?"

"Holland. Yes." Cu Zanthus's lip curled. "We had the gist of the dekatite veins, but it was Holland who discovered *how* they're getting in. Arphanium. That was never mentioned in the research. Probably too early for that discovery."

"But how is it Belzen made this discovery and not Dhavnakir?" Andrew asked.

"Well, there's virtually no arphanium in Dhavnakir. Or in most of the southern hemisphere. Every bit of arphanium we have was acquired through trading with Belzen. You know, *before* they cut us off completely."

"Can other countries do it, too? The ones that can mine arphanium?"

"We haven't seen sign of it elsewhere. Although there's been recent suspicions about Criesuce. They're doing *something*. But we don't know anything for sure."

"So if you didn't know how to travel through yet," said Andrew, "that means your army *isn't* planning to come through those mines at the base?"

"No." Cu Zanthus pulled his hand from Andrew's and sat back, looking at him thoughtfully. "But now that we do know, it's an opportunity we can't lose. Mila is on her way there now, you said?"

"The shelter we were in was hit by a bomb. Both her and Holland were knocked out. I was trying to rouse Holland, but then Mila started waking up, and I ran. So I don't know *when* she'll get there, but I know that was her plan."

"OK." Cu Zanthus nodded to himself. "If I just show up at the same time she does, she'll know you were involved. But if she expects to see a whole Dhavnak unit… Hmm. Let me make some calls. I'll make it happen. We have to keep her from blocking that entrance at all costs."

Andrew swallowed. "You won't hurt her. Right?"

"No," said Cu Zanthus without hesitation. "Even capturing her will be a last resort. Holland is working with her and I don't want to put a halt to his intel. Hopefully we can handle this without tipping off our involvement at all. Just in case, though…" He tapped a finger against his lip, eyeing Andrew. "When you left her, where would she have expected you to go?"

"She thought I'd find you and confront you. She was afraid you'd kill me."

"So she expects me to hurt you. That's something we can use." The matter-of-fact way he said it was almost chilling; just another nuance of his job. Cu Zanthus put his elbows on the table and locked eyes with Andrew. "If you're serious about doing this, you need to agree to the number one rule of infiltration. This is very important. Holland himself failed to heed it."

"What is it?" Andrew breathed.

"Never break your cover unless you're ordered to. Anytime we go into a new situation like this, things can go backwards faster than you'd believe. But no matter what happens, your sister has to believe *you* haven't changed. My cover's compromised already by her suspicions, but *yours isn't*. If circumstances arise where you have to choose, choose her. To do any differently after I've exposed myself as an agent would tell her everything. And if you let slip that we had this conversation, you're *done*. There are no excuses. Do you understand me?"

"Yes. Absolutely." Andrew nodded vigorously. But one small thing troubled him.

If there were no excuses for breaking your cover… what did that mean for Holland?

Chapter 14

BLACKWOOD
AMBUSHED

"There. Was that there when we were here earlier?" Blackwood pointed at the single empty water glass against the wall in the foyer.

Holland moaned under his breath, laying his head on the arm of the couch he had collapsed on. "I don't know, CSO."

Blackwood grimaced, and did a quick run-through of the rest of the house. Closets she'd thrown open still gaping wide, empty boxes in her parents' room still overturned, Andrew's room still a wreck. Nothing had been disturbed, as far as she could tell. But where else would Andrew have gone?

"Do you think Cu Zanthus came and got him, before we woke?" she called as she walked briskly back down the hallway.

"I don't know, CSO."

Blackwood's fists balled up. Holland would pass out on that couch, if she let him. She briefly ran the idea through her head. She *could* move faster without him.

She rounded the sofa, looking down at the bloody, matted hair on the back of his skull. She could easily see the finger-long slash beneath the dark strands, where he'd split his head open on the corner of a concrete stair. Just seeing it made the pounding pain in Blackwood's own head worse. It was almost as bad as the sharp twinge in her back every time she moved it. *Better than being dead. But still, the last thing I needed right now.*

Holland, sensing her presence, turned his head in her direction. His eyes were red-rimmed with fatigue and pain. "I'm sorry…" he said hoarsely.

She waved him off. "Don't be. Xeil knows I should stay here and take care of you. Unfortunately, I can't." Xeil. Andrew's comments, unbidden, rang through her head again. *Xeil isn't real. It's all there in those notes…* She glared at the duffel she'd left by the door. The time since Andrew had disappeared weighed heavily on her. *He's not stable. He's not safe. He shouldn't be alone out there.*

"CSO," said Holland. "You're not thinking of leaving me."

"What choice do I have, Holland?"

"I'm fine. I'm already better." He pushed himself back to sitting. To his credit, she only saw him wince because she was watching for it. "Maybe your brother has something. You know. For the…" Gingerly, he put a hand toward the gash on his head, stopping just short of touching it.

"Painkillers?"

"Yeah. I mean, yes, ma'am."

"Doubtful. But I'll check. I'll get you a rag to clean it, too." She walked back down the hall, gritting her teeth at the extra time spent. She tried to picture how it would go if Andrew returned to find Holland on his couch. Holland should be too weak to attack him again, at least. But what if it wasn't Andrew who found him? What if it was Cu Zanthus? She shook her head as she knelt at the cabinet under the washroom sink. More complications. *I have to keep him safe. Somehow. It's my job.* But her persistent anger was making it hard to think straight. Her anger at Andrew for disappearing, and at Holland for setting the fuse for all this with his pendant. *It's a good thing,* she tried to tell herself. *Otherwise, who knows how long before I'd have found out about Cu Zanthus?*

She raised her eyebrows when she discovered not just one bottle of pills, but a good dozen. Painkillers, mostly. But some sleeping aids, too. She let out a sigh. *All that money I've been sending home. Alcohol. Drugs. Xeil knows what else.* None of it would have been cheap during wartime, either. She snatched out a bottle of standard, if high-dosage, Lovatane, and poured several of the yellow grain-filled capsules into her hand on her way back to the family room. She capped the bottle, tossed it toward the duffel, and split what she had between herself and Holland. Then she grabbed the empty glass on the floor and headed to the kitchen for water. She filled it halfway, noting uneasily how little water Andrew had. How much had water rations been slashed since her last visit?

When she came back, Holland was flipping halfheartedly through the Dhavnak book still lying on the couch. He turned bleary eyes toward her. "How long did you say they'd been friends, ma'am? Since before your parents died?"

Blackwood set the glass of water on the table in front of the couch. "No, not that long. It was about a year after."

"Has Andrew always been… that way? That hard to deal with?"

Blackwood thought for a second. "He's always been emotional. But the worst time was after we lost our parents. He shut down completely. He would just lay in bed for hours, *staring*, like a twelve year-old… corpse or something. It creeped me out. All I wanted was to get out there and protect the work our parents had died for. Instead, I was stuck with this – this problem." She winced. "Bad choice of words. But I was eighteen. *I* didn't know what to do with him. When a boy close to his age moved in down the street, I invited him over every chance I got. I… I basically *threw* Andrew into Cu Zanthus's arms."

She shook her head in disgust, and headed back to the kitchen. Holland's voice drifted after her, thin and shaky. "Don't be so hard on yourself, CSO. You were just trying to help him."

Blackwood found a rag and wet it down, being as frugal with the water as she could. She headed back out to the main room. "I thought it *did* help, at first," she said, handing Holland the rag. "After a few months, they were inseparable. I signed up for the navy, I was *sure* he'd be OK. But then, when Cu Zanthus moved away suddenly, Andrew took it hard. He was moody. Passive-aggressive. It was as if he blamed *me*. Things never got better. Some things you just have to… walk away from." She closed her eyes briefly. Fifteen years old by then. Plenty old enough. *Would things be different if I'd stayed?*

She couldn't dwell on it, especially now. She dumped her pills into her mouth and took the glass from the table, grimacing at the water's stale flavor. When she handed the water to Holland, she saw his head drooped to his chest. The handful of capsules she'd given him was still in his half-curled hand.

"Holland!" she said in alarm.

His eyes jerked open. It took him several moments to find her face.

"Stay awake," she said. "Take the medicine. Clean your wound. Stay busy."

He blinked at her, processing the information slower than usual. Finally, he brought the rag to the back of his head and started gently sponging it. His breath came ragged from the effort of not showing pain.

"What's the plan, CSO?" he managed.

"Whether it happens later today or next week," she said, crossing her arms, "the Dhavnaks *will* be using that mine. I'm certain of it. I have to tell the military."

"You're sure? Even if your… your brother's Dhavvie friend did go through those notes, you're sure everything they needed to know was in there?"

"Probably not," Blackwood conceded. "But we have to assume this wasn't their only source of information. That mine there is a disaster waiting to happen. It should have been sealed off a long time ago. And now that Cu Zanthus has read about it–"

"But won't they ask how you know?"

"I don't have to mention the notes. I could just express concern over the mines being there, and the possibility of the Dhavnaks finding out about them."

"Possibility?" Holland lowered the rag, now stained with blood, and placed it with extra care on the floor. "More than a possibility, though. They won't move for… possibility. Not right now, in the middle of…"

"It's my only option," Blackwood said shortly. "If I tell them I'm sure we've been compromised, I'll have to say *why*. Because my own brother let an enemy into our house. I *don't* think Andrew's complicit in this, Holland – I think he's just going through a world of confusion right now – but our government won't see it that way. He could be executed!"

"No, ma'am. You're right." Holland picked up the water, as well as the pills he'd left at his side. "Maybe we can take care of it ourselves. Sneak into the basement under the... the..."

"FCB."

"Yeah. Keep a sentry on it or something."

"A sentry?" Blackwood frowned. "I don't know about a sentry, but taking care of it ourselves... yeah. Maybe. Cave it in. Collapse it. While there's still time. Not bad, Holland."

"Oh," said Holland. "I don't know if... wouldn't you need explosives?" Slowly, he tipped his head back and dropped the capsules into his open mouth, then followed them up with several gulps of water. A grimace of pain flashed across his face as he swallowed.

"Doubt I can get explosives on such short notice," she said, taking the glass from his hand and setting it down. "Maybe that power of mine, from the dekatite mark—"

"I think I'm gonna throw up," said Holland.

"No, hear me out—"

"Not you." Holland leaned forward, one hand on his stomach, the other over his mouth. His eyes were shut tight, and he breathed in a deep, deliberate rhythm that somehow seemed just short of hyperventilation.

As fast as Blackwood had ever grabbed the damage control kit during training exercises, she whisked to the kitchen and snatched a big, dust-covered serving bowl from under the counter. She got back just as Holland opened his eyes. His hand was still over his mouth, but his breathing was easier.

"I'm OK," he said, pulling the hand down. "It's passed."

"You're in bad shape, Holland," said Blackwood, putting the bowl down and sitting beside him. "Maybe I can leave you at a bomb shelter on my way out, so there'll be people to watch you."

"No, ma'am! I'm fine."

"You're not fine—"

"What were you saying?" Holland turned his head toward her. His eyes kept squinting, as if he was sensitive to the dim light coming from the curtains. "You were talking about that – that power? If you can call it that?"

"I didn't tell you, but I tested it. While you were outside, at the physician's office."

A look of horror flashed across Holland's face.

"And," said Blackwood, "to put it frankly, it's real. There was a flash of lightning. Right there in the enclosed space. There is, incredibly, some sort of power in this mark."

"Was there anything about that in your parents' notes?" Holland finally got out.

"I don't know. I haven't had a chance to read them."

"Well, you probably should! This is serious stuff—"

"I know! I'm aware." *The Synivistic gods are real, and Xeil isn't. That's what their research is about.* "I can't take the time to look right now, though."

What was she more afraid of? she wondered. To discover that Andrew was crazy, or a liar? Or that he'd been trying to reach out, and she had shoved him as far away as possible? Or did it go even further than that? If what he'd said was true... *then they're really and truly gone.* No. It wasn't possible. She put her hands to her heart, to comfort her mother and father's spirits within. *I have you. And I'm trying to help Andrew. I promise.*

"I can't stay here a second longer," she said. "There's too much in play."

Holland nodded and stood up, before she could try to stop him. Blackwood leapt up and got a hand on his shoulder as he swayed. He closed his eyes, his face paling.

"Did you experience that weakness again, ma'am?" he asked, his eyes still shut. "When you tried the... the lightning thing?"

"A bit," she admitted.

"You'll need someone. Just in case you do end up using it."

"You're hardly in a position to help."

"You'll need someone," he repeated. "I'm not letting you do this alone."

Blackwood let out a long sigh. "To be clear, you can't disobey orders if you come. I cannot – I *will* not – deal with that again."

Holland flushed. "I know, ma'am. Don't worry."

Blackwood's mouth twisted. It seemed to be his hatred of Dhavnaks that set him off. Could that actually come in *handy* if things went wrong?

She didn't have time to worry about it. She'd just have to trust him to keep his head. And hope to Xeil she didn't regret it.

The bombing seemed to have let up slightly, although planes of both Dhavnak and Belzene design droned by in the early morning sky almost continuously. The booms and blasts from the south grew more intense the closer they got to the heart of the city. The day before, in late morning and calm circumstances, it had taken them a good hour to get to Blackwood's house from the FCB. Now, with the heavy bag of notes on her shoulder, the dust-filled air, and the tumult of war vehicles and running soldiers, their pace was cut in half. Holland kept up a steady jog at her side, his head jerking erratically toward every slight sound or flash of light. It must be a wash of overwhelming sensations to his sluggish mind.

By the time the Federal Combat Base was in sight, the Main Sun was breaching the eastern horizon. Percussions of gunshots rang out in a nonstop salvo. Bodies littered the courtyard, and the ones still fighting seemed an equal mix of dark brown Belzene linen and black Dhavnak poly wool. On the left of the complex, several facilities were burning or already collapsed, the flames gleaming from the cobblestones of the courtyard. To the right, a huge chunk had been knocked out of the main structure. The large iron gate they'd driven through the day before was open and half-skewed off its hinges. A huge Dhavvie tank sat in the courtyard, so massive that the barrel would have easily swiveled over Blackwood's head if she'd happened to be under it. Belzene soldiers surrounded it, firing frantically.

A black Dhavnak warplane, a little farther out, dipped low and dropped explosives that erupted near the tank yard they'd escaped through the previous day. The huge report echoed through Blackwood's skull and caused Holland to clamp his hands over his ears and open his mouth in a silent scream. Blackwood grabbed his elbow and pulled him through the gate before they could change their minds, though every bone in her body begged her to run in the opposite direction.

She yanked Holland up the steps leading into the complex. Soldiers poured from the building all around them, and not a single one so much as looked at them. Right before they reached the door, Holland's legs buckled, but Blackwood hauled him back up with a violent wrench of his arm.

"You can make it!" she said. If he fell now…

"But, ma'am!" he protested. "It's too late! The Dhavvies are here! This is out of our control, Blackwood!"

She shouted directly in his ear. "No, it's *not* too late! If they take the complex today, then we *have* to erase evidence of those mines before they get to them! It could be our last chance!"

She guided him to the door without releasing his arm. He staggered as she shoved him through. All the incoming sensory data was overwhelming him, she could tell.

Another explosion shook the building, its report crashing through the thick walls. They both stumbled and Holland almost went down again. She pulled him back up. Still holding his wrist, she pushed her tired body into a run. The underside of her arm prickled painfully. She chose to think of it as evidence that the dekatite mark would be fully ready when she needed it.

They were in the hallway, almost to the stairway heading down to the basement, when someone came hurtling toward them, rifle clutched in one hand. His face was streaked red with heat and soot. He paused at Blackwood's side.

"Orders are to report immediately to the courtyard!" he shouted. "The Dhavvies are in the base."

"We're on it, sir," Blackwood said.

"You're going the wrong way!"

"Lost our rifles, sir. Heading for replacements."

"For the love of… No one has time for this." He fumbled at his waist, yanked a pistol out, and stuck it in her belt. "Get *rid* of the bag and get out there!" he snapped. Then he was gone, as fast as he'd arrived.

Blackwood pulled Holland along again, turning a corner and rushing them down the two flights of stairs to the basement so fast that Holland missed the last couple. He crashed to the hard floor, letting out a painful grunt. She leaned down to pull him up again, but he thrust a hand out, warding her off. Blackwood bit her lip. She knew she was pushing him too hard.

"Should I carry you?" she said.

He struggled to his hands and knees, gasping for breath. "Blackwood... I want to know what you're... planning. What's to stop you... striking me... with your lightning?"

"Maybe you could wait outside," she said.

"That's all you've... got? You can't... gonna kill yourself..."

"No. I can do it." She bent, ready to throw him over her shoulder if she had to.

"I'm OK!" Holland bit out. His uncharacteristic lack of respect made Blackwood blink. He really was being pushed over the edge. Holland struggled to his feet, catching himself on the wall briefly before standing on his own again.

"You said you were with me," Blackwood continued, resuming her pace. The iron door Zurlig had led them through was visible at the end of the empty hall. It seemed all the scientists had disappeared – probably into proper bomb shelters.

"I know, CSO," Holland said, huffing along at her side. "I'm just questioning your *ability* to use uncontrollable lightning to collapse an underground mine!"

The lab door had been left slightly ajar – a marked difference from the three sets of locks Zurlig had had to open on their last visit. It was dark inside except for one flickering galvanized bulb at the very far end. Shadows of clutter spread across the floor; not only all the vehicles they'd been experimenting with, but the remnants of the disaster Blackwood had pulled down on them before she'd run. In the poor lighting, it was impossible to tell if Zurlig's and Marson's burned bodies were still inside.

No Dhavvies had come through here yet. Of that she was sure. Only now that she saw the gleam of the sharp-faced dekatite mountain, comprising the whole back wall, did she feel daunted by her self-imposed task. She knew they *were* mines, although the original entrances had been covered over. A good enough explosion *should* collapse them in on themselves or at least knock down enough overhead rock to slow progress in and out. But would a single strike of lightning do it? Would multiple strikes?

"What about *your* mark, Holland?" she asked as they headed through the huge room. "Have you even tried it yet?"

"*Tried* it, CSO? Of course I haven't tried it!"

"Does that tingling I describe feel the same in your mark? Almost like an electromagnetic spark under your skin?"

"I don't know, ma'am! It just feels like… damaged nerves or something."

"You must have admitted to yourself you might be able to cause lightning too, though. Right?"

"I…"

"I'm thinking that if the two of us tried together, we may have a better chance," Blackwood said.

She skirted around a tank and paused beside a military truck facing the wall. The dark gray of the dekatite flashed eerily in the sporadic lighting. Down here, the booms from outside were muffled; it was like a different world. Their words echoed throughout the cavernous room.

She tried to focus on that tingle in her arm. It wasn't strong now, not like it had been earlier in the cellar. Not good enough. *It works better when I'm angry.* No question there. *When I'm scared.* When she'd been sure Zurlig would get Holland killed. When those bombs had been falling from the plane. Maybe it was a desperation thing. *But how on Mirrix do I explain that to Holland?*

She took a deep breath and turned to the young deckman. He was right beside her now, staring uncertainly at the dekatite wall. "Try concentrating on your mark," she told him. "On the tingling. But at the same time–"

"Stop right there, Mila Blackwood!"

The voice rang out from her right, reverberating from the walls. Holland's breath hitched, and he dug his fingers into her bicep. A figure stepped forward into the flickering patch of light. Blackwood's throat went dry. His hair was darker, his chest broader, his face harder… but she recognized him. Cu Zanthus. And he wasn't alone.

He held Andrew against his body, with a length of rope wrapped around his neck. Andrew's hands were digging at the taut rope, trying to get his fingers beneath it, but Cu Zanthus held it too tightly. Andrew stared at her through teary eyes, his dark face flushed and desperate in the lambent light. He looked stunned, as if he still hadn't quite grasped what was happening.

Blackwood's jaw clenched. Andrew had gone and done *exactly* what she'd told him not to.

"You're surrounded!" said Cu Zanthus. "Surrender now if you value your brother's life."

Blackwood glanced behind her, and saw several bodies materializing from the shadows in the dark room. "How did you…" Her gaze shot back to Cu Zanthus and her brother. "*Andrew?*"

"All he asked was if the things you told him were true. Nothing he said after that came… willingly." He glanced at Holland. "I'm interested in the stuff you were telling your comrade just now. *Very* interested."

"What do you think you'll do?" Blackwood said harshly. "You don't own Ellemko yet. You gonna capture us? Take us to whatever underground network you have here?"

"Yes, as a matter of fact. It's more forward than we usually operate, but sometimes we're forced in a different direction."

Blackwood could sense Cu Zanthus's men moving forward into a semicircle around her and Holland. Holland's gaze hadn't left Cu Zanthus; he seemed frozen where he stood. Blackwood's hand brushed the pistol in her belt.

"Don't even think about it!" Cu Zanthus barked. He pulled the two ends of the crossed cord tight. Andrew's eyelids fluttered and his mouth opened in a frantic draw for air.

Blackwood screamed. Her mark erupted in needle-sharp stabs. She tried to hurl the sudden burst of energy straight into Cu Zanthus, but either poor luck or her own subconscious fear of hitting Andrew sent the strike into the dekatite wall instead. The lab was plunged first into eye-searing brilliance, then abruptly into blackness. A huge crack sounded, and the whole room shuddered as the thunder and shock wave roared through it. Cries erupted from all around her. Another massive spark from the light bulb showed her the dekatite wall stood intact, but a crack now zigzagged down its face. The crack extended to the ceiling – and chunks were starting to fall. That was all she had time to see before the room went dark again. Her vision burned from the flash.

Disoriented, she staggered, catching herself on Holland. That same wave of fatigue and weakness from before grabbed hold of her, like she'd been hit by a concrete slab.

"Andrew…" she choked out.

"On it!" Holland responded. He extracted himself and disappeared, and Blackwood crumpled to the floor. The thunder still echoed in her eardrums, and crashes sounded from all around her. She peered through the darkness in the direction of the doorway. Lights from the well-lit hallway illuminated the entrance. The falling ceiling didn't extend that far back – not yet – but that could change in an instant. She *had* to get Holland and Andrew out, and fast. But that window of light might as well have been across an ocean.

Splinters of pain and shock shot through Blackwood like needles of ice. She tried to push herself up, but her body spasmed and she went down again. Hopelessness washed through her. Andrew and Holland would be better off than her, but not by much. They'd never make that door, not before they were captured or killed.

Still fighting her leaden body, she turned, dragging herself one painful fraction at a time toward the truck she and Holland had been standing beside.

Before she reached it, an arm latched around her neck from behind.

"Got you, you lunatic Belzene bitch!" someone hissed into her ear. She was yanked to her feet, one of the man's arms still tight around her neck and the other pinning down her right arm. Lightheadedness rocked her, threatening to pull her from consciousness. Someone was yelling. A few people. She was sure she heard Holland's voice in there, but before she could make out his words, two gunshots echoed off the walls. *Xeil's grace!* Two shots. Holland and Andrew. *No! Can't think that!*

With the hand that wasn't being restrained, Blackwood pulled her own gun from her belt and aimed it over her shoulder, then squeezed the trigger. It exploded next to her ear. She screamed as the physical pain from the bang hit her eardrum. But the man released her. Another spasm seized her almost immediately and she fell brutally back to the ground. The concrete floor slammed against her body, jarring her to the bones.

The dark, boxy shape of the truck was an arm's length in front of her. But Holland… She looked in the direction he'd disappeared, feeling the mad pulse of her heart where her chest pressed against the hard floor.

A second later, she heard pounding footsteps, barely audible over the ringing in her left ear, and suddenly, Holland was at her side.

"I have Andrew," he said. His voice came out terrified and breathless, making him sound about sixteen. Blackwood looked up. She could barely see either of them, although she could hear Andrew's labored breathing.

"You weren't shot!" she said.

"No, ma'am. But–"

"Talk later," she ordered. "Right now, help us into the truck. It's our only chance." She managed to jam the pistol back into her belt as she struggled to her knees.

"Yes, CSO." Holland opened the truck door and pushed a still-wheezing Andrew in, then leaned down and pulled Blackwood the rest of the way to her feet. His breath was coming fast, tumbling closer and closer to full-blown panic. *Firm orders. Don't let him think.*

"Grab the duffel!" she shouted. "Toss it in."

"Yes, ma'am!"

Blackwood turned to squeeze over Andrew and into the driver's seat. The keys were in the ignition. There was no way she'd get out through those narrow hallways. Garages? There must be some sort of opening to get all these huge vehicles in here… *unless they shrouded them in.* No matter. There wasn't time to look, especially not in the dark. She slid one hand over the wires and dials of the shrouding drive, installed at the dash. As she'd expected, the truck's steel body was lined with arphanium pipes.

She turned the key, and the truck came to life with a soft purr. There were no lights, but the even hum of the electric motor was enough to alert everyone to their presence. The sounds of gunfire filled the air, pinging from the steel of the truck.

"Ditch your pendant," Blackwood yelled to Holland, "and get in!"

"You're *shrouding?*" Holland yelped.

At her side, Andrew jerked, as if thinking of leaping from the truck. She threw an arm across his waist.

"Just *get in!*" she screamed. Still holding Andrew, she opened the driver's side door a crack and looked back, toward that window of light to the hallway. The last thing she wanted was to leave other shrouding vehicles for the Dhavvies to follow them.

She sent a burst of will toward the light, as strong as she could muster. Pain flared through her dekatite mark as multiple branches of lightning slashed from the doorway, sending lances of voltage through half the vehicles in the room – and hopefully, destabilizing the ceiling even more.

But the effort cost her. As she shut the door, her head spun. Her forehead cracked against the glass before she realized it was tipping. She shoved herself upright, even though the truck seemed to be spinning around her. It wasn't – it was still stationary – but she knew she'd better get that shrouding drive up and running before she attempted to drive it. There wouldn't be much time once the truck started moving.

She hit the button on the dash to cycle the solar power reserves, then threw the lever to activate the shrouding drive. She'd only ever seen it done once, when it was first installed and all the department heads had been given emergency training. She hoped she remembered it correctly. First the lever, then the two dials at the far right… Her head pounded. The truck still seemed to be turning, slowly, nauseatingly. She blocked out the screaming, the gunshots, the shaking of the vehicle as it was buffeted by bullets. She did the rest instinctually, letting her body do the remembering. And she must have done something right, because the whole dash and windscreen lit up bright blue, sending another stab of pain behind her eyes. She remembered the bright blue. It was even more searing in this dark room than it had been underwater.

No more time to waste. She pressed her foot to the treadle.

"Holland!" she said through gritted teeth as the truck leapt toward the dekatite face. "You better have gotten rid of that pendant!"

"M- Mila!" Andrew stuttered. "Holland. H- He shot him. He shot Holland!"

Blackwood looked to the right. In the wash of dazzling blue, she saw Andrew kneeling on the seat, leaning toward the half-open door. Her heart seized.

"He shot him!" Andrew repeated, his words shrill with hysteria.

"Shut the door, Andrew."

"But he–"

"It's too late! Shut the door!" Even now, the front of the truck was disappearing into the dekatite; they were already shrouding, and by the time she'd slammed the brakes, they themselves would be within the rock.

Andrew still wasn't reacting.

"For Xeil's sake," Blackwood shrieked, "we can't shroud with an open door! We'll be ripped apart!" She lunged around him and grabbed the handle, then pulled back as hard as she could. The sudden motion flooded her with dizziness a hundred times worse than before, so intense she lost any notion of up or down. The air went ice cold. Her consciousness ebbed, like a wave was pulling her away. She clawed to hold on. She couldn't... not now...

"Mila?"

She opened her mouth to answer, but the world spun away. Darkness consumed her.

Chapter 15

KLARA YANA'S CAPTURE

Klara Yana's first thought, as she stared at the dekatite wall where Blackwood and Andrew had vanished, was that none of it was real. She'd passed out on the Blackwoods' couch, the CSO had gone on without her, and nightmares had dominated her tired mind. The sensations around her were somehow *too* intense to be real: the hard concrete against her prone body, the excruciating pain in her side, the sharp smell of blood mingled with dust and cordite, the needle-sharp tingling in her palm, the incomprehensible shouts, the distant blasts, the crashes as the huge lab came apart. Even when hands grasped her armpits and hauled her up, the terror of Blackwood leaving her alone with the Dhavnaks seemed overblown. *They're on my side. No one* meant *to shoot me.*

Some of the words around her were finally breaking through. "… Belzenes in the corridor…" "…got a sample…" "…nothing to get through…" "…out this way…" Chaos. She was tossed over someone's shoulder, and felt a gush of fresh blood down her side. Everything seemed blurred, shapes changing too fast to make out before they were gone. Whoever had her was moving, running even, and it didn't help. She dug her fingers into his shoulder blade, fixating on the one thing close enough to see. The back of his head. His hair – short, dark, curly. A dark-skinned neck below that. Belzene. Soldier?

Someone on the other side of her cursed. "This way, *this way*, you fool!" The man holding her abruptly veered the other way, and the room spun again. She squinted her way through it, staring at the blood soaking the bottom half of the man's jacket. Her blood. Moments later, she realized seeing the blood meant the light had brightened. Stairs. Smoke-filled air. A breeze. Heat. Running. Nausea. A distant flicker of fear. *No. Misunderstanding.*

It hit her suddenly: it had been Cu Zanthus's voice redirecting her savior – captor? Whatever he was. He was Belzene, but he wasn't *with* the Belzenes. A collaborator. Of course. When Cu Zanthus had set up that ambush, there was no way he would have found enough Dhavnak spies on such short notice. He'd been making connections the whole time he'd been here – Belzenes who wanted favor after the takeover, who wanted high-paying government positions further along. Even then, it was unlikely he'd gotten more than ten or so. The person she'd shot, then, had almost certainly been *Belzene*, not Dhavnak. One thing to be thankful for. *And I didn't kill him.*

"This is your fault."

"Wait." Someone grabbed her by the hair and pulled her face up. She found herself looking at Cu Zanthus. He looked more enraged than she'd ever seen him. "*What* did you say, Keiller Yano?"

It had been her who spoke. She only realized it now. But those horrible moments following Cu Zanthus's comprehension that she had, in fact, been hiding something, flooded back without warning… and it no longer felt like a sensation-rich nightmare. It was real life. She was in more trouble than she'd ever been. Cu Zanthus would be carting her – someone he surely saw as a traitor after the withheld intelligence and the insubordination – to Larin Vron Lyanirus. Blackwood and Andrew had really shrouded, alone in that truck, with Blackwood barely functioning and, worse, with that dekatite burned into her arm. They were as good as dead. And in one of the most horrible ways imaginable.

"This is *your fault*," she repeated, twice as loud. Unexpectedly, it was fury that coursed through her, warming her veins. "I knew what I was doing. You should have handed over Andrew and trusted me! You've ruined everything!"

"Trusted you? After I find out you've been hiding intel? After I hear this lightning storm that attacked us was caused by *you?*"

He released her, shoving her head roughly to the side. They resumed their quick pace. The sounds of warfare were sharp and sudden again, loud enough to mask their words from anyone more than a step away. She eyed Cu Zanthus's Belzene uniform; she would look like a wounded soldier being rushed away for attention. No one would stop them.

"No! *Wasn't* me!" She could barely breathe, slung over this man's shoulder as he ran, but she *had* to make Cu Zanthus believe her. Before this went any further. "Was Blackwood. But I don't know enough yet! You can't just haul me out... middle of a mission... *shoot* me like an enemy–"

"Better than leaving you in as a double agent!" he shot back.

"No! I'm not–"

"You shot one of my men!"

"I- I didn't have time to explain! Blackwood was gonna get away. Couldn't lose her. And I knew if I brought her Andrew... would keep my cover strong. You want me to break cover, Cu Zanthus, you need to *tell* me!"

"If I ever want you to break cover, believe me, you'll know," he answered coldly.

And that's when Klara Yana knew. It was no accident that Andrew had gotten in that truck and not her. Andrew had told him about her. They had set it up together. Maybe Cu Zanthus hadn't planned it that way initially, but after hearing Blackwood's words – *You must have admitted to yourself you might be able to cause lightning, too* – he'd pulled the trigger on the operation. She'd been replaced, by Blackwood's brother of a measly seventeen cycles. She fought back the sudden urge to retch. Her one small consolation was that Andrew apparently hadn't mentioned her gender; if Cu Zanthus knew, this would have been a very different conversation.

Whether she could *keep* it that way was another question entirely.

When the person carrying her finally shoved through the door beneath the theater, she'd come up with a plan. The head wound. She hadn't been thinking straight. She'd been confused, had thought Cu Zanthus's order of "Seize him!" had been for her, telling her to grab Andrew. A misunderstanding. And when Cu Zanthus told Lyanirus about the mark, the power? *I'll just show him. It's on my hand, after all. And I don't have any power; what can he possibly do?*

"Kommandir Ayaterossi!"

Lyanirus's unexpected shout pulled her from a haze she didn't remember falling in. Fatigue pulled at her with every wave of torment across her side, and her body had gone completely slack on her captor's shoulder.

"When, exactly, were you planning to tell me about this operation of yours?" Lyanirus barked.

"I wanted to get the intel first, sir," said Cu Zanthus, somewhere off to her left. "It was a very delicate—"

"Now you've sent the chief whatever-she-is off into the dekatite without backup! What in Shon Aha's name happened in there? It was her? *She* used the lightning power?"

"Yes, sir, she did. She meant to collapse the mines. And she might as well have succeeded, for the damage she did. She mentioned having a mark. Some sort of mark that causes lightning."

"How long have you known *that?*" said Lyanirus incredulously. "Since before or after you made the decision to leave me out of it?"

"It was after, sir. I thought we'd just be watching her, maybe snatching her, if things went really backwards, but—"

"What about Hollanelea?"

Several agonizing moments passed before Cu Zanthus answered. "It became apparent that Hollanelea withheld some key pieces of information. Including the fact, sir, that he has the same mark Blackwood does. The one that creates the lightning."

"Is that him?" said Lyanirus after a second. His voice was very soft, very dangerous.

"Sir."

"He's wounded?"

"I shot him, sir."

"I see." Another pause. "Put him down."

Klara Yana felt herself lowered until her feet touched the floor. She had her words ready. *Yes, I got a mark, but neither of us realized it meant anything at all. It didn't seem worth mentioning. We didn't even know–*

"Turn around, Hollanelea."

Somehow, her legs supported her as she turned, though the room seemed to be swimming again. Those distant reports aboveground battered her skull. She blinked at the blurry form of Lyanirus. "Yes," she began. "I got–" Without warning, her legs buckled. The man behind her caught her with a surprised grunt, a second before she hit the floor.

"You *had* to shoot him, didn't you?" Lyanirus snarled. "Fine. Bring him to Dela Savene, back in that office off the southeast corner. She'll get him patched up while we get to the bottom of this. Telchimaris! Contact every soldier you can about watching the dekatite faces we know about. The chief female has to come out somewhere. Ayaterossi–"

"We grabbed a piece of arphanium, sir. It might be enough…"

Klara Yana lost the rest of the conversation as she was hauled to the back of the theater and then through a narrow hallway. The light dimmed the farther back they went. She was brought through a doorway and into an office room, then dumped on the floor. Agony shot through her side, and she couldn't hold back a hiss of pain. She saw a pair of candles flickering on a desk shoved against the far wall. By the other wall was a pile of blankets. The woman from the first meeting sat up from them when Klara Yana hit the ground. Klara Yana thought she saw her hide a book beneath the blanket.

"Bandage him!" ordered the man who'd dropped her.

Dela Savene nodded, getting hurriedly to her feet and rummaging in a desk drawer. Then she knelt at Klara Yana's right side. Unlike the men, her white-blonde hair hadn't been dyed; it hung loose over her shoulder, brushing the floor between them. Dhavnak women didn't braid their hair, or put it up, or cut it any shorter than their waists. Klara Yana unthinkingly curled her fingers around the fine strands, which had fallen into her open palm on the floor. She could barely remember what it felt like to have hair this long.

She'd been sixteen when she hacked it off. A combination of several factors had gone into that daring decision. Her step-apa's increasingly violent abuse in the three cycles since her ama had disappeared. The dawning realization that her ama wouldn't be coming home, and the knowledge that once Klara Yana had been assigned a husband, at seventeen, the rest of her life would be mapped out, and her ama would be gone forever. She'd thought about trying to convince that future husband to use his influences to find her ama. But there were no assurances her husband would be someone who had those connections. There were no assurances he wouldn't be someone like her step-apa. It had been when she was trying to build that hypothetical husband in her head – the one who had the position and the willingness she'd need to pull off such a thing – that it had occurred to her she could simply *become* that person, and cut out the middle man. What better way to assure everything was done right?

Nausea twisted in her gut at how wrong she'd been. And at how much worse things might still get.

Dela Savene had produced a pair of scissors and was cutting from the bottom hem of her jacket up toward the wound in her side. Klara Yana lay on her back, chest heaving as she stared up at the guard who'd remained by the door. He watched with a scowl, arms crossed over his chest. Klara Yana felt the scissor blades reach the level of her breast wrap. She put one hand out, and Dela Savene stopped. She looked up, catching Klara Yana's eye.

"That's high enough," Klara Yana said, her voice rough.

Dela Savene nodded, lowering her eyes again. She cut across the jacket and pulled the bottom half away, then set to work on the shirt underneath.

"How long will this take?" the guard growled. "The leuftkernel is waiting."

"Does he want this soldier to get proper treatment?" Dela Savene murmured. She cut through the shirt quicker than she had the jacket, then tore a flap away. Klara Yana could tell it was just low enough that her breast wrap wouldn't show. Would her smooth hairless skin be a giveaway? Her heart rate picked up as Dela Savene pulled out a small light and inspected the wound.

"The bullet didn't go in. Just grazed you." She looked up at the guard. "I need water."

He looked back at her with distaste. "Then go get some."

"And you'll rub on the salve?" said Dela Savene, gesturing to a jar beside her.

The man glared at Klara Yana with disgust. "I'll get the damn water," he finally spat, and walked out. The door swung shut behind him.

Dela Savene got swiftly to her feet and threw a lock on the back of the door. Seconds later, she was back at Klara Yana's side with a bottle of water. Before Klara Yana could ask, she'd wet down a rag and was scrubbing the blood from her skin. Klara Yana almost screamed at the sudden pain.

"Tell me what's going on," said Dela Savene breathlessly. "And make it quick."

Klara Yana looked from Dela Savene to the locked door and back again. "Maybe you should tell *me*," she managed.

"I need to cut the rest of your shirt off to do this properly. Did you *really* want him here for that?"

Klara Yana's whole body went cold. First Andrew saw through her disguise. Now the leuftkernel's wife. *This can't be happening.*

"Slide back against the desk." Dela Savene took Klara Yana under the arms and helped her over. There, she sliced the rest of her shirt and jacket off, in three quick slashes.

"But how did you *know?*" Klara Yana finally got out, as Dela Savene slathered salve over the wound.

The other woman shrugged, almost apologetically. "I've seen soldiers disciplined often. And every single one is *mortified* to be punished in front of a woman. But you didn't so much as glance at me. That's when I started paying attention."

Vo Hina's mercy. What if either Cu Zanthus or Lyanirus started 'paying attention'? *I'm in too deep. This is spinning out of my control...*

"So what's going on?" Dela Savene said again. "Did Larin Vron find out?"

"No," said Klara Yana. "This is about... something else. It's not *good*, no, but it's not about that."

"Thank the gods for that much, anyway," said Dela Savene. She wound a bandage around Klara Yana's torso, darting discreet glances at her face as she worked. She wanted to share more, Klara Yana could tell. What was it? Something about the leuftkernel? Anything could help. Klara Yana was about to start pressing her for intel when Dela Savene spoke on her own.

"I hardly ever see this anymore. The disguise thing, I mean. Way too many risks. Plus there are better ways."

Klara Yana blinked, momentarily derailed. "Better ways? What do you mean?"

"The truth is, we can't improve the lives of women by being men. It's like accepting we'll never be equal to them, so why even try? And that's no fight at all."

Klara Yana's breath caught when she realized what Dela Savene was saying. "Is *that* what you think I'm doing? Trying to fight the system?"

Dela Savene's eyes widened. "W- Why else would you do it?"

"Because I need connections that a woman can't get! *Yet.* And I couldn't afford to wait any longer."

"Yet?" Dela Savene's brow furrowed. "You really think a few cycles is all that separates us from… no. You can't be that naïve."

"Naïve?" Klara Yana's anger flared. "It's not *naïve* to know our government gave Ambassador Talgeron a highly prestigious position ten cycles ago! Why is it such a stretch to think we'll be allowed into military positions soon, too?"

Dela Savene sat back, looking at her closely. "You mentioned her at the meeting, too. You've been studying her, it seems."

"Some," said Klara Yana cautiously.

"Well, I don't want to… to shatter any illusions you may have. But I think it's important that you're not going into anything blind here, with the expectation that Larin Vron will go easy on you because you think 'women have it better now' or something. OK?"

A chill passed through Klara Yana as she remembered Lyanirus almost choking her unconscious. Was that what Dela Savene called "Larin Vron going easy" on someone?

"Trust me," she said uneasily, "I don't think that."

Dela Savene glanced toward the locked door again, biting her lip.

"Good. That's good. Now just stay quiet and listen a moment." She bent her head back to her bandaging, talking as she worked. "Talgeron wasn't an ambassador – not really. That treaty with Jasterus you mentioned? Dhavnakir had been trying to get it for months, but Jasterus wasn't ready to sign on with people who treated their women so badly. So our government found Talgeron and stuck her in that so-called position, as a way to show Jasterus that women were being more respected. She was a figurehead. That's it."

Klara Yana jerked back. "What are you *talking* about?"

"You think I don't pick this stuff up? I've sat invisible in enough meetings and social calls with Larin Vron. Talgeron wasn't the only one. Just one of the most famous."

"That's not true!" Klara Yana said heatedly. "She would never have agreed to that!"

"Agreed?" said Dela Savene, a note of resentment in her voice. "They had her foreigner husband in a labor camp, and tortured him when she resisted."

The words were a stab to Klara Yana's heart. Foreigner husband. That would have been Klara Yana's Criesucan father, the one who'd disappeared when she was a baby. It was this small fact that shook Klara Yana's hope that Dela Savene was wrong. The woman could say anything she liked about Talgeron, but to know she'd been married to a foreigner?

"But I heard she spoke out on women's rights!" Klara Yana protested.

"That came later. After her husband was killed, she rebelled. Rallied several Dhavnak-occupied countries before she was arrested. I met her, you know. As a teenager. I've never met anyone so *passionate*." There was no mistaking the anger that flashed across Dela Savene's face. She got to her feet and circled around the desk, pulling another drawer open.

Passionate. Klara Yana's stomach turned. She'd never known that side of her ama. Because she'd only seen her at home when her step-apa was there, drunk and bullying the both of them. It was only that last time, when her ama had told her about being chosen for Dhavnakir's program to employ females in better jobs, that Klara Yana had seen happiness light up in her eyes. She could still hear her voice. *This is a sure sign things are changing.* Why hadn't her ama told her the truth?

Klara Yana had been thirteen; she could have handled it. Or had Ama not known until a lot later, when it was too late to get back and tell her daughter? To warn her?

Klara Yana pushed herself to her feet. "Where did they put her? Which labor camp?"

Dela Savene's eyebrows rose at the question. "No idea. I know the gist of what happened, but even Larin Vron doesn't discuss her life after she was arrested. The problem was fixed, after all."

But he still harbored plenty of hate for her. Klara Yana had picked up on that during the meeting. *What in the gods'-damned-name of Vo Hina have they done with my ama?*

Dela Savene retrieved a few shirts from the drawer and placed them on the metal top. "Haven't you seen how well other cultures treat their women in comparison? Seen how much better things could be?"

"Well... yes. I mean, I guess so. But Dhavnakir is different. We have a community those other countries don't. And our women are the *foundation* of that. To say there's nothing good about being a Dhavnak woman–"

"That's not what I said!" Dela Savene said sharply. "I *love* the community we have, and I love the fact that the women provide a caring and generous base for our children. But what I *don't* love is that there are still way too many men – too many *people* – who think nothing of taking us for granted. Who treat us as if we barely exist, or can be... be *forced* into submission. Can be treated like..." Abruptly, she turned away, putting her hands to her face. Putting them over the bruises there.

Klara Yana stared at her. A vile mixture of shock and shame churned through her stomach as she remembered similar bruises from her step-apa. She put a hand to her own face, closing her eyes for a second. "But it's not *all* of them–" she began.

"No. But it's too many. Still way too damn many."

Klara Yana swallowed, opening her eyes again. "I've been living as a man for too long," she whispered. "This isn't what I had planned."

Dela Savene looked back. "Planned?"

"I hadn't planned to forget. This was just supposed to be..."

"A short job? Not an entire escape?"

"No," Klara Yana said quietly. "But it became one."

Dela Savene cursed softly, under her breath. "You haven't done anything wrong. Just live through this. And then… if you do… maybe you can come back home some day. We have a movement there, and we're making progress. Slowly, but we *are*. And we could use you. With your training and experience… don't discount it. You hear me?"

"I hear you," Klara Yana said.

She knew Dela Savene was trying to give her back some of that hope she'd come in with, when she'd thought her ama had been part of a growing change to their oppressed role in society. But she didn't feel anything resembling hope anymore. She felt hollowed out and betrayed. Everything she'd believed for the past ten cycles, about her ama, her country…

Why do this for them, when they treat women like they do? Even Blackwood's seventeen cycle-old brother had seen it, and he was actively working with Cu Zanthus. *How could I have been so blind?*

"What's this?" Dela Savene touched the back of Klara Yana's scalp. "This needs stitches. It hasn't even been properly cleaned."

"Hasn't been time," Klara Yana said numbly.

"Get changed first. Duck behind the desk."

Klara Yana did so, ripping one of the black shirts Dela Savene gave her into wide strips, then using it to replace the filthy, tattered one around her breasts and upper ribs. She tucked the dekatite pendant beneath it. Before she'd gotten a shirt on over the wrap, the door shuddered as the Dhavnak soldier tried to come in. He pounded at it when it didn't open.

"Hey! Why's this locked?"

Klara Yana crouched behind the desk, buttoning up the shirt as fast as she could. She heard Dela Savene open the door.

"Not locked, sir," she said, in her soft, subservient voice again. "You just had to push harder."

"Don't you even–" the soldier snapped, but Klara Yana stood at that moment, pulling herself up with the aid of the desk. The soldier's attention shot to her.

"Wait. You're done with him? Then why in Bitu Lan's name did you need *this?*"

Dela Savene took the cup of water from him. "Fluids. For the patient." She brought it over to Klara Yana. "I have to stitch one more wound."

"You *what?*"

"It's a head wound. The worst of his trauma will have worn off, in terms of mental effects, but leaving it untreated will invite infection or worse." Dela Savene bowed her head. "I know my husband doesn't want that."

Several tense moments passed before the soldier answered, "I'll go check with him. But if he doesn't clear it, I'm taking Leuftent Hollanelea with me, even if the Vo Hina-cursed needle is still embedded in his skull." He turned on his heel and stalked away. The door slammed shut again behind him.

Dela Savene turned back, taking a shaky breath. "Kneel down."

Klara Yana knelt on the floor while the other woman scrubbed the dried blood and dirt from her hair. Dela Savene retrieved the scissors and clipped her hair even shorter, then threaded a needle. Klara Yana gripped the top of the desk and bit into her arm, muffling her scream as Dela Savene sutured the wound. Several agonizing moments in, she heard the door open behind her.

"You done in here?" said a voice. Klara Yana didn't know whether to be relieved or alarmed that it was Cu Zanthus this time.

"Almost," Dela Savene said softly.

"The leuftkernel wants him. Now."

Dela Savene didn't answer, but Klara Yana didn't hear the door close again, either, or the sound of Cu Zanthus leaving. She realized he must be watching. Tears streamed down her face from the pain, and she was terrified he'd see. Her breath hitched with every pierce of the needle. It felt like forever, but Dela Savene finally tied off the thread, then took her arm and helped her up. Klara Yana wiped her hands furiously over her wet cheeks and dug her fingertips into her eyes, as if she could erase any evidence.

"Painkillers?" she said shortly.

"All out," said Dela Savene.

"Figures." Klara Yana turned, glaring at Dela Savene and Cu Zanthus in turn. Cu Zanthus's eyebrows were slightly raised.

"Now, Keiller Yano," was all he said.

"Sir." Her hands were shaking badly, and she felt the tremors spreading down through her body and legs, too. It was mostly adrenaline and pain, but the fear of facing Lyanirus again wasn't helping. She raised her chin, though, looking Cu Zanthus in the eye. "Let's get this straightened out, huh?"

"The sooner the better," he answered, meeting her gaze evenly.

Klara Yana swept past Dela Savene, careful not to so much as glance at her in gratitude. She was still lightheaded from the blood loss, and the room seemed to pitch around her. But with a little help from the doorjamb, she kept her feet.

"Get him something to eat, if you can," Dela Savene said.

"He'll be fine."

"Sure, just bring him right back when he passes out."

"You watch your mouth," growled Cu Zanthus.

Klara Yana started to leave the doorway, but then paused and looked back. *We can't improve the lives of women by being men.* But gods, why not try?

"Thank you, Dela Savene," she said.

Dela Savene's eyes flashed in warning, but she bowed her head and murmured, "You're welcome, leuftent."

As Klara Yana headed down the hall, she sensed Cu Zanthus's eyes boring into her. Probably ready to accuse her of becoming too friendly with Lyanirus's wife again. She turned on him, ready to defend herself, but realized he was staring at the back of her head.

"Living gods," he muttered. "She give you drugs beforehand? Mild anesthesia?"

"No. Nothing."

"You didn't even scream."

Klara Yana shrugged.

Cu Zanthus whistled softly. "There's a loaf of bread down the hall," he said after a moment. "Shouldn't cost us time to grab you a slice on the way."

Klara Yana nodded stiffly, but tentative hope blossomed in her breast. Cu Zanthus hadn't given up on her yet. The bond of their partnership was strong. She held tight to that small hint of kinship, amidst the violent upheaval her life had suddenly become.

"Any word on the Blackwood siblings yet?" she couldn't help asking.

"No. But we'll find them."

"If they're still alive."

"After what you did, Keiller Yano," said Cu Zanthus, "you'll be lucky if you live long enough to find out."

Chapter 16

ANDREW'S DEFENSE

"Mila?"

With Mila's foot no longer on the treadle, the truck was just coasting now, but the second they'd gone through the dekatite wall – with absolutely no interference – it was like they hit a dirt road, and the vehicle started jouncing over dips and rocks. Andrew, kneeling the wrong way on the floor of the passenger side, held tight with one hand on the door Mila had barely gotten shut before they'd passed through. With the other, he shook his sister – lying on the passenger seat and clearly unconscious in the blue glow from the dash.

"Mila!" he yelled.

It was *freezing*. He remembered this from his parents' notes. The other realm was cold, like being at one of Mirrix's polar caps. They'd put layers and layers on the people they sent in. They *had* known how to get in, even back then... though Cu Zanthus was right, the notes had never mentioned arphanium. Just that it was dark, cold, and dangerous. They'd send someone in with layers and a light and an imagesaver and sometimes, a gun, in the cases of volunteers rather than forced subjects. No one had ever come back to them. On occasion, pieces would... be left at the gates, as it were. Andrew felt a whimper building deep in his throat.

The truck hit something with a thunk, and came to an abrupt, jarring stop. Andrew's head smacked the dash, and he barely kept Mila's unconscious body from falling on top of him. For several moments, he hardly breathed. The only sounds were a faint clicking from somewhere behind the dash and a howling wind outside, strong enough to buffet the truck.

"Mila?" he said again. Still no response. He checked her pulse and breathing – both normal, if about half as slow as his own – then bit his lip and climbed over her motionless form. He nudged her feet aside so he could sit in the driver's seat.

The windscreen had been transformed into a projected grid of some kind: a black background with bright blue lines and dots, in different arrays and sequences. Glowing circles with overlapping borders, boxes dissected by straight lines, blinking dots scattered seemingly haphazardly over it all… It was some high-tech military chart that he couldn't begin to make sense of. Obviously, with this other realm, they weren't supposed to see out of the vehicle to navigate; they were supposed to use *this* instead.

He tore his eyes away from it and looked at the dash. Numbers, glowing bars, dials. No help there.

He tried the key next. Nothing happened. He slammed his foot down on the treadle. Still nothing. He turned the key in the opposite direction. The clicking behind the dash stopped, although the glowing network on the windscreen remained.

For a handful of seconds he stared straight ahead, his chest tight, his breaths shallow. It felt like he physically couldn't draw enough air. What if Cu Zanthus had damaged his windpipes? He put one hand to his neck, feeling the pattern of the rope like a burn in his skin. If he hadn't known better… *No. It was just an act.* He repeated to himself the words Cu Zanthus had spoken in his ear right before releasing him: "RXJ87S2. Contact me as soon as you can. Now go!"

Maybe there was a radio in here, he realized suddenly. It was a government vehicle, after all. He ran his hands over the front, looking for some sort of dashbox, but came up empty. He checked the seat creases behind him, the side of the door. His hands shook with the urgency of his task.

It didn't stop the other thoughts intruding though. *He shot Holland.*

His own partner. Because she broke her cover? Because of the things she was saying? Oh, curses, the lightning. The lightning! Is that part of this shrouding? Why does Mila–

Without warning, something crashed against the back of the truck with a resonating clang, lurching the whole frame. Andrew's face smashed into the steering wheel. Blood flooded his mouth as he bit his tongue. Several pounding heartbeats later, the truck was still again, as silent as if nothing had happened. His head whipped from left to right as the chill in the air seeped deeper into his bones.

He had to get that blue light off; it was a beacon to anything out there. He started turning dials at random. The glowing dots jumped or flickered, but didn't change brightness. Another crunch against the side of the truck, shaking them. Breath coming ragged, Andrew slapped the dials and buttons faster, trying every one he could find. Finally, he slammed down a lever right by the steering wheel, and the blue light died.

For several moments he sat frozen, waiting to see if that thing would attack them again, waiting for the searing blue glare in his eyes to dissipate. His body shook, trying to warm him. With the light gone, he swore the temperature had instantly dropped even further. Trapped in some strange world, in the cold, in the dark… except, as his eyes adjusted, he realized that with the blue light and grid gone, he could see through the windscreen. It wasn't *completely* dark outside. There was some sort of light source overhead – about as bright as nighttime with both moons fully phased, maybe – but a thin haze of drifting smoke surrounded the truck, dampening that light. Andrew leaned forward, straining to see through it.

The land was rocky and rugged. He could barely make out a series of ridges, not too far off on the left side. The space in front of them seemed flatter in comparison, although he saw several boulders and bumps as faint shadows. Stuff this big military vehicle should have been equipped to handle. The wind he'd heard was apparent, churning dust from the ground into the air.

Movement to the left caught his eye. A shape was climbing the ridge on four flexible limbs, only slightly illuminated by the moonlike glow. Then it topped the ridge and was gone.

"OK," he whispered. "It left. It'll be OK."

As if something was listening, the truck was hit again, this time from the passenger side. The wheels left the ground for a brief second before coming back down. Andrew almost choked on his sudden surge of fear. His gaze shot toward the passenger sandpanes. He could just barely see something out there – a pitch-black shadow larger than a human. And there was a sound now too, like a steady howl. He couldn't tell if it was one voice or many. He couldn't tell if it was a voice at all. He turned back to the wheel and frantically tried the key again, but even the clicking didn't resume. At least not that he could hear over that… that *sound*.

"Mila! Wake up!" he begged. Her body had slid toward the driver's side when the vehicle rocked, but she *still* hadn't opened her eyes. He grabbed her leg and shook it roughly. He thought she let out a small moan, but it might have just been the howling.

A weapon. I need a weapon. His mouth dry, Andrew checked all the same spots he'd just looked through. Still empty. *Mila!* Maybe she carried a gun or a knife. He started checking her jacket right as the truck was hit again. A sandpane shattered. Andrew let out a scream, unable to help himself. But in the same moment, his hand landed on cold metal at Mila's waist. *A gun!* He pulled it free, his hip colliding with the wheel as he jerked back and held it pointed straight out.

In the faint light from outside, he saw a dark shape squeezing through the back, one long limb bending to grip the back of Mila's seat. Stripes across its body gave off a dim, pale green glow. It was probably twice as big as a person and roughly humanoid in shape. It hissed – not like an animal, but like an irate person spitting out a curse. There were almost words in its voice. *Torthu-ara-caeg-alay.*

Andrew aimed the pistol over the seat's back and squeezed the trigger. The gun fired, explosively loud, jarring his elbows with the unexpected force. The creature jerked back, its hiss becoming a snarl. A smell like burning wires flooded the truck.

"Get out!" Andrew yelled.

"Andrew?" Mila gasped. "What in the…?"

Andrew fired again. The vehicle rocked as the huge monster tried to back out and caught a limb on a broken piece of sandpane. At least, with its glowing stripes, it looked that way. It had gone back to hissing – *Caeg-alay! Caeg-alay!* – but Andrew shot it one more time, and it finally broke free with a screech of metal and vanished.

"What's going on?" Mila said, her voice weak.

"M- Monster," he got out. "Trying to get in."

"Monster? Where – where are we?"

"We're in that realm. Mother and Father's realm."

"You mean shrouding."

"I… I think so."

"No," Mila said after a second. "This doesn't make sense. No one *stays* shrouded. You're in, you're out… it takes moments. No one stops inside!"

"Well, like it or not, we're here, and some freakish monster just tried to kill us. I can't believe *this* was your escape plan."

"Just calm down. I'll take care of it," she said. She struggled to sit up in the passenger's seat. Her strained breath was apparent. Her smudged form went still as she straightened. She was staring outside, he realized, just as he had been a moment earlier. "This is incredible," she whispered.

"That lightning," Andrew said. "Did you cause that?"

"Yes."

"*How?*"

"I don't know. A side effect of the accident, near as Holland and I…" She gasped, the spell of the strange landscape broken. "By the moons, *Holland.*"

"We'll figure it out," said Andrew. "But for now, Mila, *something just tried to get in.*"

"It's… a reaction between the dekatite in the vehicle and the dekatite outside. It happened on the submarine, too," Mila said. "Move, Andrew. Let me see what I can do. And give me that gun."

"Reaction?" Andrew repeated incredulously. "I just *shot* something trying to attack us! How are you not getting this?"

"Xeil's mercy," Mila muttered. She raised her voice. "The *gun*, Andrew. Now!" When he hesitated, she reached over and wrenched it from his hand. "What is wrong with you? I told you not to look for Cu Zanthus, didn't I? If you'd listened to me, we wouldn't *be* here! What would you have done if I wasn't there to save you?"

"Save me? What are you talking about?"

"From Cu Zanthus, you idiot!"

"You tried to kill him with your lightning. Doesn't mean you were saving me. It was *Holland* who came for me."

"I sent him!" she said sharply. "I'm his commanding officer!"

"Right."

"I don't have time for this. I told you to move!"

Andrew squeezed out from behind the steering wheel and scooted to the passenger side. The freezing air from the busted sandpane in the back enveloped him. He huddled forward on the leather seat, arms wrapped around himself. He heard Mila try the key several times.

"Gee, wish I'd thought of that," he said.

"Shut up. Did the shrouding drive die at the same time?"

"The blue lights? No, I shut 'em off with the lever. So nothing would see us."

She must have thrown the lever, because the bright blue glow came to life again within the cab. The foreign landscape outside disappeared. Andrew tensed, sure they'd be bashed again. But the truck remained ominously still and quiet.

He saw Mila now, running her finger along the network of dots, following some unknown pathway. Andrew held his breath, terrified that even now, more of the things outside were stalking toward them, but equally desperate for Mila to find a way to save them.

"If I read this right," she finally said, "we've come quite some way. Distances work differently here. The nearest dekatite vein should be only a short jaunt this way – northwest, by our own standards."

A map. Andrew stared at the glowing dots, trying to see the graphite lines from the sketched map he'd seen in the notes. *Maybe* some of it seemed familiar. He felt pieces shifting around in his mind, the way they did when he was learning a new language or adding new facts to a complex puzzle. A puzzle like their parents' research, or the Age of Fallen Light. Or the puzzle of this realm.

A puzzle, he suddenly realized, that Mila might have undocumented knowledge of.

He turned away from the map. "You said those attacks – or reactions, or whatever you want to call them – are caused by dekatite being both inside and outside the vehicle?"

"We think so," she answered, almost absentmindedly. "On every occasion we've had those bad attacks, there's been dekatite inside."

"Is there now?"

"There's a spot on my arm," she said. "Happened during the last accident. Obviously related to the lightning."

Andrew's heart almost stopped. "Wait. One of them *marked* you?"

"I don't know, Andrew! All I know is I can cause erratic lightning now and it makes me weak when I do it. It's not something I've had time to explore yet."

By the moons. Of all the things he'd expected to hear, that wasn't one of them. "And the mark's made of dekatite?" he said shakily.

"Yes," she answered irritably. "I *just* said that."

"I don't suppose it's something you can cut out of your skin."

"*What?*" Her head whipped around, her eyes pinning him.

"You just said that's why we're being attacked!" he protested.

"I…" Mila hesitated. "I suppose that's not the dumbest thing you've ever said."

"Wow. Thanks."

"But on the off chance–"

Mila didn't finish before something slammed into the back of the truck with such force that the vehicle was shoved forward. A horrendous screeching filled the cab as the metal hood wrenched up toward the windscreen, then ripped off altogether. The truck rolled down a small incline before halting again, noticeably skewed now to the left. One of the sand tires had blown, or maybe even detached completely. A horrible growling filled the air, as well as a sudden scream. Mila clapped a hand over Andrew's mouth. The scream sputtered and died in his throat. The growling continued for several more moments before petering out. Andrew reached up and angrily pulled Mila's hand down.

"What are we gonna do?" he said, his voice shrill.

"I've been through this before. Just stay calm."

"Stop telling me to stay calm! Stop trying to protect me, or shield me, or shut me up, and just admit something is trying to kill us. I'm not crazy, Mila!"

An earsplitting bang cracked all around them, and Andrew had a moment of disorientation as the truck tipped again, much steeper than before. The next thing he knew, his whole right side exploded in pain as it slammed against the metal and glass of the door. In the same moment, Mila fell on his other side, so hard he cried out. The blue lights went out abruptly, and other objects clanged around them as they fell from various parts of the truck. The vehicle had been pushed onto its side. Pain lanced through Andrew's ribs, and he could feel the chill of the ground through the broken glass beneath him.

He felt Mila push off him, and a second later, a series of gunshots broke the silence. She'd squeezed her upper body through a broken section of windscreen to fire at their attacker. The deep, rattling growl reverberated through the truck again, rattling the frame with its sheer volume. Again, it was almost growling *words. Bidzin-agabi-dethu.*

"It's running away," Mila gasped out. "Thank the Goddess. I'm empty."

She squirmed back inside, although the bent metal and shattered frame of the truck left very little room to move in. Andrew managed to get his body mostly upright again as Mila struggled to open a smashed compartment benath the driver's seat.

"So are we clear now?" Andrew said. "We agree there are creatures out there?"

She sighed – in annoyance, he thought. "It's drilled into us to keep the deckmates calm. Denial works better than you'd expect."

"Well, I'm not one of your *deckmates*, to be lied to!" he said angrily.

"Don't panic, Andrew. You're just proving my point."

"If not for me, you'd have slept right through that thing coming into the truck! I chased it off, and you tell *me* not to panic? You'd be dead! How can you–"

"Andrew!" she shouted. "Don't lose it on me! Not now!"

Andrew clamped his jaw shut and tightened his hands into fists, shaking with the effort of not screaming at her. *I went to Cu Zanthus because I'm sick of dealing with her!* He forced himself to take deep breaths. *It's not about us anymore. I'm working with Cu Zanthus. With Holland taken, I'm his partner now. Mila's just a job now. She's just a job.*

Mila had finally gotten the compartment most of the way open. "No spare bullets," she said. "No lights. But I found a pair of overcoats, for what it's worth."

A second later, a heavy garment landed on him. Though Andrew was already wearing his father's jacket, he gratefully pulled it on, struggling with the sleeves in the tight confines. It smelled faintly of smoke and a bit musty too, as if it hadn't been used in a long time. Halfway through fastening the front buttons up, he paused.

"You mean we're going outside. Don't you?"

"Yes."

"But–"

"But nothing. We're not uprighting this truck on our own. It shouldn't be far. There's just one issue."

"Getting ripped apart by savage beasts?" he said sharply.

"You can't shroud – in or out – without arphanium. I'll have to pry some from the truck."

Arphanium. Exactly as Cu Zanthus had said. Holland's discovery. But if that were truly the case, what about the mutilated explorers Mother and Father had sent in? *Lots of layers, a light, an imagesaver...* The light. An arphanium lantern. Of course. Maybe it was common enough by then, they hadn't bothered making the distinction, or maybe they'd purposely left some things vague.

Mila smashed something into the control panel at the dash. A rattling screech sounded outside the truck again, but it seemed farther away now. Nevertheless, Andrew shivered. He finished buttoning up the coat with fingers starting to go numb.

A second later, part of the panel separated with a loud crack. Andrew saw a faint glow within. Mila stuck a hand inside, blotting out the dim light. There was a soft clatter.

"Good thing we slammed into that rock," Mila said. "Broke some of these crystal pipes apart."

She pulled out a couple chunks and stuck them in her pocket. Then she turned and helped Andrew up.

His ribs sent a sharp spike of pain through his side. The fear of going outside was almost more than he could stomach. He forced himself to think of something else. Cu Zanthus's kiss. Even now, the memory of it warmed his lips and sent a pleasant heat through his whole body. He held tight to it, as long as he could.

I can do this. For him.

He climbed through the shattered windscreen behind Mila, into the smoke-tinged open air. A frigid breeze blew his hair back. As he stood, the moonlit landscape spread out before him, jolting him with the overwhelming urge to scramble back into the truck. He forced the sudden vertigo down, making himself turn and look back the way they'd come instead. His jaw dropped.

No. Not moonlit.

Between the drifting tendrils of smoke, he saw a sweeping band of light jut up from below the horizon and sweep in a gentle curve across the sky, widening as it stretched away to the right before disappearing into the horizon again. Parallel lines were visible within the light, perfectly following its angles. It looked like a black and silver rainbow, but several times too big.

"Mila," Andrew finally managed, "what *is* that?"

When Mila answered, she sounded as stunned as he was. "No idea. I've never heard anything about that."

A cold dread settled into Andrew's heart. "We're not on Mirrix anymore," he whispered.

"I never… I mean, I knew we… but this." Mila's breath hitched. *She's scared,* Andrew realized. He closed his mouth, swallowing. Mila was never scared. Something about it shook him to the core. *Admit it,* a small voice inside him whispered. *She's not just a job. She's your big sister… and you expected her to keep you safe.*

Chapter 17

BLACKWOOD'S
WAY OUT

Where are we? Inside the dekatite? Through the center of Mirrix? Holland's words on the submarine came back to Blackwood now. She'd never shrouded on land before – but with the overlaid maps on the windscreens, how many drivers ever saw what she did now? The patterns in the partially-obscured stars overhead were unrecognizable. No Richard's Maple, no Sir Tristan's Funeral Cot, nor the footsteps of Xeil walking him home. The moons… four of them. *Four.* A large one overhead, a smaller one at eye level, and two very small ones opposite one another at the horizon. One of them seemed to brush that strange band of light.

With Andrew flanking her on the right, Blackwood jogged as quickly as she dared over the rough terrain. The land reminded her of the rockier parts of Belzen to the south. But though it was often this windy in Belzen, it had never been this cold. A couple mountains nearby were clearly volcanoes, lit up red in the distance and leaking smoke. Small wonder it was so ashy and hazy here.

Even with the kaullix fur-lined hood of the military parka pulled around her face, the cold bit into her cheeks and stung her eyes. The parkas had no doubt been stored for this climate on the chance the truck got stuck, as theirs had. There had probably *been* spare bullets once upon a time, as well as guns, but during wartime, everything had been given to those who needed it. The parkas had been left only because they never needed them in Belzen. But parkas or not, Blackwood knew for a fact that no soldiers had ever staggered free from shrouding without a vehicle to protect them.

She intended to be the first.

Andrew had barely spoken a word since they'd disembarked. The strange creatures called from every side, their guttural cries echoing through the rocks and distant crags, but none were visible. Blackwood did her best to keep a sweeping vigil as she ran, though her eye caught on that wide band of light behind them every time her head turned. She carried the bag of notes again, and its weight slowed her. She'd thought about leaving it, especially since Andrew had all the information in his head, but she knew she couldn't depend on him. Even if she could keep him beside her, there were no guarantees about what he chose to share.

Andrew was lagging. Blackwood allowed her already slow pace to falter, so he could catch up. "Faster, Andrew."

"I'm sorry," he huffed. By his tone, he wasn't sorry at all. "It's my foot."

"What's wrong with your foot?"

"Nothing. Just a cut."

Blackwood rolled her eyes. "From what I saw on the chart," she told him without stopping, "the dekatite source should be in those ridges. You can make it."

"We don't seem any closer than when we left."

"Sure we do." Why did she never get stuck in these situations with proper soldiers? Even Holland and his head injury would be better than this.

"Do you always travel through the same world?" he asked.

Jogging at a pace barely faster than a walk now, Blackwood eyed him sideways. Was he actually *initiating* a conversation? Non-sarcastically, at that?

"I would assume so," she said.

"What is it? Another planet? Another dimension?"

"Don't know. No one does."

"And nobody commented on how unbelievably dangerous this is?"

I did, she thought. But aloud, she only said, "It's necessary. We can travel across Mirrix in mere moments. We use shrouding as a passage, right through... through this place. A half-mile here could equal a few hundred on our own world. Or more. All you need is a dekatite surface big enough to enter. And then another big enough to come out. Anywhere in the world."

"And of course you're using it for war. Instead of for *trading* or something."

"That was originally its purpose," said Blackwood. "But then Dhavnakir happened." *If it hadn't, our parents would still be alive.* She almost said it out loud, but Andrew and those notes and his weird thoughts about religion... No. Better not risk setting him off again.

"So you're saying we might come out in Qosmya or Narbona? Or *Cardinia?*" Andrew said.

"Well, *we've* only gone to the waters outside Jasterus," said Blackwood. "But then again, I've only ever traveled by sea. I suppose anything's possible. I got a basic course in how the thing works, but didn't get the navigation training. Not many underwater dekatite veins, after all."

"So there must be oceans in this realm. Right?"

The way Andrew saw that right off jarred her. She'd never thought about it. Never thought of it as a whole other world at all – just this black, cold, dangerous abyss that surrounded them for the precious few moments it took to get back to their own reality. She remembered her snapped answer to Holland's question on the sub: *we're dead, if you don't focus.* Even now, she was singlemindedly aimed at that dekatite vein, with little thought besides their own survival. Andrew was... *too smart for his own good.* It would do well to remember that.

"Gaba! Gaba-ruta!"

Blackwood's head whipped around. The dread that had lain barely covered in her heart blossomed into full terror as a flying creature bore down on them. It was only a little larger than a person, with leathery skin, limbs resembling arms – though far too many – and a face that seemed more sharp teeth than it did eyes or nose. Blackwood grabbed

Andrew's arm and shoved him behind her, then wrapped both hands around the shorter strap of the heavy duffel. The beast came right at her, never slowing, and when it was a little over an arm's reach away, Blackwood swung the bag with all her strength. The bag caught the creature squarely in one ribbed wing and the side of its face. The force of the collision sent a jolt of pain through Blackwood's right shoulder, and she was thrown back by its weight. She landed on her back, and wasted no time rolling back to a crouch. The creature had landed just in front of them, looking none the worse for her attack. It stalked forward on six limbs, its long teeth bared and slitted eyes fixed on Andrew, who was on his feet hurling rocks at it.

"*Caeg-alay*," it whispered. The strange words carried easily through the cold wind.

"What do you want?" Blackwood said loudly.

It clicked its teeth, and its whole mouth spread wider. The stones Andrew threw bounced from its skin without so much as annoying it. Blackwood grabbed the bag again, the only weapon she had. The creature's head darted toward her, and without warning, it sprang. Blackwood got the bag in front of her just in time. The beast slashed razor-sharp teeth into the cloth, and within seconds, had ripped it apart in her hands. Papers cascaded to the ground, spilling over her feet, lashing away in the wind, great handfuls of them already shredded to ribbons. Blackwood clenched her teeth to keep from screaming. She'd seen first-hand what the canines of shrouding creatures did to human flesh. She dropped the tattered remnants of the duffel and took several hasty steps back, removing the arphanium pipe she'd grabbed from her pocket.

"Andrew!" she said, without looking away from the monster.

"The – the research," Andrew stammered. "Mother and Father's–"

"Here!" She shoved the pipe back toward him. "I'm gonna run back the way we came. You head straight for those hills, and look for the dekatite. Just hold that and push through."

"Wait! You–"

"Take it!" she snapped. "That's an order!"

The creature was coming forward again, its claws ripping through the layers of paper drifting over the ground. Its body moved almost sideways, like a wary feline or a skittering scorp.

"*Caeg*," it hissed. "*Agay-a-caeg.*"

"Zap it," Andrew said.

"What?"

"With your lightning. Do it."

Blackwood took a deep breath. "Take the pipe."

Andrew took the piece of arphanium from her hand. *One strike*, Blackwood thought. *I can do this.* She channeled her energy through that ever-present tingling in her left arm and sent it straight forward like a bolt. The lightning hit the monster dead on, blinding her momentarily with the brightness of its flash. Thunder crashed, sudden and startling. The monster reeled backward with a horrible screech. The stench of burnt meat was unmistakable, yet somehow more foreign than anything she'd smelled before.

"*Sh- Sh- Sh- Sha- Sha–*" it stuttered furiously. It pushed itself back, and somehow got those powerful wings beneath the wind again. Then it was flying away, crookedly, obviously wounded. One of those wings was visibly smoldering. It sent a loud shriek back at them, this one with no discernible words.

Blackwood stared after it. She was still upright, with no nausea, no dizziness. Her brow furrowed, and she glanced back at Andrew.

"It didn't weaken me," she said. *Because I got the mark in this world?*

Andrew only met her eyes for a moment before turning his attention back to the papers fluttering across the land in the wind, scattering in every direction.

Blackwood shook her head. "With those monsters hunting us, it'd be suicide to try to save them, Andrew."

Andrew turned away. He took one step, then another, before dropping to his knees. He reached out and grabbed a clump of paper that had caught against a rock. The arphanium pipe she'd handed him fell to the ground with a thump.

"Andrew! We can't stop!"

He spread the pages out beneath his hands. She could see his fingers trembling even from where she stood. Gritting her teeth, she knelt at his side and swept up the arphanium. She put a hand on his shoulder.

"Shon Aha is the Dhavnak god of lightning," said Andrew. His hands moved the papers restlessly as he spoke, his eyes never leaving them. "God of the Main Sun too, obviously, but lightning as well."

Blackwood's shoulders tightened. "What are you getting at?"

"Maybe... maybe he was the one who marked you," Andrew said in a rush.

Oh no. This again. She slid the arphanium back into her pocket, then took Andrew's elbow to help him up. He jerked it away.

"Andrew, we have to go," she said.

"I knew you wouldn't listen!"

"This isn't the best time! We can discuss it later."

"Our parents were studying Dhavnak gods, Mila! And now you can magically use lightning like–"

"No, they were studying *shrouding*," she erupted. "Whatever else you think you read–"

"*I know what I read!*" he yelled. "Stop treating me like I'm stupid! I know how to read, I know the things that used to happen in this place during their experiments, and I *heard* that flying thing try to speak Shon Aha's name after you used that lightning. It's not a coincidence!"

It took Blackwood a moment to realize what he was talking about. "'*Sha*' doesn't mean it was trying to say *Shon Aha*. That's a big assumption."

"Well, where do *you* think your powers came from, if you're so smart?"

"I am *not* talking about this." She stood, a flush of anger heating her face. She didn't want to discuss Dhavnak gods, and she *really* didn't want to discuss sharing some sort of magic powers with one. Did he really believe these things? What had he read to lead him in *that* direction? What kind of things had Cu Zanthus been telling him? Now that those notes were lost to her, how would she ever know? *Maybe a psychologist. Not only to help figure out the truth, but to* help *him, for Xeil's sake. I don't know what to do...*

"Mila!"

She looked back down at Andrew. He was staring up at the sky now, his mouth open. She followed his gaze.

The landscape spread out before her, still smoky, still windy, still barren… but there was a faint glimmer just ahead and to the right now. A sun was rising. One end of the strange band disappeared into the hazy orange dusting the horizon just behind a distant volcano. With the faint hint of daylight, the striped band of light had faded from silver to white, but it was still strikingly bright; like the moons, it wouldn't be banished with the full light of the suns.

"Only one sun?" she asked. "Is that what you're telling me?"

"No! The… the light band. It's like Neutania!"

"Neutania?"

He shot her a look of scorn. "Didn't you ever study astronomy? Read a textbook once or twice?"

"Astronomy? Of – of course." She looked back up, sweeping her gaze across that arc again. She adjusted her perspective, and… for just a second… the stripes weren't above her, but around her. "Neutania. The one with the rings."

"Obviously."

She stared for several moments, stunned. She wanted to deny it. But she couldn't.

"What does it *mean*, Mila?"

"I don't know, Andrew. I wish I did. I don't…" *I don't like any of this*, she almost said, but stopped herself at the last moment. As the commanding officer, she couldn't cast doubt on her authority. He had to believe she was in total control. Even if he knew deep down she wasn't, as long as she pretended, he'd follow her. She'd seen it time and time again.

"We have to go," she said. "Now."

He got up without arguing this time, several of those papers still clutched in his hand.

"Do you need me to carry you?" she said. "'Cause of your foot?"

"No. I'm fine."

She took off at a jog again, feeling the pressure of their situation more than ever. She didn't like those rings at all, if that's what they were. And Holland… What were they doing to him? He had a mark, too; would Cu Zanthus try to force him to use it, after what he'd seen Blackwood do? Clearly, they hadn't been able to shroud – unless they'd come out in some completely different place, or passed them as she'd slept. Maybe the monsters had killed them already. None of it was good. None of it.

Andrew was falling behind again. Blackwood circled back and hoisted him over her shoulder, despite his vehement protests. He was shivering violently. Either because of that or because of his difficulty keeping up, he didn't struggle long. Blackwood picked up her pace again. Rattling cries from the rocky hills haunted her as she ran. She tried to find comfort in the thought of their Goddess, and their parents' souls within her body. But she felt distant from home, distant from Mirrix, distant from belief. It was Andrew's fault. She'd never been shaken before. When this was all over… when they could sit and talk… *then what? Since when have I ever been able to have an honest conversation with him?*

The dekatite ridge she'd been aiming for came into view eventually, its sparkling face glimmering faintly through the smoke, lit by the rising sun. Blackwood shifted Andrew's weight and pulled the arphanium pipe from her pocket. She braced herself to run straight into it. She might smash her face bloody if there was some trick she didn't know, but it was the best idea she had. *Please, please let it work.*

She was about ten steps away when something came streaking toward her from the ring side of the planet. She didn't have time to reach the rock, didn't have time to so much as turn and face the thing, before it struck her with the force of a speeding mobi. Blackwood barely registered her body being thrown. But she felt the impact of hitting the ground and spinning end over end in a series of excruciating bangs and jabs. Somewhere, Andrew screamed. Not beside her. She'd lost him. Gasping, she pushed herself up, pain stabbing from every side. The creature looked like a giant insect, long and sinuous, with hundreds and hundreds of multi-jointed legs. Licks of fire danced over its head, in varying shades of orange and blue. Enormous black pupils peered from the tight red flesh beneath, barely stretched into the semblance of a human face. One of its long spindly legs held Andrew pinned to the rocky ground. The end of the leg branched into several pieces to spread over his torso like grotesque fingers. Galvanized energy danced over its entire body – like lightning.

"Let him go!" Blackwood cried.

It whipped that huge head toward her and *spoke*, more clearly than anything they'd heard yet. "*Tor-dom-an-kross-ana-tal.*"

"Let him go," she said again. "Then we'll talk."

It let out some sort of maniacal laughter, though nothing in those sharp teeth she glimpsed seemed to be mirthful. Rather than let Andrew go, it moved another leg toward him and wrapped its flexible digits around his head. Blackwood clenched her left hand into a fist and threw the energy from her mark toward the monster as if she were hurling a ball. Lightning lanced down from three separate places in the sky, including right behind her, branching and spreading its voltage across the entire length of the beast. Thunder boomed in its wake, a crack so loud it felt like a rifle going off beside her ear. The creature reared up away from Andrew, its body twisting into impossible curls as it swung its head from side to side.

Blackwood bolted forward. She shouldered Andrew's weight again and raced for the dekatite slope. Out of the corner of her eye, the monster swayed, like it was ready to topple. Its massive body still danced with lightning. A blinding flash of light blindsided her, and the next thing she knew, lightning was *pouring* down from overhead, striking the land in every direction. Far behind them, a huge wall of sound crashed forth, encompassing them, as if from a massive explosion. The truck, she thought. The self-destruct sequence triggering when it was hit. Or maybe it was one of the volcanoes erupting. Maybe both. Fear spiked in her, so sudden it almost overwhelmed her. But she got a hand in her pocket, pulled out that pipe, and dove at the sparkling gray and black dekatite ridge.

"*Is-min-shana-hathi-midrib,*" the creature roared behind her.

Blackness enveloped her. Seconds later, she tumbled with Andrew to a jagged surface. The piece of arphanium flew out of her fingers as she tried to catch herself. She fell hard to the ground, sharp rocks biting into her knees and elbows. Andrew yelled as he rolled from her arms and came to an abrupt stop against a craggy boulder. The cold wind was gone, and without it, the air was noticeably warmer. Blackwood drew in a shuddering breath.

Andrew pushed himself to sitting, staring at her with naked terror. "You heard it. Right?"

"Yes, it has some sort of language," she said. "Are you OK?"

"It said *Shon Aha*. It *said* it!"

She turned what she'd heard over in her mind. *Is min shana... shana ha thi...* She frowned and shook her head. "You're reading too much into it."

"I'm not. I'm not!" He was so agitated, she was afraid he'd explode. "What about its head? What about that lightning? What about that volcano erupting right as we left? It was like what you did, but a hundred times more powerful!"

"I don't have Shon Aha's powers," she burst out, "and that *wasn't* Shon Aha! It's a stupid idea. Drop it!"

"It's not *stupid*, Mila—"

"Be quiet. Just *shut up* for a second! I have to figure out where we are."

She pushed herself onto her elbows, feeling every part of her body scream out in protest. She realized suddenly that the smell of the ocean surrounded them, mingled with the stench of sulfur. And when she looked up, she saw it: the sea, spreading out far, far below. They were on a cliff. In fact, the drop was a scant fifteen steps or so in front of her. Her stomach dropped. If they'd come out just a little farther forward...

But they hadn't. A narrow escape, indeed. Jagged black rocks. This was no small dekatite mine or vein. The entire ground was of dekatite. Combined with the smell of sulfur, spit forth by hot springs and other volcanic fissures, there was only one place this could be.

Blackwood scooted right to the edge of the sheer cliff. She looked down on the northern end of Kheppra Isle – somewhere she'd visited a few times after attaining officer status, especially as a chief sea officer on the shrouding flagship. Her eyes fell on the back end of a submarine, poking from the submarine pen. After serving on her for two and a half years, *Desert Crab*'s shape was unmistakable. What was she doing *here*? Then her gaze encompassed the docks around the submarine pen, the men in black Dhavnak uniforms...

She backed away quickly, gritting her teeth.

Andrew watched her sullenly, but his tongue flicked over his lips, betraying the fear lurking beneath. "What? What is it?

"The Belzene Naval Base has a research station here," she said. "Top secret."

They'd spent the whole summer shrouding and keeping the Dhavnaks from sending ships in through the Qosmya Canal, while Dhavnakir's allies in Narbona hammered away at Qosmya on the other side of the world, keeping them from coming to Belzen's aid. No one had expected Kheppra Isle to be attacked; their enemies didn't know the connection with dekatite, after all. How long had they been here? How long had they *known*?

Slowly, she turned her gaze on Andrew. "Just how long has Cu Zanthus been staying with you?"

Andrew visibly swallowed. "Why?"

"The Dhavvies have captured Kheppra Isle."

"And you think that's *my* fault?"

"I hate to say it. But yes."

Chapter 18

KLARA YANA'S INTERROGATION

Cu Zanthus led Klara Yana into a room with garish red walls, now faded and chipped. A long table against the back wall had two tall built-in mirrors lined with round bulbs, but many of the bulbs were broken and the mirrors had been covered in white sheets. A crooked chandelier hung overhead, two bulbs in it burning with galvanized power. A cloth mannequin in the back corner had Lyanirus's uniform jacket draped over it. The man himself was in a gray button-down and braces, sleeves pushed to his elbows. He stood in front of a map, which was fastened to one of the sheets. Pins were scattered across it in every country. The same man that had been present for Klara Yana's first meeting was there too, sitting on one of the two plush chairs in the room. Both men turned their heads at the sound of Cu Zanthus shutting the door. Klara Yana pushed her shoulders back, tapping clasped hands to her eyes, mouth, and chest.

Lyanirus gestured and the other man stood up, then passed behind Cu Zanthus and Klara Yana to stand directly in front of the door, arms crossed over his chest. There were no other doors in the room; his intentions couldn't have been clearer. Klara Yana held her salute.

"Sir," she said. "May I speak?"

Lyanirus picked up something from the desk – a hoop of metal, it looked like. An attached chain trailed up behind it. He approached her, and before she could so much as open her mouth to ask, he'd opened the collar and snapped it shut around her neck. She flinched at the sudden chill against her skin. Lyanirus held the other end of the chain, wrapping it around his wrist.

Fear flooded Klara Yana's body, threatening to spill onto her face. She fought with all she had to hold it back. Behind her, Cu Zanthus said,

"Sir, is that really nec–"

"Did I *ask* you, Ayaterossi?" Lyanirus interrupted. "I don't know which is worse: that you were responsible for training this unprofessional scum, or that thanks to you, our only lead on Blackwood now is a seventeen cycle-old lowlife who may or may not be a sympathizer."

"He'll come through, sir," said Cu Zanthus in a low voice.

Klara Yana started to turn her head, hoping to catch Cu Zanthus's eye, but Lyanirus yanked the chain he held, jerking her attention back to him. She met his gaze stonily. *Whatever you do, don't show fear.*

"Sir," she said, "what is the point of *collaring* me?"

"It's a precaution," he said evenly. "If you try to strike me with your lightning, the surge will travel through the metal and back to you. That close to your brain, it will surely kill you."

"I wasn't going to strike you. I don't even *have* that power! Sir–"

"Show me the mark," he broke in. "The one Ayaterossi heard Chief Blackwood talk about."

"Sir, the reason I never told you about the marks was because we had no idea they were special. They didn't seem worth mentioning. If I'd known–"

He hit her, much harder than he had the first time she'd seen him. Pain exploded through the whole left side of her face. He hauled her back up by the chain just before she went down, and the metal bit brutally into her jawbone before she regained her balance. She struggled to slow her breathing, struggled to keep tears of pain and fear back. Her throat burned with the effort. *Don't freeze. Don't cry. Don't scream.*

"Show me the mark," he repeated.

Klara Yana yanked the gloves from her hands, then held out her left one with the palm up. She heard Cu Zanthus draw in his breath. Lyanirus narrowed his eyes, returning his gaze to her face.

"Is that the Broken Eye?" he said softly.

"Sir, I... I don't know. It does resemble it, I admit, but the how and why of it is beyond me."

"Are you a Vo Hina worshipper, Hollanelea?"

"No, sir!"

"Tell me the truth."

"That is the truth, sir. I worship Shon Aha."

He smiled then, as if seeing something that amused only him. It made her skin crawl. "We'll come back to that," he said. "For now, tell me about your Chief Blackwood. What mark does she have?"

"Like a lightning bolt, sir, on her arm."

"A lightning bolt. How appropriate. When did she first use it to cause lightning?"

"It must have been the night of the invasion, sir, but neither one of us knew it at the time."

"You claimed last night that you were working with a team to discover more about the lightning attack. That implies she knew *before* the invasion."

"Sir. I... I mentioned they had an unnatural lightning attack during their early testing. No one yet had made the association between that and the marks. I still don't..."

"Have you tried to use yours yet? To do what she did?"

"No, sir."

"Why not? From what Ayaterossi told me, she *wanted* you to."

"Yes, but... but I still didn't really believe she *could*. Like I told you, sir, I was never withholding anything! It wasn't until we were ambushed in the lab that I knew for sure she could do it."

"But you must have suspected. Especially after what happened right before I last saw you."

"Sir, the very idea of it... If I'd said something, you would have laughed at me. I would have sounded crazy–"

"Intelligence operatives report anything and everything they see, and let their superiors worry about what to make of it. To do differently *is* actively withholding information, Hollanelea. It is *not* your place to decide what we do or don't need to hear. Is that understood?"

"Sir. I understand completely."

Lyanirus gestured to the other side of the room. "I want you to try the power. Aim it at the floor over there, far from anyone. Just a small strike."

So that's what this was about. He was hoping to use her as a weapon. To use her against Blackwood, no doubt. Klara Yana looked at the palm she still held out. As always, she felt that crawling sensation right beneath the mark, but it had never bothered her to the extent Blackwood said hers had. Nevertheless, she closed her eyes, blew her breath out slowly, and forced all her concentration onto those tiny prickles. Lightning beneath the skin. How did Blackwood do it, anyway? She pictured the lightning bolt – coming from her hand, from the lit bulbs, from the sky. Nothing. Not so much as an increase in the tingling. She blinked her eyes open.

"Nothing's happening, sir," she said.

"You're not trying hard enough."

"Sir, I'm doing exactly what Blackwood said. Concentrating on the tingling. But there's nothing. When we were marked, on the *Desert Crab*, she was hit much harder than I was. She was thrown. She passed out. She didn't wake up until the next morning. I never even fell. I'm sure whatever happened, it made her stronger than me."

Irritation crept across Lyanirus's face. "So Ayaterossi pulled you out of the field for *nothing?*"

A spike of alarm flashed through Klara Yana. "Sir, I still have CSO Blackwood's trust. If–"

"Let's go back to the Vo Hina issue. Shall we?"

"Sir?"

"If your so-called mark has no power, how can you prove it's not a tattoo?"

"A tattoo? Sir? Why would I have a tattoo of–"

"The rioting back home, the men sympathizing with the women, the Broken Eye symbol? You claim you're not part of that movement?"

"No, sir! I don't even... I came straight from a mission in Criesuce. I haven't been home in half a cycle. I don't know anything about–"

"Maybe that's where I've seen you." He bent his head until his face was level with her own. He was so close, she could see every hair peppering his jawline. "We arrested a whole bunch of you scuzbangers a few seasons back. Were you part of that?"

"No, sir–"

"Is that why you took this job? Access to some records, maybe? Some of your arrested comrades? Is this an *inside* job for you?"

"*No*, sir–"

His violent backhand came as a shock. Her whole body went numb from the force of it; her muscles abruptly ceased to function. He let her hit the floor this time, but she hadn't even drawn breath before his foot connected with her ribs. She doubled over, pain ripping through her side. The second kick landed right on her gunshot wound, and the only reason she didn't let out a howl was because she didn't have the air to do so. Another blow landed, and another. She had to do something. He'd kill her. But she couldn't breathe, couldn't think, she was paralyzed with terror...

"Hey, go easy, sir!" someone yelled. "We might need him!"

Another kick caught her in the chin, and pain shot through her jaw, along with the metallic taste of blood. Lyanirus wasn't listening. Her palm... no. Nothing in that mark to help. Her gun had been taken when she was captured. A weapon. A plan...

Somehow, drowning in pain, she remembered her training with the Noncombatant Intelligence Corp. *What is a spy's greatest weapon?* Not firearms. Not explosives. Not even anonymity. *Information.*

Through pure willpower, she managed to force the words between her teeth. "Blackwood's scientists think I can shroud unprotected now. Without a vehicle."

The next impact didn't come. Klara Yana lay wrapped around herself, her jaw aching with the effort not to whimper or cry out. Pain shot through her, spiking with every breath. She couldn't have moved if she wanted to. A second later, Lyanirus knelt and grabbed her bruised chin, forcing her to look at him. Her lips curled back from her teeth. Despite her desperation, she met his gaze through a mask of anger.

"Are you saying you've been withholding *more* information?" growled Lyanirus.

"I'm saying that I'm not at my best when I'm treated like an animal. Important details may have slipped my mind."

"You really are a little shit, aren't you? You aren't a Vo Hina-cursed *contractor*. You work for your government, and whatever's in your head belongs to us. It is not yours to *bargain* with. Do you understand me!"

"How could I not? You've made your opinion very clear. Sir."

"When I'm through with you, there won't be a single thing *left* in your head for you to hide."

"It's not what's in my head that you need," she answered. "It's *me*. The scientists' next experiment was to send us in without a vehicle, and see if we were attacked. It's a repeat of something they tried with Onosylvani." Lyanirus would already know about that, of course, from the notes Cu Zanthus had read and reported.

"Onosylvani!" Lyanirus spat. "Gods! It goes back to *her?*"

She blinked, taken aback by his reaction.

"It shouldn't come as a surprise, sir," said Cu Zanthus from behind her. His voice was carefully controlled now, though she was sure he'd been the one to call out while she was being beaten. "We know now what they were doing in that factory."

"We know *now* that they were experimenting with this 'shrouding', yes, obviously," said Lyanirus, scowling up at him, "but that doesn't mean we have any clue why they wanted that *woman*. Hollanelea, explain what you mean about a connection between her and your marks. And don't even *think* about talking back or lying." He pulled a knife from his belt and opened it with a snap of his wrist, then yanked her hand up. The next thing she knew, the sharp blade bit into the back of her forefinger just above the knuckle, deep enough to hit bone. Warm blood streamed over her hand, and the pain pierced sharp and hot. Klara Yana screamed.

"Answer me," Lyanirus said, "or I'll sever it."

"All I know," she said, fighting to keep her voice from breaking into hysteria, "is that the lightning storm back then was a direct result of having a Dhavnak in the lab. That's what the scientist told Blackwood. She mentioned the monsters, too. It's all connected."

"So they didn't need just *anyone* for their experiments," said Lyanirus. "They needed someone from Dhavnakir. And then you... the first Dhavnak we know of to enter shrouding... also ends up *marked* rather than killed. Isn't that interesting?" He sat back, narrowing his eyes. Klara Yana almost sobbed when he pulled the knife away. "But where does Blackwood come into that?"

"N- No idea, sir."

"So *any* Dhavnak might go in safely. Might even come out again with special powers."

She almost choked. "Wouldn't count on it. We were almost *killed*."

"But you weren't, were you? Not yet. No." She didn't like the way he was looking at her. Like he was taking in every detail of her face... *Vo Hina, help me. Why did I have to scream?*

There was a loud knock on the door. Lyanirus's officer opened it. Someone stepped in behind her, and she heard the rustle of his jacket as he saluted. If the sight of a collared, beaten soldier lying on the floor with blood pooling under his hand phased him, it didn't show in his voice.

"Sir, we think we've found them. The Blackwoods."

Lyanirus stood and stepped over her. The second he was out of sight, the tears Klara Yana had been fighting spilled from her eyes.

"Where?" said Lyanirus. "Where are they?"

"The crew at Kheppra Isle, sir, that just loaded up the captured submariners to take back to our Marine Internment Camp. They claimed to have seen a flash of light on the eastern cliffs. We believe the soldier may have been attempting to signal someone, with a mirror or some other reflective device."

Lyanirus was silent for several moments. "Is it possible?" he finally said. "Ayaterossi's boy?"

"Sir," said Cu Zanthus slowly, "I gave him a tin – a little snack tin he stuck in his pocket. Right before we left to find Blackwood. I'd say it's entirely possible."

"Well then," said Lyanirus, blowing his breath out. "Time to find out if you're right. Corporant, you're dismissed."

Klara Yana was surprised at the relief that flooded her at the thought of Blackwood being alive. But it was quickly followed by a stab of dread. *If Lyanirus gets ahold of her, she'll wish she wasn't.*

"We control the dekatite mine between here and the eastern border now," said Lyanirus. "Right, Telchimaris?"

"Sir."

"That would be quickest, now that we have arphanium."

"But, sir, we don't have a vehicle," protested Cu Zanthus. "Hollanelea specifically said we shouldn't shroud unless we–"

"*Hollanelea* brought us new information," Lyanirus cut in. "*Hollanelea* can test it for us. Telchimaris. Let's get ready to head out. Ayaterossi. Clean your associate up. And keep him out of my damn way until we need him again." The door opened and closed again, and Lyanirus was gone.

She was still lying on the floor, tears running down her face. She had to get up. What would Cu Zanthus think? But Vo Hina's mercy, the *pain...*

A few seconds later, Cu Zanthus knelt in front of her. He leaned forward, working the collar from her neck.

"What is wrong with you, Keiller Yano?" he said, his voice hard. "What were you *thinking?*"

"You stood up for me," she managed. "Twice."

"Which is exactly why you owe me some answers!" Cu Zanthus sat back, setting the collar off to the side. His face, which had been tight with anger, softened into something closer to alarm. "Your neck's rubbed raw. He was really digging this thing into you, wasn't he?"

Klara Yana didn't answer. Cu Zanthus took off his Belzene uniform jacket and bunched it up under her head, so the soft folds held her injured neck from the hard floor. Then he looked to her hand. He sucked in a breath between his teeth.

"This one'll need stitches. I'll get Dela Savene. She's gonna get sick of fixing you up, at this rate." He started to get up, then paused. "If you're a sympathizer or a rebel mole, just tell me now, Keiller Yano. You're making me look really bad here, and I can't take much more."

"I'm *not,*" she said. "I never had plans to betray our government or country. I never participated in any sort of riot or rebellion. I have no friends among those who do. Spying is my life, and everything I've done has been for the good of our citizens."

He frowned at her words, clearly uncomfortable. And why shouldn't he be? Men didn't talk like that. They'd get it down to three words, then tell you to piss off. But Klara Yana was so tired and in so much pain, she almost didn't care anymore.

"Did you intentionally withhold all that information?" Cu Zanthus said.

"I shared what seemed necessary. I never thought of it as *intentional*. Just… irrelevant." She hesitated. "Holding stuff back isn't always a bad thing, you know."

"Better rethink that attitude right now, or I'm through with you."

"For example, I know about you and Andrew."

"*What?*" Cu Zanthus said sharply. "What *about* me and Andrew?"

"I saw you kiss him."

His face went still. Several moments passed before he answered. "The leuftkernel is right. You really *do* store everything until the perfect moment, don't you?"

"This is not blackmail," she said. "This is me asking for help. And offering mine in return."

"Well, it's out of the question. What you saw was part of my *job*. None of it was real. You *do* understand that, right?"

"Collaborator or not, you know there's a good chance they'll kill him. He's too close to Blackwood. Too easy to compromise. Too young."

"He's three cycles older than me when *I* was recruited," Cu Zanthus argued.

"And he's Belzene. If you think that makes your pasts comparable, you're out of your mind."

He stared at her for a long time. "I told you," he finally said, "it doesn't matter. He's nothing to me."

"I believe you."

"I'm not throwing away everything I live for. Not for him, not for you, not for anyone."

"I'm not asking you to."

"What *are* you asking me for, then?"

"Not to give up on me. That's all."

"I'll do what I can, Keiller Yano, but you brought it on yourself. I can only go so far before I'll be right down there with you. I will *not* betray my country for you." He stood. "Take a moment to collect yourself while I get Dela Savene. If you clean up your attitude, you might get through this. If you don't…" He shook his head and walked out of the room, leaving the thought unfinished. The door shut with a click behind him.

The second he was gone, Klara Yana slid his coat out from under her head. Her ribs sent waves of pain through her with even that small movement. So as not to leave bloody handprints behind, she used her good hand – the same one with the dekatite mark on the palm – to pat the folds, looking for any sort of weapon she might secret away for next time. If she didn't freeze. If she was willing to throw away any chance of claiming innocence. But if Lyanirus found out she was a woman – which was beginning to seem terrifyingly likely – then there'd be no turning back anyway. Might as well kill him.

She found something. A hard lump. She turned the cloth until she found the opening for the pocket, then put her hand in. As soon as she grabbed it, she knew it wasn't a gun or a knife. It was cool, smooth, with jagged breaks on both top and bottom. The piece of arphanium pipe Cu Zanthus had taken from the lab.

But she never had the chance to consider what she might do with it. The second her dekatite mark pressed against the arphanium, her palm sparked, as if by a shock. The small, underground room went dark. Cold air pressed into her skin. She lay suddenly on rocky ground, a harsh wind whipping around her. Klara Yana dropped the pipe with a cry. She had no idea what had happened… but there was really only one place this could be.

Far from a dekatite source, with only her marked palm and a shard of arphanium… she had shrouded.

Chapter 19

BLACKWOOD
BETRAYED

"Are you really gonna force me to carry you down this cliff?" Blackwood growled, rounding the dekatite boulder she'd just stashed their parkas beneath. Andrew sat with his back against the other side, arms crossed and face turned away. The position put his face directly toward the midday Early Sun. It couldn't have been comfortable, even with the sea breeze pushing his fine hair off his forehead, but he made no move to divert his eyes. Maybe he'd closed them.

"Andrew!" she snapped. "I do *not* have time for this. I have to get down there and figure out how the Dhavvies got the *Desert Crab*. Figure out why my crew never triggered the suicide switch. See if they're still alive."

"Then go." The wind almost robbed his low words; by his motionless body, he might not have spoken at all.

"What, and leave you up here? On the top of an island in the middle of *nowhere?*"

Andrew shrugged without turning his head.

"Are you still upset about the Shon Aha thing?"

He did turn his head then, but only enough for her to see him in profile. "I'm fine. Go check on whatever you need to. It's my fault they're here, right? Just like it's my fault *we're* here. Anything else my fault, Mila? The Dhavnak gods, maybe? Your freakish lightning powers?"

"What did you want me to say?" she said angrily. "The Dhavvies wouldn't have come here if they didn't know this island was special!"

"There's nothing about this island in the notes!" he shot back. "So it couldn't have been Cu Zanthus!"

"Yes, but it's made of dekatite. And there's plenty about *dekatite* in there!"

He turned to look at her, his face pinched in suspicion. "The whole island is made of dekatite?"

"Yes."

He turned his head fully, taking in the steeply-climbing dekatite face that rose to the summit behind her. A thin plume of ash drifted from the top, though it dissipated quickly in the morning sky.

"Not just island," he said softly. "Volcano."

"Yeah."

"You have a research station on a volcano."

"It makes a good hiding spot." She waved her hand at the plume. "And it's been doing that for years. There's no danger."

"Is that a fact?"

Blackwood gritted her teeth. "Yes. It's a fact. Get up, Andrew! *Now!*"

He glared at her, but shifted his weight to push himself up. Something flashed in his hand, bright enough to blind her for a second. She bolted to his side, knelt, and snatched it from him. It was a round tin, the kind used to package dried travel snacks, depicting a Belzene Ptero R-12 biplane on the lid. She pried off the top and confirmed that the rattle inside was, in fact, nuts, dried fruit, and meat.

"Why do you have this?" she said.

"Why do you think?" he said tightly. "In case I get hungry."

"Why were you holding it? You didn't eat anything just now."

"Well, I was about to."

She sneered. "That's about as likely as the Dhavvie gods being real."

"What are you—"

"Shh." Blackwood pressed a hand over his mouth, pushing his head against the boulder. "I hear something."

It was voices. She could barely pick out snatches over the wind, but what she could hear carried the flowing, melodic tones of the Dhavvish language. But why under the suns would they have come up here? Her eyes flicked down to the tin she still held and she got a sick feeling, down in the pit of her belly. *No. Please, no.* She met Andrew's eyes. He stared back calmly. Was that what this was about? He'd been trying to *keep* her here? No. It wasn't possible.

The men were coming closer, and she could hear the distinct clank of shifting rifles in hands. How many were there? One was clearly giving orders, and it was the responses that gave her the rough count. At least four. Maybe six, although the second voice and the fifth may have been from the same man. Now that they were near the top of the cliff, they were probably spreading out. There was nowhere to run. She had no weapons – the empty pistol had been left behind in shrouding, and she had no idea where the arphanium pipe she'd used to escape the shrouding realm had ended up. All she had was that lightning. The lightning that would surely weaken her now that they were back in their world. The lightning that hadn't killed anyone at the lab due to her utter lack of control. The lightning that would erase any doubt they were there.

The lightning that may have been given to her by an enemy god. *Xeil help me.*

"*Hai! Arras ansela!*"

Blackwood's head snapped to the right, where a soldier in black had come up on a rise nearby, and stood with his rifle trained on them. Slowly, Blackwood lowered her hand from Andrew's mouth. Very softly, without taking her eyes from the soldier, she said, "Cu Zanthus tried to kill you. Why did you do this?"

"Who says I did?" Not a hint of surprise showed in his voice, at either the soldiers or her accusation.

Anger burned a slow heat in the back of her head. Her own brother had betrayed her. How had they come to this?

The lightning came easily this time. Too easily. The soldier with the rifle was flung backward from the rock, his clothing and skin singed and smoking. Thunder rolled in the wake of the lightning. Dizziness washed over Blackwood, and she staggered back from Andrew, who was shouting and pressing himself into the boulder. She kept her feet, and sent another lightning strike directly into the soldier running around the other side.

Somewhere in the crash of the second thunderclap, a rifle shot sounded. White-hot pain erupted through her thigh. She went down, still clutching at the energy for whoever appeared next. Someone yelled out, "*Staj! Staj!*"

She looked up to see Andrew standing in front of her, both hands out in front of him. "*Staj!*" he cried again. "*Chanha marba! Cu Zanthus thurnadh ea chanha marba!*"

Hearing Dhavvish come out of her brother's mouth was almost more than Blackwood could take. How far back did this go? It was hard to focus, as the dizziness pulsing through her was compounded by lightheadedness. She gritted her teeth and struck again, aiming for the soldier approaching on her left. This time, the power didn't rip through her as easily as it had the last two times, and a wash of weakness threatened to pull her from consciousness. But the soldier still fell.

Again.

She didn't let the fourth strike fall, though. One of the soldiers had run forward and yanked Andrew back, spinning him around. He pressed a huge knife to the kid's throat. "*Goncor!*" he shouted. Another Dhavvie ran up on her right and pressed his rifle to her temple, hard enough to shove her head to the side.

"*Ea thurnadh ea chanha marba!*" Andrew screamed again.

Blackwood drew in a deep breath through her clamped teeth and raised her hands in the air, just above her head. She was shoved onto her stomach and her hands were tied behind her. But as she lay against the jagged dekatite, it was the desperation in Andrew's voice that she honed in on. After seeing many sailors through their first moments of combat, she knew exactly what it was.

Andrew had been enthralled by the novelty of what he was doing, and had treated his subterfuge with Cu Zanthus as a game. Even as Cu Zanthus had choked him, he'd probably thrilled in his role in helping. But seeing his sister shot right in front of him… it had destroyed the fantasy. She knew what he'd yelled almost as clearly as if she spoke

Dhavvish. *Cu Zanthus said he wouldn't kill her.* And Andrew had believed it, with all his heart.

She was yanked to her feet, but before she could regain her balance, the craggy rocks pitched around her like waves on the sea. At first she thought it was her own vertigo from using her power, but the Dhavnak soldiers were reeling too, thrown from their feet to the sharp rocks. Blackwood went down again. With her hands bound behind her, her face smashed into the rocks with a force that left her stunned. She struggled to breathe, and her stomach churned with nausea.

The tremor lasted only seconds. By the time she'd finally caught her breath, she'd been forced up again and tossed over a man's shoulder. Loud shouts in Dhavvish filled the air, and Andrew's panicked yells were among them. His hands had been tied now too, and the knife was back at his neck. Another soldier grabbed Blackwood's face with one hand and gestured angrily toward the dead Dhavvie soldiers with his other. He growled something, pointing back at Andrew. *You kill anyone else, and we'll kill your brother.* She thought about spitting in his face. But angry soldiers with knives and guns might take it out on Andrew – or on her. She couldn't forget the way Dhavnaks treated their own women. She was sure they wouldn't hesitate to treat her the same.

This is good, she tried to tell herself as they started down. *I needed to find a way to get onto the research base anyway.* It was also impossible to ignore the fact that she had purposely struck three soldiers, and hadn't even passed out. Dhavvie god's powers or not, she was learning to use the lightning to her advantage. She'd have to worry about the implications later. For now, it was all she had.

She raised her head. Andrew was cooperating now, but his mouth hung slightly open and his eyes darted from person to person too fast to possibly take anything in. What was he thinking? Surprised they weren't treating him like a hero? Or was he just still reeling from the tremor? Probably a little of both. Blackwood looked away in disgust. *I'll kill him. The second I get away–*

But no. She halted the thought in its tracks. It wasn't too late. Without his precious Cu Zanthus there, the romance of his collusion was gone. Once Cu Zanthus showed up – and she knew he would, eventually – Andrew would be lost again. She had to reach him before then. Somehow.

The research base was built into the side of the island, so only a long concrete dock was visible on the outside. The dock was split to allow sea access into two large square openings with ironwood supports, where submarines could seemingly disappear right into the mountain. Two bulbous Dhavnak submarines floated in the water just off the docks, looking dark and impenetrable without the solar cells that Belzene subs carried on their surfaces. The *Desert Crab* herself was halfway into one of the pens.

They were brought into the submarine pen on the right. The temperature rose the second they stepped into the shaded tunnel, and the smell of sulfur intensified. Steaming water dribbled from the inwardly-curving walls in several places and pooled in small pockets on the rough concrete. The wind was nonexistent in here, and even the sound of the breakers against the dekatite shore were muffled, giving way to the softer laps of the water between the two walkways.

The soldiers dumped Blackwood and Andrew onto the concrete. Blackwood lay gasping, her thigh pulsing in hot pain, as the soldiers tied hers and Andrew's wrists to the rails right above the waterline – the ones at ground level that sailors used to help lower themselves into the dry docks when the water was drained. Blackwood was lying on her back, and Andrew sat with his legs tucked beneath him and his hands bound at the floor. A soldier came forward and wrapped a bandage around Blackwood's wound several times, right over her trouser leg. Blackwood kept her legs bent, making sure the wound was above the level of her heart, and put pressure on it with her opposite leg to minimize blood loss. She thought the bullet had just grazed her – maybe even purposely, if the soldiers had been told to capture them alive – but the thought didn't make the pain any better.

She could just see through the wide concrete supports into the other submarine pen. The *Desert Crab* was being stripped of its arphanium. The crystal pipes glowed against the other pen's wall, sending a soft white light throughout the tunnels and barely illuminating their own. Blackwood grimaced. Clearly, they had the inside scoop on arphanium now as well. But why take it out of the boat? Why not just *use* the boat, if they wanted it for shrouding? And what had they done with the *Desert Crab*'s crew? Were they still onboard?

She watched the Dhavnaks for several more moments. No, they *weren't* stripping the boat; not anymore. They were loading something on. Big, obviously heavy, black blocks were being carried from the outside dock into the *Desert Crab*. Blackwood's mouth opened slightly as she saw the loops of wires on their surfaces, as well as the warning labels stamped on the sides. Explosives.

Her breath came short. All this time, she'd thought if the Dhavnaks discovered shrouding, they'd use it to take Belzen. But their plan was so much simpler. They'd stripped the arphanium to keep for themselves and were planning to send her old submarine back to Marldox. Marldox would let the *Desert Crab* in, unaware that it had been compromised. And the Dhavnaks' explosives would level the entire naval base, and maybe a good chunk of the city in the process. With Ellemko already fighting for its life, the surprise attack on Marldox would give the Dhavnaks the last push they needed. Belzen would be theirs.

I should strike them with my lightning, Blackwood thought. *Right here, right now.* But there were five soldiers close by with guns trained on them. She didn't think they'd kill her for trying – they would want her alive, so she could be trained to use her power for their own ends – but she had no doubt they'd kill Andrew. It wasn't a risk she could take.

She shifted her weight and pulled herself to an awkward sitting position, with one foot brushing the water and the other propped at her side, so she wasn't squeezing any more blood from the wound. Andrew hadn't moved; his legs were still tucked beneath him, his bound hands in tight fists by the floor. His eyes were fixed on the pen entrance behind her. She knew exactly what he was watching for. For Cu Zanthus to come walking in and save him.

Honestly, Andrew, Blackwood thought, *what did you* think *was gonna happen up there?* She suppressed the words, though, waited a moment for the flash of anger to dissipate, and then spoke, just loudly enough to be heard over the surf and the loading of the soldiers in the other pen.

"Andrew. We need to talk."

He didn't look away from the entrance. "No danger, you said. There was an *earthquake*."

"Yes, a tremor," she answered. "They're common in places like these."

"This place could… this whole island could…"

"Andrew, it won't. The shrouding has been making it somewhat worse, but it's not gonna blow."

Andrew set his jaw and gave a quick shake of his head, as if he didn't believe her. Or maybe it was just his way of ending the conversation.

Blackwood closed her eyes and took three deep breaths before speaking again. She kept her voice as calm as possible. "I need your help."

Andrew's lips thinned. He looked down at his hands.

"The notes are gone," Blackwood continued. "You've read them. If we stick to just the bare facts… just exactly what you've read, not interpretations or anything like that… do you think you could help me?"

Andrew didn't look up, but his breathing was slow enough that she knew he was listening.

"Onosylvani," Blackwood said. "Did she have a mark like mine? Made of dekatite?"

It seemed like an age passed. But Andrew finally gave the barest of nods, so small she would have missed it if she'd blinked.

"Was there anything about her having powers?" she asked.

"No," Andrew said softly.

Damn. Another dead end.

"But there is a Dhavnak legend."

Blackwood sucked in her breath. She tried to catch Andrew's eye, but he was still staring at his hands. "About someone with a dekatite mark?" she said. "Having powers?"

He nodded again.

"Can – can you tell me?"

"It's not from the notes."

"It's OK. Tell me anyway."

Across the pen, something clanged loudly against the *Desert Crab*. Behind them, one of the Dhavvie soldiers was telling his companions a story, or at least detailing a long explanation of something. The steady crashing of the sea drifted in as an undercurrent to it all. Andrew finally spoke, layering his words into their surroundings so effortlessly she had to strain to hear them.

"His name was Galene Marduc Craniamanthe. He was an explorer. Legends say that on one of his expeditions, down in a deep South Polar canyon, he ran across a secret entrance into the Aphotic Fields – where Synivists go after death. Accounts differ on what he saw there. The souls of the dead. Fields of rock. A land waiting to be shaped. Not much of a paradise, to us anyway. But to them... there was a community there. A community of labor and – and kinship. Galene Marduc mapped it, over the course of seven years, going in and out freely. He spoke with the gods there, but Vo Hina... this was before the Betrayal, so she hadn't been exiled yet."

Blackwood felt chilled. OK, so the kid was smart. He *could* talk without flying to pieces. But only when he was talking about Synivistic religion, it seemed. She didn't like the implications.

"The Betrayal," she said. "Wasn't that something like a hundred thousand years ago?"

"Yes. Galene Marduc became too close to Vo Hina during his studies. He laid with her in a dekatite crevasse. Came away with godlike powers, and a streak of dekatite burned into his back. This was most likely the source of the legend about gods granting blessings through dekatite, and dekatite being a holy substance. Afterwards, Shon Aha tried to kill them both."

"What kind of godlike powers?"

"It's vague. Leans toward earthquakes, volcanoes, traveling between life and death, that sort of thing. In any event, the resulting battle was powerful enough to rip off a section of Mirrix. The chunk ended up in the sky as the Shattered Moon, which to them *is* Vo Hina. Banished after Shon Aha destroyed her eye."

"But I thought she was punished for *hoarding*," said Blackwood. "Not laying with some human."

"Right. Galene Marduc was supposedly only one of several humans she got too close to – the final one that pushed Shon Aha over the edge.

Vo Hina didn't allow the other gods access to *any* of the humans. She wanted to keep them all for herself."

Blackwood's eyebrows rose. "She was hoarding… people?"

"Souls," said Andrew, nodding. "She was hoarding Mirrix's souls from the other gods."

Blackwood whistled beneath her breath. That was a twist she hadn't seen coming.

"Galene Marduc returned to Mirrix, pregnant with her child. This is how Vo Hina's curse was introduced into the female population–"

"Wait, wait, wait," Blackwood cut in. "*Galene* was pregnant with her child? How?"

"It's in some of the more obscure records. Galene Marduc was neither fully man nor woman, although Dhavnak mythology has shoved him firmly to the male side in modern texts."

"But how do they reconcile that with…" Blackwood stopped herself. Now wasn't the time to get pulled into a debate about Synivistic mythology. "What happened after Shon Aha banished Vo Hina?" she asked instead.

"The battle left Mirrix devastated. The planet was cast into darkness for seventeen hundred years. They call it the Age of Fallen Light. Three-quarters of the planet's population died. It wasn't until the gods returned, in the forms of the suns and moons, that they were able to save the remnants from the darkness and cold."

Blackwood nodded slowly. "OK. So there's an ancient darkness in Synivistic legends. And it was inadvertently triggered by this Galene guy getting a magic mark."

Andrew blinked. His gaze darted to her arm and back again. "That… yeah. That is sort of how it happened. But…"

"But what?"

"But it was Vo Hina's *betrayal* that caused the darkness. And there hasn't been a betrayal this time, has there?"

Blackwood frowned, caught off-guard. "What?"

"Unless you count Belzen betraying Dhavnakir by hoarding product… cutting off the arphanium trading…"

"Wait. Betraying Dhavnakir? What are you talking about?"

"I'm trying to think of what could trigger another period of darkness!" Andrew said. "And your mark, I- I hadn't even *thought* of that…"

"Trigger another period of darkness?" she echoed. "Andrew, you're talking about a Synivistic legend here!"

Andrew shook his head. "No! It's not just a legend! Galene Marduc existed. His map existed. Several sources mention the eternal darkness, *and* the resulting mass extinction. Onosylvani was marked. You have divine powers! Who are *you* to say none of it is real?"

"Who are you to say any of it *is?*" she countered.

"Not me. Mother and Father."

"No. You said this wasn't from the notes. So what did the *notes* say?"

"They said the Age of Fallen Light could happen again. They said we could *cause* it! What if this is what they meant? The betrayal? The war?"

"The *notes* said it could happen again?" she broke in. "Our parents' *scientific* notes?"

"Yes!"

"I don't believe this!" Her anger spiked, hot and sharp, before she could stop it. "How much has Cu Zanthus been telling you? Can I trust anything you just said?"

Andrew's eyes widened. "You asked me! Mila, you *asked* me!"

"That was before I realized Cu Zanthus had completely converted you!"

Andrew stared at her, stricken. A moment later, he backed away, as far as his bonds would allow. "Leave me alone, Mila! Just shut up!"

"But I should have known. You sold out your own *sister*, after all–"

"Stop! You can't just *ask* for my help then ridicule everything I say! You can't believe only the things you want to–"

"*Hai!*" one of the guards roared. "*Socrach faseos!*"

But Andrew's voice rose, overriding the guard's. "You can't assume everything I say has been *tainted* because of him, you can't pretend you care when it's *convenient,* you can't hate me one second then ask for my help the next–"

The guard stepped forward and bumped him on the head with the butt of his rifle, and Andrew screamed as he almost pitched into the water. The guard caught him around the shoulders at the last moment and hauled him back. Andrew kicked wildly, still yelling at the top of his lungs. The guard got a hand over his mouth and pinned him down on his stomach, his knee in his back. Andrew breathed so hard and so fast against the man's palm, Blackwood knew he was hyperventilating.

"Let him go!" she cried.

The guard shot her a scornful look, a condescending curl to his lip.

"It won't happen again," she said. "I promise."

The guard answered her in clipped Dhavvish. He removed his hand from Andrew's mouth and shoved his face into the walkway before stepping back. Andrew kept his face down, his hands still tied above his head, and gasped into the concrete.

Blackwood tried to slow her own suddenly quickened heartbeat. *Andrew is not my enemy. Cu Zanthus is my enemy. Not Andrew. Not Andrew.* It was hard to force herself to believe it. But she had to. His time was running out.

"I don't hate you," she said, hoping he could hear her.

"*Channil a bruidthe!*" the guard snapped.

Andrew turned his head just enough to stare at her through red-rimmed eyes. He looked too exhausted to respond. Blackwood gave him what she hoped passed for a smile.

Keep it together, she told herself. Ignore the voice that says he deserves it. Ignore the voice that says it's too late. Ignore the voice that wants to hurt him for what he's done. *Keep it together, or you will lose him. For good.*

Chapter 20

KLARA YANA'S COMMUNICATION

Klara Yana stared at the black-streaked rock wall directly in front of her. Sharp rocks jabbed into her side, her shoulder, and her head, where Cu Zanthus's coat provided a thin cushion under the stitched gash on her scalp. Pale sunlight made a bare splotch far away, on her right, but where Klara Yana lay was heavily in shadow. She was in some sort of giant cavern, she realized, with a chunk knocked out of its ceiling. Wind whipped at her from the dark depths of the cave, sending a substantial chill through her thin shirt. An ashy smell hung thick in the air.

Shrouding. This was the same place the submarine had gone… or at least somewhere similar. There'd been water pouring in there, just like from a real ocean. But the realm – the realm itself was the same. It had to be. She looked at the dekatite mark on her palm, then closed her hand around it, fast and instinctive. The implications were mind-blowing. Nowhere near a dekatite source, with only a piece of arphanium. But where *was* the shrouding realm, exactly? She'd never gotten a straight answer out of Blackwood about that. It certainly didn't *seem* like the center of the world. Nor was the rock surrounding her dekatite, which could hardly make it *inside* the dekatite.

But it was out of Lyanirus's grasp. And for now, that was all that mattered.

She pushed herself up. Her body reminded her with a thousand stabs of fresh pain what she had just gone through. She moaned through her teeth, but managed to stay upright in the biting cold. She pulled on Cu Zanthus's Belzene jacket, buttoning it and rolling up the sleeves.

The arphanium pipe. She'd dropped it the moment she'd landed. Her stomach turned over. She'd almost assuredly need it to get out again. In the haphazard rock field, it could have rolled off anywhere – could have easily fallen beneath some boulder too huge for her to move. Painfully, she knelt, peering in the dim light for even a hint of its glow.

She finally saw it, under an overhanging edge of rock, and ducked down to retrieve it. She was careful not to use her dekatite-marked hand. That might send her right back into Lyanirus's clutches, and even this desolate place was better than that. Her other hand, though, was drenched with blood and left the crystal slick with it. She slipped the arphanium into her coat pocket and huddled under the big rock for a moment, sheltered from the wind, and evaluated the damage.

Even through the blood, she could see the gaping gash across the base of her forefinger, the ragged pieces of flesh barely attached. If she didn't get it cleaned and bound, she *would* lose the finger, if not the hand. She ripped a strip from the bottom of the drab shirt she wore and wrapped the wound as tightly as possible, passing the cloth around her palm a few times before tying it off. A lightheaded buzz hummed through her ears; shock and blood loss battling for control. But at least she was no longer losing blood, and her training at the NIC had taught her how to push the pain aside until later. How to embrace it, even, as evidence she was alive.

That's what she did now: the wound on her head was proof the cement step hadn't killed her. The gunshot wound was a fortunate distance away from her stomach. And the finger… well, hey, she still *had* it.

She ran her other hand over Cu Zanthus's coat, and smiled when she found a military-issue chocolate bar in an inner pocket. She ripped the foil off a corner of it and sank her teeth in, remembering just in time to welcome the shooting pain in her jaw as a sign that it wasn't broken.

She sucked on the bitter chocolate to soften it as she considered her options. Her relationship with Lyanirus was beyond repair. Even if he didn't suspect the truth yet, he'd never trust her again – and that was *before* she'd vanished without a trace, taking Cu Zanthus's arphanium shard with her. Because of Lyanirus's high rank, her chances of retaining her position at all were almost nonexistent. Her hope of getting the clearance she wanted… gone. Her hopes of finding her ama… gone. And these things, she reminded herself, were best-case scenarios. If Lyanirus *did* suspect the truth about her…

Then sooner or later, she knew she'd end up in the same nightmare that Blackwood would. Imprisoned, abused, violated, forced to use these powers to increase Dhavnakir's empire. And yes, she'd planned at one point to help be part of that change, but now… now all she could think about was her ama and Dela Savene, such strong women, mistreated and used by their own government. Something inside her couldn't bear the thought of CSO Blackwood ending up like that, too.

Although Klara Yana had repeatedly scorned her for discarding and sending away her comrades, Blackwood had also prevented Vin from beating her on the submarine. She'd saved her life in the lab. She'd forgiven her for bringing dekatite on board. And every time she'd struck out on her own – *every time* – it had been because she was putting herself in danger while trying to protect others.

Klara Yana let out a slow breath. How had she ever thought Belzenes had no sense of camaraderie?

She finished the rest of the bar numbly. The harsh truth was, no one else could help Blackwood. No one else *would*. If Klara Yana didn't want her falling into Lyanirus's hands, it fell on her and her alone to do something about it.

And after she got Blackwood safe, she decided, she'd kill that sadistic psychopath Lyanirus. Before he had the chance to ruin her career. And, more importantly, before he ever got his hands on her again.

The cavern suddenly darkened, as if in response to her mood. It wasn't just cloud cover; it went from being shadowed to nearly pitch black in a second. Klara Yana's head darted up, her eyes sweeping the dark confines. She suddenly realized how *quiet* it had gotten, too. The wind had died, or at least cut back to the point where it felt like silence after the incessant howling. No… not silence, exactly. There was a subtle rasping from all around – part scrape, part slither – as soft as autumn leaves being blown across a road.

Klara Yana crept up the jagged rock jutting from the depression her arphanium had fallen into. She turned her head toward where the patch of sunlight had been, and barely held back a scream. Something was submerging into the cavern. As she watched, the giant head – or was it a body? – had just cleared the opening, sending a slash of light through again. The head… body… was about the size of a small house, and shaped like a balloon. It was covered top to bottom in some sort of drooping spikes. Giant eyes ringed its girth, blinking out of synch with one another.

The body was supported not by legs, but by tentacles. It was these that made the rasping sound. They spilled all throughout the cave, draped over rocks, climbing the curved walls, wrapped around huge slabs. All of them were in motion, sliding slowly in every direction as they lowered the heavy creature. Klara Yana watched as one muscular tentacle, almost as thick as her body, glided over the boulder she'd sheltered under and flowed back toward the monster. Klara Yana took her gaze from the creature only long enough to confirm that she had already been surrounded. She inched her hand toward her right pocket, where the arphanium pipe was.

Something opened beneath those myriad eyes – a mouth of some sort. And it spoke, in a deep, resonating voice.

"*Torthu-ara-caeg.*"

Klara Yana's mouth fell open. A language. Should she try to answer? Was it talking to *her*, or just talking?

The safest option seemed to be to stay quiet. She resumed sliding her hand toward her pocket, moving as little as possible. The huge body lowered even closer to the rocky floor, until it hovered barely above head height, its impossibly long tentacles stretching as far as Klara Yana could see to hold it aloft. Everywhere she looked, they writhed like giant highland snakes, making loops and curls on every side. The end of one approached her face. Even in the dim light, she could see wide suckers when the tapered end flicked up – and what looked like sharp, black barbs lining it. She ran a tongue over dry lips as she finally got a hand into Cu Zanthus's coat pocket and wrapped it around the smooth chunk of arphanium pipe. It was her wounded hand rather than the dekatite-marked one, unfortunately. She started pulling it out.

As if the monster sensed it, the closest tentacle shot forward. Before she could react, it had wrapped twice around her body, pinning her right arm to her side. Her hand spasmed open, and the arphanium dropped back into the deep pocket. The tentacle lifted her, bringing her closer to the thing's body. It crushed her so tight, she could feel every bruise in her ribs. The gunshot wound in her side erupted in torment. The spikes she'd seen pricked through in a few places, but thanks to Cu Zanthus's thick coat, not as badly as they might have. Yet. She struggled to breathe through the pulverizing strength, terrified the creature would bring her straight to its mouth and eat her. But instead, it kept her hanging some distance away, narrowing or widening its various eyes at her.

"*Yola-krona. Niss-machi. All-ono.*"

Klara Yana's marked hand was still free, but her other hand completely blocked the pocket with the arphanium and was pinned down. Even if she got to the pipe, would she be able to get away? Would the shrouding technique work again? She tried not to think about Blackwood's words at the lab – *I saw the bodies in* Desert Crab*'s first accident. They were torn up, mutilated…*

"*An-mal-da-caeg!*" The creature shook her, rattling her to her teeth. Another tentacle whipped up to join the first, grabbing her left leg. Klara Yana screamed as she pictured it being ripped clean off.

With a start, she remembered the shrouding vehicles were attacked when someone brought dekatite onboard. It must be what the creature wanted. Frantically, she fumbled under her coat and shirt, and pulled the Broken Eye out from under her breast wrap. She thrust it out in front of her, holding it between her fingertips so it was fully visible.

Several of the eyes swiveled pointedly toward it. The creature's mouth opened wider, terrible teeth bared and massive.

Then, before Klara Yana could react, something huge and dark dropped through the cave's opening directly above the creature's head. The monster bellowed as its bulbous shape was hit, and the tentacles gripping Klara Yana's body suddenly loosened. She plummeted through the coils. Pain erupted as her battered body hit hard rock, and she immediately began sliding down the slanted face of the boulder she'd landed on. She grappled for a grip, barely clinging onto the Broken Eye with her marked palm. Somehow, the hand with the injured finger saved her, snagging on an outcropping and halting her descent. The finger pulsed in red-hot pain. She gritted her teeth and looked up.

The creature that had grabbed her was being *dragged* away, tentacles flailing against the walls in a desperate, but futile, attempt to stop itself. Then, without warning, they abruptly ceased. The tentacles fell to the rocks around her with heavy, grotesque thumps. One of them barely missed hitting her foot.

Klara Yana peered down the tunnel, her heart thumping. A dark smoke swirled toward her. She jerked back as tendrils of it reached for her. No, it wasn't smoke… more of a dark mist. It left beads of moisture across her face and hands. Shivering in its chill, Klara Yana managed to pull herself up to a flatter part of the huge boulder and climb back to her feet. The hand not holding the pendant hovered over the pocket with the arphanium in it. But she didn't grab it yet – whatever this was, it had saved her from the other monster. Still… that didn't make it a friend.

A form began to take shape from the mist, although not a completely solid one. It slightly resembled a person sitting in front of her rock, with legs bent to either side. But there were at least four legs, and while two arms gripped the rock's surface, another propped up the vague shape of a head. Long ethereal hair drifted down in waves of mist, breaking off continuously like spray from a waterfall. Only a deep gash showed where one of its eyes should have been. The other eye was deep green with bright golden flecks. Not *exactly* the same shade as Klara Yana's, but definitely close. Klara Yana's gaze went from the one remaining eye to the missing one and back again. *What in the name of the gods…?*

"*Kinnen,*" the creature said. "*Redit-itres-kora-caeg.*"

"Um… this?" Klara Yana held out the dekatite pendant again.

A distinct look of irritation flashed across the being's face. She brought

230

up a massive hand and used it to close Klara Yana's fingers back over the pendant. The giant hand was warm and rough, despite the cool mistiness of the being herself. Its grip was strong enough to make Klara Yana gasp. It was, without a doubt, the same hand she'd felt in the submarine.

"You," she whispered. "That was you. Outside the submarine. Wasn't it?"

"*Da. Caeg.*" The creature repeated the words slowly, as if speaking to a child.

Caeg. The same thing the first creature had asked for. It must not be the dekatite, then. Reluctantly, Klara Yana put the dekatite away and brought out the piece of blood-stained arphanium instead. "Is the caeg this one?"

The being's head jerked back, and a hiss escaped her lips. One of the huge hands shot forward. Klara Yana stepped back, burying it in her pocket again.

"No. I need it," she said. "I need it to get back."

"*Norg-ahelb-caeg-machi!*" the creature snarled.

Klara Yana's heart pounded. Blackwood had said the creatures were drawn to dekatite. But even if that were true, clearly it was the *arphanium* they wanted. And there were only two things Klara Yana knew arphanium was used for: lights... and getting in and out of the shrouding realm. What if *that* was what these creatures wanted? What if that's why the submarine had been attacked?

She took another step back, until her heels hung over the edge of the flat boulder. "No," she said shakily. "No, I can't let you come back to Mirrix. I've heard what you do. The people you kill. No one would be safe!"

"*Okel-mara!*" The monster's hand lunged for her again.

Klara Yana took another step back, pitching her body forward and digging her boots in for traction as she slid down the steep decline of the huge rock. She leapt off halfway down, twisting and landing deep in the crevice between two boulders as big as tanks. By the time she hit the ground, her body was screaming in pain again, but she had the arphanium clutched in her non-marked hand.

"*Galene!*" the creature said from behind her, her voice urgent.

Klara Yana froze. Slowly, she turned around. The creature was up on the rock she'd just jumped from, staring at her with that one eye that seemed so bright even in the shadows.

"Did you say *Galene?*" said Klara Yana.

"*Galene. Da-caeg.*"

It's just a coincidence, thought Klara Yana. *Some sound-alike word from their language.* And yet… there was no denying the similarity of the creature's face and its single eye to Vo Hina's – to Klara Yana's own goddess. Vo Hina, whom Galene Marduc had slept with. *No. It's not possible.*

"*Icseni. Peraga.*" The creature was back to speaking very clearly now, as if she could somehow drill the words' meanings into Klara Yana's head. She pointed one finger to the arphanium Klara Yana held. "*Da-caeg.*" She reached down and picked up a craggy rock from the ground, small enough to fit in her hand. "*Peraga.*" She closed her fingers and squeezed tight. A sharp crack echoed through the cavern, followed by a muffled grinding. The being opened her hand and particles of crushed rock fell in a cloud of black and gray dust.

Klara Yana's mouth went dry. "You want to *crush* my arphanium? Destroy it? I'd be *trapped* here!"

"*Norg-bivorna.*" The being pointed to the creature she'd killed, behind her.

Klara Yana felt a headache coming on, nowhere near the gash on her scalp. What was the creature trying to tell her? She wanted the arphanium. No doubt there. But to *destroy* it? Was it a ruse, to trick her into handing it over? It *had* been the hand from the submarine, she was sure of it. Had she been trying to get the arphanium then, too? *But why destroy it?*

A sudden flash of light lit up the cavern, searing into Klara Yana's retinas as strongly as Cu Zanthus's shock grenade had. Klara Yana staggered back with a yell, an arm flung over her eyes. She could still see the bolt of lightning that had come through that hole in the ceiling, like an afterimage burned into her brain. Rock shattered with a deafening crack as the strike hit the ground. Just over the noise of the rolling thunder, Klara Yana could hear the voice of the creature she'd been speaking with.

"Galene! Falb! Falb!"

Klara Yana blinked her eyes open, squinting through tears. She could just make out the creature with the single green eye.

"Norg. Bivorna!" the creature said again, gesturing frantically overhead.

Bivorna. Klara Yana looked from the dead creature she'd first pointed at to the hole overhead. The space had darkened again. Another monster? Were *they* the Bivorna? With that lightning, it had seemed like gods-cursed Shon Aha!

Shon Aha. What if *he'd* been the one to strike Blackwood? And this creature – Vo Hina? – had been the one to… *No. Not possible!*

"Galene!"

Klara Yana wrenched her gaze back to the creature. It slowly dawned on her that every time the creature had used that word, she was trying to get her attention. Like a name. *Does she think I'm Galene?* But what sense did that make?

The shrouding creature looked overhead one more time, then back at Klara Yana, and stabbed with a single finger at one of her own palms. *"Da-caeg!"* she shouted. *"Falb! Falb!"* Then she threw her arm out in a frustrated gesture that surely meant the same thing in any language: *Go! Get away!*

Klara Yana didn't wait to be told again. She hastily transferred the arphanium to her dekatite-marked hand and closed her fingers around it. The world went dark.

Chapter 21

KLARA YANA'S
INFILTRATION

Klara Yana fell to her knees in a crevice of stone, her eyes squeezed shut against the sudden brilliance and warmth of the midday suns. Waves crashed nearby, and the air was humid and salty. The abrupt change from the shrouding realm was disorienting enough to send her head spinning. She'd only been thinking one thing as she closed her hand around the dekatite pipe: *Not back to Lyanirus! Not Lyanirus!* Blackwood's face had flashed through her mind, and Kheppra Isle on its heels, where she was sure the leuftkernel was heading after his soldier's report. She slowly squinted her eyes open again, taking in the craggy black dekatite surrounding her, the pair of crabs on the rock close by, the plume of smoke swelling high overhead and hazing the pale blue sky. To her left, the sea sparkled as far as she could see. *Kheppra Isle.* Without even intending to, she'd directed her own shrouding. She tucked the arphanium into her trouser pocket and slowly lowered herself until her hands touched the solid rock, anchoring herself firmly back in her own world.

The creature in the shrouding realm had saved her life. Almost assuredly for the second time. Because Klara Yana had gotten the gist.

The creature had wanted to destroy the arphanium. She'd pointed to both the dead creature and the one who'd shot lightning into the cavern. *Norg. Bivorna.* Then... then she'd told her to run. She'd wanted her gone – wanted, Klara Yana thought, to *protect* her.

She couldn't help wondering how closely that scene had mirrored the one that had happened just outside the *Desert Crab*.

She touched the Broken Eye beneath her jacket and whispered a small prayer her ama had taught her, one meant only for the Informer. *May Vo Hina watch my back this day. May she keep me safe should I lose my way.*

Maybe... maybe...

Something flashed just at the edge of her vision, reflecting Shon Aha's light. Klara Yana turned her head. A submarine was rounding the island from the north. She remained motionless, barely breathing, and watched it for several moments. It looked like the *Desert Crab*, though she'd only seen it a couple times. She knew it was Belzene, at least; the Dhavnak ones she'd seen in Jasterus were rounder, bulkier, blacker, and of course, had no helio cells on top. Why, then, had Lyanirus mentioned a Dhavnak crew here?

She watched until the submarine was out of sight, heading south – back toward Marldox. She wondered if it carried reinforcements for the battle. Or maybe it had just come back from a shrouding expedition. Strange. She shook it from her head. She'd wanted to come to Kheppra Isle for a reason. And she didn't know how long Blackwood had.

Her body was too abused to hike over the whole island and track down Blackwood and Andrew. Her right forefinger was barely mobile. Pain arced through the gunshot wound in her side every time she moved. *If I can't walk,* she thought, *maybe I can shroud.* She fixed her eye on a point as far to the north as she could see, then grasped the arphanium pipe. Again, the cold of the shrouding realm hit her. She was in a canyon this time, with a roaring river before her and a sun so high overhead, it was no bigger than a marble, barely visible through a high sheen of smoke. Shivering, she took her hand away for just a second, then gripped the arphanium again, focusing all her thoughts on the place she'd picked out in her mind.

It worked. She recognized the depression in the rocks with a pool from the ocean spray, and the ax-shaped protrusion above. She took only enough steps to pick out another place to hop to. Continue heading north, where the submarine had come from. She figured she'd eventually have to hit a dock or base of some kind… and then she'd find out what she was dealing with.

Four more dips into shrouding – a band of light across the sky, a volcano exploding in the distance, a gawking monster with enough hair, legs, and eyes to haunt her dreams for a lifetime, and a spit of sand overlooking a deep black sea – and she found herself only fifteen or twenty feet above a narrow dock pressed into the cliffside. Black-uniformed Dhavnak soldiers came and went from a vast cave leading back under the island. She sat back against the rocks, thinking.

She could hop down to the dock and head back into the island, see where it took her. But she'd be noticeable. Lyanirus's shirt might be military-reg, but it was certainly no uniform, and leaving Cu Zanthus's Belzene officer's coat on would be no better. Even if she continued using her shrouding as she had been, constant disappearing and reappearing would send the whole place into a swarm trying to catch her. Too brash.

Instead, she waited until a soldier broke off from the others and stepped to the side for a tobie break. Then, holding the arphanium between her thumb and forefinger, she dropped off the ledge and landed on his back. The instant she touched him, she closed the rest of her hand around the pipe.

The soldier yelled, staggering to the side, but he lurched to a halt when he noticed the dirt terrain around him and the distant suns above, not to mention the sweeping band of light. Before he could react, Klara Yana wrapped her right arm around his neck and used her other arm to pull it tight. She yanked back as hard as she could, finally getting her feet on the ground and pulling him off balance. He tugged at her arm, but she scrambled back, keeping him from regaining his control. It didn't take long for him to lose consciousness. Klara Yana lowered him to the hard ground, struggling to catch her breath. She'd been lucky; he was on the smaller side, barely larger than she was. Combat training or not, she wouldn't have been able to handle someone stronger, not in her current state.

In the privacy of the alien world, she changed into the knee-length belted jacket, tight trousers, and boots, finding them only a little big. She pulled the folded garrison cap over her short hair and straightened the collar to cover the raw marks on her neck. The only thing missing was a weapon – the soldier had probably set it down somewhere while he'd been loading equipment. Nothing to be done for it. She left the man on the south side of Kheppra Isle in nothing but his underclothes, then shrouded back to the docks.

She saw Blackwood and Andrew immediately. They were sitting on the concrete next to the wide waterway, their wrists bound, surrounded by four armed soldiers. Blackwood stared toward the other tunnel, watching armfuls of arphanium pipe being loaded into a Dhavnak submarine, which had navigated into the passage. Andrew glared at one of the guards, who paid him no attention. Klara Yana strode toward the group, doing her best not to hold her side or move too stiffly. She wished the Dhavnak uniform had gloves, to hide her bandaged hand as well as the dekatite mark; but at the same time, she *needed* the dekatite mark free to escape. She thought maybe she could just grab both of them and go. But what about their bound hands? Would they slip free of the ropes, or would they be trapped? She was painfully aware there'd only be one chance.

The braided brown cord on her shoulder named her a low corporant, but the guards' black cords made them even lower ranking primers. The closest one looked up as she approached. He straightened, frowning. His salute came hesitantly, and it took her several moments to realize he was staring in fascination at her face. Her heart seized. Had he noticed she was a woman, that fast, that easily? The other guards had looked over by now and added their own salutes, but she distinctly heard one laugh under his breath and mutter, "*Someone* stepped out of line."

Vo Hina's mercy. The bruises. With everything else, she'd forgotten what her face must look like. She fixed a murderous glare on each of them in turn.

"Hand over the prisoners. Leuftkernel Lyanirus is waiting in a 'rotor up top."

Blackwood looked up at her voice. Her eyes widened. Klara Yana knew what she was thinking. *He speaks Dhavvish? He got his hands on a Dhavvie uniform? He escaped?* There would be a lot of explaining to do after this. For now, Klara Yana just hoped Blackwood didn't inadvertently expose her. Andrew didn't look surprised to see her, just... wary. The last he'd seen, she'd been captured by her own partner; for all he knew, she was a renegade agent now. If he thought that, he was absolutely right. As the one who'd turned Blackwood in, he could be a lot of trouble. *Just go along with it, kid. Please.*

"We weren't notified, sir," said the same guard who had laughed.

"You're being notified now. Untie them."

"Tizantuck. Go clear this with Kommandir Nimoresa," the soldier ordered. His smile was gone. The man he'd spoken to jogged off, not even checking with Klara Yana first.

"The leuftkernel is waiting *this second!*" Klara Yana said sharply.

"Your pardon, sir, but I think the leuftkernel himself would tell us to question anyone who gets punished as often as you."

"So that's what this is about."

"With due respect, sir, we're aware how important these prisoners are. No way am I turning them over without his explicit orders."

Klara Yana coolly lifted an eyebrow. "Consider your objection noted. We'll wait on Primer Tizantuck then. Until then, I'll make sure you haven't mistreated the prisoners." She stepped toward Blackwood and Andrew, but the soldier swung his rifle up and trained it on her.

One of the other guards stuttered out, "Urmensias!"

"Urmensias," Klara Yana repeated, her eyes never leaving the uncooperative guard's. "Good to know." She stepped past the gun, pushing it out of the way with her hand, and knelt by Blackwood. Instantly, she saw why the chief sea officer was sitting so awkwardly. She'd been shot. Klara Yana gritted her teeth. *This just gets better and better.*

Blackwood stared at her, not daring to utter a word. Andrew's eyes darted between her and Blackwood. He was probably dying to ask if Cu Zanthus had sent her, but couldn't do so in front of his sister without exposing Klara Yana.

She reached into her pocket and wrapped just her thumb and

forefinger around the arphanium pipe. She glanced at the siblings, making sure they were close enough for her to grab at the same time. *One chance.*

"Lyanirus hasn't contacted us!" a voice hollered across the walkway. Out of the corner of her eye, Klara Yana saw Tizantuck running toward them. "Seize the corporant!"

Klara Yana lunged forward, grabbing Andrew around the waist with her right arm and Blackwood with her left. Andrew screamed as her force pushed them from the ledge. But Klara Yana got her palm around the arphanium... and instead of plunging into water, they slid down the side of a slick hill, headfirst, snow spraying into their faces. Blackwood hissed in pain – definitely her leg – and Klara Yana howled as a rock struck her in the side. Fresh blood gushed beneath the bandage. She finally skidded to a stop, pain pulsing through her as intensely as it had after Lyanirus had finished with her. She lay wheezing, unsure if she'd ever be able to move again.

"By the moons!" Andrew gasped, somewhere to her right. "That ring! We're back here? What are we doing back here?"

"I'll get you out again!" Klara Yana croaked. "Just... give me a second." She felt around in the shallow snow for the piece of arphanium she'd dropped. The sweeping river of stars arced through the haze above her – the ring, Andrew had called it. Was it? She'd taken several trips back as she'd shrouded around the island looking for Blackwood and Andrew, and that strange arc of stars had been in a different place every time.

"How did you *do* that, Holland?" said Blackwood.

"The mark," Klara Yana answered, still staring at the sky. "I touch the dekatite to arphanium, and I shroud. From anywhere."

Blackwood whistled. Andrew scrambled to Klara Yana's side, feet slipping in the accumulation. He spoke Dhavvish in her ear, hissing out his words in a desperate whisper.

"Did he send you? Why didn't those soldiers–"

"*Yes*, he sent me!" Klara Yana said through her teeth. Vo Hina's mercy, did he want to get her killed? If Blackwood realized that Deckman Holland had helped compromise her parents' research, she would strike her with that lightning in a second. No explanation on Mirrix would save her.

She spoke her next words louder, but gave them as much implied weight as possible, for Andrew's sake. "Find the arphanium. We *need* it. OK?"

He nodded vigorously. "OK. I'm on it."

Blackwood was breathing very deeply and deliberately somewhere to Klara Yana's right, obviously trying to get up. Klara Yana put her hand to her wounded side, closing her eyes tight at even the thought of wrenching it again.

"Holland," Blackwood said. "You speak Dhavvish."

Klara Yana's heart jumped before she realized Blackwood was referring to her rescue of them, rather than her short exchange with Andrew. "Yes. Yes, I do, CSO. I taught myself Dhavvish after my home was attacked. Just in case."

"How did you escape? How did you find us?"

Klara Yana rolled onto her side, gasping at another stab of pain. "I stole the arphanium piece from the officer who captured me and instantly shrouded. But while they had me, I heard them talking. I heard them mention Kheppra Isle."

"Look at me, deckman."

Klara Yana looked over her shoulder, bracing herself. The CSO was standing now, her hand gingerly over the bandage on her leg and her long curls blowing free in the cold breeze. Her eyes drilled into Klara Yana's.

"Were you sent here?" she said, her voice hard. "It all seems very convenient. The escape. The uniform. The Dhavvish."

"Are you *serious*, CSO?" Klara Yana choked out. "Do you think I let myself be shot, too? And beaten nearly to death? Maybe you'd like to see my finger? It was almost cut off. I can take off the bandage, if you don't believe me."

Blackwood studied her for several moments. Finally, she let out a small sigh. "You really do look like kaullix shit. Was it about your mark?"

"Yes, CSO. And where you had gone. Why I couldn't do the lightning thing."

"What *did* you tell them? Anything?"

"Nothing. I swear, CSO. I stayed quiet, right up until I got the arphanium and escaped."

"And then you came here?" It was Andrew who spoke this time, looking up from where he crouched in the snow. "To this realm?"

"Yes."

"Did you see any... any of the beings here?" he asked. There was something almost hungry in his gaze.

Klara Yana looked between him and Blackwood, trying to read their moods. The way Blackwood's face tightened at Andrew's question could mean anything.

"Yes," she answered cautiously, keeping her eyes on Blackwood's face. "I actually sort of... spoke with one."

"What?" said Blackwood sharply.

"I mean, kind of. I couldn't understand it, but–"

"They've never done anything but try to *kill* us before!" Blackwood said.

"No, CSO, that's not true!" said Klara Yana. "One of them *did* attack us, yes, but it was a different one that grabbed my hand on the submarine. It was... I think it was the one..." She stopped, forcing herself to take a deep breath. "One of them saved us. Not all of them are bad."

"You're saying there were two monsters outside the submarine?"

"Yes, ma'am."

"I hadn't realized that," Blackwood said after a moment.

"I didn't figure it out until much later, ma'am. But I'm almost positive it's true."

"Is that the one you spoke with?" said Andrew.

Klara Yana dipped her head in a guarded nod. "It was the same hand I felt on the submarine. I'm sure of it."

"You mean when you were both marked," he said.

"Yeah."

Andrew's gaze slid to Blackwood. Her eyes narrowed. Andrew swallowed and turned back to Klara Yana. "Shon Aha, the Marshal, the god of the Main Sun and lightning. Vo Hina, the Informer and the goddess of the Unseen." Blackwood started to say something, but Andrew talked over her, his words tumbling faster from his mouth. "If Mila was marked by Shon Aha and can now use lightning, maybe *Holland* was marked by Vo Hina. What if the legend of her being

Unseen was because she could shroud? Like Holland can now?"

"Andrew!" Blackwood said forcefully. "Holland doesn't want to hear this any more than I do."

"Why *not*, Mila?" Andrew said, his tone edging closer to agitation. "Shrouding came from *somewhere*! Why *not* Vo Hina?"

"It *came* from the arphanium that was buried miles belowground and only recently discovered. It's a new technology–"

"Or an ancient *lost* technology!" Andrew insisted.

Blackwood sighed through her teeth. "Yeah. Maybe. But so what? What does that have to do with Dhavvie gods coming to life?"

"What does it have to *do* with it? Vo Hina's betrayal? The fact that she *hoarded* souls by preventing the other gods from getting them? If she could shroud – if she could trap them all somewhere and destroy the arphanium so they couldn't get back–"

"Xeil's sake, Andrew, are you *listening* to yourself?" Blackwood burst out.

Klara Yana's gaze went back and forth between them, her breath coming fast. *Destroy the arphanium.* That creature with the single eye had told her to run. *What if she could trap them so they couldn't get back…?*

"But where would she put them?" she found herself saying.

Blackwood's attention snapped to her. "What was that, Holland?"

Klara Yana managed a small laugh, breathy and disbelieving. "Just… Andrew's theory. Makes no sense. I mean, where *would* the Dhavvie goddess trap them?"

"Anywhere!" Andrew said. "Anywhere that has dekatite, right? Isn't that how you said shrouding works?"

"Anywhere?" echoed Klara Yana. "What do you mean, anywhere? Another plane of existence? Another planet? Inside Mirrix?"

Andrew blinked. He mouthed something under his breath as his gaze flicked back to Blackwood.

"Andrew…" Blackwood began.

"Another planet," he said. "Mila, the notes said… they said there were dekatite veins all over the galaxy. The Shattered Moon. The Shipora Belt. Mittdreck. *Neutania.*"

Blackwood opened her mouth. She started to shake her head.

"It's colder," said Andrew. "The suns are farther. No vegetation. More moons. It has *rings*. If you can shroud to *any* dekatite vein on Mirrix, Mila, why not any dekatite vein in the galaxy? In the universe, even? Just admit it. It's not impossible!"

Blackwood closed her mouth again. Her gaze swept up to that starry band. "It's not," she finally said. "It actually… almost makes sense."

"But why Neutania?" said Klara Yana faintly.

"Probably because that's where Galene Marduc went," said Andrew, "and that's what his map was based on. When Belzen stole it and used it for shrouding, they *built* it into those vehicles to shroud here. Otherwise, you could probably go anywhere." He turned to Klara Yana, his eyes widening. "I bet *you* could go anywhere, if you tried!"

Living gods. Blackwood's little brother could put stuff together faster than Klara Yana could even think of the questions. She was starting to see why Cu Zanthus had been so excited to see him again. If it weren't for the boy's emotional immaturity, he'd make a formidable partner for Cu Zanthus. She was burning with questions, and realized that, against all odds, Andrew might be the best person to talk to. But she couldn't come out and *ask* him, not in front of Blackwood. What would Deckman Holland care?

She had to look like she was siding with the CSO. Very carefully, she said, "But that creature I met… it wasn't *really* a god. That's impossible."

"But maybe it was!" Andrew said. "In the past, if the gods could come from Neutania to Mirrix–"

"Wait," Blackwood cut in. "We're not talking about this."

"But, Mila, the creatures! The similarities!" Andrew protested. "We saw the one like Shon Aha, right? There had to have been some crossover, early on. This could have even been where Vo Hina was banished to!"

Klara Yana almost choked. "Shon Aha?" she whispered.

"Andrew, no!" said Blackwood. "I'm begging you, for all our sakes. Do *not* start again!"

"Why won't you just *listen*–"

Blackwood's voice rose in anger. "The Dhavnaks have taken our parents' lives, our city, my submarine and crew. They're close to taking

Belzen, they've got half of Mirrix, and now you want to give them the shrouding realm, too? *And* the afterlife?"

"It's not about what I *want*, Mila," said Andrew, a note of pleading in his voice. "It's about what I've read and seen first-hand. You think I'm biased? Well, you're afraid to admit it could be true! You're just as bad. *Worse*."

Several moments of tense silence passed. Andrew finally lowered his head and continued looking for the arphanium pipe. Klara Yana climbed painfully to her feet and started up the slope to help him look. Blackwood spoke as she passed. Her voice was tight with underlying fury.

"I'd rather be blind to the truth than betray my own country and family."

Klara Yana froze. Andrew looked up from the snow, his eyes flashing. She didn't think he was quite close enough to hear what his sister said, not as low as she'd spoken. But there was no way he could miss the tone she'd used. Klara Yana held out a hand toward Blackwood, her heart pounding.

"CSO, let's not jump to conclusions. He's a seventeen year-old kid—"

"Our crew is probably on that boat, Holland. The one filled with explosives that's heading to Belzen as we speak. I'm trying to save our people, and all my Xeil-cursed brother can do is glorify our enemy's folklore! I can't help him. I can't *do* this anymore! He is Cu Zanthus's puppet and I just – cannot – get *through* to him!"

Klara Yana took in her commanding officer's clenched hands and her short, quick breaths. Was there *actually* a charged sizzle to the air, or was that just Klara Yana's imagination?

"Andrew!" she snapped. "Find that arphanium! *Now!*"

"But Mila won't even—"

"No! Don't argue. Don't even talk. Just do it." She walked as quickly as possible to Blackwood's other side and took her shoulders, facing her away from Andrew. Blackwood glared at her.

"Holland, you have no idea what—"

"CSO. Please. Calm down. Just… just listen, OK?"

Blackwood stared at her, her breath still coming way too fast.

"You don't want to kill him. Right?" said Klara Yana.

"No! Of course I don't!"

"You killed Zurlig."

"Zurlig was gonna kill *you*, Holland—"

"I get that. But what if the same thing happens to Andrew? Then will it *matter* whether he trusted the wrong guy, or made a dumb decision because of it? Will it even matter if you save your crew? You won't be able to go back and change it! Ever!"

"Are you giving me a reprimand?" Blackwood said incredulously.

"I'm sorry, ma'am. I'm just trying to help. Honest!"

Blackwood cursed and threw Klara Yana's hands off her shoulders. She turned away, crossing her arms over her chest. For several moments, she stared toward Andrew, her chest heaving. Andrew glanced back once, quick and furtive, before jerking his attention to his search again.

"I thought you hated him," Blackwood said under her breath. "After you attacked him in that basement and everything."

"Wanted to punch him in the face, sure. Doesn't mean I want the kid dead."

"What about our crew? What if he was responsible?"

"Then he was responsible. Maybe he pays for it someday, maybe he doesn't. But you don't want him killed because *you* lost control."

"But what if I can't help it?"

Vo Hina's mercy. What would Deckman Holland say to a question like that? He'd be dazzled by his opinion being asked in the first place. He'd say something like, *I know you wouldn't do that, CSO. I believe in you.* But that wasn't what Blackwood needed. She harbored a very real fear that she might hurt her brother. No matter how much she didn't want to.

Klara Yana spoke softly. "Just step back from it. Remember that his thoughts – his fears and worries and desires – they're just as real to *him*. No matter how stupid or wrong they are to you. Maybe you remember that often enough and you'll get inside his head better. Make less of an enemy out of him over time."

Blackwood turned back, eyebrows raised. "Xeil's grace, Holland. That was right out of an analyst's textbook or something." She frowned. "Just how old are you, anyway?"

Klara Yana threw on a crooked grin, trying to slide back into the twenty-one cycle-old Blackwood knew. "Did a bit of acting when I was younger, CSO. That's one of the first rules in understanding your character. It sometimes works in understanding another person, too." It was barely even a lie. The Noncombatant Intelligence Corps had all kinds of tips for getting into their roles.

Blackwood studied Klara Yana's face for several moments, most likely taking in the bruises there. "Don't know what to make of you sometimes, Holland."

Yeah, Blackwood was still suspicious, all right. But at least she'd gotten her temper under control. *If not for that mark on her arm, I'd almost consider telling her the truth,* thought Klara Yana pensively. *But if she thinks* Andrew *didn't do right by her, what in Vo Hina's good grace would she do to me?*

"I found it! I found it!" Andrew came running down the snowy hill then, holding up the arphanium pipe triumphantly. Klara Yana breathed a sigh of relief. Blackwood turned and held her hand out.

"Give it here," she said.

Andrew glanced at Klara Yana, and waited for her slight nod before handing it over. Blackwood frowned at them both as she took it. She rolled up her sleeve and pressed the pipe to her mark. Nothing happened.

"Different powers," she said finally. "Curious."

Different gods, thought Klara Yana.

Blackwood handed the pipe to Klara Yana. "Holland, do you think you can shroud us directly onto the submarine?"

Klara Yana blinked. "But… but what do think you can do? Commandeer it? Sink it?"

"I don't know yet. But I can't let it reach Marldox. And if some of my crew *are* still on it, I can't let them die."

They weren't. Lyanirus's corporant had mentioned the *Desert Crab*'s crew being sent back to a Marine Internment Camp – probably the big one in Jasterus, near Lake Lassinder. But she couldn't say that. Blackwood was suspicious enough as it was.

"Deckman Holland," said Blackwood. "Consider it an order."

Klara Yana took a deep breath. Lyanirus was still looking for

Blackwood. Until he was dead, Blackwood might still end up in his grasp. And Klara Yana had vowed not to let that happen.

She pulled herself into a Belzene salute, fist to her chest. "Andrew too, ma'am?"

"I'm not letting Andrew out of my sight. Yes, he's coming with us."

"Understood, CSO."

Chapter 22

ANDREW'S REUNION

Even bracing himself for the transition, Andrew had to throw out a hand for balance as they landed in a dark, stuffy room lit only by red lights along the ceiling. He steadied himself on a nylon bed jutting out from the wall, his eyes flicking over the unfamiliar space. A submarine. He'd never even seen one, much less been inside one. His nose twitched immediately at the smell, like too many bodies and not enough showers, like clothes left unwashed and sweaty sheets. He felt the press of its walls around him; maybe it was illusion from the emergency lighting, but the space was smaller than he'd pictured. With the beds out, two people wouldn't even be able to pass side by side in the central corridor. Something in his chest loosened. The smell didn't bother him in the least, and the feel of the close walls seemed like a barrier against the outside world. The soft hum of the motors was another layer of security. A small, dark, muffled space, like his own house, his own bed. No wonder Mila liked it here.

"By the goddess," breathed Mila. "I didn't know if that would work."

"Me neither, CSO," said Holland, sounding more than a little shaken herself. "It seems to help when I can picture a place."

At the open doorway at the other end of the room, someone let out a yell. Mila cursed and started toward the opening, leaning heavily on the lowered bunks as she dragged her leg behind her. Shouting rose in

Dhavnak, from more than one voice. "Intruders!" "…missing prisoners from Kheppra Isle…" "…radio the leuftkernel *immediately!*"

"CSO, let me!" Holland hissed. "I'm in uniform!" She halted her commanding officer and tried to squeeze by her.

"The uniform won't fool them!" Mila snapped. "They'll have heard by now what you did. Just secure the hatch! Hurry!"

Holland reached the doorway – the hatch – at the same moment a Dhavnak soldier appeared on the other side. He started to raise a pistol. Almost faster than Andrew could follow, Holland slammed her palm up into the man's chin, snapping his head back, then grabbed the thick oval-shaped door at her right and swung it shut. She needed her whole body to heave its weight around. The man managed to fire off a shot, but the door was almost shut by then, and the bullet pinged off the edge of the thick steel. Holland slammed the door closed with a clunk and spun a wheel on the back side. It creaked as it locked tight. She looked back in the low red lighting, looking simultaneously startled and terrified. Muffled shouts and bangs were barely audible through the thick steel behind her.

"Holland," said Mila. "That was… really good."

"Thanks, CSO."

"Here's the plan," said Mila. She kept her back to Andrew. *Could have at least pretended to include me*, he thought, rolling his eyes.

"First. Find out if there are any Belzenes on board, and if there are, *get them off*. Holland, you can do that with your arphanium. The Dhavnaks, too. The less in our way, the better. It'll be dangerous, because they'll realize what you're doing right away and try to set a trap."

"I can do it, CSO."

"Second. I find out what went wrong with the self-destruct system. The *Desert Crab's* already packed with Dhavnak explosives, but I'd need the detonator to set them off. No good. I have to fix our self-destruct and get rid of the boat long before it's close enough to cause damage."

Andrew sank down on one of the lower beds, arms wrapped around himself. Explosives? Soldiers shooting Mila, holding him hostage? *I agreed to report where Mila went, not to assist in blowing up one of our own cities. How far does he expect me to go?*

He looked up, licking his lips. Holland. He had to talk to her. If this was all part of Cu Zanthus's plan, she'd know. *Unless she lied, and she's running from him.* But she hadn't confessed anything to Mila, and that struck Andrew as a sign she was still working from within. Maybe it had *all* been an act, from her own capture to the incredibly believable evidence of being beaten. Maybe Cu Zanthus had wanted Andrew alone with Mila, to test him.

I don't hate you.

Mila's words echoed through his skull, yet again. He ground his teeth. *But only until the next time I make you mad, right, Mila?* Her love was too fragile; even if he tried every moment of every day to be perfect, he'd fail. With Cu Zanthus, he didn't *have* to be perfect. *What does he want me to do?*

"Andrew! Why are you sitting down?"

He looked up, heart pounding. "Just... just resting."

"Well, get up! They *will* get through that hatch eventually, and I know for a fact they've called for backup. Holland, can you get Andrew and I down to the lower flat of the forward power room? I can check the connections on the self-destruct system there."

"I'm not sure I can shroud somewhere I haven't seen before, CSO," said Holland.

"You used to sneak down there all the time when you were feeling overwhelmed, during your panic attacks," said Mila.

Holland flushed, the perfect image of an embarrassed young soldier. "You're right, CSO."

"Good. Get us down there, then start getting the Dhavvies off the boat as fast as you can. Leave them in the shrouding realm, drop them in the ocean, I really don't care. But whatever you do, *be careful.* If we lose you, Andrew and I are trapped here. Got it?"

"Yes, ma'am."

"Stand up, Andrew," said Mila again.

Andrew pulled himself up, trying to catch Holland's eye as she put her hands in the pockets of the long, belted Dhavnak coat and positioned herself between them. She didn't so much as glance at him.

"You know I can only take care of one soldier at a time," she told

Mila. "Maybe two, at the most. So you'll have to be prepared to hold off any in the compartment until I can clear it out."

"Understood, deckman."

"Maybe I can help," said Andrew.

Both of them turned their gazes on him. Andrew shrugged.

"If I go along with Holland, I can help. Maybe make it easier to take care of two soldiers at a time."

"No, because then he'd be grabbing *three* people at a time instead of two," said Mila. "That makes no sense."

"But–"

"You're staying with me, Andrew, and that's that. Holland. Now."

Holland linked her elbows into both of their arms. Her chunk of arphanium pipe was clutched between her fingers at Andrew's arm. Andrew got his mouth as close to her ear as he dared without making it obvious.

"What does he want?" he whispered.

Her eyes darted toward him, then away again. Abruptly, the boat disappeared. A flash of lightning lit up the sky. The wall of sound crashing into his eardrums could have been either the resulting thunder or the terrifyingly close volcano spewing lava and sparks hundreds of feet into the air. A dark cloud of smoke rushed toward them. Just beneath it, a giant fleshy creature was dead on the ground a stone's throw away, body ripped open, blood and innards pouring out. Three hairy black creatures tore into it, matting their coats with blood. One of them looked back. It roared something, and both it and another one leapt from the carcass, running toward them so fast they seemed a blur. Andrew screamed, lurching back. Holland lost her grip on him. She lunged for him, snagging his coat.

"Don't move!" she shrieked. Then, just as abruptly as they'd arrived, they were back on the submarine. Andrew stumbled, spilling down into a bank of pipes and knobs. Nausea rose up, fast and powerful, and he rolled over, retching. Nothing came up, but it left him weak and dizzy.

When he looked up, Mila had already gone from his side. He saw her a few steps away, throwing a punch into a Dhavnak soldier's face.

Andrew's still-sore cheek twitched in sympathy. He saw Holland grab another soldier and vanish into thin air. He gritted his teeth and pushed himself up, using some metal black boxes off to his side. When he noticed the warning labels on the sides, he jerked his hand away. It reminded him that whether he chose to help Mila or not, this submarine *would* explode.

He stood and hurried down the slight ramp of treaded metal flooring to join Mila. The soldier she'd taken out was slumped unconscious against a cylindrical brass tank at the base of a ladder heading up. No one else was in the compartment. Mila looked around at the black boxes stacked against the walls under the jointed pipes.

"This was all arphanium in here before," she said with a disgusted gesture. "They've ripped her apart."

"Ripped who apart?"

"The *Desert Crab*. And now we're gonna have to scuttle her. Xeil's grace. After everything we've been through." She turned on her heel and limped back the way they'd come.

Andrew followed, glancing nervously behind him. It was loud down here. The hallway was so narrow, he had to pull his shoulders in. They passed another ladder and squeezed into a space smaller yet, where the narrow pipes were orange instead of brass and a rhythmic hissing pumped out somewhere above them. A single galvanized light burned above, chasing away the shadows.

Mila pointed in front of her, down at a corner. "You can kneel down there."

"Mila, I'm not gonna—"

"Please, Andrew. It's the best out of the way spot, and I don't want to trip over you."

"Right." He sighed and lowered himself to a squat where she'd indicated. The space felt comfortingly close around him. He watched as Mila dropped to one knee, hissing as she folded her leg beneath her. She pried a panel from the floor, then carefully pulled a tangle of wires from inside.

"Are you sure that auto-destruct, or whatever it is, is broken?" Andrew asked. "Maybe your captain just didn't trigger it. I mean, your ship wasn't shrouding at the time, was it?"

"It's a boat, not a ship. And no, they wouldn't have been captured while they were shrouding. The Dhavnaks would have taken them beforehand."

"So why *would* your captain have self-destructed?"

A look of annoyance crossed her face, but she didn't turn away from her work. "Because we were *captured* by *Dhavvies*, Andrew."

"I always thought…"

"What?"

"I mean, in Mother and Father's notes, they discussed the possibility of self-destruct systems, but it was always so the things in that other realm of theirs – whatever it was that ripped the test subjects apart – didn't get the technology. They talked about never leaving anything from here *there*, in case something got hold of it. I…" He shrugged uneasily. "I got the feeling they thought those shrouding creatures might get out if they did."

Mila did look at him then, her eyes a bit wider than normal. "Is that true? That's what it's for?"

"I think so. I thought so."

She cursed under her breath and bent back to the wires. Andrew listened to the rumble of the motors, felt the soothing vibration of the submarine against his back and under his feet. He couldn't see anything from the tiny room, couldn't tell if Holland had picked up the other soldier's body yet.

He closed his eyes for a moment, remembering Cu Zanthus kissing him against the loading truck. Would he ever do it again? Would he do more? Not if Andrew let him down, he wouldn't.

Andrew let his eyes drift open, looking at the barely visible ladder beyond Mila. Down here, no one would hear him even if he *did* try to give her up. No one except Mila, who'd knock him out in a second. Besides, those soldiers at Kheppra Isle had almost *killed* her; the ones here might do the same. Once Cu Zanthus was involved again, it would be OK. He'd tell them not to hurt her. He'd tell them he and Andrew had talked about it, about just keeping her prisoner if they had to.

"There *is* a broken wire!" Mila exclaimed. Andrew looked over to see her holding the two pieces in her hands. She picked up some of the others, shuffling through them with her thumb. "Why would this one have gotten such worse wear than any others? It almost feels like it's been *scraped*. With a knife."

She sat back, a tense look on her face. "I told you one of my deckmates had dekatite, right? And that's why we were attacked during shrouding?"

"No…" Andrew said cautiously. But Mila wasn't talking to him, not really. She was still staring at the wire.

"This department could have had one, too," she said. "A saboteur. A spy. It would've been hard for anyone *outside* the department – like Deckman Vin – to get down here, at least not without landing in the captain's office." She raised her eyes to meet Andrew's. Her dark face had gone a shade paler.

"What?" Andrew said warily. "What is it?"

"Holland was found down here at least twice," she said softly.

"Holland? *Your* Holland?"

"Yes. Deckman Holland. He had dekatite, too. And he… he speaks Dhavvish." A slow look of horror was spreading across her face now.

"Just because he speaks Dhavvish–" Andrew began.

"No. Not *just* that," Mila cut in. "It's the way he walked onto that submarine base and ordered those men around. It's the fact that he chased down a sniper, when a rookie like him should have been scared stiff. It's the way he cracked that man's head back, just now in the torpedo room!" Her eyes had gone distant, as if she were picturing those things in her mind right that moment.

Andrew swallowed. "What are you thinking?"

Her eyes slowly focused again. Something dangerous had awoken in them. "There's no way Kyle Holland is some kid fresh out of the academy," she said. "He's just very good at *pretending* to be."

"You're not saying–"

"Yes. I am," she growled. "And if I hadn't been so cursed distracted lately, I would have seen it sooner!" Her head snapped up, eyes locking on his.

Andrew stiffened, his back pressing harder into the wall.

"Please tell me you didn't know," Mila said, her voice low and furious.

"What? No! Of course not!" Andrew stammered.

Blackwood's mouth twisted and she turned back to the wire. "Get me some banding tape for this. Tool locker, other side of the compartment. It's silver. Hurry!"

Andrew jumped up and opened the locker four steps behind her, just outside the tiny room. He found the skinny roll of tape and passed it back, running his eyes over the still-empty compartment as he did. Mila tore off a piece, binding the two broken ends together. Andrew was still standing in the doorway, watching the far ladder, when Holland appeared without warning halfway down the compartment. She ran straight past Andrew and through the doorway, pausing with her hand on the jamb.

"CSO!" she gasped. "They're here! The backup. They were lowered from an autorotor. The... the one who captured me, his commanding officer, a whole bunch more, and they know where you are, they're coming–"

Mila shot to her feet, stumbling only slightly on her wounded leg. She grabbed Holland around the neck and slammed her against the orange pipes. With her other hand, she slapped the arphanium pipe from her grip. It rolled across the floor, toward the wire Mila had just repaired. "Of course they know where we are. Because you *told* them, didn't you?"

Holland's eyes flicked to the bound wire to the arphanium pipe, then back to Mila, her breath coming quick. "CSO, I'll tell you whatever you want, but if we don't leave *now*–"

"Leave? Leave this submarine of explosives to hit Marldox? You'd like that, wouldn't you? You've set it all up very nicely."

"*I didn't set this up!*" Holland burst out. "I have nothing to *do* with this! I'm trying to save your life, CSO, you and your brother both–"

Andrew crept away while Mila's back was turned and clambered up the ladder the unconscious soldier had been below earlier. He found himself at the floor level of another narrow corridor lined with white steel containers. The room was just as noisy as the one below, if not more so. From his left, he heard the ring of boots along the metal floors. He looked up and saw a small group of men headed his way. A man with dark wavy hair led them. Cu Zanthus was at his side. Andrew's breath caught when he saw the gun at his friend's waist. There was something about it that made him seem so... so much *older*. He couldn't place whether it was a good feeling or a bad one, but it shook him more than he expected.

"Andrew," Cu Zanthus said sharply. He glanced at the man beside him, who sneered down at Andrew. Cu Zanthus knelt, grabbing his wrist. "You're gonna blow your cover," he said through his teeth.

"Oh. Right. I just–"

Still holding his wrist, Cu Zanthus wrenched him from the ladder, then swung down the short distance to the lower room. Andrew clanged against the brass tank as he fell from the ladder. Mila looked back. From the angle they were at, Andrew couldn't see Holland. Cu Zanthus's associate and the soldiers following him poured into the compartment between them.

"There she is, Leuftkernel Lyanirus!" one of the soldiers said.

"Yes, I *see* that!" the man beside Cu Zanthus snapped. "Grab her!"

Right in front of Andrew, one of the men pulled a pistol before running forward. Andrew yanked his hand from Cu Zanthus's grip.

"They won't kill her, right?" he said.

"Holland has arphanium, doesn't he?" said Cu Zanthus.

"Yes, but–"

"That's how he escaped. It's that mark. Can he do it without, or does he need the arphanium?"

"I think he needs it–"

"Where is he? Is he still with you?"

Andrew looked again toward the little room they'd been in, but the soldiers were blocking the way now. *Was* she still there? Or had she managed to grab the arphanium and get away? He turned back to Cu Zanthus.

"So you *didn't* send h- him to get us?"

"No! I need to *find* him and take that arphanium before he can get away again!"

"I'm on it!" said Andrew. Before Cu Zanthus could answer, he darted forward, scrambling up the bombs and pipes to squeeze between the ceiling and the top of a tall locker midway through the room. He wriggled on his stomach toward the back, through a space so cramped he couldn't even raise his head. From his vantage point, he saw Mila yanked from the small room and slammed against the other side of the corridor, one soldier on each arm. She was lunging and kicking, and one of them already had a bloody nose. The other one threw an elbow into her stomach. Mila buckled, vomiting over the slatted floor.

Before Andrew realized what he was doing, he swung his legs from the locker and jumped into their midst. He shoved the man who'd hit Mila.

"Don't *hurt* her!" he yelled.

The man pushed him back and he crashed into the front of the locker door. Cu Zanthus's commanding officer stormed forward. He pulled a gun and pressed it against Andrew's forehead, forcing his head back against the locker. Mila screamed.

"Sir. Sir!" yelled Cu Zanthus. He ran forward, shoving soldiers away to place himself in front of Andrew. He pushed the gun aside. "Leuftkernel, don't! I'll take care of it."

"I *don't* have time for this!" the other man snarled.

Cu Zanthus grabbed Andrew by the back of his neck and pulled him away, toward the back of the compartment. Behind him, Andrew heard Mila cry out again. He tried to turn his head, but Cu Zanthus tightened his grip on his neck, keeping his face turned forward.

"You promised you wouldn't kill her!" Andrew said.

"We're *not*! We want her alive. Pull yourself together."

"You swear?"

"Yes! *You're* the one who's gonna end up dead, acting that way!"

Delayed adrenaline surged through Andrew. He put a hand to his forehead. "I'm sorry–"

"*Focus*, Andrew. We were talking about Holland."

"Holland!" He looked forward, where he could just see her feet. She appeared to be on her hands and knees, no doubt trying to find the arphanium shard Mila had knocked from her hand. Mila's shouts were fading; he thought they were probably taking her up top. Andrew hesitated, but only for a second. Cu Zanthus had said they wanted Mila alive, probably because of that mark she had. Holland also had a mark. They wouldn't kill her, either.

He bolted forward and rounded the small doorway. Holland was on her stomach, her hand out of sight in the section of floor Mila had removed. She looked back at the sound of his footsteps, her eyes wide and terrified. Andrew ran forward and grabbed her other hand, the one with the makeshift bandage on it. He tried to pull her away from the compartment. She shoved him off, baring her teeth. He could see her other hand in the darkness, illuminated by the slight glow of the arphanium pipe. Her fingers were barely gripping it, as if she'd just stretched far enough to reach it.

Cu Zanthus came in right behind Andrew. He grabbed Holland's legs and yanked her out. Holland howled in pain as her battered body slid across the rough floor. But she was still clutching that arphanium within her fingertips.

"Andrew! Take it from him!" Cu Zanthus shouted.

"Kommandir! What's the hold up?" called Leuftkernel Lyanirus from the bigger section.

Andrew lunged for Holland's other side. She chopped the blade of her hand down on the bridge of his nose. He reeled back, half-blinded by pain. Holland freed one of her feet and kicked Cu Zanthus in the jaw, snapping his head back. Then she curled her legs away from him – and was gone.

Andrew peered up, hands over his bleeding nose and tears of pain standing in his eyes. Cu Zanthus was raising himself to a crouch, one hand against his jaw.

Lyanirus stood in the doorway, staring down at them in fury. "*Hollanelea was here?*" he roared. "Why didn't you say something?" His gaze shot to Andrew. His lips thinned and he raised the gun again.

But before he could fire, Holland appeared behind Lyanirus. She grabbed his shoulder. Andrew only had time to see her murderous glare, pinned directly on him, before she vanished again, taking the officer with her.

Andrew pulled his hands down. He used his sleeve to wipe the blood away, though his arm was shaking badly. "I thought–" he began.

Cu Zanthus leaned forward and slapped him across the face, hard. Andrew jerked back in shock. He stared at Cu Zanthus, trying to remember how to breathe.

"How could you let him go?" Cu Zanthus snapped. "What is *wrong* with you? Now he's taken the *leuftkernel!* Do you know how bad this is?"

Heat washed across Andrew's cheeks, followed by a crippling wave of shame. "I'm sorry! I tried–"

"Did you? If you hadn't stopped back there to check on your sister, we would have made it before he got away. This isn't *good* enough, Andrew! If you want to be my partner, you need to act first and think later, and you *damn* well don't worry about whether your target got bruised while they were trying to kill you! Do you hear me?"

"I'm sorry. I'm sorry! I just – everything happened so fast–"

"Where did he go? *Where did Holland go?*"

Andrew struggled to get himself under control before Cu Zanthus hit him again. "Sh- shrouding! That shrouding realm, the one from the notes."

"The one with the *monsters?*"

"Yes! And the ring and the smoke and the volcanoes and the…"

Cu Zanthus cursed, cutting him off once more. Andrew turned away and put his face between his knees, pressing his hands as hard as he could to the sides of his head. He wanted to keep pouring out apologies, excuses, to say how much he hated himself, *anything* to make Cu Zanthus forgive him; but he was also sure that Cu Zanthus would strike him again at any moment, so he forced himself to hold the words and the panic back, though he felt it would kill him. He just wanted to be gone. Gone somewhere so far and so small that he'd never have to look at himself or anyone else again – somewhere he could cease to exist at all.

He felt Cu Zanthus's hands around his wrists, pulling them down. He tried to push himself away, but Cu Zanthus wrapped his arms around him and drew him close. Andrew found his head pressed close to the Dhavnak soldier's chest, the man's heartbeat strong and steady in his ears.

"Calm down," said Cu Zanthus quietly. "I know you'll do better next time."

Another wave of humiliation washed over Andrew. He closed his eyes tight. He felt like he couldn't breathe.

"Yes," he finally choked out. "I will. I promise."

Chapter 23

KLARA YANA'S RETALIATION

The bullet meant for Andrew shattered the still silence of the shrouding realm, sending a spray of rocks from the sheer cliff rising straight above them. Klara Yana let go of Lyanirus immediately and took two quick steps backward, lifting her palm from the arphanium just long enough so she could make the connection again and shroud back out. But Lyanirus whipped around, faster than she would have thought possible, and slammed the pistol down on her left wrist. Her hand went numb, and the pipe tumbled from her fingers. Lyanirus shoved the barrel of the gun under her chin, pushing her head back, and forced her backward until she hit the cliff wall. One of the suns, smaller than even Bitu Lan, shone weakly through the smoke overhead. The wide starry ring arced across the sky beneath. She didn't think Lyanirus had even noticed it. Somewhere above them, a low moan sounded, ending after several moments in a screeching cough. Lyanirus didn't seem to notice that, either. He just stared down at her, his green eyes glittering in the shade from the cliff.

"I didn't think it was possible," he said. "I thought I was imagining things. But now that I see you again..." He shook his head, laughing under his breath. "You're a woman. And not just any woman. You're Ambassador Talgeron's daughter. Aren't you?"

Even though she'd half-expected it, the confirmation still came as a shock. She fought her sudden surge of fear down, but she could tell by the leuftkernel's smirk that he'd seen it on her face.

"What have you done with her?" Klara Yana said.

"What have *I* done with her?" Lyanirus raised his eyebrows. "Your ama *broke the law*. She used government funds to incite movements and rebellion from Dhavnakir to Vassis to Descar. How is this about what *I've* done?"

"She did all that?"

"Oh yes. And even then, I would have been happy to let her serve her sentence out in one of our lighter labor camps. But she hadn't been there even five cycles before she broke free, changed her name, and fled to Belzen. I suppose she thought *they* could help get her daughter out of Dhavnakir. Well. She was wrong."

Something turned over in Klara Yana's stomach even before Lyanirus spoke his next words, watching her closely as he did.

"Belzen killed her."

The ground seemed to rock beneath Klara Yana's feet. "No," she whispered.

"You and your partner brought us the information yourselves," he said. "Idyna Larine Onosylvani. That was the alias she used. Sound familiar?"

Klara Yana heard Zurlig's dying words in her head, as she'd struggled to make Blackwood understand. *President Wixxer gave her to SAI, for studying. It was because of her...*

She shook her head, trying to shove herself farther back into the cliff. Trying to get away from the things he was saying. "You're lying."

"Denial is such a cowardly trait. No wonder you were a terrible agent."

"No!" she shot back. "I mean, you're *lying* about Belzen killing her! It was a Dhavnak assassin! Everyone knows that."

A slow smile spread across Lyanirus's face, very like the one he'd given her right before beating her. "You might call it a combination. There was an accident in the lab, but it triggered the explosives wired underneath. If it's any consolation, Kommandir Ayaterossi never knew he was partnered afterward with the child of the woman he killed. Then again, how could he have?"

"Cu Zanthus?" Klara Yana said sharply. "But he was just a kid then!"

"Yes, and only a child's body could fit in the conduits beneath the laboratory. Why do you think we recruited him at fourteen?"

"I figured it was because of Andrew…" she began.

"No. That wasn't until later. After we found out we needed the research from the scientists who worked there."

"So you sent him to befriend the boy whose parents he'd murdered?" Klara Yana felt sick. "That's just…"

"Befriend? We sent him to *target* the kid. You really don't understand this whole agent business, do you? But then, you were never expected to. There's a reason we don't employ *women* in these positions, after all." His hand came up, wrapping around her neck and shoving her farther into the rocky cliff. The gun was still tight under her chin. "That's what this was about, wasn't it? Finding your ama? What a sad stupid ending to your pathetic story."

"You'll never get back to Mirrix without me," she said, putting as much force into the words as she could.

Lyanirus barked out a laugh. "I can still use your palm if you're dead. In fact, I can cut off your hand and carry it around with me. Might be easier than hauling *you* around. Although… gods, I'd get such better use out of you with a whole body." His eyes roamed down her dirty Dhavnak uniform. He licked his lips. "It's liberal bitches like you that are stripping our whole culture of its fertility, by blaspheming against the gods. Maybe Shon Aha would reward me if I dragged one of you back into line."

Her stomach clenched with nausea and fear. *Grab the gun! Do something! Don't freeze! Not now…*

"Feel good about this, Hollanelea," said Lyanirus, running the gun barrel over her bruised cheek. "If you provide your country with *my* child, I'll let it be known to all that Shon Aha himself forgave you. It will be a godsent sign that it's not too late for Dhavnakir to turn back to the ways of the brotherhood. *You* would be an example to every man or woman who's gone astray."

She drew in a strangled breath, her teeth clenched over a scream. Weapons – none. Anonymity – gone. *Blackwood will die if I don't get back*, Klara Yana thought desperately. *She's been captured. She's counting on me.* But she kept flashing back to Lyanirus choking her, kicking her, the knife digging into her finger, her certainty he was going to kill her. She dug her teeth into her lip. *If Klara Yana isn't brave enough to go for that gun, I need to be someone who is.*

Her eyes drifted closed. And she put together a new character. A woman. One who did what she had to, no matter the cost. Like Chief Sea Officer Blackwood. Like Dela Savene. Like Ama. A woman who would never be paralyzed by fear, especially in front of a scuzbanger like this.

She opened her eyes. Fear flickered for just a second, but she pushed it aside. *Just a character. Like any other mission.* She grabbed the barrel of his pistol, shoving it to the side. With her other hand, she punched him in the face, putting all her strength behind it. His grip on the gun loosened just enough for her to tear it from his grasp. He cursed and lunged for her, but she was already scooting away along the face of the cliff. She raised the gun.

But as she twitched her finger to fire, excruciating pain shot from her fingertip to her wrist, and the finger itself failed to respond at all. Vo Hina's mercy, the injury! She struggled to readjust her grip before he reached her. She'd just transferred the gun to her left hand when Lyanirus's fist slammed into her skull. The sheer force of the blow drove her against the cliff. Pain exploded through her side and ribs. Frantically, she got the pistol into position again, and squeezed the trigger. The noise of the gunshot left her ears ringing. Hot blood poured over the hand holding the gun. He fell, his weight bearing them both to the ground. Klara Yana fired again, her breath coming in short, sharp gasps. Another gush of blood spilled over her stomach, and his body sagged over hers. She finally scrambled free, not taking her eyes off him for a second.

Lyanirus was pulling himself up, one hand over his stomach. His features were distorted in rage.

"You're just like your ama," he spat. "An utter disgrace to your country and your gods."

Klara Yana raised the gun, pointing it at his head. "This has nothing to do with our *gods*, Lyanirus. You brought this on yourself. Not Vo Hina. Not Shon Aha. You."

Her finger tightened on the trigger. But her eye fell on something behind him the second before she squeezed it. A segmented body, materializing from the cliff's side. It looked like a long snake, with grotesque, multi-jointed legs spreading from beneath, giving the ground the look of a broken window, riddled with cracks. Her gaze followed the body forward. Long, sinuous curves, and a massive head at the end of it all… tight crimson flesh, huge black pupils, flames wreathing its scalp. Klara Yana froze. There was no denying it. The creature looked like Shon Aha.

Lyanirus, noticing her attention drift, looked over his shoulder. His breath came out in a croak. "It can't be. Is that…" His gaze shot back to Klara Yana. "What *is* this place, anyway?"

"*Niss-mala-strana!*" the creature growled. Its voice, though pitched low, reverberated from the landscape around her. Klara Yana's gaze flicked between the monster and Lyanirus. It hadn't asked about the *caeg* – the arphanium – as she'd expected. Not yet, anyway. Nevertheless, she cast her eyes over the rocky ground for the dropped arphanium pipe, her heart beating faster. If this monster found it before she did… there was no saying. It might go back to Mirrix. It might go on a murderous rampage. And she herself would be trapped here…

The creature snarled again, twice as loudly as before. "*Niss-mala-strana-shonaha!*"

Klara Yana's gaze darted up. "Shonaha?" she repeated.

In response, a bolt of lightning shot from the murky sky, striking the towering cliff on her left and sending shards of rock flying all around them. The sudden flash left her eyes burning. A crack of thunder rolled through like a wave. The creature's voice sounded over the crash, forming words in its barely-comprehensible tongue.

"*Niss-mala-shonaha!*" it roared, gesturing with its flaming head where the strike had hit. "*Niss-mala?*"

Klara Yana drew a ragged breath. It wasn't talking about itself, she realized. It was talking about the *lightning*.

Shonaha was its word for lightning.

It left her reeling. If the name of the Synivistic main god was just a term to these creatures, then who *was* the monster before her? Actually a Synivistic god? Or something else? *Vo Hina, help me. By the gods. Vo Hina...*

Another strike of lightning cracked the sky. Somewhere, an explosion sounded, ten times louder than the thunder she'd heard previously. High above, at the top of the cliff, a mounting rumbling echoed over the barren land, like massive rocks grinding together. Klara Yana's breath came short, her gaze moving faster. She *had* to find that pipe.

Lyanirus let out a sudden gasp. Klara Yana's head jerked up. Another creature had appeared in front of him, seemingly without warning. It was the same one she'd spoken with – the one that just might be Vo Hina. The creature was glaring at the leuftkernel with her one green and golden eye. A second later, she looked up, pinning that gaze on Klara Yana.

"*Rana-illum-mala-hiri?*" she said, her voice crisp.

Lyanirus looked from the creature to Klara Yana, his jaw clenching. "That's *Vo Hina!*" he ground out.

"I..." began Klara Yana.

"Your eyes. By the gods! Your betrayal..."

"What are you talking about?" Klara Yana said. She held her gun out, not even sure where to point it anymore. The first creature – the one resembling Shon Aha – had slowly turned its serpentine body to face the other one.

"*Vo Hina's Clannama*, that's what I'm *talking* about!" Lyanirus spat the words out like a curse.

"*What?*" Klara Yana said incredulously. "The hypothetical descendants of... of Galene Marduc and Vo Hina? Are you serious?"

"Such a massive betrayal to our country could only have been committed by Vo Hina's own children," Lyanirus hissed. "That's why you lived, isn't it? You and your ama both? Because Vo Hina *came* for you? Saved you, when everyone else who ever shrouded ended up dead?"

Klara Yana went cold. *Shared blood.* That's what he was saying. It was hard to believe, but her eyes... they matched that creature's. Her ama had had them, too – and she, too, had survived an encounter during shrouding. *And Blackwood?* Would the chief sea officer have ever survived if not for Klara Yana being there? As Blackwood had pointed out, every previous encounter had ended in slaughter. *If Lyanirus is right, it could be my presence that saved their lives!* But it was small consolation; it had been Klara Yana herself who'd brought in the dekatite and caused the attack in the first place.

Unless Blackwood's government was *wrong* about the monsters being drawn to dekatite. It was arphanium they wanted. *The black and white gems of the valleys and mountains.* Those were the elements that Vo Hina had hoarded, along with humankind's souls. The goddess would have needed both dekatite *and* arphanium to trap the gods away from the humans, as Andrew believed. After all these hundreds of thousands of cycles… were the gods still drawn to *both* substances? *Maybe it draws them strongest when they're together.* And Vo Hina herself – drawn to Klara Yana, but barely in time to save her.

Vo Hina's Clannama. The genes of a god. Or… something else, maybe. *Another life form.*

Klara Yana was pulled abruptly from her thoughts as the first creature *moved*, as fast as the lightning it commanded. One spindly leg shot forward and seized the leuftkernel, wrapping its finger-like appendages around his body and squeezing tight. Lyanirus let out an excruciating scream as blood ran in crimson rivers over the jointed limbs. Klara Yana stumbled back with her hands over her mouth, barely holding back a scream of her own.

"*Galene!*" the other creature snapped. Her wispy hair blew and broke like clouds as she whipped her head around. "*Rana-urtezi-falb!*"

"I… falb. Yes. Run." Klara Yana wrenched her gaze away from her commanding officer, searching desperately for the crystal. Lyanirus's shrieks grew louder, pummeling her skull. Beneath it, she could hear her creature's – Vo Hina's – voice, yelling something at the other one. Another strobe of lightning danced just outside her field of vision. As it faded, she finally saw a faint glow in the craggy rocks, nestled deep in a wide crack. She knelt and reached her fingers in, trying to wiggle the chunk of arphanium to the surface. It held fast.

"Hollanelea!" Lyanirus howled. "Help me. Please. *Please!*"

She couldn't take it anymore. She brought the pistol up, turned, and emptied the magazine into the bleeding mess that had once been the leuftkernel. After the third shot, his screams ceased abruptly. For a second, the only sounds were the echo of the gunshots and that terrible grinding high overhead. The fire-haired creature's huge head swung in her direction, big red eyes narrowed. A thick blue-green mist hung opposite him, where Vo Hina had been, but Klara Yana could already see her form coalescing again behind the creature. She was moving through reality unseen. *Like shrouding,* Klara Yana thought. But it was more ethereal than anything Klara Yana or the submarine did, and it certainly wasn't through Mirrix.

Then again, Vo Hina didn't have arphanium.

The fire-headed creature – Shon Aha – seemed to sense Vo Hina's presence, and started to whip around. But Vo Hina solidified with her arms latched around his upper body. She wrenched him toward the cliff, twisting his body violently, and Klara Yana saw something tear within his sinuous folds. An awful yellowish-black goop streamed down his skin and onto the craggy ground. Shon Aha roared, and the world flashed suddenly and blindingly bright in every direction. Her heart stuttering with fear, Klara Yana turned her attention back to the arphanium, prying with her fingertips to get it loose. Why wouldn't the cursed shard come out?

Another crack of lightning split the sky, with thunder crashing behind it like an aerial blast. Klara Yana flinched, expecting to be ripped apart any second. A loud cry sounded from above her. She looked up and gasped.

Vo Hina stood over her. The top of her misty head was seared black, and the smell of burning was overpowering. She'd *blocked* the lightning bolt – surely one that would have taken Klara Yana's life.

Third time. This was the third time she'd saved her life. *Because she came for you. Saved you, when everyone else who ever shrouded ended up dead.* Klara Yana gazed up at her and felt her throat tightening with a gamut of emotions. Ten cycles she'd lived without her ama, and she'd known only a scant handful of people since who cared whether she lived or died. And now one of them – her own guardian from another realm, never mind whatever else she was – would be gone too, nearly as fast as she'd found her.

Snatched away. Just like her ama.

"I'm sorry," she whispered.

"*Galene*," Vo Hina said, her voice low and deliberate.

"I know. I… I promise I won't let him have the arphanium. No matter what happens."

Vo Hina started to answer, but then she darted her head back just in time to see Shon Aha slam into her with a meaty thunk. No trick of evanescence saved her this time. Tendrils of lightning danced across both their bodies, leaving brilliant afterimages flashing across Klara Yana's sight. Far overhead, at the top of the cliff, a churning mess of red and black sludge tipped over the edge.

Klara Yana turned back to the ground. With one hard jerk, she broke the arphanium. One piece fell back into the crevice, but the other slipped free, barely grasped between two fingers. She stumbled back, curling her fingers inward to press the crystal against her left palm.

She cried out as an appendage whipped out and snagged her wrist. The shrouding realm vanished around her.

Chapter 24

BLACKWOOD'S BATTLE

The Early Sun sank toward the western horizon, as the Main Sun burned a late afternoon heat onto the reinforced metal deck. Kheppra Isle was barely visible to the north, over the Trievanic Sea's sparkling ripples. A steady trickle of smoke rose from the top of it, leaving a slight haze and an ashy smell in the air.

Blackwood, spent from struggling, slumped against the anti-aircraft gun in the center of the deck. Only a single soldier held her hands behind her back now, though another stood nearby, rifle at the ready. Blackwood glanced at the conning tower where another pair stood, one on a radio, the other peering through a small scope. The atmosphere was tense. She heard the word *leuftkernel* being tossed around a lot, as well as *kommandir*. For the moment, she gathered, they were waiting on that autorotor to return and hadn't expected to be out here without a commanding officer. They knew there were enough explosives beneath their feet to blow up a small island, and wanted to be off the boat.

Another surge of nausea churned Blackwood's stomach. Again she pictured the black-jacketed officer with his gun pressed into Andrew's forehead, and again she heard the bang in her head that had never come. She heaved, but she had nothing left in her stomach. The soldier holding her wrists made a noise of disgust, and muttered something to the man on the left. Something about women's weak stomachs, no doubt.

Blackwood tried to focus. The lightning. If she hit the submarine right now, in the right place, the whole thing could blow, long before reaching Marldox. If it weren't for Andrew down there somewhere, she'd have done it already. *If I'd never joined the navy? If I'd been a better listener? If I'd chosen not to trust him with a fifteen year-old Dhavnak boy, merely because of the rumors of a war?* She shook her head violently. She couldn't change the past, and wouldn't know where to start if she could. The bottom line was, Andrew was in over his head, and no one else would save him. Not any of these soldiers, not that traitor Holland, and *definitely* not Cu Zanthus, no matter what Andrew thought.

The access hatch near the conning tower opened, and Cu Zanthus climbed up. Blackwood still wasn't used to this older, harder-looking version of him, with the dark hair. Not someone *she* would have called handsome, with his too-large ears and square chin, but it was still easy to see why Andrew had gone for him. It wasn't just the looks, though; she knew that instinctually. Cu Zanthus had been exactly who he needed. Someone who listened and didn't judge, and told him what he wanted to hear. A combination of disgust and guilt turned her stomach.

One of the soldiers on the conning tower yelled to Cu Zanthus. *Something something leuftkernel something something something*, ending in a gesture at the hazy sky. Cu Zanthus got his feet on the deck, and leaned down to pull Andrew up behind him. Blackwood started breathing again. Andrew caught sight of her halfway out, but jerked his eyes away quickly. Once fully out of the access hatch, he slunk to the base of the conning tower and huddled against it, eyes fastened on Cu Zanthus. There was a red mark on his cheek she didn't remember. Blackwood's jaw clenched, and she slid her eyes back to Cu Zanthus.

He was answering the soldier. No gestures from him, just a commanding tone with an edge of anger. The soldier saluted with that strange combination that crossed both face and chest, using only one fist, then went back to scanning the sky. The soldier beside him got back on the radio and made a vague rounding-up gesture toward the other soldiers on the deck – some ten of them just on the bow, with who knew how many on the other side of the conning tower. They wouldn't all fit in an autorotor. Some of these had been on the boat already and would leave on inflatables, so the officers at the base wouldn't suspect anything. The submarine was probably already running on auto-pilot, as they all prepared to disembark. Blackwood hadn't seen anything to indicate there were Belzenes on board. At this point, she would just have to assume there weren't.

But where was Holland? Were both he *and* the leuftkernel missing?

Blackwood watched Cu Zanthus, striding across the deck and barking commands to the soldiers at the rails. Now that she was looking for it, she saw his agitation. He slid into the role of commander easily, despite looking younger than almost anyone there, but his body was too stiff, his words too forced, his face too tight. He hadn't been expecting to do this alone. The leuftkernel was gone, and it hadn't been either him or Andrew who had done it. That left only one possibility: Holland had shrouded the leuftkernel away. Double agent then? Or had he just received contradictary orders?

The beating sound of blades hit her ears. The autorotor was finally in sight, coming from the direction of the island. A few of the men cheered. Others looked uneasily at the access hatch, as if still waiting for their commanding officer to return. Blackwood looked to Andrew again, and caught him staring at her. Glaring, as if everything were her fault. *If I'd made Holland take him somewhere else, where Cu Zanthus wouldn't have found him?* No. Here and now. Cu Zanthus would take Andrew on the 'rotor, she was certain. At some point, whether Blackwood herself was still on the boat or not, Andrew *wouldn't* be… and *that* was when she could strike it with lightning. When he was just far enough to be safe.

After that, Andrew would be on his own with Cu Zanthus, one way or another. *I have to get through to him before then. But* how?

What had Holland said? *His fears and desires are just as real to him.* How could that help her? Andrew feared her, and desired Cu Zanthus. Or… no. That wasn't quite right. He got agitated at her often, but he wasn't *scared* of her, not really.

An image came back to her, of twelve year-old Andrew motionless in bed and staring at the wall. *Fears and desires.* To lose both parents at that age must have made the whole world feel unstable, as if anyone could vanish at any second. No wonder he'd been afraid to reach out again. But five years ago, Cu Zanthus had made it happen – he'd brought back light and hope, and maybe even tentative trust. And then both he and Blackwood had left, almost simultaneously, leaving Andrew reeling all over again.

No. It wasn't his sister Andrew feared. He'd *told* her his worst fear, right in that basement in Ellemko, and it had rolled right past her. *They're gone, you're gone, and I'm alone, Mila.*

Blackwood's next thought hit her like a blow. *I shouldn't have left.* It wasn't the familiar guilt that spoke this time, heavy with excuses, but a deep conviction that she'd taken the last vestige of solidarity in his life and thrown it away. And there was nothing she could do to fix it. She couldn't promise him she'd always be there, especially not now. But she'd be damned if she left him thinking for the rest of his life that no one had ever cared.

Andrew is not my enemy. Three deep breaths. *He's my brother.*

She looked away from the 'rotor and back toward the conning tower. "Andrew! I need to tell you something."

Both the guard holding her and the one nearby glanced over at her voice. But either the Belzene words meant nothing to them or they didn't have orders to keep them from talking, because they turned back to the approaching autorotor after just a second. Only Andrew kept his eyes fastened on her, his expression even harder than before.

She pitched her voice loud enough to carry over the approaching 'rotor. "I shouldn't have left you to raise yourself at fifteen. And I'm not just saying that because of Cu Zanthus. It wasn't fair to you. It wasn't fair to *either* of us. I'm sorry. I hope – someday – that you can forgive me."

Andrew's brow drew down, as if Blackwood had said the last thing he expected. He straightened, his gaze flicking to Cu Zanthus at the other end of the boat, then back to her. "*Someday?*" he repeated, an edge to his voice.

"You're not alone," Blackwood said. "You're not alone in still trying to figure the world out. You're not alone in learning. You're not alone if you think things should have been different. Whatever happens, from here on out, remember that. You are *not alone*. And you never have been."

The sound of the autorotor's propellers thrummed louder as it came directly overhead. The blink of a solar cell from its tail flashed into Blackwood's eye. The force of its blades sent a windstorm over the whole deck, tossing her curls into her face. Blackwood didn't dare look away from Andrew.

He took a single step closer. A look of urgency had come over his face. "Mila!" he said, clearly straining to make his voice heard. "What are you gonna do?"

"I'm still with you, Andrew," she said. "Don't forget it. You hear me?"

"Mila, *no*, you can't just *stand* there and tell me you—"

Suddenly, Cu Zanthus was at his side, taking his arm. Andrew flinched at his touch, and clammed up instantly. His eyes stayed on her, wide and frenzied. Cu Zanthus barked something at the guard who had her wrists, ending with an angry jerk of his head toward her. The guard answered, his expression terse. She couldn't hear their words, and couldn't imagine they could hear each other, either. Cu Zanthus shook his head. He jabbed a finger first at her, then at the rope now dangling from the autorotor. The guard shoved her forward.

Blackwood glanced back just long enough to make sure Cu Zanthus was planning to bring Andrew up behind her. How far away would they need to be before she risked that strike? Would Cu Zanthus kill her afterward? Right in front of Andrew?

But what about Holland? Her breath suddenly came short. She didn't know anymore. If he'd taken the leuftkernel, maybe she'd been wrong about him. He might come back. And if the submarine was in the process of blowing up, or was sinking to the bottom of the ocean, Holland would be dead. As fast as that. *Xeil's grace. Could I live with myself?*

She was almost to the rope when the submarine bucked beneath their feet. Blackwood's foot slid and she slammed to the deck. Her thigh erupted in pain. A couple soldiers were thrown over the rail. Blackwood, her hands free now, clawed herself to a halt as the boat righted itself. Her foot dangled over the edge. She looked around wildly for Andrew, and found him wrapped around one of the ladder rungs leading up to the conning tower, his face ashen. Cu Zanthus, at his side, was already back on his feet, gesturing emphatically for the soldier who'd let go of Blackwood to continue loading her up. The soldier leaned down to grab her, but his lips were moving in some desperate prayer – *like Holland*, Blackwood couldn't help remembering – and his hands shook as he tried to pull her up.

Blackwood shoved him off and got to her feet, limping as fast as possible toward Andrew. She expected the guard to grab her again, but he didn't. She started to glance back, but the boat lurched a second time. She kept her weight low and didn't go down. She could hear the shrieks of the men now; the autorotor had backed off, no doubt because of the pilot's fears of the submarine exploding. *No. Not yet. Not yet!*

The access hatch burst open as Blackwood passed it, and Holland poked his head out. He spotted Blackwood immediately.

"CSO!" he yelled. "I shrouded back – he touched me right when I – he was throwing lightning and – and then this lava came down, and he grabbed me – I tried to send him back, but he got away–"

Blackwood leaned over and took his arm, hauling him out in one swift move. In his right hand, Holland clutched his chunk of arphanium, his bandaged forefinger the only one not closed around it. His garrison cap was gone and his Dhavvie uniform jacket was covered in blood – not quite dry, by the look of it.

"Did you take the leuftkernel? Did you shroud him?" Blackwood shouted.

"Yes, ma'am!"

"Killed him?"

Holland glanced down at his jacket, then back up. "Yes, ma'am!"

"Are you *with* us? The truth!"

"Yes, ma'am! I swear!"

The boat swayed in the other direction and Holland staggered back, stumbling as one foot fell into the open access hatch. Blackwood caught herself on the hatch door, throwing another quick look around the deck. It was madness. Some soldiers clung to the rails, while others leapt into the water and swam away as fast as possible. No one was paying the least bit of attention to her or Holland.

The minute the boat was even slightly upright again, Blackwood pulled Holland away from the hatch.

"Those creatures want to get back here, CSO!" Holland said urgently, staying at a low crouch. "I'm sure of it! I'll tell you everything, I *promise*, ma'am, but right now–"

"It talked to you, did it?"

"Yes, ma'am. We don't have much time. Please, we have to go!"

Blackwood ground her teeth and glanced toward Andrew. He was clinging to Cu Zanthus's jacket and staring at the two of them wide-eyed. He was close enough that he'd probably heard every word. Cu Zanthus was screaming into a radio, while his free hand beckoned vigorously for the autorotor to come closer. The pilot seemed to be ignoring Cu Zanthus as completely as Cu Zanthus was ignoring Andrew.

Which meant there was almost no chance of Andrew getting off the submarine on that autorotor. Blackwood was out of options. Dhavvie spy or not, Holland was all she had.

She turned back to him. "Get my brother and get him out of here!"

"I can take you first, CSO–" Holland said.

"*No*! Get Andrew safe. Now!"

"I can bring you both!"

"Right now, this boat is set to hit Marldox. I *will not* leave until I personally see it stopped or destroyed. Whether there's a monster on it or not. Whether I'm on it or not. But I *don't* want you or Andrew here. Is that clear?"

Holland gaped. "Are you saying the second we're gone–"

"Don't argue, Holland! And don't you dare shroud back to this boat once you're gone. I can't have the distraction. *Am I clear?*"

Holland hesitated, then saluted. "Ma'am." He turned and took off across the deck without looking back. Blackwood limped in the other direction to open the access hatch over the aft power room. Halfway there, she heard Andrew start screaming.

"Mila! The lightning! Don't let it use the lightning! The darkness–"

And then his voice cut off, as abruptly as it had begun. Blackwood darted a look over her shoulder. Andrew, Cu Zanthus, and Holland were gone. She drew in a shaky breath. *Don't let it use the lightning.* What was he trying to tell her? How could she *stop* it from using it? And why was that his focus all of a sudden?

Blackwood turned back to the hatch. Andrew was barely reliable, and now was hardly the time to worry about it. She lowered herself and braced her feet on the gauges of the control panel, then pried open the overhead slats. The submarine life rafts were in here, in big yellow canvas bags. One at a time, she heaved them onto the deck. Four of them – enough for twenty-four people. She doubted any of the Dhavvies would get far, but it was a chance she was willing to throw them, if only because it was a chance for her too.

She was just pulling herself back up when a huge, muscled creature crashed headlong through the interior wall at her left, just beneath her feet. The boat heaved with its weight. She clung to the lip of the hatch, staring back down into the submarine. The same burning head she'd seen before, huge teeth, wide black eyes. Sparks danced over its body, sending equipment hissing and sizzling. Blackwood cringed. If Holland had shrouded this thing to the lower flats where the bombs were, instead of the aft torpedo room, they'd be dead already.

One of those crimson eyes latched onto her, where she hung half-in, half-out of the access hatch.

"*Tre*," it breathed through its jagged teeth. "*Tre-ta-oncho-okmi*."

Blackwood scrambled from the hatch and slammed it shut behind her, closing the monster inside the sub.

"OK. OK," she whispered under her breath. Dhavnak men still ran rampant over the deck, but several had jumped overboard and were swimming toward the autorotor. Two of the life rafts she'd tossed out had been dragged to the rail, and one was even half-inflated. Thank Xeil; some of the men up here were submariners that had been sent to pilot the boat, and knew what they were doing. It lightened her work load. She opened the straps of the closest bag and yanked out the high pressure cylinder and pump, then hollered to one of the other men.

"Get this operational! *Quick!*"

She left him to try to figure it out, and jogged – or rather, limped briskly – across the deck toward the conning tower. Something slammed against the underside of the deck, sending vibrations through the metal planks. The submarine tossed sickeningly. Blackwood caught herself on the huge barrel of the anti-aircraft gun, using it to anchor herself as she checked both sides of the conning tower as best she could. No one; even the soldiers nearby had taken flight now. Bobbing heads speckled the water, swimming away as fast as possible.

She turned back to see whether any life rafts had been launched yet – and saw the monster from the shrouding realm rearing its gigantic body through the access hatch. Just the part that was out was twice as tall as she was, its body bulging far too wide for the small opening. The steel of the hull, thicker than the interior bulkheads, creaked at its pressure. Beyond it, she saw the barely-filled life raft bobbing in the ocean, several men crammed onto it, and another completely packed one, floating with two hangers-on just behind. She didn't think there was a single man left on the boat now. At least not on the deck.

Lightning crashed down from the sky, hitting the conning tower behind her. The galvanized energy from the strike washed across the steel and up through the AA gun she held, jolting her whole body. She felt her muscles lock tight as the energy coursed through them. Horror filled her. The monster was going to take her out, right now; she wouldn't have time to swim to a life raft, wouldn't have time to kill it, wouldn't have any way to stop the *Desert Crab* getting all the way to Belzen if the monster didn't blow it up beforehand. Whoever had that detonator could still get there and trigger the explosives, if they didn't find some other way to ignite them. She had waited too long.

No. The mark on her forearm was buzzing with energy, almost as if responding to the monster's power. *Don't let it use the lightning.* Well, it was too late now. And that lightning – the power she may have gotten from this very monster during the attack – was the only weapon she had. She would *use* it to kill that beast, if it was the last thing she did.

Her whole body began to tingle in resonance with the mark, from the soles of her feet to the palms of her hands. Intense cold flooded her. She gritted her teeth and sent her will up toward the sky, clutching intangibly for the energy she'd used before.

A bright flash of light lit up the sky to her left. Stabbing pain erupted over the burn mark. Blackwood slid down the AA gun, her body trembling violently with sudden weakness. She saw the creature clinging to the deck now, its chitinous legs scrabbling madly to pull its body from the hatch and get to her. It was only about a body's length away now. Lightning seared in front of Blackwood's eyes, splashing against the nose of the submarine with a loud crackle. She felt the backlash from the strike wash over the steel of the boat, jarring her to her teeth.

She'd hoped to hit the beast. She'd hoped to blow up the boat around it. But the submarine had been hit at least a couple times now, and the bombs hadn't gone off. It wasn't working.

Slowly, painfully, Blackwood pulled herself back toward the open hatch directly in front of the conning tower. There was still the self-destruct system. She'd fixed the severed wire. She just had to make it to the control room – or, more likely, into the conning tower above that, where the captain would have been during battles. If she could get to that, she could take care of both of these problems, once and for all.

A bolt of light streaked from overhead again, washing the world blindingly white. The boat pitched, and Blackwood rolled. She threw out an elbow and stopped herself, her back scraping excruciatingly against the steel deck. But she didn't have time to recover before her body went rigid, as galvanized energy poured through her. Thunder erupted like a sonic blast. The lightning had struck dangerously close; maybe it had even struck her.

She tried to get up, but she seemed to be glued to the steel deck. Currents of voltage coursed through her body. She tried to move her arm, her leg, her head, *anything*, but the muscles stayed locked. Her own body had become a prison. She knew, without a doubt, that she was about to die.

Move. Just move. The conning tower is right there. All I have to do…

The monster was suddenly above her, huge eyes narrowed, jagged teeth bared. "*Chenel-gabell-mo-cumachas-beaatha!*"

Blackwood focused, harder than she ever had before. She focused on bringing energy forward from every switch, every wire, every solar cell and humming motor, every battery and generator, within the *Desert Crab*. She focused on pulling the power *up* through the surface of the deck and concentrating it all on this center of gravity that stood over her. She focused on the flash powder and dynamite inside the Dhavnak explosives.

She felt a surge of energy, more powerful than anything yet. The blinding light in the sky pulsed, held a beat too long, then fluttered and died. Thunder washed over them in one last earsplitting crash that seemed to shake the boat like a piece of debris. The creature reared and let out a roar. Its head whipped from side to side. The deck beneath Blackwood's back heated so fast and so hot that it was like being dropped on an oven. Clouds of black and orange surged toward her from either side.

Then suddenly, Holland was sliding beneath the beast. He threw his body atop Blackwood's. The *Desert Crab* vanished. The monster vanished. There was a flicker of stars, a painful stab of cold after the excruciating heat, then hard cement beneath her back. In the distance, Blackwood heard the low boom of the explosives, ripping apart both her submarine and the mysterious creature from another world.

Chapter 25

KLARA YANA'S DECISION

Klara Yana pushed herself up from Blackwood's prone body. They were far back in Kheppra's submarine pen, deeply hidden in the shadows. At the entrance out to the ocean, Klara Yana could see Dhavnak soldiers running over the ramps connecting the dock to their one remaining smooth, black submarine. The air was stiflingly hot. Hollow booms sounded from somewhere outside the dekatite walls, sounding distant and surreal.

Klara Yana started to step forward, but Blackwood's fingers snagged her wrist at the last second. She glanced down. She could barely make out Blackwood's glare in the dim lighting. The chief sea officer was still rigid with paralysis from the galvanized shock she'd received, but she forced a word through her locked jaw, just as she'd forced those fingers around Klara Yana's wrist.

"*Andrew.*"

"Yes, I'm getting him, ma'am!" Klara Yana hissed in a whisper. "Just hold on!" She pulled her wrist free and stood, peering anxiously toward the entrance for Blackwood's brother. None of the soldiers were looking in their direction, but that wouldn't last. She regretted her snap decision to bring Andrew and Cu Zanthus here to the Kheppra dock, where she'd been bringing all the other soldiers she'd shrouded off, but there hadn't been time to *think*. Now she'd just have to hope she could snatch Andrew back before Cu Zanthus–

"We have to get off this island! *Now!*"

That was Andrew's voice, shrill and panicked. Klara Yana stepped over Blackwood and jogged forward. She stuck close by the jagged dekatite wall, clutching her arphanium in her non-marked hand. As she neared the soldiers, a tremor rocked the whole walkway beneath her. She threw her arms out for balance. The sound of grating rocks sounded from above the tunnel somewhere. Klara Yana looked back, terrified, but she could still make out Blackwood's body. No rubble had fallen back there.

The men ahead were yelling frantically, but Klara Yana could still make out Andrew's hysterical voice over them.

"Because this volcano is unstable, and Mila, and the monster, the *darkness*, we have to go, we have to go *now*–"

Klara Yana broke into a run, shoving through the Dhavnak soldiers now with reckless abandon. *I should have brought Blackwood somewhere else. I shouldn't have even* attempted *this.* But the CSO would never forgive her if she left her little brother in Cu Zanthus's hands.

Forgiveness? Is that what I'm looking for? But what else *was* there? Her ama was dead. The leuftkernel was dead. Her partner wanted *her* dead. She had nothing.

Nothing.

Something uncomfortably close to a sob caught in her throat. She shoved the despair back brutally. *By all the gods, figure it out* later!

She finally spotted Andrew's dark form in front of the bulbous submarine, his eyes darting from soldier to soldier in desperation. None of them seemed to be listening to him. Cu Zanthus was nowhere in sight.

Klara Yana raced toward Andrew. She *should* be able to grab him, flash back to Blackwood's side with the arphanium, then get the three of them off the island before it blew. It would mean leaving Blackwood alone and paralyzed on the dock with her enemies, but only for the split-second Klara Yana was in the shrouding realm…

Andrew's gaze fell on her and his eyes widened. He opened his mouth. Klara Yana reached out for him. But just before she touched his jacket, an arm wrapped around her neck from behind, yanking her momentum to a jarring halt. She gasped as her left arm was suddenly wrenched up behind her back. Cu Zanthus's voice spoke in her ear.

"Nice of you to show up, Keiller Yano. I almost thought we'd have to leave without you."

Her left hand instinctively curled inward, toward that dekatite mark in her palm. But it was no good. That was the hand Cu Zanthus held, and the arphanium was still in the other one. It might as well have been miles away. Cu Zanthus pushed her hand higher up her spine. She moaned through her teeth at the sudden spike of pain in her shoulder.

"What did you do with the leuftkernel?" Cu Zanthus said in a hard voice.

"He's gone," she ground out.

"You Vo Hina-cursed bastard! You killed him?"

Klara Yana's free hand went to her waist. No gun. Gods, she was caught in the same situation all over again. And Blackwood was as helpless as–

"Let Holland go!"

Klara Yana's head shot up in time to see Andrew Blackwood stumbling back. His hands were wrapped around the grip of the sidearm he'd yanked from Cu Zanthus's hip holster. He pointed the gun at Cu Zanthus.

"What did you say?" her partner said incredulously.

"Holland's the only one who can help Mila!" Andrew said, his breath coming short.

"Help Mila? But–"

The ground shook again, harder than before, and several soldiers screamed and went down. A gust of wind, stinking of sulfur, blasted against them from deep inside the submarine pen. The strong breeze was uncomfortably hot. Klara Yana tried to jerk free from Cu Zanthus when she felt his sudden unsteadiness, but his arm tightened around her throat until she struggled to breathe.

Andrew was still yelling. She didn't know if he'd ever stopped. "You promised you wouldn't let her die! You *promised*! But she's still on that submarine with that monster and this volcano's gonna blow, and unless Holland helps her–"

"Primer Trimesseni! Take the gun!" Cu Zanthus snapped.

One of the soldiers lunged toward Andrew, but Andrew danced backward out of his grasp. The pistol barrel whipped wildly from Cu Zanthus to Trimesseni and back.

"If she's dead, I'll never forgive you!" he said. "Never!"

"I didn't take her away from you!" Cu Zanthus growled. "You did that to yourself, Andrew!"

Andrew took another step back, the gun shaking in his hands. "Because I thought you *loved* me, Cu Zanthus! But that was exactly what you wanted, wasn't it? You saw I was young and dumb and I'd fall for *anything*! And you were right! And now… and now you…"

Klara Yana's breath caught. He'd mentioned their relationship, right in front of all these Dhavnak soldiers. Klara Yana was sure Cu Zanthus would drop her and kill Andrew with his own hands, right then and there.

But he didn't. He just let out a long, slow breath. This close to her ear, she could hear how uneven that breath was.

"Trimesseni," he repeated, his voice rough.

Once more, the young soldier stepped forward. Andrew started to swing the gun toward him again, but the soldier moved faster this time. Andrew cried out as he yanked it from his hands. His red-rimmed eyes stayed locked on Cu Zanthus's as another soldier grabbed his elbow from behind. He seemed to have finally run out of words. He didn't resist as they shoved him up the ramp toward the waiting submarine.

Klara Yana's heart sank. She hadn't expected Andrew to save her, necessarily, but she'd been hoping Cu Zanthus would slip up enough to give her an out. But he hadn't. And now she had to choose between leaving Blackwood paralyzed on the side of this active volcano or giving up her location so she'd be taken prisoner along with her. *After everything we've gone through, I have to betray her after all.*

Unless…

What is a spy's greatest weapon? The same one that had kept Lyanirus from beating her to death on the floor of that theater. Information. She knew – she was positive now – that Andrew Blackwood had been more than just a job to Cu Zanthus. She had heard it in that ragged sigh before he'd disarmed Andrew. *Use that.*

She pitched her voice just loud enough to reach Cu Zanthus's ear alone. "Call off your men. Or I'll tell Andrew that you killed his parents."

For several moments, she thought Cu Zanthus hadn't heard her. But then he finally answered, his voice low and furious.

"How could you possibly know that?"

"I'm a spy," she said evenly.

"That was classified intel!"

"Tell Andrew that."

"I should never have–" he said, but Klara Yana drew in a deep breath and shouted out before he could finish.

"Andrew!"

The boy looked up from the deck of the submarine, his eyes wide and terrified.

"Cu Zanthus ki–" she began.

Cu Zanthus dropped her arms and shoved her away, so hard that she sprawled to the concrete dock. He yelled loud enough to drown out her voice.

"Let the boy go! Now!"

"Sir?"

"I said release him!"

The soldier holding him cast a doubtful look between her and his commanding officer, but he obeyed. After one last glance over his shoulder, Andrew ran back toward the access ramp. Klara Yana pushed herself to her feet, but clamped her arphanium pipe between the fingers of her left hand this time, so she could easily curl them in and touch it to her mark if she needed to.

But Cu Zanthus made no move to recapture her. He just glared at her hatefully.

"How could you betray your country like this?" he bit out. "By Shon Aha's mercy, *how?*"

"*You* killed Ambassador Talgeron," Klara Yana answered shortly. "Your own countrywoman."

"The ambassador?" he said with a sneer. "She was a traitor, too!"

"She was my ama," said Klara Yana.

"Your ama? But Talgeron didn't have a son! She had a…" He trailed off. The color drained from his face as he studied her. "Living gods," he whispered.

"My ama started something," said Klara Yana. "With her women's movements, and her involvement of the other countries. She started something this world badly needs more than any war. So I *will* be back. Not because I'm a traitor to our country. But because Dhavnakir belongs to *all* of us, and it's time we started treating it that way."

Cu Zanthus's jaw set. "I'm not saying you're wrong," he said, "but a traitor is a traitor. You killed your CO. You lied to your partner. You made *me* an accomplice when I stood up for you. These are things I can't forgive. Not ever."

She started to say that *she* wasn't the one who needed *his* forgiveness… but something kept the words locked behind her teeth. For the past two cycles, Cu Zanthus had been her partner and her friend. She'd gone through stretches where she'd considered him her *only* friend. But he'd killed her ama before they ever met. She'd never known the man he really was. And he hadn't known the first thing about her. She wondered if there was a part of him that felt as betrayed by that as she did.

She felt a hand on her arm and turned to see Andrew at her side, breathing hard. His eyes were pinned warily on Cu Zanthus. Cu Zanthus finally tore his gaze from her face and turned toward Andrew. He half-raised a hand toward Andrew's face, where a red mark was barely visible. Andrew flinched.

"Don't," he said tightly.

"Andy," Cu Zanthus said. "I never–"

There was another tremor, the biggest one yet. Klara Yana lost her balance, and hit the concrete dock with a force that sent every injury in her body screaming in pain. She gasped, relieved to see that she somehow still clutched her shard of arphanium. When she looked up, she saw Cu Zanthus pulling Andrew to his feet. Her partner held the boy's hand for just a second, and the way he looked at him made him appear younger and more vulnerable than she'd ever seen him before.

He said something too soft for her to hear over the rumbling of the mountain before letting go of Andrew's hand and turning away. He strode toward the submarine without looking back.

"Load up!" he yelled to his men. "We're leaving!"

Andrew turned to Klara Yana, swallowing. "Mila?" was all he said.

"She's alive," said Klara Yana. "Follow me!"

Chapter 26

BLACKWOOD'S NEW ALLIANCES

"Deckman Holland," Blackwood said weakly. "You came back."

Galvanized energy still rippled through her, making it feel as if all her muscles were tensed simultaneously. But at least words came easier now. Holland had shrouded her again, she realized, though it had been so smooth she'd barely noticed it. She took in an adobe ceiling and shuttered sandpanes. A coarse rug pressed against her burning back. Low booms still echoed from some far-off place. Andrew's house. *Her* house. Holland had brought her home.

"Holland, why isn't she moving? What's wrong with her?"

Andrew was suddenly kneeling in front of her, his eyebrows knit in concern.

"Holland found you," Blackwood managed. "Didn't... betray me."

Tears ran down Andrew's cheeks. "Mila, I'm sorry, I'm so sorry, I thought you were dead, you *would* have been dead–"

"Not dead," Blackwood forced out. "Alive. We're both... alive. Where's Holland?"

Andrew looked up, just over Blackwood's shoulder. Blackwood tried to follow his gaze, but Holland circled around into her line of sight. He knelt at her other side, opposite Andrew.

"Are you OK, ma'am?" he said.

"You saved him," said Blackwood. "Saved me."

"Yes, ma'am."

"I want… truth from you. Now."

"I…" He faltered, staring at her uneasily.

"Say it," said Blackwood.

Holland swallowed. He held her eyes for several long moments before speaking again. "I'm a Dhavnak spy."

Blackwood let out a slow breath. An unexpected tension released in her shoulders. She struggled to string her thoughts together coherently.

"How much… happened… your fault?"

"Probably most of it," he answered quietly.

"Andrew, too?"

"Not entirely. But I didn't make things better."

Andrew's gaze flicked between her and Holland, but he didn't break in to correct him. Anger simmered just beneath Blackwood's surface. She fought to keep it contained. Erupting at Holland wouldn't help anything, not in this state.

"Why… save us?" she asked.

"The beating I received was real. I was ripped apart for withholding information. Afterward, my reasons for needing this position… were all obsolete. I've lost everything." There was no shame or remorse in Holland's voice. Just bone-tired resignation. "You've done right by me. Not just once, but over and over again. It was the least I could do."

"Withholding information," Blackwood repeated.

"Yes, ma'am."

"About me?"

"No, ma'am. About myself. My mark. My gender."

"Your gender?" Blackwood blinked as his words sank in. "Oh, Xeil's grace. You're a woman."

"Ma'am."

"So your commander…"

"I killed him. He had my mother murdered, and tried to come after me next. I wanted to save her. I thought if I got the intel…" Holland looked away, blinking hard. "You and your brother have nothing to fear from me," she finished roughly. "Not anymore."

The red-hot anger spiking through Blackwood was suddenly and unexpectedly paired with another emotion. It took her a moment to recognize it. Sympathy. She tried to cling to the familiar pulse of anger instead. Holland had destroyed their *lives*. She'd almost gotten both her and Andrew killed, and stolen everything Blackwood cared about from right under her nose.

But she'd been faced with a decision. Either stay home in Dhavnakir, oppressed and abused, wondering for the rest of her life what had happened to her mother… or take matters into her own hands. It seemed like an impossibly foreign situation to be forced into, and yet here it was in front of her, and Blackwood couldn't say for a second that she wouldn't have made exactly the same choices.

"My condolences," she finally said.

"Thank you, ma'am."

"It's Blackwood. I'm not your CO."

Holland hesitated, then took a deep breath. "I'm Klara Yana. Klara Yana Hollanelea."

Blackwood's lips parted in surprise. Different responses ran through her mind. How very *Dhavnak* that name was. How it was such a huge risk in her line of work. How telling Blackwood her real name wasn't something she'd had to do.

In the end, though, Blackwood simply took it for the gesture of trust it was. "Thank you," she said softly.

Klara Yana nodded, her eyes still fastened on Blackwood's, and pushed herself to her feet. Blackwood saw that lithe grace differently now – not a boy barely out of his teens, still waiting to gain his muscle mass, but a lean woman with a confident agility. She looked older too, without that feigned uncertainty she'd had ever since Blackwood had known her.

"I'll leave you and your brother to recover," Klara Yana said. "But… if you want me to… I'd like to help make it up to you. We're the only two people in the world who've been marked by those creatures. We have a bond, whether we like it or not."

"Make it up how?" said Blackwood.

"Your submarine crew. I have some connections that might get them out of the internment camp. I'll do my best."

Blackwood's eyes widened. Klara Yana held up a hand.

"I can't promise anything. Except to try."

"Find me," Blackwood said. "When you have information. Need help. Anything."

"I will, Blackwood. I'll be in touch." Klara Yana brushed a fist to her opposite shoulder in a casual Belzene salute.

Blackwood blinked, her breath catching.

"You're the best officer I've served under, CSO," said Klara Yana. "And that's the truth." Then she was gone.

With Andrew's help, Blackwood got the gunshot wounds on her arm and leg cleaned and redressed, grateful there were no signs of infection. Andrew made tea and brought pillows and blankets out to the couch for her, along with some painkillers, which she took gratefully. The absolute worst agony was the one on her back. Her skin had suffered severe burns from the flash-heated steel deck. They left her feeling feverish and weak, with a fatigue deeper than she'd ever experienced. She knew that she and her brother needed to leave the house – Cu Zanthus knew where they lived, and she had no doubt he'd send someone for her, and maybe Andrew, too – but the excruciating pain in her back was hard to think past, and she found herself lying motionless on the couch instead, drifting in and out of consciousness as explosions racked the city.

It might have been hours. It might have been days. All she knew was that at some point, her mind gradually let go, and she slept. She slept in the dreamless oblivion that only severe fatigue can bring, and that she'd often longed for in those final few weeks on the *Desert Crab*. She slept far away from the pain and the fear and her constant responsibilities. She slept in a place without bombs, without war. Without betrayal or guilt or regret.

When she finally surfaced again, some indeterminate amount of time later, and found Ellemko eerily silent around her, she thought herself still sleeping. But moments later, dread filled her.

"We were taken," she whispered.

Andrew looked up. He was sitting on the floor beneath the sandpane on the far side of the room, a book open in his lap.

"Andrew," she said. "Tell me. *Were we taken?*"

"No," he said.

She let out her breath. "We beat them. I can't believe it."

He opened his mouth, but closed it again without answering. He pushed himself to his feet, one finger holding his place in the book.

"Andrew?"

"How are you feeling?" he said, without meeting her eyes.

"I'm OK," she said warily. "How about you?"

"Yeah. Fine." He started to walk past her, either toward the kitchen or his bedroom. As he passed the couch, she reached out a hand and snagged his wrist. He paused, staring at the floor.

"What's wrong?" she said.

"I'm fine."

"No. I'm not accepting that. When you and I got back here – with Klara Yana – I *saw* you. I saw that you did care. So why do you do this? Go back to hating me?"

He flinched at her words. "It's not… It's about what I… Will you just…" With one hard jerk of his arm, he broke her grip and stalked off to the kitchen. The book he'd been reading fell to the floor with a thump.

Blackwood managed to pull herself to sitting. Her back still felt tender against the rough fabric of the couch, but it was bearable. She stared in the direction Andrew had disappeared. Damn him, why was he always so *hostile*? Surely he wasn't upset about the outcome of the invasion. He hadn't *wanted* Dhavnakir to win the war. Had he? Not anymore, at least.

Not anymore. But he had helped Cu Zanthus. In doing so, he had helped Dhavnakir… and almost gotten her captured or killed. It was practically the first thing he'd said when they'd gotten home. *I thought you were dead, you would have been dead…* She'd stopped him before he finished, but she knew how that sentence would have ended: …*and it would have been my fault.*

She sucked in her breath. Because for the first time, she understood. His terse silence, his resentment, his refusal to look her in the eye…

It wasn't hostility. It was shame.

She pushed herself painfully to her feet and made her way to the kitchen. Andrew was standing back by the sandpane, staring out the narrow crack between the shutters. There were a million things she could say. A million things that wouldn't get through. He'd already passed his judgment, and hers would be swallowed up by the power of his own. She knew this. Part of her even understood it.

"You knew about Klara Yana," she said quietly. "Didn't you?"

Andrew stiffened at the sound of her voice. But slowly, he nodded.

"That she was a woman, too?"

"Yeah."

"Did she tell you? Did Cu Zanthus?"

"No," said Andrew. "I figured it out. Why?"

She blew out her breath. "How long did it take you?"

"It was in the basement—"

"After you'd just *met* her?" she broke in incredulously.

He looked back, eyes flashing. "If you're trying to say something, just say it."

"Do you really think they're Dhavnak gods?" she said.

He started to answer, then blinked as he processed her words. "W-What?"

"You can figure things out," she said. "In a way I can't begin to understand. I'd written your theories off as biased speculation before, but I see now that's not how you operate. So I want to know what you really think. I'm listening."

He stared at her for a long time. She couldn't remember the last time he'd held her gaze that long. "No," he finally said. "I don't think they are."

"Is that the truth?"

"Yes. But the resemblances… they're *real*, Mila. And they're substantial."

"So? What's your theory? I assume you've been thinking about this."

"You *really* want to hear it?"

She nodded, leaning against the doorjamb and crossing her arms over her chest. Andrew licked his lips, turning away from the sandpane.

"OK. Well. What if they *are* Synivistic gods… but only because the legends sprouted from a real event in the distant past and got distorted along the way?"

Blackwood's eyebrows rose. "A real event? Like what?"

"Like shrouding. From Neutania to Mirrix. Aliens who were actually *here*, on our planet, at some point."

"Aliens with powers? That were turned into gods by Dhavnak mythology?" she said.

"Yes, exactly. But not *just* Dhavnaks. In Cardinia, for example, they believe the Providence Spirits sequestered themselves beneath Mirrix's surface to escape from the cruelty of humans, and took the world's light with them. It's a similar twist on the same theme. The gods – the creatures – disappearing one day and leaving nothing but darkness behind."

"And Xeil?" said Blackwood.

"Xeil collected and transported souls back to the bodies of living loved ones. And Vo Hina *hoarded* souls – collected them. So I think both Xeil and Vo Hina are different interpretations of the same creature – the one that saved our planet from the invading ones. Probably the same one that rescued you and Klara Yana on that submarine. Or at least one of the same kind."

"But what about our marks?" said Blackwood. "The powers they gave us? Was that intentional?"

"Doubt it. In Galene Marduc's case, he was touching Vo Hina when Shon Aha found them, and it was a sort of anomaly that happened during the attack. Afterward, it's implied that Galene Marduc could throw lightning like Shon Ana *and* travel spontaneously to Mirrix like Vo Hina. Something similar may have happened to Onosylvani, right? After all, it would never have been mentioned in Mother and Father's research if her powers manifested on the very day they were killed. But you and Klara Yana…" he paused, his mouth twisting in thought, "…were different. It's almost like you *each* got hit by one of them. Maybe if… if the one resembling Vo Hina was closer to her, and Shon Aha was closer to you? It's hard to say. I don't see how we could ever know for sure."

"Doctor Zurlig told me that Onosylvani was marked *because* she was Dhavnak," Blackwood said.

Andrew frowned. "Well, they were also only halfway through their experiments when disaster struck. If that was the first time someone hadn't died, they might've assumed certain things as a factor – race, gender, age, and so on. Probably something they'd narrowed it down to… or thought they had, anyway."

"Do you think she was right, though?" said Blackwood. "I mean, Klara Yana was Dhavnak, too. They may have had a point."

"Were there any other connections between her and Onosylvani?"

"Not that I know of. But… but then again, I didn't know anything about her. Did I?"

Andrew shrugged. "We don't have all the pieces. Those scientists didn't either."

"So the reason Doctor Zurlig was so bent on telling me Onosylvani was Dhavnak…"

"She was probably trying to tell you that Klara Yana caused the lightning," said Andrew. "Which… you know. Didn't turn out to be true. Still. Logical conclusion with what she knew."

"So what do you…" Blackwood began, but trailed off when she saw how carefully Andrew was watching her. Almost as if he were bracing himself for her next question.

"What is it?" she said slowly. "What am I not asking?"

He let out a sigh, barely noticeable, and looked down at the floor. Irritation rose in her, that he was so damn *selective* about what he chose to answer. She could push him, sure, but he'd either end up shutting down completely or screaming at her, and she didn't think…

Screaming at her. His last words on the submarine came back to her now. *The lightning! Don't let it use the lightning! The darkness–!*

"Andrew?" she said, suddenly apprehensive. "Why did you say that? On the submarine?"

He didn't ask what she meant, which told her she'd hit on exactly what he'd been avoiding. She waited for him to tumble out of control. But instead, he spoke, his voice softer than before.

"Klara Yana's the one who made me realize their lightning actually *triggers* the volcanic eruptions. It happened when that Shon Aha-looking creature attacked us in the shrouding realm. And it almost happened when you used your lightning on the Kheppra volcano."

"Triggers it," she whispered.

He nodded, still staring at the floor. "So… so the Age of Fallen Light. The one I told you about?"

"Yeah?" she said uneasily.

"If I'm right, then those monsters caused it by setting off volcanoes using their lightning, and filling the sky with dark smoke and ash for centuries to come. I think that's why the shrouding realm looks the way it does. They've *ruined* it."

"But the Age of Fallen Light wasn't *on* Neutania, was it? It was here."

"Yes. I think when Galene Marduc traveled to Neutania, they followed him back with arphanium or something, and used their powers then. But what if one of those creatures – the one resembling Vo Hina, for example – later betrayed them by destroying the arphanium and keeping them from returning? Remember what Klara Yana said when she came back from the shrouding realm? *They want to get back here.*"

"And the darkness?"

"I…"

She gestured to the shutters. "Open them."

It took him a second, but he reluctantly ducked his head in a nod before turning to the sandpane and swinging the shutters wide. It was late evening, with both suns already beyond the horizon somewhere. A drab fog had permeated the backyard and blurred the nearby houses into dusky shadows. Something resembling black snow drifted in flurries against the glass.

"It's gotten gradually worse since this morning," said Andrew hesitantly. "Not long before you woke up, I even briefly saw the Main Sun rise, before… before the smoke obscured the eastern horizon, too."

Blackwood took a couple steps forward, her eyes glued to the falling ash. "Are you saying it's not even *midday* yet?"

"Right. I was out all morning, getting what information I could."

"The Kheppra volcano," she said after a moment.

"No. I mean… yes, obviously. But not *just* Kheppra. Last night, the number was at… fifteen eruptions, I think? In the surrounding region? But that was before the radios went out. The signals are gone now. By the time I came home again, a lot of the mobies were already… I mean, the helio panels. Most of our stuff can't operate without the suns."

"Why didn't you tell me this earlier?" she said sharply.

His head snapped up, and she knew immediately she'd hit some nerve he'd barely been holding onto.

"I don't *know*, OK?" he said, his voice rising. "I… I figured you didn't need to see it right after what you went through, and it's not like you can do anything *now*, and you never believe anything I say anyway, and I didn't want to have to *deal* with–"

"It's OK!" she broke in, her heart pounding. "Andrew. It'll be OK." She didn't know if she believed any such thing, but she said it anyway.

"No, you don't understand, Mila! This darkness was in almost *all* the religions I read about. But it *wasn't mentioned in Xeil's*. If it's happening – if it's *really* happening – then it's proof, isn't it? It's proof that Xeil never existed, and that our parents are *gone*, and I've tried, I've tried so hard for that *not* to be true, but it happened anyway, and I don't know what to *do* anymore!" He put his hands to his face, against his temples, and shut his eyes tight. She could see him shaking from where she stood.

She drew an uneven breath and limped across the kitchen. Tentatively, she put an arm around his narrow shoulders, feeling awkward the whole time. After a moment, Andrew lowered his hands and turned his face into her shoulder. Blackwood put her other arm around him and held him close, and it suddenly didn't feel so strange anymore.

"Listen," she said softly. "I talked to Mother the morning she died. It was after you'd finished breakfast and gone to get dressed. I was upset because the boy I'd been seeing at school… Edwin. You remember him?"

Andrew shook his head.

"Anyway," said Blackwood, "I'd just found out he'd been stealing drugs and selling them to students. He was caught in the act and arrested. He called asking if *I* could help him out. I'd never been so angry. Never. I wanted to march right into lockdown and punch his teeth in, bash his head against the bars until he passed out. Honest to Xeil, I had plans to, as soon as school let out." She shook her head, swallowing. "But Mother, she said, 'Mila, that's not the way Xeil would want it. With our ancestors inside us, we have no room left for hate. Remember that. Kill your enemies with kindness. Kill them with love.'" Her voice trailed almost to a whisper as she remembered. *What happened? How did I forget that? How did I end up consumed by my anger, and Andrew crushed under his despair? What happened to us?*

For a moment, the only sounds were the wind against the sandpane and Andrew's ragged breathing. When he spoke, his words were barely audible.

"I remember her saying that, too."

"Do you understand my point, though?" said Blackwood, just as quietly.

Andrew tensed. "You're saying I've failed her? Is that it?"

"No, Andrew. It's that even with what our mother knew, or recorded, about Xeil not being real, she still *believed*. Not because she had the science to back it up, but because she had the faith. It didn't *matter* to her whether the Dhavvie gods were real and Xeil wasn't. What mattered to her was which one made her into a good person."

Andrew didn't speak for several moments, but he'd stopped shaking and his breathing had slowed. "I… I want to believe that," he finally said, his voice muffled against her shoulder. "But I almost got you killed. I'm not a *good person.*"

"And I lost control of my anger and almost got *you* killed," Blackwood answered. "I'm not, either. But I don't think Mother would agree. She'd tell us there's always hope. No matter what."

"But *what* hope, Mila?" Andrew said pleadingly. "The Age of Fallen Light almost wiped out life on this planet! There's no reason it won't be just as bad or worse this time. If I'd figured it out in time, I… I could have told you. I could have stopped it. But I didn't. And now… now…"

"This darkness," said Blackwood. "It's from an ancient Dhavnak mythology. And, like you said, all mythologies come from somewhere. They build on things that actually happened."

"Yeah. And?"

"And Xeilak religion doesn't have this darkness. So... wherever Xeil originally came from – whatever culture, whatever part of the world–"

"Southeastern Criesuce," Andrew muttered.

"– maybe they didn't *have* this darkness," Blac kwood finished. "Maybe it wasn't worldwide."

Andrew sucked in his breath. He turned his face up to look at her. "By the moons," he whispered. "Mila. What if you're *right?*"

"Can you find out?" she asked. "The same way you figured out everything else?"

"I can try," he said cautiously. "But I've read almost everything I can get my hands on. I'll need to get more information somehow."

"What if we went down there? To South Criesuce?"

Slowly, something lit up behind Andrew's eyes. "Cu Zanthus said there are suspicions that Criesuce has shrouding technology, or something similar. Who knows what we'd find there? They might have all *kinds* of knowledge that I haven't even..." But then he trailed off. "You couldn't come. Could you? Because of the navy."

"For one," said Blackwood, "the Kheppra volcano erupted. I'd be surprised if Marldox hasn't been wiped out by a tsunami by now, and our whole naval fleet with it. For two, I was stripped of command, killed two military scientists, and vanished in the aftermath, so I hardly think returning to the base is a good option right now. And for three... I told you that you're not alone, Andrew. I'm not leaving you again. I mean it."

Andrew licked his lips uncertainly, his eyes never leaving hers. "But what about the war? Dhavnakir knows about shrouding now. And they were close to taking most of Mirrix even *without* it."

Blackwood nodded. "Which means they're about to find out just how dangerous shrouding really is. Mirrix isn't gone yet, Andrew. Not to Dhavnakir *or* this Age of Fallen Light. And you're the one who's gonna help me keep it that way."

He swallowed. "Are you sure you trust me?"

She tightened her arm around him. "Yes. Don't ever ask me that again."

A tentative smile crept across Andrew's face. It was such a different expression than she was used to seeing on him that it almost took her breath away. *I should have been here.* She stopped the thought in its tracks. It was done. She hadn't saved their parents' research, but that hadn't been the most important thing they'd left behind. She just wished she realized it sooner.

I'm here now, she thought. *And that's what matters.*

ACKNOWLEDGEMENTS

The journey of this book has been complex, and the fact that it got this far is due largely to the people who've helped along the way. No one deserves more credit than my husband, Trever Peters. He knows that writing is the glue that holds me together, and goes to great lengths to give me the time and support I need. My fantastic agent, Cameron McClure, read my book in four days flat, and then became the partner I'd always dreamed of to make it shine. My editor, Lottie Llewelyn-Wells, helped me push it that extra mile, and has been a joy to work with. Marc Gascoigne, Penny Reeve, Nick Tyler, Gemma Creffield, and the rest of the team at Angry Robot offered me an incredible opportunity with their Open Door program, and I am grateful to them for inviting me into their world. I am also thankful to Eleanor Teasdale, my commissioning editor, and Francesca Corsini, who created my awesome cover.

I owe a huge thanks to my two earliest critique partners, William Tracy and Ken Hoover. This book was a mess when they first read it, and it would never have gotten further without their invaluable feedback. I also received great feedback from RJ Taylor and my dad Patrick Hogan, who helped smooth out the rougher patches. Thanks to my mom, Kathy Campbell, for being a devoted fan; my good friends Anna Cummings, Jada Maes, and Joshua Carter for helping pull me through the darker times; and Mary Ann and Marianna DeBoer, who have encouraged my writing since the beginning. The podcasters and alumni of Writing Excuses also deserve my thanks for having such a knowledgeable and welcoming community.

Lastly, I am thankful to my two insatiably curious kids, and to my brother Michael. It's because of him that I know how special the brother/sister bond is, and how important it is to nurture and protect it.

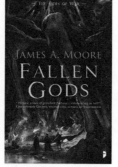
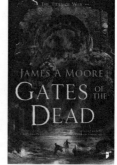
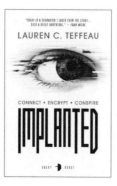

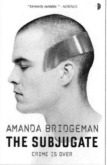

UNDER THE PENDULUM SUN BY

JEANETTE NG

PAPERBACK & EBOOK
from all good stationers and book emporia

Two Victorian missionaries travel into darkest fairyland, to deliver
their uplifting message to the godless magical beings who dwell
there… at the risk of losing their own mortal souls.

*Winner of the Sydney J Bounds Award, the British Fantasy Award for
Best Newcomer*

Shortlisted for the John W Campbell Award 2018 & 2019